HARD QUESTION, MOMENTOUS ANSWER

He wore only a loincloth and a scarlet head-band. His hair was to his waist. There was a long, jagged scar across his chest from his left shoulder nearly to his navel. His skin was copper-colored, and beneath it muscles rippled with each breath and small movement. He was tall for an Apache, taller than all but a handful of the white soldiers back at the fort, and his black eyes stared out over high, sharp cheekbones. His nose was straight and unusually narrow, his forehead high and smooth. He was a younger man than she had imagined.

"Who are you?" he asked.

"I am Mary Hart and I demand that you release me."

"Who are you?" he repeated.

And she could only answer with the truth she no longer could escape in this man's presence, in this man's power. "I am Cheyenne. . . ."

Annie—
Now those I meet may
Look upon my face and say,
"He has lived in joy"

PUBLISHER'S NOTE

This novel is a work of fiction. Names, characters, places, and
incidents either are the product of the author's imagination or are
used fictitiously, and any resemblance to actual persons, living or
dead, events, or locales is entirely coincidental.

NAL BOOKS ARE AVAILABLE AT QUANTITY DISCOUNTS WHEN
USED TO PROMOTE PRODUCTS OR SERVICES. FOR INFORMA-
TION PLEASE WRITE TO PREMIUM MARKETING DIVISION, NEW
AMERICAN LIBRARY, 1633 BROADWAY, NEW YORK, NEW YORK
10019.

SIGNET TRADEMARK REG. U.S. PAT. OFF. AND FOREIGN COUNTRIES
REGISTERED TRADEMARK—MARCA REGISTRADA
HECHO EN CHICAGO, U.S.A.

SIGNET, SIGNET CLASSIC, MENTOR, PLUME, MERIDIAN AND NAL BOOKS
are published by New American Library,
1633 Broadway, New York, New York 10019

First Printing, February, 1986

1 2 3 4 5 6 7 8 9

PRINTED IN THE UNITED STATES OF AMERICA

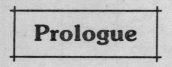

Prologue

Her blood was Cheyenne, but she had seen the ways of the Cheyenne die. She had seen tragedy and she had suffered for being an Indian. Her mother had named her Akton, but she had taken another name, another way so that she might be white, so that she might survive. She had nearly succeeded in forgetting.

Her blood was Cheyenne.

1

The land was raw and savage, a barren and endless expanse dotted sparsely with broken red mesas and wind-sculpted, crumbling spires. The stage stop was the only man-made thing for mile upon empty mile. Even that structure seemed ready to give up the uneven struggle against time and the elements. Made of adobe blocks oozing mortar at the seams and of raw, unpeeled poles, the stage stop was surrounded by a grove of yellow-green cottonwood trees that provided the only relief from the glare and heat of the sun.

The young woman was dark and lovely. She wore a blue skirt and jacket over a ruffled white blouse. Her hair was a glossy blue-black coil, pinned expertly under a small matching blue hat. She clutched a black reticule in both gloved hands. As she moved, the toes of her dusty button shoes kicked up puffs of fine pale dust.

"Miss Hart!"

"Yes, I'm over here," the woman answered.

"We'll be pulling out in ten minutes."

"All right, thank you."

The stage driver nodded. He removed his huge stained hat and mopped his forehead with a large red kerchief. He squinted toward the trees and his young passenger, then into the distance, his pale and weathered eyes narrowing. Mary Hart turned too, and saw the smoke rising from a far-distant fire. It was a thin column of black smoke, scarcely wavering on this windless day. The stage driver walked to the coach, where fresh horses stood ready to be off. He snatched his rifle from the box and tucked it under his arm.

Mary Hart didn't see that. She was still watching the smoke, frowning as if with disapproval. It was an expression which made her handsome face seem tighter, older, more coarse.

She had come this far—to Clay Springs, Arizona Territory—with only the company of an older man in buckskins and a drummer who seemed to carry nothing but whiskey in his sample case. The man in buckskins was pleasant enough but he hadn't wanted to speak much. The drummer slept most of the time, waking only to peer out at the desert, shake his head, and take another drink from his sample case.

Now, as Mary walked to the stage, she was glad to see three new passengers waiting beside the dilapidated building. One of them, thank heaven, was a woman. Mary had only seen two other women in the last two hundred miles. This one was narrow, matronly, conservative in dress and demeanor. There was a young army officer standing beside her. Cavalry, Mary knew from the yellow stripe on his pants leg. The silver bars on his shoulders proclaimed him to be a lieutenant. Those two would be a welcome addition to their little party.

There was now also a cowboy in leather chaps carrying a saddle, a lean leathery man with a yellow mustache. He had apparently lost his horse somewhere. He watched as Mary Hart climbed up into the stage and sat waiting for their departure. Then he spat into the dust at his feet and said loudly, "I'm damned if I'm riding with a squaw."

"Next coach ain't for two days, Charlie," the driver told him.

"I don't give a damn if it's a week. I'm not riding with no squaw Indian."

With that he turned away, tramping back into the stage station, the door banging shut behind him.

The older woman stood frowning in perplexity. The army officer, young, redheaded, and freckled, watched the closed door for a long while. Mary Hart sat woodenly, anger buzzing in her head. She had heard it all before. First in Dakota and then in Maryland where she had gone to school and discovered what an Indian's lot was in a white world.

"Ignorant trash," she finally muttered between compressed lips.

"That's right, miss," a voice agreed. Mary turned sharply toward the sound. Grinning, the man in buckskins clambered up. He winked and Mary turned her eyes down.

"He *is* ignorant, so why let it rile you?"

"Mr. LaPlante, is it?"

"Yes, miss. William LaPlante." The man touched his hat brim and settled onto the wooden seat.

"I appreciate your understanding. However, I seem to detect a note of pity in your voice, and that is even less welcome than simple antagonism."

"Yes, miss," the man answered. Then he tugged his hat down, folded his arms, and slept, or pretended to sleep, a faint smile on his lips.

While they talked, the army officer and older woman had their luggage lifted to the top of the coach and tied down. Then the woman was helped in. The lieutenant followed.

"I'm Mrs. James Shore," the older woman announced. Her features were sharp and clean, with only the slightest sagging of flesh beneath the chin and under the eyes to speak of her age. The eyes, too, were sharp, birdlike. She was a determined woman, one who had seen a great deal. "My husband is Colonel James Shore. Since I take it we're all proceeding to Fort Bowie, I thought I might tell you that before you start discussing the famous man."

"Is he famous?" Mary asked.

"In some circles," the woman said dryly. "Ask the lieutenant or Mr. LaPlante here . . . I didn't get your name."

"Hart. Mary Hart." The women exchanged a gloved handshake.

"BIA?"

"Yes, that's right. I'm going to establish a reservation school at Fort Bowie."

"I wish you luck, dear. I heard that this was in the works. I can't say I envy you. You can't imagine what you'll be up against."

They were waiting now only for the drummer. He arrived moments later, looking up into the coach with red eyes, blinking as if astonished to find the newcomers inside the coach.

"Malcolm Avery," he muttered. "Notions, novelties. Denver."

Then, his foot slipping a little, he clambered aboard and wedged himself in between LaPlante and the lieutenant. The door was closed, the driver and shotgun rider climbed up into the box, and the stage rolled on. Mary Hart sighed quietly and looked out the window at the billowing red dust, at the stage station vanishing behind the cottonwood trees, at the endless miles of empty land.

"You have experience in this field, do you, Miss Hart?" the young army officer asked. "Permit me. I'm Lieutenant Scott Sampson. There's no one here to introduce us, but things are a bit informal here."

"Yes," Mary Hart murmured. She was aware of the young officer's appraising eyes. He was very polite, quite handsome in a youthful way, but there was something disconcerting in those eyes. "I have experience. I was on the Pine Ridge reservation teaching the Sioux and Cheyenne for nearly a year before this offer came through from the Bureau of Indian Affairs."

"Well, it will be different here," Scott Sampson said. His eyes continued to evaluate her in a too-frank manner.

"Apache are different from any other human beings on this earth," LaPlante volunteered from beneath his hat.

"That's ridiculous," Mary Hart responded with some heat. "All people are the same."

"I always liked that theory," LaPlante drawled, "but I never could see that it held much water. Much of what a person is is in his blood, to my way of thinking."

"Then I must say that I don't admire your way of thinking," Mary Hart said. She was aware of the flush creeping across her skin but could do nothing about it. The gray eyes of Mrs. Shore sparkled with ... Amusement? Admiration? Mockery? "We are what we wish to become, and that is that," Mary Hart concluded.

"Can't change what's in the blood," LaPlante said again. He tipped his hat back and sat up straighter, resting his hands on his narrow knees. "Ask anyone who knows an Apache. They're savages who like hurting other living things, other people. They're cruel and sly. Lie every other word."

"*If* that were so, there would be a reason for it. Education and environment are what make a person into what he is."

"Think so? You don't know 'em, miss. We got us a man down here called Thumb who'd like to take every one of us aboard this coach and slaughter us—slowly—and would if he was given half a chance. I suppose you ain't seen that smoke out there. That's Thumb. By now there'll be a lot of people dead. Everywhere he touches there's death. We got us a man named Geronimo down here and one called Victorio, an Apache named Cochise and one called Mangas Coloradas—others I could name. They all live just to see that other people die."

"Then it is their training, their way of life which has produced this bloodlust," Mary Hart insisted.

"Can't get that out of their blood."

"But you can." Mary leaned forward intently. "If I didn't believe that, I would give up teaching right now."

"You're Cheyenne, aren't you?" LaPlante said.

Mary Hart sat up stiffly. "Yes."

10

"Now I understand why that cowboy acted so rudely," Mrs. Shore said. "Yes, you are Indian, aren't you?"

The drummer opened an eye and peered at Mary.

"Yes, I am Cheyenne. But don't you see—this is my point! I have my education. I dress as you do, I have been told I am well-spoken. My mother was Indian, Indian through and through. She lived in the old way. I am part of the new generation, looking for a way to benefit the Indian wherever he lives—however he lives—and bring him forward into this modern age." She had grown impassioned, but now with a look around at the curious faces of her fellow passengers, she settled back in her seat, hands clasped.

"I must say I admire your attitude, your courage and ambitions," Scott Sampson said.

The man in buckskins glanced sideways at the army officer. "Been down here long, Sampson?"

"No, sir. I've never been in the Southwest before."

Mrs. Shore said, "This is Lieutenant Sampson's first field assignment. He requested it. He was given Fort Bowie—no doubt as a less-than-subtle form of punishment," she added ironically.

"I am happy to be here," Sampson objected.

"You won't be," the colonel's wife replied.

"Point is," LaPlante went on. "that you can admire the lady's attitude, her courage, but it won't do a thing to make what she wants to do possible." LaPlante leaned forward. His eyes were amused but tolerant. He liked what he saw in this young Indian woman, but, still, he was doubtful. He had seen the Indian try to adapt to white ways before, had seen him do it out of idealism, had seen him do it out of compulsion. He had never known it to work.

"Maybe I'm wrong, miss, but I've seen a few Apache—something you haven't done yet. The Apache is a fierce and savage creature. He's been bloody and he's been noble, but he won't turn white for you. If he does that he's dead in his own eyes. I admire you for trying to run an Apache school, but I'll promise you this—an Apache won't learn unless he wants to. He'll resist you right down the line. His blood won't let him become what you or what any of us would like. Docile, I mean. That's what we want, isn't it?"

"Are you saying an Apache can't learn or won't learn?" Mary demanded.

"It amounts to the same thing." LaPlante leaned back. "Maybe I'm wrong, but as well-meaning as you might be, miss, you'll do no good here. The Apache won't learn."

"*That* is what you believe?" Mary Hart was incredulous.

"It is my considered opinion, miss."

"Nor, I suppose, can a Cheyenne or a Sioux learn."

"I guess you're proof that a Cheyenne can," LaPlante said cautiously.

"Yes, I like to think I am."

"But I still say it's in the blood . . . what you are is in the blood. An Apache's an Apache. It shows in his manner, just as what you are shows in those black eyes of yours, that black hair."

"The idea of the Bureau of Indian Affairs and of the education department, Mr. LaPlante, is that we are not merely what we are born to be. The idea is that this country is sprawling, growing, and we are what we wish to become. I may have had an Indian father and mother, but I am now an American—as you are! I have made myself into what I am. As for blood telling, the theory is outdated and fatuous. You, Mr. LaPlante, have a French surname but one doesn't expect you to be able to speak French merely because of that. You are an American. And so, Mr. LaPlante, am I."

The stage hit a rock and bounced into the air, landing roughly. By the time everyone had gotten settled again the thread of the conversation had been lost. Mary Hary sat looking out the window at the endless red desert. They were nearer to the smoke that rose in an unwavering column into the white sky. Nearer to the Apache. Mary watched the smoke, fascinated by it. She didn't even hear William LaPlante murmur: "*Dans la grande maison de vitres les enfants en deuil regardèrent les merveilleuses images.*"

They reached Fort Bowie at dusk, just as the purple shadows were collecting beneath the clumps of brush and stretching out crooked fingers from the bases of the tall, thorny ocotillo that flourished in the sandy washes and out on the brown rock desert. Bowie itself might have been abandoned but for the small rectangles of lantern light showing against the muted background like winking bright eyes.

They had to go into the town of Bowie, which was no more than a jumble of adobe-block buildings along a crooked central street. In the near-darkness they switched their luggage to a buckboard which then took them to the fort. The drummer was left behind where he stood in the middle of the rocky, rutted street and muttered one dynamic curse before opening his sample bag once more.

Mary saw a few soldiers in the streets and saloons. The night was warm, dry. Each breath filled the lungs with fine dust.

Mary also saw Mexicans, dressed in tight vaquero jackets and slash-cuffed pants, with sashes around their waists and huge sombreros. They stood smoking cigarettes, watching from the dark corners.

There were other dark faces as well. Indian faces of tribes exotic and small, proud, and some nearly extinct. Mary didn't know them by their faces or by their dress, but she knew they were in and around Fort Bowie, brought there by their fear of the desert war and the Apache, or by the hope of opportunity. They were Navajo and Hopi, Zuni and Keres, Tonto and Yavapai, Pima and Papago, all the sere, sun-branded people of the harsh and lonesome land.

Mary saw nothing to read in their eyes, and the buckboard went past them quickly, the shadows of the town swallowing them up, hiding their eyes and thoughts and culture.

"It's only five minutes to the fort," LaPlante told Mary. "Just across the wash there."

"And what's that?" Mary asked, pointing toward the fires burning low against the foothills.

"Your people," LaPlante said. "All those people waiting to be guided into your future."

Mary grew briefly angry, but that emotion was overwhelmed by curiosity and the excitement of stepping into a new world of her own, a land far from the northern plains where her mother and father had lived among the buffalo, where they had warred foolishly, inexorably, and died. The north, where she had left a brother, a sullen, prideless man trapped between two cultures; where she had lost a sister who had traveled north in the winter and never returned.

Those had been the bad years for Mary Hart. Her father had been a Cheyenne war leader until the soldiers had come to the Rosebud and slaughtered him, just as they slaughtered the many, leaving them lying against the snow dead and dying. Her twin, Hevatha, had been lost in the storm, or killed, or captured—they never found out for certain.

Then Mary's mother had taken them to the fort. Mary and her brother, whose name had then been Dark Moon, were taken there so that they might live. That was all far away in another universe in Dakota.

There the land was flat too, but in Dakota it was cooler, and flowers dotted the long plains and grass grew tall and silver-green. This arid, dreamless land was something out of a beggar's imagination.

The wagon jounced its human cargo down along the sandy bottom of the dry wash and then crawled up the slope before them, winding briefly across a hillside dotted with nopal cactus and shaggy mesquite. Then they arrived at the fort itself: desolate, dry, crooked, and stolidly businesslike.

"Home again," Mrs. Shore said sardonically. "And

14

why, having gotten as far away as Tucson, I ever came back is beyond me."

They rolled on through the high palisaded gate under the eyes of armed troopers, crossed the hard-packed parade ground, and halted on swaying springs. The fort was dark and still and empty. Mary Hart sat in the darkness for a long minute wondering what had brought her to this desolate place, to an alien land. But it was only a traveler's qualm and the feeling passed quickly. She took a deep breath and rose to be helped out of the wagon by Lieutenant Sampson, who held her hand just a fraction of a second too long.

"Thank you very much," she said.

"You're entirely welcome."

He hadn't caught the faint disapproval in her tone. LaPlante was helping Mrs. Shore down from the wagon on the other side. Looking up, Mary saw a vast sweep of stars against a black sky. It was still quite warm. A haze of light along the eastern horizon promised an early-rising moon.

A log door was suddenly opened and a tall officer who was hatless and graying, emerged from the office behind him.

"Edna, welcome back," he said to Mrs. Shore. Mary saw the insignia of a full colonel on his uniform as James Shore stepped to his wife and they embraced stiffly, nearly at arm's length. Lieutenant Sampson had moved near them and held himself ready for an introduction. The colonel looked them over and said, "Come inside, all of you. That's a long journey."

"Don't mind if I do," LaPlante said.

"Sir," Sampson said formally, saluting, "Lieutenant Scott Sampson reporting for duty."

The colonel, who had taken his wife's luggage, stopped, looked the young officer up and down, and nodded. "Well, welcome to Bowie. Who's mad at you?"

"Sir?"

"Never mind. And who's that?" The colonel squinted at Mary.

"That's the teacher, dear," Edna Shore said. "The one BIA sent down."

"Oh, yes. Well, she might as well turn back and go home if she wants my opinion, but I guess she doesn't. Come in teacher."

"Miss Hart."

"Yes, come in. I've cracked a bottle of bonded bourbon for the men. Edna can have her woman make some tea. Maria makes a good pot."

Mary hesitantly followed the others up onto the plank walk. The colonel was not what she had expected. A little unorthodox, a little reserved, but used to being obeyed. They walked past the office door and down the walk to another door, which the colonel pushed open with his toe.

Inside, a low-burning lamp illuminated the colonel's quarters. There was a faded red settee, a braided rug on the wooden floor, and a wall draped with various military gear: old muskets, Indian hatchets and lances, a war shield. A maple sideboard held glassware and a stock of liquor. Beyond the door was a kitchen where a brighter light burned and brass kettles hung gleaming on the wall. A large Mexican-Indian woman appeared, her face broad, dark, and curious.

"Maria, tea for the ladies," Colonel Shore said.

She nodded and vanished again. In the meantime, Edna Shore had turned up the lamp and was now removing her hat, leaving her guests to their temporary discomfort. Sampson was doing his best to look competently military, but only succeeded in looking like a rather tall, gangly freckle-faced boy. Mary Hart clutched her reticule tightly, as if the contents of her purse provided reassurance.

Edna Shore placed her hat on the shelf, patted at her gray hair, and finally offered her guests a real smile, as if by entering her home they had earned her warmth.

She even took Mary's hand and led her to the

settee. "Old as the hills. This is the third post its been at—I've a new one on order from Santa Fe. Been on order for six months. Thumb's probably sitting on it out at his rancheria," she added with a dry laugh.

"Thumb is . . ."

"Thumb is Chiricahua, Mary. He's quick as a fox and savage as a wolf. My husband wants him so badly he can taste it. It would guarantee a star on his epaulets."

"That is not the reason I want him," Colonel Shore said, apparently miffed. Maybe it was the actual reason. He walked to where LaPlante and Sampson stood and gave each a short glass of whiskey.

"Thank you, sir," LaPlante said.

Sampson looked uncertain. Perhaps because he wasn't a drinker, perhaps because he was in his commanding officer's presence. As he took the whiskey he fumbled for something in his tunic—his orders, perhaps—but he didn't manage to get it out before Shore had turned away to face Mary and his wife.

"He's a killer and everyone knows it. Do you want to count up the number of people he has injured, killed, captured, or driven out of Arizona . . . and the ways some of those people were injured . . ."

"Please, James," Edna Shore said as if her husband were committing a table faux pas, with an air of weariness and slight embarrassment. "I apologize. The army has good reason for wanting Thumb, and it goes beyond the desire for glory."

"No sign of him lately, I take it" LaPlante said.

"No. Just his shadow—death." The colonel shook his head. "Lieutenant Sampson, I take it you've met Bill LaPlante here, but you don't know how fortunate you are to have done so. He's my chief of scouts. We've got four Navajo scouts, two Hopi, three Apache. Bill knows them all and he knows their language. He is respected by them—they know he can find a mule track in a sand drift after a three-day blow, or at least they believe he can," the colonel said with what might have been a chuckle, or maybe just a short cough. "When you do take the field, you will have a more seasoned officer with you and a damn good corps of enlisted men. And you'll have Bill LaPlante." The colonel finished his whiskey. The others were watching, expecting more from the officer, but the speech was ended, apparently.

His eyes went to Mary Hart and halted there. "Sioux?"

"Cheyenne," LaPlante said.

"Well, it's good an Indian wants to do for other Indians. Can't count much on anyone else, can you? You'll find things are different here, however. Hart?" He was momentarily thoughtful. "Isn't that the name of the Indian Affairs man up in Washington? Related, are you?"

"No." Mary turned her eyes down. "I adopted the name. My own would be too difficult for most people to pronounce."

"Fine idea. Mary Hart . . . Well, Miss Mary, have you got any thoughts on where you're going to build your school or how you're going to come by the funds or how you're going to get the reservation Indians to go to the school once its built, and how you're going to teach them to sit still and speak English and wear stiff collars?"

There was a goading tone in the officer's voice, but also a hint of compassion. Mary glanced to the scout, who was finishing his whiskey, to Scott Sampson, who was warming his between his freckled hands. Mrs. Shore nodded encouragement.

"Colonel Shore, I was given to understand that there was already a school here and that it was being administered by a Ralph Justin, the current Indian agent."

"You were given to understand wrong," the colonel said. "I haven't seen Justin for months. I haven't seen him sober for a year or more. He's got a Navajo assistant that hands out the rations that sometimes—

even our system can't misfire endlessly—arrive for the reservation. There's a pile of gray lumber out there that was brought in from Tucson and dumped on the ground. At government expense. That is the Indian school."

"It was never built?"

"No, but on paper it looks good. On paper Justin's record is sparkling."

"But then . . . no one has come down to evaluate his progress here?"

"Come to Bowie? From Washington? Not likely, Miss Mary," the colonel said, pouring more whiskey into his glass.

"Surely you have mentioned this to the authorities?"

"It's not my business," the colonel said frankly. "I'm telling you because it concerns you, because you're here to do a difficult job—maybe an impossible one, I don't know. I'm speaking to you as a guest, an acquaintance. Officially it's hardly army business what the Indian agent does with his funds, his time, his obligations. My superior doesn't want a report from me on the conditions at the reservation. He would never forward it. I'd likely be admonished for wasting his time."

"But the Indians are being shortchanged," Mary objected.

"Miss Mary, that is something that only you can correct. I wish you luck. Caught between hostility on one hand and bureaucratic indifference on the other, I can only say that you will *need* luck. I do not envy you." He downed his whiskey and looked at the empty glass. He reflected, "It is much simpler to wage a war against the body than to rehabilitate the mind. If I could shoot Thumb—as my wife has pointed out—I would be rewarded. I don't think there's anything you can do that will earn you a word of thanks here, Miss Mary."

"I don't want thanks."

"Of course you do. We all do. Anyone who tries to do the right thing wants thanks. Well"—he shrugged—"where can we put Miss Mary for the night, Edna? The guesthouse?"

"Yes." Edna rose, smiling, but it was a worried smile. "I'll see that there's linen. Lieutenant Sampson will be in the BOQ? And, Bill, you're back home."

"I sure am. And ready for my bed," LaPlante said, rising and putting his empty glass down on the table. Sampson stood hat in hand, awaiting instructions.

"Commander's call tomorrow at eight o'clock," the colonel said. "You'll be briefed and introduced around then."

"Thank you, sir."

"Bill, I wish you'd come along too."

"Sure." The civilian scout put his hat on over his long graying hair. He looked at Mary again, squinting as if he were looking into the desert sun. It seemed to be a habitual expression with him. He told her, "You need any help, miss, you ask me. You'll be running into some odd characters and some downright dangerous ones, I'm afraid."

"Thank you, Mr. LaPlante, I'm sure—"

"That's not an idle offer, miss. Politeness or some such. If you need help, you ask."

She looked at him again, seeing the sincerity and concern in his pale eyes. Finally she smiled. "Thank you. I will."

LaPlante winked and walked out then, lanky, catlike.

Lieutenant Sampson had his hat on as well. He stopped before Mary. "I suppose I'll be busy for a time, but I too would be happy to assist you in any way possible—so long as it doesn't interfere with military obligations," he amended hastily with a glance at Colonel Shore, who seemed to be beaming with warmth and interest. Mary realized suddenly that the colonel had had more than a few whiskeys.

"Thank you," she told Sampson.

"Five or six doors down to the bachelor officers'

quarters," the colonel said. "You'll see the sign. Granger and the others'll show you how to set up."

"Thank you, sir." Sampson saluted, did a smart about-face, and strode out.

Mary watched him go out and close the door. She heard, although she probably wasn't supposed to hear, the colonel mutter, "Kid's walking unarmed into hell."

Mary hadn't time to turn that over in her mind before Edna Shore took her arm and guided her toward the door.

"I'm sure you're tired."

"I am. I don't know if I'll be able to sleep, though."

They were outside. The closing door shut out the lamplight, and the stars peered down, pulsing slowly. Distantly they heard the laughter of a hysterical man, drunk or wounded or both.

"It's a long way from anywhere," the colonel's wife said. "Come on. Maria will bring whatever you need. I don't suppose you'll be staying here long, though, will you?" She answered herself. "Against regulations. Civilian personnel will be shown every reasonable courtesy insofar as lodgings, sustenance, and transportation go, but their presence cannot be encouraged, not being conducive to the efficient operation of a military installation." Edna Shore squeezed Mary's arm. "That's a quote, dear. I'm army. My father was army. But I'm damned if I can understand their English. Here we are. This is what we call the visitor's cottage."

It wasn't a cottage at all, but another apartment built into the long log building. Somewhere, once, there must have been a cottage on the army base and so these rooms had earned that title.

The colonel's wife opened the wooden door and led Mary into a room which was neat but Spartan, apparently designed not to encourage the presence of civilians. There was a bed of puncheon, a thin straw-filled mattress, a washbasin on a small corner table. A zig-zag patterned Indian rug in red and gray completed the furnishings.

The colonel's wife looked around, smiled unsuccessfully, and shrugged. "This is it. Maybe it's no punishment to find yourself pushed out in a day or so."

"At any rate," Mary said, "I was going to sleep at the school as soon as possible."

"But there is no school!"

"There will be," Mary said firmly. "I promise you that. I'll find this Mr. Justin and see that there *is* a school."

There was confidence in her voice, but later, when Mrs. Shore had gone, when the night grew dark and empty, it had all seeped out of her. Mary Hart lay there, her hands clasped on her abdomen, watching the sliver of moonlight on the ceiling and wondering whether she too was going "unarmed into hell."

The dawn restored her spirits. She hastily pinned up her waist-length, heavy dark hair and dressed in a comfortable divided skirt, high boots, and a white blouse. This was the first day, and she would make it count. She found the papers authorizing her assignment to the reservation school and put those in a wallet which she placed in the large pocket of her skirt. Then, with a last glance at her hair, at her own dark but sparkling eyes, she went out into the morning.

She stood for a moment and watched the dawn fade to blue-white day. A party of soldiers was riding from the camp while another group stood at attention across the parade ground. The desert air was so clear that the mountains, which were miles distant, seemed to be just beyond the wall of the fort.

She turned at the sound of boots on the plank walk and saw Scott Sampson, scrubbed and shaved, approaching in the company of a sallow, weary-looking captain.

"Good morning, Miss Mary," the lieutenant said.

"Good morning," she answered, bowing her head slightly.

"May I introduce Captain Walter Granger."

Granger just grunted and Mary guessed he was the first of many she would meet who would have no use for a schoolteacher, much less an Indian.

"I hope you rested well," Sampson went on, flushing beneath his freckled skin.

Before Mary could answer, Granger interrupted. "Damn near late now, Sampson."

"All right. I'm sorry. Perhaps . . ." Sampson stumbled, shrugged, and said good-bye, touching his hat. The two officers went off together, Scott Sampson glancing back once. Mary smiled faintly, cocked her head thoughtfully, and then went on, the smile lingering on her lips.

She went to the colonel's office and entered to find herself face to face with a corpulent, red-faced sergeant with many stripes on his sleeves, who was staring back at her from behind a scarred oak desk.

"I'm Mary—"

"Colonel told me you might be by. He's having officers' call just now." The sergeant cleared his throat and shifted in his chair, accidentally knocking half a dozen sheets of paper from his desktop. "He said to give you what you need."

"Thank the colonel for me. What I should like is to borrow a horse and have someone show me the way to the reservation school."

"Sure you don't want a buggy, miss?" Then Mary saw his eyes change and realized he was thinking that she was Indian, after all, and not only would know how to ride but also would probably prefer it. That wasn't strictly true, but for this particular trip Mary wanted the freedom of a horse.

"I'll get you a mount saddled. Don't need a side-saddle, do you? Haven't got one anyway. I'll have someone find Kemo, too. He's a Navajo kid. Bright as a jay. Also a little thief—have to watch him." He turned to a nearby corporal. "Hear that, Killian?" The corporal grabbed his cap and scurried out the door.

"Thank you." Mary found a seat in the corner of the office and waited, listening to the complaints of an enlisted man who wanted to go home, the excuses of another who had been involved in a drunken brawl.

A little while later a Navajo scout appeared, trail-dusty, carrying a repeating rifle and wearing cotton trousers, a white loincloth, and a black shirt with silver buttons. He glanced at Mary, frowned, and then reported to the sergeant, who sent him into the colonel's office.

The corporal, Killian, had returned, and in tow was a boy of nine or ten, his silky dark hair clipped straight across in front and in back. He wore moccasins, a print shirt, and a red headband.

"Found him, Sarge," Killian reported. "He was in the back of the grub hall. Doing guess what?"

The sergeant didn't want to guess. "Got a horse for the lady, Killian?"

"Yes, Sarge, out front. One for the kid as well."

"All right. Kemo?"

The Navajo boy smiled and stepped forward, saluting. "Yes, boss?"

"Take this lady out to the reservation school, will you? She's going to be your new teacher."

"What school, boss?" Kemo asked, spreading his hands.

"Where the school is supposed to be—you know. Where all the lumber was dumped."

"The firewood?" Kemo asked.

"Is that what's happening to it? Yes, the firewood pile."

"Sure," Kemo said, his expression clearing now that he knew what was required of him. "Come on, lady, I'll show you. Say—you are an Indian lady, don't you know where the reservation is?"

"I'm not from around here."

"No? What did you do, jump the reservation?" he asked.

"Something like that. I went to school and they

let me leave. You can do the same thing if you like. You can be anything you want, did you know that?"

"Anything?"

"Certainly."

"I want to be like the boss sergeant, just like him," Kemo said.

"A soldier?"

"A white man," Kemo replied, and Killian laughed out loud. Kemo grinned. Mary wasn't sure if she was being made fun of or not, and so she simply gestured toward the door and followed Kemo out. The day had grown hot while she sat inside the office. She squinted into the distance briefly and then went to the big bay horse which had been left at the hitch rail for her. She untied the reins and swung up easily.

"You've seen a horse before," Kemo said.

"Yes, and I'll bet you have too."

"Me? I ride like the wind. I always ride."

"Is that your own horse?"

"This one?" Kemo said disparagingly. "Look at him. Failing in the quarters, roached in the back, ewe-necked. Got ring hoof starting on the left fore." Kemo wagged his head. "Not like mine. I've got a spotted stallion. Run all day and all night too. I caught him myself—wild stock. It took me three weeks to break him."

"Where is he now?"

The boy waved a hand toward the horizon. "Out there. I let him go. Couldn't stand to see him tamed."

Then he leapt onto the back of the small horse the corporal had found for him, turned the head roughly, and heeled it, lifting it into a run which stirred up the dust and caused the soldiers on the parade ground to turn their heads and shout after him. Mary rode her own bay a little less flamboyantly to the main gate and followed the boy out onto the desert. Kemo was vanishing in a funnel of distant dust, away from the jumbled, untidy town and out onto the empty land.

She had seen nothing but desert for days on the

stagecoach, but it was a different land entirely from horseback. Likely it was still more different afoot.

Kemo had slowed his horse and turned it. As she waited for him to rejoin her, she studied the broken, rugged land around her. Deep arroyos cut across the red-rock desert. Distantly she could see white dunes against the red background of a giant mesa. Saguaro cactus raised supplicating arms to an empty sky. In the shade of a mesquite a pale sidewinder buzzed a warning that caused Mary to turn her horse. There was some sage, some greasewood, but no trees visible for mile upon mile. It was nine in the morning and the temperature had already climbed over a hundred. Mary regretted bringing no hat.

Kemo was back, exhilarated, beaming, and dusty. "Very slow horse," he said deprecatingly.

"Your own spotted horse must be much faster."

"Champion? Oh, yes!"

"Is that his name—Champion?"

"Sure. Because he is the fastest of them all. I named him Champion when he beat a wild black stallion. That black horse had a harem of fifty mares. When he lost the race he left in disgrace."

"Was that when you let Champion go?"

"Yes, so he could have his harem and make more wild horses."

"You speak English very well, don't you?"

"Sure. The best. And I never went to school, either."

"Wouldn't you like to?"

"What for? I'm going to be an army scout when I grow up, and lead the soldiers to kill Thumb."

"Perhaps Thumb will have already been caught by then—you have to prepare for all sorts of things."

"Then I'll find Geronimo, and the soldiers can kill him."

"Perhaps there won't be any more Indian wars when you grow up, so we won't have to have anyone killed."

They dipped into an arroyo where some dry wil-

26

low and much chia crowded together and insects hummed busily. After the horses had climbed the far side of the arroyo, Kemo answered.

"There will always be wars against the Apache. The Apache will never surrender."

"Even after you kill Thumb?"

"Not even then."

"Who taught you English?"

"Me? I learn it myself. I hang around the fort."

"Did you jump the reservation?" Mary teased.

Kemo grinned. "No. I'm not a reservation Indian. Some Navajo, yes, but not me."

"Your family . . ."

"No. I have no family," Kemo said, "only an uncle in Mexico."

"Then your band . . . "

"I have no band."

"Why not? You mean you don't choose to live with them or . . . ?"

"I choose? I have no choice. They are all dead." His young oval face was suddenly too grave, too old. "Thumb killed them all. Chiricahua Apache killed them all."

Which explained the wish for revenge that Mary had accepted as merely an adolescent's violent fantasy. She had seen much of that in her teaching. Young boys who saw themselves as braves, as leaders, heroes who knew how to express those traits only in terms of gore and brutality.

They rode silently after that. It was another half-hour before they began to see signs of human habitation around them. Here and there stood a mud hut or a shack of cast-off lumber. Faces that were tanned, aged, lined by the sun, emerged to peer out at Mary.

There were fields where plows had been left at the end of an unfinished row to rust, where native brush had recaptured the land. There were scattered sunflowers with their faces turned toward the sun in unison or bowed as the great weight of their huge yellow heads proved too much for the slender stalks. Crows sat with folded wings on the humped dry earth, cawing to each other for no intelligible reason.

"Zuni," Kemo said as they passed a family working at trying to harvest a crop of withered cotton. He seemed to sneer.

"Don't you like them?"

"Their language is funny. They aren't like me."

"Nor are you like me," Mary said.

"No. Not at all. You are tame. Tame woman. I thought a Cheyenne would be different."

There wasn't time to delve into that. Nor how he had heard she was Cheyenne. A low white house, peeling and sun-baked, appeared before them. Around it stood half a dozen cottonwood trees, indicating water below the ground. To one side was a pile of weather-grayed lumber. Several Indians were digging through it, taking a piece now and then.

"Is that my wood?" Mary asked.

"Firewood." Kemo shrugged.

"Is that my lumber for the schoolhouse?" she demanded, and her voice was sharp enough to make Kemo turn to her with surprise.

"That is your wood. The school."

She lifted her horse into a trot and rode toward the Indian men. "You there," she called out. "Stop that. That's not firewood, you know. It's for constructing the new school."

A few of them turned their heads, but no one answered. "Do they speak English?" she asked Kemo.

"I don't know. Hopi men."

"Can you tell them what I said?" Mary watched as one man shouldered two long boards and walked away with them. "You! You can't have those!"

Mary swung down and started marching toward the Indians. Their eyes were coldly hostile or indifferent. She walked to the nearest man and took a board from his hands, throwing it down.

"You can't have that! Don't you understand, this is for the school!"

The man bent to pick up the board, and when Mary tried to interfere he simply pushed her back and she landed on the ground, her legs spread before her.

She rose sputtering and dusted herself off. She tried shouting again but the men were utterly indifferent to her. She watched the pile of wood shrink by the quantity of seven sawn planks, watched as they walked away. Then, throwing out her fists in frustration, she uttered a muffled shriek and turned to stalk toward the white house which dangled a weathered sign from its porch reading "Indian Agent."

She marched up the steps and in through the unpainted wooden door. A sleepy-looking Indian rested in a rocking chair beside a desk which looked unused though it was overflowing with papers.

"You can't come in here like this," the Indian said.

"Where is Mr. Justin?"

"He can't be disturbed."

"He is here, then?"

The Indian's eyes shuttled toward an inner door and then returned to Mary. "No," he answered. Mary was already walking toward the door, however, with Kemo in her wake. She knocked once, opened the door, and recoiled. The stink was overwhelming. The room was airless, smelling of whiskey and sour manhood. Sprawled on an unmade bed was a short, balding man of forty, his collar turned up, one arm draped over the side of the bed allowing his hand to dangle near an overturned whiskey bottle.

Mary strode across the room to the window. She struggled with it for a minute before it finally slid open and a blast of hot, clean air rushed into the room.

The Indian from the outer office stood in the doorway silently. He didn't try to stop her, he simply watched with frank curiosity. Kemo was grinning. He looked to Mary, then to the bed, where the Indian agent stirred sluggishly.

The man wiped at his mouth and rolled onto his side. "What . . . ?"

"Mr. Ralph Justin," Mary said as if Justin were fully awake and sober, "allow me to present myself. I'm Mary Hart."

"What . . . ?" Justin came to a sitting position and remained there, his head hanging, hair in his eyes, breathing through his mouth.

"I am certain you were expecting me. I'm the woman who has been assigned to establish a reservation school."

"Mary Hart." Justin rubbed his hand across his mouth and reached for his bottle, which rolled away under the bed. "Yes. Schoolteacher. Actually showed up, did you?" Justin lifted red, round eyes to Mary.

"Of course I showed up. I feel an obligation to do my job, an olbigation quite a few people do not share, it seems. You were supposed to have the schoolhouse constructed, Mr. Justin."

"Yeah, but—"

"Instead I find the lumber outside in a disorderly pile which shelters rats, not schoolchildren. That is, the lumber which remains after the depradations of the local people." Justin started to speak, but she went on. "This is happening virtually on your doorstep and yet I see no effort at security. In fact it seems to me that you are inviting people to take that lumber and use it as they see fit—and I can't imagine that lumber, sawn lumber, is easy to come by in an area with no forests and little reliable transportation. I only hope there is enough left to proceed with the planned construction."

Justin just stared. He rubbed an eye with the tip of his index finger and shook his head. "Lady, I know you're very young, but tell me: where did they come up with one like you? No, the schoolhouse ain't built. Who's going to build it? The Indians? They never seen a hammer or a saw. I got no funds to hire anyone. They sent me a load of lumber and said it's a schoolhouse. All right. There it is, use it. . . . Wait a minute, don't answer yet . . ." He held up his hand. "Even if you could get it built, there's no way you're going to get any of these Indian brats into it. No way their parents are going to force them to come. No way you're going to teach them if you don't speak their languages—four separate languages, by the way—and no way you're going to find them a place in white society if you could get through all of that. Get me?"

"I'm certainly not going to give up before I've started! I didn't come all this way to sit around and ignore my duties—to get drunk and sleep my time away."

"No?" Justin rose to his feet at last and stood there wobbly-legged, looking pale and insignificant. "Maybe you will eventually, lady. Maybe after you've given ten years of your life like I have to try to get something from a government that doesn't want to give a hand to the Indian who doesn't want to take, maybe you'll sleep a little more just so you don't have to open your eyes and stare out at that damned desert and the damned ignorant bastards who live on it."

Mary listened patiently. When Justin was through, she asked, "Will you assign a guard to that lumber?"

"You're going to build the schoolhouse?"

"I am," she said. "I am going to do it. One way or another, if I have to do it with my own two hands."

Justin studied her bleakly. Dull thoughts seemed to flicker behind his eyes, but he voiced none of them. At length he said, "All right. All right, lady, I'll watch your lumber for you. You go on and do it—I'd be proud to see it. You build this damned school."

There was a trace of mockery in his voice, but there was also a challenge. Justin looked at his Indian secretary. "You heard that, Charley. Get Coscobo or One-Eye or someone to stand watch over that wood. Give them a double tobacco ration. Then bring me a bottle."

Charley left and Mary Hart, with a last glance at Justin, followed. Outside it was over a hundred, the dry wind lifting the light soil, drifting it across the reservation. Mary Hart stood on the porch of the Indian agency, taking it all in, the dry, reddish earth, the gray-green of the scattered sumac and greasewood, the slanted shacks and mud huts, the few wind-ruffled cottonwoods, the far hills. The poverty was all too obvious. Poverty not only of the purse—for when had these Indians had wealth? —but also of the soul, of the spirit, of the mind. They did not ache to do, to improve their lot, as Mary herself had, growing up on a reservation. They did not seem to want to grow, to gain stature, to meet a changing world in the only way possible, on its own terms. Their view had to be an illusion. She would open the eyes of the young, she would show them the way out of this poverty.

"You will build the school," Kemo said.

"I'll build it." The school, a temple to the mind, to the spirit, the door upward and out and onward. Mary Hart would build it. She would people it, she would make it work. She had to.

Kemo was still watching her, his habitual smile now absent. "How are you going to build it?" he asked. "How are you going to do these things?" He paused, staring at her strangely, then said, "Know something, Miss Mary—Justin was right. Everything he said. Do you know what these people want? To be left alone. I know. I am Indian."

"And I am Indian," she snapped. "How can you forget that? That doesn't mean I am going to sit down and cry over the past. We are going forward, Kemo. Forward and into the future, the rich future, the better future."

"Yes." Kemo just stared at the pile of lumber where an old Indian with one eye now sat smoking a pipe, a rifle across his lap, staring into the infinite distance between the reservation and the long ago. "Into the future."

"Don't you believe me, Kemo? Don't you believe

this thing can be done? I see it in my mind, I envision what will be. How it must be."

"In my mind," Kemo replied quietly, "is a great spotted horse. This I see. This I ride in my mind's eye. I believe in it, I see it, yet no one else does."

"But I do," Mary Hart said, looking toward the far hills. "I see a spotted stallion as quick as the wind, and his name is Champion. He runs free with his harem, his prize for defeating the emperor of the wild horses, a great black horse. I see all of this, Kemo. I see the spotted horse."

His name was Thumb. He lay unmoving beneath the white sun, the sand beneath him baking his mahogany skin. He lay still and he watched the white settlement.

The sudden movement beside him caused his eyes to flicker to one side. It was nothing, only Sagotal, his face painted a dark yellow ocher, his eyes ringed with dark paint. The big man slid closer to his chief, his friend.

"There are but a few guns," Sagotal reported. "The men with the beards have gone somewhere. Two men are in the small house, the others you see."

"After I have done what I must do," Thumb said, "poison the well water. They must not drink our water, they must not live on our land and scratch at it with their iron plows."

Sagotal nodded. He squinted into the sunlight at the small white community of Coyote Wells. He and Thumb were alone. There were more Apache in the hills to the south, but they were not needed for this.

Thumb's black eyes shifted to those of Sagotal, and then with a nod the Chiricahua chieftain rose and darted off through the sagebrush and sumac below them, leaving Sagotal to check his bow, his arrows, his flint and steel. He could no longer see Thumb—the man was a ghost, a shadow. The whites would never see him, not until the time Thumb chose to show himself. Then it would be too late.

Sagotal watched the settlement patiently. It was very hot, but he was Apache. He had the patience of a warrior. He would wait a little while yet and then he would do as he had been told. Poison the water, burn the houses.

Thumb worked his way through the brush. It was hot and his throat was dry. Perspiration trickled down his throat. Gnats swarmed around his face but the Chiricahua war leader ignored them. From the settlement a child called out, but no dogs barked—it was the dogs Thumb was wary of, always the dogs who heard what white ears could not.

"Women," he murmured to himself as he crouched in the chia and sage, staring down into the settlement. He was suddenly sure that he had made the right decision by coming this way, just himself and Sagotal.

He crouched and waited and watched as the women hung up their wash on a rope strung from the side of the house to a broken cottonwood tree. It took a long while but finally they picked up their baskets and went into the houses. Then Thumb went on, working his way to the creek bottom, scrambling over the dark boulders there, weaving through the nopal cactus which clotted the far bank, and finally emerging just south of the little house, the one that Sagotal said had two men in it.

Farther on, Thumb could see two other men in the field. They were both armed. One had his rifle slung on his back, the other had his in a scabbard strapped to his plow. Thumb looked to the hill rise, toward Sagotal. He waited a minute longer, his eyes searching the surrounding country, the red empty land, and then he worked his way up out of the wash and crossed boldly toward the house.

He moved quickly, running in a crouch, taking advantage of the few trees to conceal his approach, but the whites could have seen him, should have. Perhaps they slept.

34

They would not sleep much longer.

Thumb reached the wall of the house and hunched down, looking to the window above him. Raking up a handful of cottonwood leaves, he bundled them and struck fire to them. Rising, he threw the bundle of smoldering leaves into the window, and heard the immediate startled yell.

Thumb unslung his bow and notched an arrow Two men burst from the front door as Thumb rounded the corner. The Chiricahua shot the first man in the thigh. He was a very big white man, nearly as tall as Sagotal. His pale face registered shock and horror as the arrow penetrated his leg. With a bellow the big white man fell back into the house. Glancing across his shoulder, Thumb saw the men from the field racing toward them. He smiled faintly, put another arrow into the open door of the house, and then sprinted away, hearing one wild shot fired.

Thumb jogged on, weaving through the nopal cactus which spilled out onto the flats from the arroyo beyond the trees. Then he slowed his pace deliberately, looking back toward the house.

The whites were on horseback now. Thumb heard a joyous yell, the thrilling battle cry which lives deep in the throats of all races. Smiling still, he ran on.

He zigzagged through the head-high cactus, not hurrying, letting the occasional shots the whites fired strike near. There was some risk involved, but from the back of a running horse few men can hit anything at all.

Thumb let them keep him in sight. Teasing them, he wove uphill and then down. Now the smoke began to rise over Coyote Wells and the Chiricahua heard a shout of chagrin and fear as the whites realized that they had been led away from their settlement so that the buildings might be burned. They feared for their women, and after a hasty loud argument, one man turned back.

The others continued the pursuit. They would have Thumb's blood.

The Apache was running in earnest now, down a sandy wash and then onto the flats, where a jackrabbit raced away. Thumb saw the hollow ahead of him beneath the creosote bushes and he ran that way. He got down on his belly and began throwing sand over his back.

When the whites came, they saw nothing.

Thumb was there. Only his eyes showed. He was lost in the shadow and the sand and they did not see him. They rode past and Thumb heard their muttering, the frustration in their voices. They looked for a little while more, so near to the Chiricahua that he could have risen up and put an arrow in both their hearts before they could so much as blink. But Thumb had not come to kill. He had come to tell them that they must leave his land, that they must not drink the Apache water, that this desert was his and not theirs.

After a while the whites left and Thumb rose, dusting himself off, brushing the sand from his hair. He jogged toward the rock with the two holes in it where he was to meet Sagotal.

The big Apache was sitting in the rock's shade, waiting.

"I had to kill one man," Sagotal told him.

"What needs to be done is done in war," Thumb said.

"I cut the throat of their calf and put it in the well. One woman shot at me. She was not such a good shot." Sagotal grinned. "When I set fire to their houses they ran into the canyon beyond the corral."

"Good, it is good," Thumb said.

Sagotal looked at his war leader and said, "They will not leave, these men. That is what the others will say."

"What others?"

"You know who I speak of. He will say they must be killed, every one of them."

"Let him say what he will." Thumb watched the smoke spiral into the white sky. "I am war leader. I am the one who says what must be done."

"And if they do not leave, and if the army comes into our stronghold again, Thumb?" Sagotal asked.

"If they do not leave, they must die," Thumb said. His obsidian eyes were expressionless. "And if the army comes, then the blue soldiers must die . . . and if they plant corn on my land, they must die . . . and if they take our children, they must die."

Thumb said nothing else. He had spoken.

2

She stood watching, arms folded, as the men sawed and drove nails and painted and cursed in five tongues. Scott Sampson found her there in the shade of the cottonwoods, standing by as the school went up, the gray, splintering lumber finding form and life.

"Success," Sampson said, swinging down from his bay horse.

"We're trying, Scott. Trying."

The army officer let the reins drop and the horse began nibbling at the young bright green grass beneath the trees. Sampson walked to stand beside and slightly behind Mary, studying the line of her jaw, her long lashes, her strong curved neck, the wisp of dark hair which curled back over her ear. He liked the determination he saw on her face, the curve and tilt of her body, the concentration as she watched her work crew. He stood closer to her, a little too close, Mary thought.

"I still don't see how you did it. Amazing. The colonel says you must know the black arts."

Mary smiled. "I asked them to come, that's all. I walked into the cantinas and the shops in town and I told them what I wanted. Some of them laughed. A few came. Then I searched the army ranks for soldiers who had had experience as carpenters, and some of them promised to come when they were off duty. I knew this Indian Agency building didn't put itself up either—there are Navajo and Hopi craftsmen here who could learn any job if they wanted to, but they didn't care about the school building. No one did. No one ever asked for help or tried to build it."

"What about the children? Have you got any promised?"

"The children will come."

"Does that mean no, you haven't got any students?"

Mary turned toward him, her eyes sparking a little, then settling to quiet resolution. "They will come. Once the people understand that education means the difference between poverty and a decent future for their children."

"I hope so." Sampson sounded unconvinced. Well, he wasn't the only one. Mary Hart's ideas were considered praiseworthy, but there weren't many around who believed a reservation school was going to change much. "Would you like to take a walk with me, Mary?"

"Now?"

"Yes." Sampson's eyes met hers, and the corner of his mouth lifted in an uneasy smile.

"All right." She shrugged. "They don't need me watching. They know their job."

"Are you still sleeping here?" Sampson asked, looking around at the building site. "Yes, you must be—but it hardly seems safe."

They went through the cottonwoods and down along the sandy wash which cut across the reservation behind the agency building. There cicadas sang and blue drangonflies droned.

"It's safe enough. Who would bother me?"

"I don't know. I just don't like it. There's not even a roof over your head."

"But there will be, there will be soon."

Sampson looked across his shoulder at the back of the agency building, at the cottonwoods. Then he stopped. Mary halted as well, watching him expectantly.

"Yes?" she prodded gently.

"There's a dance," he began, his words coming

out in a rush. "Mrs. Shore organized it. Some of the prominent local families and the officers. I'd like it . . . I was wondering if you wouldn't go with me."

"Oh, Scott, I don't know."

"It could be a valuable opportunity for you to meet influential people. People who might be able to help you with what you'll need out here. Books, for example."

That was a point to consider. Despite her luck in getting laborers for her project, Mary had much left to do. There were no desks or chairs and nothing to make them from. Ralph Justin had done a thorough job of spending every cent designated for the school and its supplies.

"I'll let you know," Mary answered.

"Please, Mary." He stretched out a hand and rested it on her shoulder lifelessly, not gripping her but letting it lie there like a perched bird. Then the hand fell away. He smiled once quickly and then turned and walked away, his step springy.

Mary watched him go, feeling a little amusement and some uneasiness. But she didn't have time to dwell on the young lieutenant's intentions for long. Kemo was waiting for her when she got back to the schoolhouse. The boy was in the shade sitting against the trunk of a bent cottonwood. He jumped to his feet when he saw Mary.

"Good morning," he said. He grinned and came toward her.

"Good morning, Kemo. All ready?"

"This will do no good," the boy said.

"How do we know unless we try?"

"I know," he said pessimistically. "I know the people of the reservation."

"We'll see. The schoolhouse will be completed Friday. Monday, school begins."

"They will not come."

"They will. If I have to drag them. You'd better make sure you're there," she teased.

Kemo seemed shocked. "Me! But I have to help my uncle. With the sheep."

"I thought your uncle was in Mexico."

"That was my other uncle. This one has sheep and he needs me."

"On Monday?"

"Yes."

Mary shook her head with mock sternness. "And then on Tuesday. And Wednesday—you'll never be able to come out of the hills except when there's no school. And think how lonesome you'll be, sitting up there by yourself."

"Yes, I know," Kemo admitted. She had caught him off guard and he hadn't had time to think of a really good story.

"Besides, I would miss you," Mary Hart said.

"Really?" He brightened a little.

"Certainly. And I was counting on you to help me out in the classroom."

"I don't know about that."

"Maybe?"

"We shall see." He shrugged. Then his grin was back and everything was all right again. They went to their horses and started at a walk toward the heart of the reservation.

The Navajo lived on the southern boundary. They had sheep and their carelessly made shacks and little else. They had been brought to the reservation at their own request. In the hills the Apache had raided them constantly, stealing their women, killing their men. They had come voluntarily, but the collection of huts and trash had the aura of a defeated people.

"Whom should I talk to, Kemo? Who is head man?"

"Long Ears, but you can't speak to him."

"Why not?"

"He will not listen. He is a sour man, very old but very strong still. Once a great warrior. There are tales of Long Ears filled with blood."

"Then the people will listen to him," Mary said.

"They would, yes, Miss Mary, but . . ."

"Where can I find him?"

Kemo was doleful. "Over there. That is his house with the two red dogs in front of it."

Mary turned her horse that way, walking it through the scattered huts and mud houses. Dogs yapped at the horse and nipped at its hocks. Black-eyed people stared at her from behind blankets hung across doorways, wondering at this Indian in white dress, this interloper.

She swung down at Long Ears' hut and the two red dogs rose, stretched, and came lankily forward to sniff the hand she proffered. One sat down and howled at length, perhaps in welcome. The other walked in a lazy circle, pausing to sniff occasionally.

"I don't want to wait," Kemo said.

"You'll have to," Mary said with more sternness than he had ever heard in her voice. "Someone will have to translate."

"Long Ears speaks English. Very well. He was a scout for General Baker long ago."

"All right." Mary waved a hand. "Go on, then."

Kemo turned his horse and rode away. Mary waited until the dust had settled and then, taking a deep breath, walked to the hut, the dogs followed to flop down in the dirt. She called inside, "Is Long Ears, the head man of the Navajo, inside this hut?"

There was no answer for a long while. Mary heard something move, making a scratchy small sound. At last a voice as distant and flat as her own northern-plains accent answered.

"Long Ears dwells here."

"May a woman enter to see him?"

"What woman is this?"

"Her name is Miss Mary, the woman who has come from the land of the Cheyenne to teach school to the Navajo."

There was another long pause before the voice answered, "Enter."

She ducked under the low sill, pushing the zigzag-designed blanket aside. Within, the air was close and smoky. There was no furniture, only an old man with long white hair sitting on the floor. He wore a red shirt and a turquoise necklace. His face was carved by wind and summer heat and cold rain. His ears were indeed very long, almost abnormally so, like those on the ancient carvings of Mexican Indians. His eyes were dark, bright, and strong, holding the memory of a virile past.

"Long Ears?"

"That is what I am called, woman. What have you come to bring me?"

"I have come to bring news for you," Mary said. "News that should cheer you."

"I could use cheering news." Those virile eyes grew darker. "What news could you bring me from the far north?"

"I told you, Long Ears—I am here to teach school to your children."

There was only silence after that. Long Ears was still watching Mary but he seemed also to be looking through her, to the future or the past, to distant places.

"Don't you understand? I am here to teach the Navajo to read, to write, to understand the world around them."

"Our children learn the old ways."

"They cannot read the white man's language."

"They read the skies. They read the soft track of a cottontail in the sand and know that their supper has passed that way, that it will return, that they will snare it and eat it. They know when the coyote is near and where the quail nests its eggs. They know sunrise will follow darkness. They know the signs in the stars, the truth of the sand paintings. They need to know no more."

"They did not need to know more—in the old world."

"It is the same world, divided red and white." His hand made a chopping gesture left and then right. "But the same world."

"You have come here." Mary spread her arms.

"But we will leave. When the Apache are dead."

"Will you? Or will you stay?"

"I have said we will go. Home. To the Mesa Grande, where we have lived since the first star fell."

"Then I believe you," Mary said. "But still you need to know the white language, the way to write their symbols, the way they think."

"I know the language. I am the head man. Children do not need to know these things. What does it benefit a child?" Long Ears asked.

"It opens his mind!" Mary took a step nearer and bent forward at the waist. "It opens a child's mind and lets the world enter it. The world of the white man, yes, but this world is one world, as you say, and if the Navajo knows more about the wild things, the spirits that dwell in the desert, still there is much to learn from the white. The white knows nature in a different way, he knows how to prevent diseases and how to raise better crops, how to breed healthier sheep—these are not unimportant things. They can mean the health of a people, of a nation. In old times you needed lances and bows. Now you need knowledge—knowledge is a weapon against poverty and the whims of those who would dominate you. This is true! You must see this, Long Ears. You have seen many skies, many rains. Let your wisdom examine what I have said, turn it this way and that, see if there is not the kernel of truth in it."

"The children of the Navajo do not need school," the old man answered. "But," he added with the faintest smile, "I will consider what you have told me. I will say this, woman from the north: if you have learned to speak from the white education you have had, then it is a good thing. No wise man has presented his argument more strongly to me than you. Not for years."

"I have strength in my words only because I feel the truth of them." Mary touched her breast with her fingertips. "I haven't come to take from the Navajo, but only to give. Please—if you want to give to your people's children, consider deeply what we have discussed."

Long Ears didn't answer. He sat so still that he might have been asleep. Yet his eyes were open. His eyes watched, they knew. Mary backed away from the hut, let out her breath, and squinted at the bright sunlight. The dogs didn't bother to rise again as she mounted her horse and rode slowly from the Navajo camp.

Kemo was waiting for her on the outskirts and he fell in silently beside her. Eventually he asked, "Did he strike you?"

"Who?"

"Long Ears. He is a fierce man. Did he strike you?"

"No! He was polite."

"And he said he would send the Navajo to school?"

"Not exactly that, no. But," she repeated, "he was polite."

"But that is over. Good. Now we can—"

"Now we can see the Zuni leaders and then the Hopi."

"Miss Mary! All of this is a waste of time."

"Nothing," she replied, "that has a worthwhile objective is a waste of time."

"Still," he said, "we cannot go to the Zuni camp."

"Why not?"

"Who will speak to them? I don't know their tongue. Only a few speak English."

"Then we will find the few," Mary said firmly. "The school will open Monday, and it will have students in it. Even if we have no books and no chairs and no desks, we will still have school! This is what I have come here for, and, Kemo, do not tell me that it is a waste of time. What is a waste of time is to live day by day without using the mind, without trying to form a future, without trying to be someone worth being."

"And what does all that mean?"

"It means," she said, "that we are going to the Zuni camp. "Which way is it?"

The day grew hotter. Distant blue thunderheads hovered above the red desert. They could see lightning occasionally, but coolness never touched them; there was a hot devil wind blowing. The horse was a heavy, stolid presence between Mary's legs. She couldn't take a breath without inhaling dust. The sun was pale and angry.

They saw the Apache a few minutes later.

Several hundred of them were living in a collection of shacks built in a depression where nothing but nopal cactus grew. There was nothing else green, no sign of grass or planted crops; there were no animals, no dogs or chickens or sheep. Cavalrymen with rifles in their hands stood on the high ground ringing the camp, watching the desert, the Apache, the approaching woman.

The corporal came forward. "You can't ride this way, Miss Mary."

"Why is that?"

"These are prisoners of war. Chiricahua."

"Isn't this the way to the Zuni camp?"

"Yes, Miss Mary, but you'll have to circle wide around. You don't want to go down there anyway."

"Is it dangerous?"

"Yes, very dangerous," the corporal said.

"But they have children—I can see children down there."

"They can cut your throat as well, Miss Mary, and would."

"But you don't understand—I must talk to all the reservation Indians and get them to send their children to the school."

The corporal was adamant. "Not to them, miss. Not to the Apache."

"I shall speak to Colonel Shore about this, soldier."

"Fine, miss, that's fine," he answered. "You talk to him. But until you do, I can't let you go that way. Colonel Shore's orders, you see. No one goes unescorted or unauthorized onto the Apache

46

reservation— and, Miss Mary, you just ain't authorized."

There was no arguing with the soldier, but she stared at the camp for a long while in silence before turning away with Kemo.

"What are we going to do about that, Kemo?"

"I don't understand."

"The children, the Apache children, must come to school too."

"No. There would be trouble."

"Not in my school," she said fervently. "I just won't allow that."

"No," Kemo said dubiously.

"But the first thing is to get them there. They're in army custody, aren't they?"

"Prisoners, Miss Mary."

"Yes. We shall see, then. Perhaps Colonel Shore can order them to school."

Kemo turned his head away so that Miss Mary wouldn't see the dismay on his face. She was suffering from some madness. Others laughed at her or shook their heads in amazement, and Kemo had even been in a fight sticking up for her. Now he wondered if the others weren't right, those who laughed at the folly of a reservation school and at the proud woman who had more determination than good sense.

Putting Apache in school! And next she would be looking for Thumb so she could sit him at a desk and teach him English manners.

"There's just the man I've been wanting to see," Miss Mary said. Kemo looked to where she was pointing. He was riding toward them from the Zuni camp, a lanky, graying man on a black horse.

"LaPlante?"

"Yes, Bill LaPlante."

"Going to make him come to school too?" Kemo kidded.

"No. I'm going to ask him to teach me," Mary said. She began to wave her hands, calling out to the army scout, who held up his black horse and then started toward them.

" 'Morning, Miss Mary."

"Good morning, Mr. LaPlante. I need help."

"Anything at all." The scout removed his hat and dabbed at his forehead with a folded bandanna.

"You're the only one I know who can speak all of the tongues here."

LaPlante nodded. "I guess I am. If you can call it speaking. What I know, I've picked up over the years from the Indian scouts. I don't suppose it's all real polite talk."

"I don't need polite talk. I need to be able to tell a boy to sit down, to be quiet. A Zuni boy, a Hopi boy, an Apache."

"You haven't given up on all this yet, I take it?" He put his hat back on, tugged at the brim, and frowned into the sunlight. His horse shifted its feet and blew loudly.

"I haven't even begun."

"Well, I suppose I got the time. Or I will have when I get back. I'm taking some scouts out this afternoon. Captain Granger and Lieutenant Sampson are going along. Down toward Coyote Wells. They've got an idea Thumb is staying in that area. When I get back, though, sure. I'll do my best, Miss Mary. I can probably get you started."

"That will be enough, Bill. After that my students will teach me."

"Why don't you just teach 'em all English? Make it simpler, wouldn't it?"

"For me. But I want to know more than a few words, Bill. I want to understand them."

"Well, Miss Mary, if you get that far, you let me know. Anyone that can understand an Apache is miles beyond me. I'm satisifed if I can just keep 'em from taking my hair."

"It can't be so difficult to understand them," Mary insisted. "They are men, women, and children, walking the earth like the rest of us."

LaPlante smiled a little indulgently. "The Apache

isn't the same, Miss Mary. Don't take that to mean that I think he's less, now. That's not it at all. But he's not the same. An Apache thinks different. His life is war and the hunt. He thinks different about his women. Most times a woman is to be used like a dog."

"These cultural differences are superficial, Bill! That's all. With education, with understanding . . ."

"You can make him almost white. Like you."

Mary wasn't pleased with the remark. "Are you deliberately trying to anger me?" she asked.

"No. I'm not, Mary. Just trying to tell you something you might have forgotten, might not have wanted to recall—you're Indian. The Apache's Indian," he added, "and I do speak French." Then with a wink he touched his hat brim and started his horse away at a walk. He glanced back, over his shoulder once to where the tall young Indian woman and her guide continued toward the Zuni camp. He watched them for a long minute, then shook his head, and whistling dryly, rode on toward Fort Bowie.

Yellow Sky was a half-Navajo scout with hands twice the size of a normal man's, narrow eyes, and a long chin. He wore his hair to the middle of his back. As LaPlante reached Bowie, Yellow Sky, who had been crouched in the shadows of the high wooden water tank, rose and walked forward to meet him.

"When do we go?" Yellow Sky asked.

"As soon as the soldiers get formed up. Have the boys pack their war bags."

"They say Coyote Wells," Yellow Sky said. He peered up at the white scout, holding the bridle to the black horse in that slightly aggressive way he had. LaPlante did not trust him entirely.

"That's what the report was."

"Not Thumb. Not to the south. He will not be there."

"Well, we'll see. All I know is what the colonel says."

"The colonel is . . ." Yellow Sky broke off abruptly. The army paid him after all. "When General Clark takes over, then we will have Thumb, then we will have the Chiricahua beaten."

"Clark? Here?"

"My cousin was by the telegraph office. He heard the soldiers talking. Clark is coming from Sante Fe to relieve Colonel Shore."

"Well, dammit all," LaPlante said with passion. He knew General Warren C. Clark. He knew him and disliked him. Clark was a warrior, all right, but he was also affected, pompous, and somewhat ruthless. What he wanted to come to Bowie for was beyond LaPlante. The last he had heard, the general was living soft in the capital. Well, there was glory to be had if a man could clean up the Apache trouble, bring in Thumb. Maybe Clark was looking for a third star.

LaPlante said good-bye to Yellow Sky and rode to the orderly room. First Sergeant Lou Hazleton, a bad-tempered grizzly of a man, looked up from a mountain of paperwork.

"Oh, hello, Bill," Hazleton said glumly.

"The colonel in, is he? He sent for me."

"Yeah. He's in. In a bad mood, too."

"Because of Warren Clark?" the scout asked.

"Well, dammit, what kind of grapevine have you got? The orders just crossed my desk thirty minutes ago."

"I just read some of Thumb's smoke, that's all," LaPlante said with a wink. Then, with Hazleton's suspicious eyes following him, he knocked on the commander's door and went in. Colonel James Shore was behind his desk, his hands clasped thoughtfully. In those hands he held a folded sheet of yellow paper which LaPlante recognized as a telegraphic dispatch.

It was a minute before the colonel seemed to notice the scout. "Sit down, Bill," he said at length. He placed the paper on his desk, smoothed it out, or tried to, and shrugged. "I'm being relieved, Bill."

"Well, you'll be off the damned desert."

"Relieved. You always wonder why, you know. Is this a promotion or a slap on the wrist?" The colonel rose, went to his window, and stared out at the parade ground where a company of men was going through mounted drill. The shouted orders of their NCO were just barely audible.

"Sir," LaPlante said, "I'm sure this ain't no slap on the wrist. Who's got a better record than you?"

"If unspectacular. It looks like I'm afraid to take a risk, doesn't it, Bill?"

"You mean with Thumb."

"With Thumb, yes."

"Sir, I recall a man called Custer who took a risk. It's not always the wisest thing to do."

"We've never even engaged Thumb. He snipes at us, strikes the isolated communities, fights with guerrilla tactics."

"That's his way, and it's suited to this country, to his type of force, that's all. You can't predict where he's going to strike and I don't imagine the textbook has so much as a chapter on how to counterattack when you can't locate the enemy."

"No. But in Washington they haven't any understanding of our problems, Bill, and what Washington perceives is all that matters."

"Maybe we'll have some luck today, sir. The scouts seem to have a pretty good idea where Thumb is now."

"Then why . . . ?" The colonel was irritated.

"Yellow Sky is lying. Leastwise I think so. I've known him for some time. He prefers getting his pay every month to actually finding Thumb or any other hostile."

"By God, I'll run that beggar off this post!"

"No, sir. No, I prefer havin' him around. If Yellow Sky says Thumb is north, you can bet your ears he's likely south."

"How could he know?"

"Yellow Sky knows. He's read sign with the best. The reservation Indians all know where Thumb is anyway. He's a hero to most of 'em. They talk among themselves, but no white ears are going to hear what they know. But maybe today, Colonel. Maybe we'll run that killer down."

"Doubtful, isn't it Bill?"

"Yes, sir," LaPlante admitted with a quick smile. "It's doubtful."

"It doesn't matter, really," the colonel said. He returned to his desk and sat heavily. "Well, Edna has always hated Bowie—or she says she does. Denver—I'm going to Denver. Lovely country. Very lovely."

"Yes, sir."

"This will give Edna's party a reason for being. Welcome the new commander, farewell to the Shores."

"Yes, sir." Bill didn't feel the need to speak up and tell the colonel how they would miss him and his lady, how much having him at Bowie had meant. Things weren't done that way. Besides, James Shore knew. The colonel made a small sound of disgust that seemed to banish his despondent mood.

"Granger isn't riding with you this afternoon. I'm sending him north to Catclaw. There's been a house burned, a settler killed. It's possible that it's Thumb's work, but I doubt it. I place him south, as you do. Still, I can't ignore the possibility. I'm giving you Scott Sampson—take care of him, Bill. He's a good kid but he's green as grass. He doesn't know a damn thing about desert fighting."

"I'll watch him," LaPlante said quickly. "I can't imagine we've much of a chance of catching up with Thumb anyway. Bunch of uniformed men riding together, sabers clanking . . . but we'll try, sir. We'll try, but we'll be lucky if we find his tracks in the sand."

"You're probably right." The colonel rubbed his cheek with the back of his hand. "I think," he announced, "that I'm going to spend the rest of the day trying to forget Thumb and all the other bloody Chiricahua."

"Leave them for Clark."

"That's it. If the general thinks he can do any better, well, dammit, he's welcome to try. Good luck to him. And now, if you'll close the door on your way out, Bill—the men shouldn't see their commanding officer with a whiskey bottle in his hand."

Bill winked and started toward the door.

"Take care of the kid, Bill," the colonel said. "Just in case."

"I'll watch him like he was my baby brother."

"Thanks. As you say it's likely Thumb has drifted away . . ."

"I'll watch him, Colonel."

Then LaPlante went out, closing the door softly. Sergeant Hazleton was away from his desk. The duty corporal glanced up and then went back to staring blankly at the roster in front of him. Outside it was glaring and dry, with a slight breeze blowing. LaPlante started toward his black horse, but he was hailed.

Turning, the scout saw Lieutenant Scott Sampson hurrying toward him. The kid looked just a little tense. When he caught up with Bill LaPlante he was flushed and slightly breathless.

"I guess I'm taking the patrol out alone," Sampson said.

"That's what the colonel just told me."

"You know . . ." He hesitated. "This is my first time in the field."

"Everyone has a first time for everything. You'll be an old hand in no time."

"I suppose it's natural to worry about it . . . what might happen."

LaPlante told him, "There's ninety chances in a hundred that nothing will happen. We'll spend a long hot day in the sun with the wind whipping sand in our faces, leg-weary from the horse under us, half-sick, and mad as hell. Then we'll drag ourselves back to report no contact and fall onto our bunks. There's nine more chances in that hundred that we'll make some sort of hostile contact—probably tracks in the sand a day old, a burned house, maybe a murdered settler or vaquero. We'll get our blood up then and start out after Thumb, but we won't come from here to New Year's of him. Then we'll ride home to report hostile contact and fall onto our bunks."

"There's one more chance in that hundred," Scott Sampson said.

"Yes, there is. The chance that we meet Thumb in armed combat. When that happens, we won't do much thinking. We'll ride like hell or squeeze a lot of rounds through the barrels of those Springfield rifles. It's a slim chance, so slim I wouldn't worry about it—worrying won't help anyway. We'll fight the best way we know how. That's what we've all been trained to do—you included, Lieutenant Sampson. We'll just fight and hope for the best."

"You're right. I just wanted to talk about it. How many scouts will I have?"

"Three. Me, Yellow Sky, and Tall Man Running. Captain Granger will have the others."

"In an hour?"

"One hour, Lieutenant."

Then LaPlante said good-bye, swinging aboard his black horse, riding out of the fort toward the town, where they said he kept an Indian woman.

Sampson watched him go. One hour. Everyone told him that the chances of actually engaging a Chiricahua force were minuscule, but it did nothing to settle his nerves. No, he wasn't a coward, he didn't even consider that as a possibility. He was just nervous, wary of being shown up as an inexperienced officer. The country was new, he was new to it. Desert warfare wasn't something they taught at West Point. There was no textbook to learn from, and anyway, textbook information was of no real use in the field—that was what his instructors had admitted. Events were too quick, too unpredictable. A man either had it or he didn't. Some responded well and quickly—others failed, and if a man failed his first time out, he might as well resign his commission. They said you never got your nerve back.

He turned and started walking toward the bachelor officers' quarters to gather his gear.

Mrs. Shore emerged from her quarters to greet him. "You haven't forgotten about tomorrow night, Lieutenant Sampson."

"No, ma'am, not at all."

"And you will have a lady on your arm?"

"I hope so, yes."

"Let me guess who," Edna Shore said with a smile. Samspon's eyes shifted hastily away. "Don't be embarrassed. I think Mary Hart is a fine woman. She's noble, dedicated, and strong. Yes, she's strong, is Mary. I don't know how Laura Clark is going to react, though."

"Laura Clark?"

"Yes—General Clark's wife." Edna Shore peered more intently at the young officer. "Why, haven't you people in the officers's ranks gotten the word yet? Every Indian scout and enlisted man on the post knows that General Warren Clark is due to arrive tomorrow."

"A visiting general, here?" Sampson couldn't help asking.

"Why would anyone visit here?" Mrs. Shore laughed. "Although General Crook once stayed with us for a month. But this is more than a visit. General Clark is going to take command of Fort Bowie. My husband and I, thank God"—she looked skyward—"are going to Denver . . . Fort Vasquez, actually."

"I didn't know. I'm sorry."

"Don't be sorry! I'm sorry for all of you who have to stay here under Warren Clark. I know him, of course. He's ambitious, too ambitious . . . Well, it's not my place to talk about him to a junior officer, is it?"

"You said something about the general's wife."

"Yes." Edna Shore frowned. "Laura Clark is a lovely thing. Twenty years the general's junior. She's blond and green-eyed and apparently her figure is appealing to men. She has a degree from a moderately respected women's college—history is her specialty, I believe—and she has made the grand tour of European cultural shrines . . ."

"However?" Sampson prompted.

"However, she despises Indians. Her parents were killed by the Sioux in Minnesota. A reservation uprising, I believe. They were missionaries, if I recall. In her husband she has found a perfect match—or perhaps I should say her perfect complement. For I don't think General Warren Clark hates the Indians—he doesn't seem to perceive them as human enough to be hated. They are simply obstacles, items to be cut down so that the reward for having done so can be obtained. Silver stars, chiefly," she sniffed. "He is very good at his work and Laura seems to find it all most exciting and gratifying in a way that is distinctly unhealthy."

"Are you," Scott asked tightly, "advising me not to bring Mary Hart to the dance?"

"Why, no!" Edna Shore laughed at the idea. "I love to see sparks fly. Especially if one of the annoyed people can be Laura Clark. Anything that upsets her pleases me greatly."

But then Edna Shore's expression sobered. "Seriously, it might not be fun for Mary, but I think she can deal with it if it's worth it to her. I can't really imagine that she's too anxious to attend our little excursion into hypocrisy and sham anyway, is she?"

"She hasn't given me a definite answer."

"I hope she does come. She's certainly better company than most of the ones I've invited. Señora Fernandez and Señora Diaz might be very interesting women, but I've never been able to determine for sure, as neither speaks English. All in all, I'd prefer Mary Hart. It might offend the general and his wife, but then we're leaving, and it looks now as if James is never gong to see a general's star of his own no matter what he does. . . ." She was briefly silent, then cast the subdued mood aside and brightened again. "And so please do bring her if she'll come. *You* be sure to come anyway, Lieutenant. Don't you dare duck the party— very bad for a young officer on his way up the ladder, you know."

"I'll be there," he promised. "And Mary, too, if I can convince her."

"You're going out on patrol this afternoon? Bring back Thumb's ears. Though . . . no, that would defeat you in the general's eyes. He wants the Chiricahua war leader himself. And he'll have him," she said with a quick nod. "If I know General Warren Clark, he will have that Apache's hide—and that, Lieutenant, is called giving the devil his due."

She left then, bidding Scott a hasty good-bye. Colonel Shore had appeared on the plank walk before his office and she was hurrying to catch him. Scott Sampson watched her link her arm with the colonel's and stride off across the post with him. Scott was still thinking about the dance, about Mrs. Laura Clark.

Maybe he was making a mistake by taking Mary Hart. She was Indian, after all. Some of the other officers had given him an odd look when he told them he had asked the new schoolmistress to the dance. But then, they understood that there just weren't that many women around. Laura Clark wouldn't.

He turned and walked on sullenly. It wouldn't do his career much good to infuriate the new commander's wife. He still had two years ahead of him at Fort Bowie.

Maybe volunteering for Bowie had been a mistake. He was going out today to fight a blood-crazed Apache. No matter what LaPlante said, Scott knew that Thumb was out there waiting. Then, if he survived, he was going to take an Indian girl to the party for the new commander. It wasn't fair. Probably Mary would refuse to go and thus settle everything. She certainly hadn't seemed eager to go with him. He doubted she would go—she was an intelligent woman, after all. She must have known that

Scott's impulsive invitation was a mistake—that an Indian wouldn't be welcome.

Feeling slightly ashamed as these disturbing thoughts wound through his mind, Scott entered the BOQ, took off his boots and tunic, and began to prepare his bedroll.

Thumb.

The very name was enough to cause a tiny ache in the back of his skull. Sampson tried not to think of Thumb, of anything at all.

He peered at the polished steel shaving mirror and saw a slightly distorted, puffy, freckled face peering back. Someone's face, some soldier's face. Everything had an air of unreality about it.

He found his sidearm and strapped it on, checking the loads in the Schofield pistol. Polished, oiled, deadly, until this moment it had always seemed nothing more than a decorative accessory, like the dress saber that hung in his locker, which he would wear to the dance tonight if Mary Hart decided to accept his invitation. That thought caused a knot to develop in the pit of his stomach, just below and beside the other stony lump which was nascent fear. His mouth remained dry even after he poured and drank two cups of water from the canteen on the wall; his entrails felt loose, his eyes dry and hard. He finished dressing, picked up his Springfield rifle, and went out into the dry day.

There was smoke rising from the grub hall, and the scent of frying beef and toast filled the air, but Scott knew he couldn't keep anything down. He walked instead to the paddock, where a lanky young private brought out his horse and saddled it while Scott stood watching, feeling weak-kneed and small. To the east the sky seemed faintly darker and the breeze off the hills to the south and west had stiffened.

"All ready, sir."

Scott turned toward the private and nodded, returning a careless salute. The horse was held as he swung up with the creak of leather and the slight chink of the bridle chain.

"Goin' after Thumb, are you, sir?"

"That's right."

"Good luck, then. Hope you bring back his hide."

"I hope so too," Scott said. He wondered if he sounded at all sincere. The bay horse walked forward and out onto the parade ground, where Sergeant Sherman Hollister was starting to form up his men. Now and then the grub-hall door opened and the soldiers, in pairs or singly came out to walk toward the formation, chatting and laughing. They had filled their bellies. No one anticipated much trouble on this patrol.

Hollister was a big man with a booming voice, and from time to time he shouted to the laggards who were still checking their gear, mounting.

"Jefferson, we don't wear our cuffs rolled up in this army. Can't you control that horse? Don't let him back in ranks!"

Then the rows of soldiers were filed and orderly, the corporal with the guidon beside the sergeant. Hollister called roll and gave a few last perfunctory commands. Bill LaPlante came toward them, leading his black horse, which moved silently, unlike the cavalry horses, which chinked and squeaked and rattled their gear with each step. LaPlante himself moved easily, confidently. The man knew his work.

Yellow Sky and Tall Man Running, the two Indian scouts who would be with them, arrived from the opposite direction. They stood, rifles cradled in their arms, the slight breeze shifting the feathers in their hair, waiting with all the patience of a desert people.

Theirs was the patience needed to outwait the prey nearing the snare, to remain still and silent while the hunt was in progress, to wait out the long, long season of drought and heat, to watch and accommodate to the desert, which always reclaimed its own. It was a patience which sometimes decided life and death, a patience the desert warriors had in abundance and which the Apache possessed in an untoward degree.

But it was also a quality that escaped Scott Sampson completely, as the horses tossed their heads and blew, as the soldiers shifted in the saddles and coughed or whispered. Sergeant Hollister called the last few names on his roll before turning and walking to meet Sampson. He saluted as he reported, "All present and accounted for, sir."

"Forward, then," Scott Sampson said mechanically. "Form a column of twos, Sergeant."

Scott Sampson rode at the point of his wavering blue column as they rode out of Bowie, Bill LaPlante beside him, Hollister slightly behind with the guidon carrier. The Indian scouts had ridden out to either side, searching for hostile sign, which could hardly be expected this close to Bowie.

The patrol rode through the white sand dunes crowding the rocky wash south of the town of Bowie, which now appeared only as a dark smear against the desert. The wind of the evening before had sculptured the dunes delicately—they appeared as ocean breakers frozen in silver motion.

Here and there ocotillo could be seen, twelve to fourteen feet tall, whiplike, tipped with crimson flowers. Their spiny stalks cast crooked, menacing shadows against the sand, which had grown hot, troubling the horses. Heat veils rose before them, obscuring the vast distances where eroded red mesas and turrets carved by wind and time rose from the flats.

LaPlante took a drink of water from his canteen and spat most of it out again.

"How far to Coyote Wells?" Sampson asked.

"Fifteen miles or so. Hard miles," LaPlante told him.

"The men should be alerted."

"Sir, they've been alert all morning. Most of these boys have seen some fighting. They know."

Scott nodded. "What's at Coyote Wells?"

"Not much now, since the last raid. There's

the wells, of course. Sweet water—but Thumb's likely poisoned them. There was a trading post and the six families—three of 'em related, the MacCormacks— and a few dozen head of cattle. Nothing else.''

"Where are your scouts? Shouldn't they have reported in by now?"

"They'll come when they've something to report. No sense in them riding in to tell us they haven't got anything to tell us.''

"The procedure . . .''

"Sir, in the first place, procedure means nothing to those Indians. Trying to get them to do something that makes no sense just because some white soldier a hundred or two years ago thought it was proper procedure is butting your head against a wall.''

"And in the second place?" Scott asked.

"And in the second place, the man who wrote that book never seen a desert like this one, never seen the Apache fight.''

"I've been told they fight afoot.''

"Mostly, that's right. They'll use cavalry if it seems to their advantage, but the Apache have more use for a horse as something to eat. Hard enough for a man to find water out here, without trying to forage for a horse.'' LaPlante added, "But don't let that give you any false hope. *N'de* can outrun a horse through the heat of the day. *N'de* can hide behind a rock that you'd think couldn't hide a kangaroo rat. He can smell water and live without if he has to. He's a man, sir, a soldier.''

"*N'de*?" Sampson asked blankly.

"Yes, sir. That's what the Apache call themselves. *N'de*, or sometimes *Dine*—means the same thing: 'The People.' Like a lot of other races, the Apache think of themselves as the chosen people, or the only people worth mentioning, the superior race. We call 'em *Apache*: that's the Zuni word for 'enemy,' that's all. You call 'em what you like—they're warriors and an adversary to be reckoned with.''

"You actually sound like you admire them, La-Plante."

"I admire strength. Maybe not admire—I *respect* the Apache. I respect Thumb, though you give me a chance and I'll cut his throat."

"A peculiar attitude."

"Is it? Maybe I'm a passionate man, Lieutenant. All I know is that Thumb wants to kill me, all of us. It's best for me if he dies first. It don't mean I can't respect a man who fights for what he believes in."

"And what does Thumb believe in, LaPlante?"

The scout smiled crookedly. "That I couldn't exactly tell you, sir. All I know is that the Blue Jackets don't fit in with it, whatever it is."

They sighted Coyote Wells shortly after that. There was the scent of smoke in the air, lingering, like a memory. The fires had been put out days ago. The MacCormacks, guns in hand, were out working again, trying to clear away the burned timber and the dead stock Thumb had dumped in the wells to poison the life-giving water. The whites' cattle had strayed, and two of their houses were burned.

Angry eyes lifted toward the cavalry contingent. Three men, all with red hair and bulky shoulders came forward to meet them.

"You're too late. LaPlante," the oldest of the three said. "Too late by three days. Thumb's been and gone—what the hell kind of protection are we getting from the army?"

"You know, Harry, the army can't be everywhere," LaPlante said soothingly.

Harry MacCormack wasn't so easily placated. "No—and the army can't find Thumb. Years of this, we've had. We lost Gregory and Ned Phillips this time. Who'll it be next time? A man don't walk outside without his rifle. A woman in Coyote Wells don't walk outside, period. We do the fighting, and three days later the army shows up to offer condolences. And who's this?" he asked, looking directly at Scott Sampson as if he would like to yank him from the horse and lead him to the graves of the dead. "And what is he going to do about it?"

"Easy, Harry, this doesn't go," LaPlante warned him.

"Still army, are you?"

"So long as they pay me."

"I don't need your protection," Scott Sampson said, suddenly angry. "You can't blame the army for this, Mr. MacCormack, and I'm sure you know it. All we need from you is any help you can provide as to which direction Thumb was heading, where he might be now."

"And you're going to ride him down!" MacCormack chided.

"Yes," Sampson replied, "we are, with any luck at all."

MacCormack looked him up and down. "I'll believe that when I see it," he grumbled.

"You or any of your people see which way he went?" LaPlante asked.

" 'Course we seen which way he went. We was shooting at him."

"Then?" Sampson prodded.

"South. Toward the border."

"You sure?"

MacCormack flared up again. " 'Course I'm sure! I told you I saw him go."

"We had a report he was up north, toward Catclaw."

"Maybe he is. Don't take much to change directions, does it?"

"No." Sampson was still staring southward, across the narrow belt of grassland toward the foothills beyond. "Where would he be if he had kept riding southward, LaPlante?"

"I couldn't say for sure. Carrizo? There's water there, up in the tinajas along the gorge."

Scott Sampson continued to stare, giving no indication that he had heard his scout. He stared toward the salt flats, the red hills beyond, savage raw hills where nothing seemed to grow out of the jumble of stone and sand.

"He's there," Scott said. "I know he is."

LaPlante frowned, his eyes narrowing. One of the MacCormacks snickered. The nearby privates cast sideways glances at their lieutenant, thinking: So he *knows* Thumb is there, does he? Curious, considering they had all been searching for just a hint of the Chiricahua without success for a long time now.

Sampson said it again. "I know he's there, LaPlante. Where are the Indian scouts? Let's ride. MacCormack, good day." He touched his hat brim, touched spurs to the flanks of his big bay horse, and they rode out, splashing across the silver ribbon of a stream running down from the wells above the settlers' houses.

Sampson rode alone in the front of the troop briefly. The guidon carrier, urging his own mount on, was struggling to keep up. LaPlante had drifted out to the right flank; his black horse was growing lathered and he was determined to slow up on his own if the black showed any sign of faltering. Some devil had taken hold of Scott Sampson and was riding him now, driving him toward the hills to the south.

LaPlante had seen a case like this before. It was fear, he believed, which made the lieutenant madly anxious to engage the enemy. He was afraid of his own fear and he wanted somehow to banish any thoughts someone else might have that he was a coward.

Not that there was much hope of finding Thumb, of fighting him—inside, Scott Sampson must have known that—but the little fillip of bravado was bolstering the young soldier's courage. Who knew, maybe it was helping the men as well.

Sampson had slowed his mount. The hills were as far distant as ever—on the desert everything seems nearer, everything recedes as it is approached. The clarity of the air causes that illusion, and many men have died from believing they were nearer to a landmark than they were.

The column of cavalry soldiers slowed to a trot and then to a walk, Sergeant Hollister's hand going up as Sampson eased his pace. Then they were trudging forward, toward the far hills, their horses' hooves sending up clouds of dust that were visible for miles. LaPlante's mouth tigtened and he shook his head—the army would never take Thumb or any other Apache leader with these tactics. Crossing the flats en masse, loaded down with steel and silver gear which chinked and rattled and caught the sunlight. They might as well have beat drums and blown trumpets as they went.

He looked again to Sampson, seeing that the mood still hadn't passed, that he was still gripped by the excitement, the wish for combat. His eyes were bright, his head thrust forward eagerly, his shoulders and arms tense. From time to time he touched his holstered belt gun. LaPlante turned his head, spat, pulled down his hat brim, and settled in. It was going to be a long hot ride.

At midday the desert was a white furnace. The sun was merciless, punishing. From time to time LaPlante looked up, seeing the red hills draw nearer, seeing the desolate and broken land, wondering how even the Apache could survive there.

The scouts came in shortly after noon. Yellow Sky was whipping his horse furiously. Tall Man Running sat crookedly on his paint pony's back, apparently holding his side. LaPlante felt his heart quicken its pace. He looked toward Scott Sampson, seeing a strange and violent spectrum of emotions on the young officer's face.

Tall Man Running tumbled from his horse onto the sand before anyone could help him. He lay faceup, writhing in agony, blood staining the deep blue silk shirt he wore.

Yellow Sky's horse stumbled to a stop and he started reporting very rapidly. "Thumb. We found his camp. A rancheria along the gorge where the tinajas collect water. Two Apache found us. Tall Man Running was shot. We rode back."

"War camp?" LaPlante asked. "Did they have women and children or not?"

"Women and children." Yellow Sky nodded. "Yes."

"Then they can't run fast. Lieutenant," Bill LaPlante said, "it appears you've got your wish."

3

It was as still as death in the canyon. They climbed higher but there was no cooling breeze. They had left the horses below, and now, glancing back down the long, sheer red canyon, Scott Sampson could see the animals bunched, waiting, held by two impatient troopers chosen by lot. No one had wanted to miss out on this.

Sampson scaled a ledge, crawled along it on hands and knees, his pistol in his hand, and then stood to inch forward up a trail no wider than a spread palm. Above him he could see LaPlante, intent, hatless, his face dusty, reaching for one handhold and then another. In front of LaPlante was only Yellow Sky, angry now—Tall Man Running was dead; the Apache had killed his friend.

Sampson's boot slipped and he bit his tongue, fighting back a curse as he regained his balance and continued to climb upward. His shirt was stuck to his back and chest with perspiration. Sweat trickled into his eyes, burning them. His legs were cramped from the climb.

The hope was to circle behind and above Thumb's rancheria—his mountain camp—and attack before the Apache could defend themselves or run. If they had women and children with them they would have to break camp gradually, traveling slowly. But Thumb had had warning. When Yellow Sky and Tall Man Running had encountered the Apache lookouts, one of the Chiricahua had escaped. He was wounded, Yellow Sky said, but he had undoubtedly reached the rancheria and raised an alarm.

The wind had come up in the gorge and it gusted against them now, tugging at their shirts, slapping at them as they crept upward. Sampson looked up again, still not seeing the way over the ridge that Yellow Sky swore was there.

Behind the officer a man slipped and went down, cracking his knee against the red stone. He cried out with muffled pain as hands reached for him, pulling him back onto the narrow ledge, where he sat doubled up, holding his leg. No one spoke. The following soldiers just stepped over him and advanced. The wounded man could be seen to later. There wasn't going to be a second chance like this to trap Thumb.

Scott saw the notch against the sky. The red rock parted as the trail ended against the crumbling ridge. Yellow Sky was already out of sight and now LaPlante followed, throwing a leg up and over, rolling onto the ledge with Yellow Sky helping.

Both men yanked the officer up, and moving in a crouch, Yellow Sky led the way across the flat rock toward the canyon beyond. The soldiers were scrambling after them now, eyes intent, faces flushed, their hands knotted around the rifles they carried.

Yellow Sky flung himself to the ground suddenly and LaPlante and Scott Sampson followed instantaneously. They crept ahead on their elbows and knees. There was a thin screen of dry gray brush and then a gradual slope down into the canyon proper. Below, Scott could see cedar, some pine, grass in patches along the shadowed foot of the canyon wall opposite.

And near that the Apache camp.

Something was wrong. The Apache didn't seem to be stirring. They seemed to be going about their normal activities, unaware that the soldiers had arrived in their area.

"He didn't make it back," LaPlante guessed in a whisper. "The Apache lookout bled to death before he got in."

"What do we . . . ?"

"It's your war, Lieutenant. I'd just advise we do it quick."

Scott looked around for Sergeant Hollister, found him, and waved him over. "We'll try to flank him south and north. Send out six men on either side. Tell them to move cautiously but quickly—"

Scott was interrupted by a shout from below, a distant pained, small sound. His heart leapt into his throat. LaPlante was straining to hear, to see.

"The lookout," Bill LaPlante said. "He just came in."

Below, all was suddenly frenzied activity. Men ran through the camp, women dragged children after them, dogs began to yap. LaPlante was looking at Sampson, as were Hollister and Yellow Sky. They wanted to know how it was going to be.

"Form a picket line," the young officer ordered. "Advance downslope and through the trees. Hold your fire until we are within range and you hear my command—or," he added grimly, "until we are met by hostile fire."

They rose and started scooting, slipping, walking down the slope, advancing raggedly. Still the Apache hadn't spotted the blue uniforms on the canyon wall.

A moment later they had. The soldiers heard a shout and then another, and then a fusillade of rifle fire. Bullets danced their way across the red slope beneath them. They were still out of range, but the distant puffs of smoke, the pinging of lead against stone, the dust rising from the red rock around them was eerie and frightening. One soldier fired in return and Hollister's booming voice barked out: "Obey your commands. Hold your fire until you're in range."

A dozen Indian ponies raced toward the mouth of the canyon. On their backs were women and children, one older man. The two men Scott had left at the foot of the gorge would have a surprise coming when that party rushed toward them. Unless there was another way out, a feeder canyon—there probably was. Thumb wasn't one to get himself trapped in a box canyon.

Scott Sampson began to feel panic—had he handled this right at all? Maybe some of his force should have come mounted up the gorge, trapping Thumb. But they would have been seen much sooner, losing the advantage of surprise.

Hollister was staring at him now, as was LaPlante. It was a minute before he figured out why. They were well within rifle range and the bullets from the Indian camp were singing around them.

"Fire," he yelled but his voice emerged strangled and weak. He cleared his throat and a hoarse, fierce bellow leapt from it. *"Fire!"*

The cry hadn't faded away before it was drowned out by the reports of the army rifles behind and to the sides of Sampson. The Indians who had been standing on position or kneeling as they fired, covering the retreat of the rest of their tribe, now broke for the rocks and trees beyond the camp. Army rifle fire took two of them down and they lay twisted against the field as the soldiers approached.

Sampson's heart felt twice its normal size, filling his chest with wild exultation. The pistol in his hand kicked against his palm twice, three times. He thought he hit an Apache in the back of the neck. He cried out, the thrill of battle sweeping over him, washing away all doubts, all thoughts besides pursuing, killing.

He was running now, holding his saber to his side with one hand, firing with his sidearm, urging his men forward. Sergeant Hollister was beside the lieutenant, and then he wasn't—crumpling up, Hollister fell. There was blood on his face. Scott Sampson didn't even slow down. He waved his pistol-wielding hand toward the sergeant and shouted for someone to take care of him.

He was into the oak trees now, and he paused, his breathing ragged. Leaning against a tree, he shakily reloaded his pistol. His men were advancing in an uneven picket line, firing as they came. Fire, reload. Fire, reload. From the Indian camp there was only sporadic fire.

"They're in the rocks," LaPlante said. The scout had come up on Sampson without his realizing it.

The lieutenant turned wild eyes on LaPlante. "We'll get them out, then, by God!"

"Easy, Lieutenant, that's like chasing a rattlesnake into the rocks."

"I won't let Thumb escape."

"We're drawing blood, and we've got some of their force cut off. Even if we don't get Thumb, we can get some hard information," LaPlante shouted above the roar of the guns. "But you go into those rocks and you'll lose half your people."

Scott's eyes were wide. The pistol in his hand was clutched tightly. That hand was trembling, trembling with war fever. He needed to fight desperately—then suddenly the mood passed. He nodded to LaPlante. "All right. I welcome your advice, Bill. Show me where we've got some of them pinned down."

They went on through the trees, finding another dead Apache—his scalp was gone.

"Yellow Sky," LaPlante said. Scott, who would have thought he'd be revolted by the idea, found it only fascinating. Yellow Sky had gotten some measure of revenge for his friend's death. "Best not to dress him down over this, sir. It's his people's way."

"No. No, I won't."

A brief spate of gunfire caused both men to hurry on, emerging from the trees into the ruined Apache camp. Three soldiers were firing down into the canyon from a stack of yellow boulders before them, and they trotted that way.

"What is it?" Sampson asked.

"There's three, four of 'em down there, sir." An answering shot rang off the boulder, drifting stone dust. "See what I mean? Best keep your head down, sir."

"All right. We'll root them out of there. Keep

firing, soften them up." Sampson turned to another private, one with a scratched face and a stained uniform. He was young and exhausted. Sampson himself was euphoric, feeling no weariness, no fear. "Get across the camp, call those men off that pursuit. We'll never get the Apache out of the rocks. These we've got cut off," he said, as if all this were his own line of reasoning, not LaPlante's. Bill LaPlante didn't begrudge him the use of the logic. A lot of soldiers could be killed climbing around those rocks looking for Apache.

They just might have found more than they wanted to find.

The soldier took off at a loping run while the others emptied their rifles into the brush in the canyon below. Sampson saw a rifle fired in answer, marked the puff of smoke which rose from a thick clump of red-tipped laurel-leaf sumac, and calmly emptied his pistol into the bush.

The cry of pain sounded from the brush and Scott Sampson's mouth lifted in a tight little smile. A moment later the bare-chested Apache, blood smearing his face and chest, burst from the brush, wildly firing his Winchester repeating rifle. The soldiers cut him down and he lay still in the silent canyon where smoke drifted away on the dry breeze.

Behind Sampson many footsteps sounded and he glanced over his shoulder to see his men running toward him, dusty, some of them in torn uniforms, their faces blackened by gunsmoke. They crowded around him, awaiting his command, and he could read it on their faces now: they had accepted him, they trusted him as a leader. A part of it had been chance. On his first patrol he had found Thumb; he had promised them that he would find Thumb and he had. Now they had apparently beaten the Apache in this skirmish. Scott Sampson was suddenly not a green lieutenant from back east, but a war leader. He liked the feeling.

"They're down in the canyon," he told his men, not stiffly, but as if he were one of them. "Let's soften them up a little more and then we'll go down and see what we've got. How's Sergeant Hollister?"

"He'll make it, Lieutenant. They've got him bound up and resting."

"Fine." He looked at the eager, half-frightened faces around him. "Let's put some lead into that canyon."

The soldiers clustered on the rocks and began methodically firing into the brush in the canyon. Only occasionally did the cries of pain rise, but it was enough to bring a smile of satisfaction to Scott Sampson's lips, knowing that they had another dead Apache to report.

The shooting went on for most of an hour. After that time Bill LaPlante, looking inexplicably sour, ventured a comment: "Maybe it's time we went down there and mopped up, sir."

"That might be like going in after rattlesnakes, wouldn't you say, Bill?"

"It might be." LaPlante's eyes narrowed. "But I doubt there's many rattlers alive down there."

"Let's make sure. . . . Corporal, see if that brush won't catch fire. Let's smoke 'em out."

LaPlante turned away. Sampson couldn't see his tightly compressed lips, the tautness of his expression. The soldiers, who hadn't relished going into the brush after the Apaches, no matter how few they were, started a fire at the upper end of the canyon. The dry brush—sumac and sage—caught quickly and the wind pushed the fire down the canyon, crackling and snapping, red and yellow flames leaping into the air and spreading a cloud of smoke for more than a half-mile into the air. Sampson, his pistol holstered and arms akimbo, watched. Excitement still quivered within him, moved through his arteries, knotted his muscles, filling his heart. He had come here a boy, an uncertain leader, and he would return a warrior. He had found the Apache. He had won.

It was a long while before the canyon was considered cool enough to attempt entering. The fire had burned itself out against the dark rocks at the lower end of the gorge, although as they started down into the brush, they could still see a few tongues of fire against the darker background.

The rocks were hot underfoot, the ashes warm, stirring with each step. The soldiers were silent, grim, walking through the aftermath of hell. They watched their officer constantly.

"Oh, Jesus," Scott Sampson said and he leapt back. LaPlante, surprised at the exclamation, stepped forward.

The Apache was lying in a shallow ditch, his blanket over his head and shoulders. He was very dead, his body badly burned. They couldn't even tell if it was a man or a woman. Sampson wiped the back of his hand across his mouth nervously. He needed someone to reinforce him and he got support from Yellow Sky.

"This man," Yellow Sky said, kicking the blanket away, "wanted to kill you, to kill me." His toe touched a rifle, the stock charred. "Fire killed him. It was good. He would have shot us. Fire or bullet, you are still dead."

Sampson wanted to hear that, and accepted it. He turned around, managing a sickly grin. He called attention to the body as the soldiers approached. "There's one that won't be firing back, men. I knew there were some alive down here yet."

He heard someone say, "I told you the lieutenant knew what he was doing." When he looked again at the blackened body, he was able to see only the remains of an enemy soldier.

That Apache wasn't the last they found. Some had obviously been dead before the fire swept over them; others—like one woman—appeared to have been alive. Finding the dead woman bothered no one. Everyone knew an Apache woman was as dangerous as an Apache man—they were as bloodthirsty, as filthy, as treacherous.

There was no sniping; none of the enemy seemed to have escaped the fire. The men relaxed a little.

Now and then a joke passed between them, nervously told, nervously received.

"Prisoners," LaPlante said to the lieutenant, "were what we needed."

"We don't need any more reservation Chiricahua."

"We need someone to tell us where Thumb is."

"Why, he was here!"

"Doubt it. Small camp, lots of women and kids." LaPlante shrugged. "Didn't look like no war camp. Thumb would travel quick and light. And if you'd of found Thumb, he wouldn't have taken to the rocks so quick."

"You're telling me this wasn't Thumb's camp?" the lieutenant asked with some hostility.

"Might have been." LaPlante shrugged again.

"You know damn well it was," Samson said hotly. It was important to him, important that it was Thumb he had met.

"Could be," LaPlante said again. He walked off to the right while Scott Sampson went to the left.

Then LaPlante found the live Apache, the prisoner he had been hoping for. He had started past the rocks and was halted by the smallest of movements. He brought his rifle around, paused, and then went forward.

He moved cautiously toward the rocks, glancing back toward the soldiers who still advanced, following their lieutenant away from LaPlante.

LaPlante cocked his weapon. The wind shifted the ashes in the canyon. It was hot, very hot. The rocks, huge yellow boulders, were stacked together randomly. And beneath the rocks there were deep shadows, a depression, and a pair of glittering eyes that stared out at LaPlante.

The scout called out, "Lieutenant, we got one! We got him alive!"

When Kemo found Miss Mary she was in the back room of the schoolhouse, where she had made her bed for the past week. Usually she was hard at work there, writing letters or making lists—of what,

Kemo didn't know. He still hadn't much interest in school or its business. Besides, he had heard everyone say that Miss Mary's letters would have about as much effect as a leaf falling on the earth.

This afternoon Miss Mary wasn't working at her mail, her lessons, her lists. She had on a blue dress with long sleeves and a high neck. A narrow lace band circled each wrist like a delicate bracelet. Around her neck was a small black stone flanked by half a dozen bone beads. Kemo was surprised by that—he had never seen Miss Mary wear anything that an Indian had made. Her hair was piled high in braided profusion. She was a very handsome woman, he decided. There was something in her eyes that made her almost beautiful. Some knowledge, not of her own, but some racial knowledge, some wisdom which must have passed into her through the blood of her ancestors . . .

Kemo chased away that fragment of a dream. He told her, "I have brought the buckboard, Miss Mary."

"Thank you, Kemo."

"I wondered why you didn't ride your little pony. Now I see." He nodded at her skirt, and Miss Mary laughed.

"Eight petticoats, I couldn't ride unless someone threw me across the saddle." In a lively mood tonight, she lifted her skirt three or four inches and revealed her white petticoats. Kemo laughed, partly from embarrassment.

"You are going to the dance, then?"

"Yes. Poor Lieutenant Sampson had his heart set on going, I think. I will go."

"The general has arrived. Him and his yellow-haired wife."

"Did you see them?"

"Yes. A little after noon. A big man."

"And his wife is very pretty."

"Too young," Kemo said, making a flat gesture with his hand. "A man needs a woman who knows how to weave and tan hides and cook. What does a young one know?"

"You've been well taught by someone," Miss Mary said with a smile.

"Everyone knows that. A man needs an older wife."

"Yes." Mary looked at the boy again, touched his hair, and smiled more deeply. "Perhaps."

"The necklace you wear . . ."

Mary touched it nervously. "Yes?"

"I have never seen it before."

"I always wear it. Inside my blouses. It . . . was my mother's."

"The Cheyenne woman."

"Yes. The Cheyenne woman, Amaya."

"She is dead?"

"Yes."

"What happened to her?" Kemo pressed on with the bluntness of youth.

"Why, she died."

"Of old age?"

Mary looked into the shadows of the room. A stray beam of light reflected in one eye. Her profile was sharp and clean. "She was ill."

"She died on the reservation up north."

"Yes—there's really no point in talking about this, Kemo. I don't know how we got onto it."

"Does it hurt you to talk about it?"

"Yes. Of course."

"Then I will be quiet. I am foolish." Kemo smiled and Mary returned the gesture, but he noticed that for a long while after that she fingered the necklace unconsciously.

They went out into the dusk, which glowed with a strange red-violet light as the desert withdrew into darkness. Kemo helped Mary up into the buckboard. Waiting for him to clamber up into the driver's seat, she sat for a long minute watching the big oak against the sunset sky before she realized the old man was there. He hobbled a little as he moved, his hair was snow white. Long Ears was no longer young. He stepped to the wagon and rested his hand on the dashboard as he looked up at Mary Hart.

"They will be here," Long Ears said. "I will send the Navajo children here to school."

"Long Ears—"

"Wait." He held up a hand. "This is for a little time. To see if they learn anything useful. Some of the things you told me made sense. I have decided this."

"Thank you," Mary said. "I thank you for the children's sake. You are a wise man."

"No." He shook his head. "Only uncertain which way the future turns for my people. Only uncertain which road we must walk." He started away, then halted and with his back to Mary said, "I hear you are learning our language."

In the Navajo's own tongue she replied, "I am trying. I want to be a good teacher. I must learn as well."

Long Ears started away, walking into the sunset, being covered by the deep liquid shadows beneath the oaks.

"Kemo! Isn't that wonderful!" Mary hugged him, astonishing the boy. She pulled away and smiled, squeezing his shoulders. "What a victory for the school! Doesn't it make you happy for me?"

"For you, yes. All it means is that I will have to come as well. For myself I am not happy."

"Kemo, I think you hoped the school would fail . . . I think you believe it will!"

Kemo didn't answer. He looked sideways at her, snapped the reins, and started the team forward. He was dejected, but Mary didn't notice. She was happy—no, thrilled. It would work, it must work now. The school building was nearly complete, at least enough to begin classes, and now there were students. The books and slates could come later. She could teach without them; they could learn without them. Nothing could stop her now, nothing.

By the time they reached Bowie, the sky was fully dark, with just a faint deep purple glow in the west. The lanterns were lit around the camp. Surreys from town had arrived, bringing the elegantly dressed Spanish women and their husbands. A black horse trapped in silver stood regally among the smaller ponies of the less aristocratic. Mary looked around, but the patrol didn't seem to be in yet. That meant Scott was still out on the desert, probably scared to death—or maybe that wasn't a kind thought. Anyone, she decided, would be frightened in combat.

Combat. War. Futile, debilitating conflict, bringing death and hurt and hunger and pestilence. She abhorred war, the thought of it, and all those who would make it. It was never justified, never.

"Not yet," Kemo said, concurring with her own thoughts. "The lieutenant is late."

"It appears so. That's what I expected, really."

The colonel's quarters were brilliantly lit, as was the dining hall, which for tonight would serve as the ballroom. Kemo halted the buckboard before the hall and looped the reins around the brake handle before leaping out to help Mary down. Several men stood outside smoking. Two were Mexicans in silver-ornamented sombreros, two others army officers. Mary had seen none of them before.

The men all watched her coolly as she lifted her skirt and went into the hall unescorted. Inside, bunting in red, white, and blue hung from the walls and from the wooden uprights. On a long table, punch was being served. Men stood together in groups: the American civilians; the teamsters, sutlers, providers, local cattlemen together; the Mexican civilians together; the military men in their own groups. There were a few exceptions, but for the most part people congregated with their own. The women were segregated as well. Spying Mrs. Shore with two very large Mexican ladies, Mary started that way. Edna Shore waved at her with a small handkerchief, urging her on.

"My dear, you look marvelous," the colonel's wife said. "I envy you, and that is God's truth. So lovely, so lovely. May I introduce Señora Fernandez and Señora Diaz."

"How do you do," Mary said with a small curtsy. The women nodded back.

"How is your Spanish, dear?" Edna Shore asked.

"I'm afraid I haven't any."

"Then things will have to proceed as they may," Edna said. "Our friends here don't speak English. How is everything on the reservation?"

In a rush Mary told Edna of the news Long Ears had brought, and of her plans to open the school Monday.

Edna Shore listened, nodding thoughtfully. "You're strong, Mary. Very strong. I didn't think you could have brought things this far along. No one did. I'm proud of you. I don't envy you your future, though. Not out here on this godless desert, not with these children, twisted and dirty, mistrustful."

"But you can't—"

"I don't condemn them all. I don't blame them. They are children of war, Mary, that is all. I just wonder if there's anything at all anyone can do to change them beyond bringing back the past."

The Spanish women interrupted and Edna listened patiently to a stream of words she couldn't understand. Finally, with much fluttering of fans, the black-clad women left and Edna shrugged. "Every year. Every celebration—you'd think one side or the other would have broken down by now and learned the other's language, but I've always been sure James's border time would end soon. Maybe it was my way of bolstering my wish to leave Bowie. And now," she said contemplatively, "we shall."

"About the school . . ." Mary began.

"Yes, that consumes most of your time, doesn't it? What is it you need?"

"I wondered if your husband couldn't somehow compel the Apache children to come to the school."

"The Apache? I'm sure he *could*, dear, but I don't think it would be in anyone's best interests."

"But it *would*. They must come. How can we discriminate against them?"

"Very simply. *They* are the enemy. *They* are the

troublemakers. They aren't Zuni, Hopi, or Navajo. They are wild, savage, and untamable. You would be lucky if they didn't assault you in your schoolroom. At the very least, they would disrupt the others' learning."

"The colonel could compel them to come?" Mary pressed on.

"Dear," Mrs. Shore said, shaking her head in wonder, "I will talk to him." She gave a little sigh. "As one of his last acts of command, perhaps he will do what you wish."

"I'd nearly forgotten. The general."

"The general. He comes and we depart. And good luck to General Warren Clark. And may his lady fry her brains out in the desert sun—don't look so shocked, dear, if you knew her you'd wish worse for her, believe me."

But Mary ignored the comment. Scott Sampson doesn't seem to be back yet.

"No." The colonel's wife looked a little worried. Maybe she had seen too many patrols come back with empty saddles or fail to come back at all. "He's overdue, but no one can maintain a strict schedule on the desert. But if he doesn't hurry," she said more brightly, "I'm afraid he'll miss the general's party and miss the lovely girl who's waiting for him . . . God, there they are."

Mary turned toward the door. A tall narrow-faced graying man stood there in a dress uniform. Silver stars gleamed on his broad shoulders. He wore a long curling silver mustache and squinted with one eye as he surveyed the room. On his arm was an exquisite, tiny blond in a yellow dress edged with black lace. She was cold, aloof, ivory-complexioned. Her eyes swept past Mary without seeming to notice her. The regimental band struck up without warning, a strident, brassy welcome, and the general smiled, walking into the room to the strains of "Hail the Conquering Hero."

The guests stirred expectantly, the soldiers coming to attention unconsciously moving forward slightly as if eager to be noticed. Behind General Warren Clark, Colonel Shore entered like a shadow. Mary studied the colonel's expression, finding it enigmatic. Amused? Tolerant?

The general had paused to say hello to Bye Courtney, the town's big merchant. Apparently the two knew each other from way back, giving each other an extended handclasp. During the interval the colonel caught up with Clark and his wife, and then he could be heard making a few introductions. Ralph Justin, his cheeks glowing red, was trying to insinuate himself into the group, but for the moment the Indian agent was being thoroughly ignored. It was another ten minutes before Colonel Shore managed to bring the new commander to his wife's side. Mary had tried to inch away, feeling out of place, but Edna Shore took her hand and gently pulled her back.

"Hello, Edna," the general said. "It's been a long while."

"Too long, Warren."

The general's lady stepped forward, smiling a smile that didn't touch the expression in her green eyes. She hugged Edna briefly, and her lips pursed beside Edna Shore's cheek. She stepped back, still smiling.

"You're still lovely, Edna. Where did you get that dress?"

"Out of a catalog, and you know it."

"Still the same Edna Shore."

"Let me present our friend Miss Mary Hart, who is running the school on the reservation. Mary, this is Laura Clark."

"How do you do," Mary responded.

"I can't believe it came from a catalog, dear, not the way it fits you. Do turn around once." Laura Clark was still smiling brightly. Colonel Shore frowned. The general tugged at his mustache. Edna seethed.

"Are you growing deaf, too, dear?" she asked. "Or are you only still rude? This is our friend Miss Mary Hart."

"And, Warren," Laura said to her husband, pointing across the room, "isn't that Captain Holt? Remember the fun we used to have racing his blue roan against all comers at Fort Riley?"

"By God!" the general roared. "It *is* Holt. I'd forgotten he was on Shore's post. Has he still got the roan, I wonder? Nice to have seen you again, Edna, we'll have dinner tomorrow night. Holt!" And the general strode away as the band played on. His yellow-haired wife was on his arm, her ringlets bouncing as they walked toward Captain Holt, who indeed still had the blue roan. The horse was the regimental racer on which entire payrolls had been wagered. Edna Shore just stared. She was white with anger.

Her husband touched her shoulder and shook his head. "It's not worth it, Edna."

"There's no excuse for that kind of rudeness. None! Mary, I'm sorry, it's . . . ."

But the corporal of the guard burst into the hall just then, clutching a rifle by the barrel. Even above the crash of the band they heard him distinctly as he yelled, "Patrol's coming in! Sir! Colonel Shore. Lieutenant Sampson's patrol is coming in and they have wounded. They also have a prisoner."

It was a ragged report, but the corporal was excited. The response was less than disciplined as well. The colonel glanced at General Clark and then led the rush toward the door.

Edna Shore took Mary's hand. "You'll want to be there as well."

"It's not my—"

"He's a friend of yours."

Then Mary was being steered toward the door, where the press of bodies was close and she was jostled and steadied, then propelled forward.

Ouside, the evening was warm. Only a few stars were visible in the hazy sky. Those who waited could just make out the head of the cavalry column, the horses' heads hanging, the guidon fluttering darkly like a night bird.

Privates were emerging from the sutler's store, where they had been drinking beer, smoking, and cursing the officers' army. They needed to know who among them had been shot or killed, who would not return from the desert. The company surgeon had left the ball to hasten to his office and was now returning on the run, his bag in hand.

They could see the wounded men now. Three of them, Mary thought, supported by their comrades. One of them was Sergeant Hollister. His face was a mask of agony.

She saw Scott Sampson then and relief washed over her. She started forward, checked herself, and stood beside Edna, feeling the older woman's arm around her.

Sampson was giving his report. "Colonel Shore, I must report casualties sir. We engaged the enemy, Thumb, at—"

"Later," Shore snapped. "Get those wounded men into surgery. Easy there, Sergeant! That's a man, not a sack of potatoes."

"I don't see any prisoners. I heard they had prisoners," a voice cried out.

"A prisoner", someone answered. "Yes—I see him. Look at Bill LaPlante!"

There was a spate of laughter despite the nearness of danger and pain. Bill LaPlante was marching toward them, and beneath his arm was a boy of nine or ten kicking, clawing, biting, and screaming. The scout approached Colonel Shore, and with a glance at the general, who was at the colonel's shoulder, LaPlante said, "Brought him right in here, sir." Bill looked at Mary Hart and said, "Here's one for you, Miss Mary. Think you can tame him?"

The boy spat at LaPlante, screamed, and kicked still more vigorously. His face, she noticed, was fire-smudged, his clothing ruined, his hair singed.

The colonel waited patiently. He knew LaPlante and knew that Bill hadn't dragged the Indian boy to the fort for no reason.

General Clark, however, didn't know the scout.

"Why bring the boy here?" he demanded. "Belongs on the reservation, doesn't he, filthy little thing."

"He does. I just thought you might want to take certain precautions. You see, this here is Thumb's boy."

"He's what!"

"Thumb's kid."

"How could you know that?" Clark demanded.

"He told us, that's why. Told us what his father's going to do to us for taking him."

The boy had stopped struggling, seeing that even if he got free there was nowhere to run. He hung limply from Bill LaPlante's arm, staring at them like a trapped wolf cub.

"And you believe him?"

"I believe that he's Thumb's kid, yes, sir. He was wearing this necklace—sign of pretty high rank." LaPlante handed over a necklace of silver and turquoise. It was delicate work for the time and place, Mary noticed.

"By God, that gives us a negotiating tool, doesn't it?" Clark said. He was ebullient—briefly. As he stepped forward, the Apache boy spat in his face. Swearing, Clark leapt back and then slapped the boy across the face so hard that it sounded like the crack of a pistol shot. Blood flowed from the Apache boy's nostrils, but he didn't so much as whimper. If Clark hadn't stepped back again, Mary thought the boy would have spit again.

"That was uncalled for, sir," Bill LaPlante said. It wasn't a wise thing to do, speaking up like that to a general, but it revealed LaPlante's finer instincts.

"Take the little bastard away. Lock him up."

LaPlante didn't move. He stood watching Colonel Shore, who still commanded the post, until Shore nodded. Then LaPlante turned, striding away with two privates as an escort.

"Where are they taking him?" Mary asked.

"To the stockade."

"They can't do that!" She moved beside Colonel Shore. "He's just a boy."

"He's Apache."

"Still only a boy," Mary insisted.

General Clark angrily threw away the handkerchief he had been dabbing his face with. Turning to Mary, he said "The boy's a valuable hostage. He'll stay under lock and key. I can understand why *you* would have sympathies for the boy."

"Because I am a teacher?"

"Because you're a squaw." There was a hard, dark silence which seemed to fill the night. "You *are* a squaw, aren't you?"

"I don't know what you mean," Mary said through clenched teeth.

"Indian, you know—squaw woman."

What Mary would have said next, she didn't know. Fortunately they were interrupted by the arrival of Scott Sampson, who had rinsed off a little and dusted his clothes haphazardly.

The general spied him and said, "Damm it all, Lieutenant! Stealing my thunder in the war against the Indians are you? Congratulations!" The general beamed.

Scott saluted and smiled boyishly. They shook hands. "Welcome to Fort Bowie," Scott said.

The general studied Sampson by the dim lanternlight. "You went out there and found the devil, did you? Found him and engaged him and came away with his boy—and some Indian blood, I'll wager."

"The enemy suffered casualties," Sampson said, trying to remain modest despite the fact he was obviously bursting with pride. He had gone out to prove himself and he had done so. Now the man who mattered, the Father, the war leader, had approved and commended him, praising him in front of the entire post.

"Gentlemen, shall we return to the ball?" the general said. They started that way, General Clark's arm slung over Sampson's shoulder.

They went away one by one, Edna Shore and the colonel, the Spanish women and the officers. One by one. Until Mary Hart was left alone in the night staring toward the stockade, where a young and frightened boy had been taken.

She bit at the inside of her cheek. She was angry and confused and upset all at once. "They won't keep him there," she promised the night, "not if I can do anything about it." She looked toward the hall from which the sounds of brassy music reached her ears. She hesitated and then started that way. There was nothing to be gained by walking away with her injured pride.

They had begun to dance inside, the Spanish men and their ladies taking the floor first. Colonel Shore and Edna joined them. In one corner Mary saw Scott Sampson, still dusty and glowing, recounting the events of the day. The general nodded with apparent satisfaction from time to time. And watching Sampson with more than casual interest was the general's young wife.

Mary watched for a minute, unsure if she was imagining the situation. But no, Laura Clark was glowing as brightly as Scott Sampson with his battle flush. Her glow, however, had another source.

Bye Courtney appeared before Mary just as she was ready to force her way into the group. The merchant was drunk—very drunk. Courtney, they said, had begun his fortune by selling Comanche scalps in Texas. Then the whiskey trade had carried him for a time. Now he was older, grayer, stouter. Life had brought him to an age and a position where he could think of little that he didn't already possess, and so he spent his money on whiskey. He was the army's main supplier of goods in the territory. He had wangled or purchased every major contract offered in the past five years. He dealt in grain and firearms, in liquor and dry goods, in hardware and farm implements. If he did not have it, they said, it wasn't to be had.

Now he reached out, and without warning gripped Mary's shoulder, pulling her to him. Before she could protest, he had swept her out onto the dance floor. He reeked of whiskey. Each step he took threatened to be his last as he reeled from side to side. Other couples moved aside, glaring or laughing as the corpulent trader spun dangerously through the dancers.

"You've never danced like this, I'll wager!"

"No. Please, Mr. Courtney," Mary answered, trying to escape from his firm grasp.

"Used to dance all night! Every Saturday night at the schoolhouse! Younger then . . ." He stumbled and Mary had difficulty keeping him up. Across the man's broad shoulder she saw Edna Shore watching them with some apprehension. She tried to signal Edna, but Courtney turned her in a constant circle and they careened on.

"Please, Mr. Courtney—I'm getting very dizzy."

"Too close in here? Outside, then," Courtney said, his voice very slurred.

She was unable to stop him or even slow him down. With his massive arm around her waist, he made his way to the door and led her outside into the starry night. Then Bye Courtney turned her suddenly and pressed her against the wall of the building. His thick, whiskey-flavored lips mashed themselves against Mary Hart's and she struggled free, twisting her head away.

"No," she cried.

"Not here? Let's go out on the desert, then, girlie. Or I'll show you my house. Ever seen my house?" Mary was trying to wriggle free, but Bye Courtney's hand was wrapped tightly around her arm.

"Please let me go. This is inexcusable," she said in frustration.

His hand held her still more tightly. He laughed out loud. "They told me you were a high-toned squaw. You talk real highbrow, don't you? That don't mean a thing, you're still an Indian woman. I can have any squaw I want, and I've had plenty."

His lips were near to hers again and she slapped him hard, so hard her fingers ached, but he only laughed. He had her pressed against the wall with the bulk of his body. She turned her head from side to side, anger and shame rising simultaneously within her.

"Let her go, Bye." The voice was hard, but Mary heard it with a trembling sense of relief.

"Nothin' but a squaw woman, Bill."

"Fine. Let her go now," Bill LaPlante said again. "You had a little too much liquor. Why don't you take a walk and cool down? I'd hate to shoot you."

"Why, damn me, Bill LaPlante, would you shoot me over this?" Bye Courtney asked in true surprise.

Bill's answer was calm, certain. "Yes, I would, Bye. I'd shoot you over it. Leave the woman be, now."

Bye looked at Mary a long minute more, then with a shrug released his grip and stepped back. Mary saw that Bill LaPlante had changed. He wore a gray suit, that was quite rumpled, and a string tie. He still wore a gun, however, and looking at it, Bye licked his lips nervously. He managed a grin and a wink.

"I believe I will take a little walk, then, Bill."

"Do that."

The big man started uncertainly off the plank walk.

Mary found she had been holding her breath for a long while, and now she let it out. "Thank you," she said finally.

"Welcome. Liquor gets him that way."

"You apologize for him?"

"Explain for him, that's all," Bill LaPlante said. "I thought the lieutenant was your escort for the night—where is he?"

"Still inside with the general." Mary glanced toward the hall and smiled. "He seems to be enjoying his big moment."

"Yes," LaPlante said ambiguously, "the big moment. Well, I guess I'd better go in and make an appearance. Not my sort of shindig, though. Like to go in with me?"

"No," she said. "No, I think I've had enough socializing for tonight."

"Can't say I blame you. You got a way up to the reservation?"

"Kemo brought me. He's gone now. It's all right. I'd like to walk, I think."

"Want me to walk along, Miss Mary?"

"No. It'll be all right. I'd prefer to be alone."

"If you're sure. Good night, then. Want me to say anything to Lieutenant Sampson?"

"No. I really don't think it would matter just now. Tell Edna Shore thank you and good evening, please."

"I'll do that, Miss Mary. You're all right, aren't you?" LaPlante asked, peering at her.

"Yes. Quite all right." She hesitated. "The boy—is he really in the stockade?"

"He is, yes, miss."

"But he's just a child."

"He's secure in there. In case . . ."

"In case what?"

"In case his father comes looking for him."

"Surely he wouldn't dare!"

"No telling what Thumb might dare. He's a bold one, and he's plenty smart. And, just now, plenty mad."

"Still, you can't place a boy in prison."

"That's where they wanted him, Miss Mary, so that's where I put him. I might agree with you, but the army pays me."

"And that's the way it is," she said a little roughly.

"And that's the way it is. I cut my way. I do my job."

"Yes," she said quietly, distantly. "We do our jobs."

"There's not much else we can do, is there, Miss Mary?"

"I suppose," she said, "we can do whatever we choose to do in this life. We choose to do what we perceive our duty to be."

"To teach."

"Or to scout," she said.

"Or to make war, like Thumb or General Clark."

"I can't believe people *choose* that as a way of life," Mary said.

"Maybe not. I don't much believe," Bill LaPlante said, "that we choose anything. We try and we fool ourselves into thinking we make choices, but we're pretty much what we have been given, what we are told we are, what . . ."

"What our blood makes us," Mary said.

Bill smiled in the darkness. "You know how I think on that."

"That we are born to be . . . what we must be."

"That's about it."

"Perhaps," Mary said. It hadn't been a happy night, and her head buzzed. She liked Bill LaPlante, but his theories were antiquated. She was what she had chosen to be; she would be what she decided; she would do what must be done.

Mary's mother had felt much the same way Bill LaPlante did. A Cheyenne was a Cheyenne, an Indian an Indian. To try to be otherwise was an offense to the universe. It was a primitive thought, a primitive concept. Mary herself disproved such theories. She was no longer Indian, she was no longer . . . Akton.

"Miss Mary?" Bill LaPlante was looking at her with concern and curiosity. "Are you all right?"

"Yes, Bill, thank you."

"I'd be glad to walk you back if you want me to."

"No," she answered, touching the scout's hand gently. "I need to be alone. Thank you."

"All right. Good night, then, Miss Mary. If you're sure . . ."

"I'm sure." Then, still hesitant he slowly turned and walked away.

Mary watched him saunter away, hearing the sudden increase of sound as he opened the hall door, and then the near-silence as it closed behind him. She waited, looking at the closed door, the brightly lit windows, the couples whirling past in silhouette. Then she turned and started away, away from the fort and the dance and the whirl and sound.

91

She passed the stockade, which looked dark and forbidding with the soldiers standing before it, rifles in hand. They tensed slightly as she passed them. Inside there was no light; in her mind's eye she saw only a boy awake in the darkness.

The desert was dark and sterile. The moon was rising later these nights and the stars seemed dim and sleepy behind the haze. Miss Mary walked on, happy to be alone, to be invisible in the night, to be only a single person beneath a towering sky.

The town and the fort died away, sinking into the sand. There was only the desert then, soundless and still. There were strange, mammoth silhouettes against the skyline, the distant Mesa Grande and the Devil's Tower, an eroded red spire. Now and then something whispered with menace or amusement.

Akton, she thought as she walked on, hands behind her back, her eyes on the stars and the distant landforms. "My name is Akton."

It wasn't really, not any longer. She had voluntarily discarded that name. It was an Indian name, and since she was no longer Indian, had chosen not to be Indian, she had no use for the name her mother had given her. It sounded strange now even to say the name, to think of it, to remember the little girl growing up on the reservation, skinny, wide-eyed, ambitious.

Mother had always told her that she was the serious one. Her sister, Hevatha, who had been lost during a winter battle with the soldiers, was the laughing child. Hevatha was lost and Akton was the one whose spirit demanded that she achieve something, become larger somehow, outgrow what she was, become . . . whatever you became.

She had decided to be a teacher, to escape the reservation drudgery in that way. There had been a teacher she admired, a white woman named Clara Bourke. She had been dignified, erect, British. She had taken the fever after six months and died. Her bones lay on the reservation; no one knew where in England she was from.

92

Mary stopped. Distantly a coyote yapped. The land was shadowed, seeming to undulate gently, though that was far from the truth. Night had softened the land, turning it into a dream.

She waited a long while as the stars slowly wheeled over. Waited for something that never occurred, could not occur, since Mary—or was it Akton—had no idea at all what it was that she waited for.

Her mood, timeless, soft, yearning, was broken by another distant sound; and although it couldn't have been, not at that distance from the fort, it sounded too much like a child's sobbing for Mary to be comfortable in the darkness any longer.

His back was sore from being slapped, his face glowing with liquor, his eyes bright with success. The general had already promised Scott Sampson a promotion the moment he had officially taken command of the post.

"Dance with me," the blond woman said softly, and Sampson looked with surprise at Laura Clark, taking in the glow of her green eyes, the creamy flesh of her shoulders and throat.

"I've never had a woman ask me to dance before," Sampson said. He tried to make his voice light, but wasn't successful.

"Put your drink aside," Laura said, "and dance with me."

Sampson glanced to the corner of the hall where General Clark was reliving yet another battle to the ostensible interest of a knot of uniformed junior officers.

"All right." Samspon hesitantly put a hand on Laura's waist and clasped her right hand with his left. The small military band tramped on through its number, and Scott, his head swirling, spun across the floor with the general's wife.

"Where is that Indian girl?" Laura Clark asked.

"What girl . . . Mary Hart?"

Laura's hair was soft and scented. The lanternlight streaked it with shifting pale bands.

"The Indian girl—they said she was your date," Laura prodded. She was dancing much too close to him.

"Yes. Mary Hart."

"An Indian!"

"There aren't many women . . ." Sampson stuttered. "Out here."

"And a man gets lonely," she said, and Sampson felt a flush creep up his neck and stain his cheeks with color. Before he could answer, she laughed out loud, showing her white even teeth, her pink tongue and mouth.

The band staggered to a stop and the general's wife said, "Take me outside. It's so hot in here."

"Certainly—I'll ask the general."

"Ask him? What for?"

"Mrs. Clark, it isn't done."

"I do what I want to," Laura Clark said. "What's convention but bondage anyway? I can't think of a reason in the world why I should ask that old man if a handsome young officer can take me outside for a breath of air."

Sampson again glanced toward the general, who was regaling the others with still another tale. "All right," he said quietly. What else could he say? The night was a dream, a heady blend of blood and valor and liquor and success. "Outside, then," and she hooked his arm and walked out with him past the scrutinizing eyes of Mrs. Shore.

Outside it was cool, the night empty.

"Walk with me a way," Laura said.

They stepped off the plank walk and started across the parade ground. The skies were bright with huge silver stars. The wine was working in Scott's head. As he looked up, they seemed to spin a little.

They halted near the side gate. They could hear the sounds of the dance only as a distant muffled murmuring. Scott stopped and the general's wife stood before him; then with a smile she stepped against him, her breasts meeting his chest, her thigh pressed against his.

"You're a hero, Scott Sampson," the lady said.

"Your husband . . ." was all he managed to reply. The scent of her hair rose into his nostrils and heated his body. She knew what she was doing, damn her, but why . . . ?

"This post, this desert. What can you do here? Do you know what it's like for a woman—a place like this? Conversation with boring, bored wives, teas with the officers?"

"I'm sure you'll find the people here congenial," Sampson said, trying to make a return to propriety.

"You're a warrior, Sampson. You're young." Her fingers dug into his upper arms. "Strong. We'll be friends." Someone was coming toward them, a guard walking his slow round of the wall. "You'll see," Laura whispered, and then, rising to tiptoes, she bit Scott's lower lip, bit it so hard that blood flowed from it and he yanked his head back, touching his mouth.

The general's wife smiled in the night, the starlight showing the dark pleasure on her face. Then she turned, lifted her skirts, and was gone, leaving Sampson to finger his bloody lip, to wonder what sort of woman she was and what he would have to do to have her.

4

When they came, it was reluctantly, in small bands or singly, barefoot and dirty, hostile, curious or frightened. There were a few Zuni boys and several Hopi. For the most part they were Navajo—Long Ears had sent them all. He had kept his word; now it was up to Mary to keep hers, to make the education of the Indian children worthwhile. She stood on the porch of the newly painted white schoolhouse and watched them as they eyed each other warily, cast sideways glances at their new teacher, and looked wistfully out at the open land beyond the reservation. There, they had run and played and made their mock wars, and hunted jackrabbits or dug for crawfish along the creek, or swung from ropes tied to the limbs of the cottonwoods above the creek and dropped shrieking and laughing, twisting into the water to swim or fight or run back for another turn.

They stood and watched and waited.

"Now?" Kemo said. He looked no happier than the rest.

"Not just yet," Mary answered quietly.

"It is time. What are we waiting for?"

"Be patient."

They had to wait another fifteen minutes. Then they saw the wagon with the canvas top winding its way toward them, three cavalry soldiers flanking the wagon, a fourth driving.

"What is that? Books?" Kemo asked.

"You shall see."

Kemo watched with curiosity as the wagon pulled up to the school. The soldier in charge, Corporal Killian, swung down and walked to the teacher, his face lined with disapproval.

"Where do you want this bunch, Miss Mary?"

"Let them out."

"They'll run away."

"Not if you watch them carefully, I'm sure."

"Now, wait a minute! The colonel didn't say anything about standing guard over them."

"I'm sure he doesn't want you to lose them," Mary said confidently. "Let them out. You, Private! Let down that tailgate."

Killian swore under his breath and shrugged. The tailgate was lowered and they emerged. The Apache. Slowly they climbed down, eyeing the soldiers and the school with equal mistrust.

"Come, now," Mary said in their language. "We'll have fun here. This is your new school and I am your teacher."

Three of the Apache children immediately broke into the predicted run. They scattered through the trees, with the soldiers chasing them while the other children laughed or threw rocks or shouted to the soldiers, "Shoot them!"

Killian cast one more poisonous glance at Mary, who seemed unmoved, and he too took off to round up the scattering Apache children.

It took most of an hour. The last one was found hiding in a dry well, holding a pointed stick which he tried to poke through a trooper's eye. Killian's uniform was filthy. Two buttons were missing from his shirt. He walked forward with the two young Apache boys he had by the collar and threw them into the school, banging the door behind them.

"All right, now," Mary said, clapping her hands, "school is in session."

Kemo could only stare. He watched in bewilderment as the children, the Najavo, the Zuni, and the

Hopi, who had all been so recalcitrant before, now marched into the schoolhouse.

"Amazing," one of the soldiers said.

"No," Killian, who was working his sore fingers, replied. "These kids fear the Apache, hate 'em. But they respect 'em, too. They seen the Apache make a break for it, seen us just drag 'em back. They know Miss Mary'll send us after them if they try it as well."

"I didn't enlist to become no truant officer," the soldier said. "But all in all," he said, leaning against the upright of the porch, "I guess it beats fightin' growed-up Apache on the desert."

Mary watched as the last Indian, a Navajo who was no more than five, with a hole in the seat of his twill pants, went in. Then she turned, nodded her thanks to the soldiers, and swept into the classroom.

There was utter silence inside. The Indians, sitting on the floor in tribal groups, lifted black eyes to her. They barely stirred as she walked to the raised portion of the floor in front of the room and turned with a smile.

She spoke first in Apache. "Good morning. I am Miss Mary. This is your school. We will all learn to speak English here so that we can communicate among ourselves and with the white authorities. We will have certain rules here—"

An Apache boy made a dash for the window, but Mary lifted her skirt and with two strides overtook and tackled him as he tried to leap out. He was a strapping boy of eleven or twelve, and strong. He turned, slapping at her face, trying to kick her. Mary got hold of his wrists, and panting, struggling, rolled him, bringing both arms up behind his back. The Apache stamped down hard on her toes and she grunted with pain. When he tried to bang his skull into her face, she was quick enough to dodge it. She continued to lift his arm, to bring his hand up between his shoulder blades until his mouth opened wide with silent pain.

He spun then and tripped her and they went

down in a heap together. Mary realized the other children were screaming with delight now, jumping up and down, but she paid little attention. She was wrestling on the floor with the boy, who was still trying for the window.

He tried to get to his feet, and Mary dragged him back by an ankle. With his other leg he kicked out at her, and a solid moccasined foot struck her skull above the left eye.

Still she managed to hold on, and now, panting with exertion, she climbed up onto the boy's back and knelt there, one hand on his neck, the other renewing the hammerlock she had on his right arm.

He wriggled beneath her, kicked at the floor, and yelled, but her grip was sure this time, and she held him tightly.

For five minutes they remained there on the floor, the Apache boy struggling to escape, Mary gradually tightening the grip on the boy's arm until her own shoulder ached with the effort. Finally she felt him give up. He just lay there, one eye glaring at her.

In one quick movement Mary was on her feet, yanking the boy up after her, leading him back to the circle of Apache, where he was unceremoniously plopped down to sit glowering. Mary glared back, trying to pin up her hair, which was all snarls. She watched the boy for a long minute, their eyes dueling, until they reached a silent understanding. Then with a little nod she returned to the front of the classroom, turned, smiled, and began: "Good morning. I am Miss Mary. This is your school . . ."

She kept the lessons short for that day. At noon they left, hardly convinced, hardly eager, but they would learn. She would see to it. They would learn to protect themselves, to move forward.

"What did you think of it, Kemo?" she asked.

"Too much sitting still."

"You have to sit still at times."

"Why? The brain works when we move, too."

99

Mary laughed. "Just try reading a book while you're running sometime."

"I'll never read a book. Who wants to? Besides, we have none."

"But we will have. And you would too want to read a book—about castles and battles and dragons and kings."

"Maybe so." He shrugged. "But I don't have a book."

"I'll get you one." She rubbed his head. "You get discouraged too easily."

"Did Nochay hurt you?"

"Nochay—he is the Apache boy?"

"Yes. Did he hurt you?"

"No. It was a good fight, wasn't it?" She laughed out loud, shaking her head in amazement. "I didn't think I had that in me, but when he tried to leave, I knew I had to stop him. Why, all the boys and girls would have left, wouldn't they, if Nochay had gotten away."

"He won't come back to school anyway."

"Well, he'll have to."

"Never. If they kill him, he won't come."

"Why? What do you mean?"

"After a woman beat him in a fight and made him stay in school? An Apache? A Chiricahua?"

"But surely it won't seem so serious to him tomorrow."

"But it will. He will hate you always. He will never forget. He will be shamed forever before his friends."

Then Kemo said good-bye and rode off on his little pony. Mary watched him go, her thoughts on Nochay, on what she had done. Ignorance was no excuse. She should have foreseen this—the soldiers should have been allowed to stop him, not her. There wouldn't have been shame attached to being caught by the soldiers.

"I am sorry, Nochay," she said aloud. Sorry, because if he did not return he would spend the rest of his life in ignorance on this reservation, his mind only half-open, his eyes half-seeing.

A memory came to her then, a memory she had thought lost, buried in the past. The white lady with the long nose, her lips pressed together so tightly that rays of lines showed around her mouth. And she was pulling a girl by the wrist, pulling her and beating her with a switch, dragging her to a school she did not want to go to.

"My God," Mary whispered. "I had forgotten. Forgotten."

The girl had been Mary Hart.

Saddling her own horse, Mary rode into Fort Bowie. Two soldiers were placing Edna's faded red settee into a wagon outside the colonel's quarters.

Mary swung down from her horse and watched for a minute. She turned at the sound of approaching footsteps, to see Scott Sampson walking toward her. His expression was odd, perhaps because he had abandoned her at the dance the other night. She smiled, lifted a hand, and started to speak.

Sampson spoke first. "Hello, Miss Mary." He touched his hat brim and then was past her, walking on down the plank walk.

Mary stood watching him in disbelief. Is that how it is now? she asked silently. All right. Fine. I wasn't chasing *you* to begin with. She watched him awhile longer, then brushed aside her pique and went into the colonel's office. Sergeant Hazleton was at his desk, looking blankly at some report he apparently found incomprehensible.

"What in hell's a maenad?" he asked pleadingly. "This says one of our troopers was tangling with some maenad in Tucson."

"I believe it is a loose woman, Sergeant," Mary answered.

"Yeah?" He frowned and then brightened a little. "Why they can't say so, I don't know. Well, I'll give that to the colonel, then. I didn't know if it

101

was plague or pestilence. You going to have all them Indian kids knowing those words, Miss Mary?"

"I'd like to think we will, one day."

"Well, I hope you do it. Maybe I ought to come over and sit in school for a time. . . . Maenad?" He shook his head. "The colonel's alone if you want to see him. Just tap on the door and go on in if you like."

She thanked him, stepped to the office door, tapped, and was summoned. She found the colonel putting a whiskey bottle away. He had a sad, nearly tragic expression on his face. His eyes were ringed and sunken. He wasn't taking being relieved very well. His career was over and he knew it. It was causing him more pain than Mary—and perhaps Edna—had guessed.

He looked up, then composed himself quickly. Standing, he asked, "Well, how did the first day of school go?"

"Well enough, I think. But I can't have the soldiers guarding them forever, can I? Now comes the hard part—making them *want* to come."

"I don't think it can be done, but then, I keep saying that to you, don't I?" The colonel sat down again, as Mary did. She leaned forward, hands clasped, and told him what was on her mind.

"I've been thinking about the other boy. Most of the night I worried about him."

"What boy?"

"Thumb's son."

"You don't have to worry about him. He's being well fed, he has blankets enough."

"But he doesn't belong there!"

"He belongs where he can be held securely."

"So that you can use him as a bargaining tool?"

"Hopefully. Now, don't sit there fuming, Miss Mary. We might very well be able to save some lives by using that boy."

"By holding him, you might cause the loss of some lives too, it seems to me, if Thumb chooses to retaliate."

"He won't. Not while we have the boy."

"But he's not a chess piece. He's only a small boy. A live, confused, innocent boy."

"What would you have us do, Miss Mary, send him to school?"

The colonel was being sarcastic, but Mary answered, "Yes! That is exactly what I want to do. Teach him."

"No."

"He should have the same rights as the other boys."

"No."

"He's done nothing! Even if his father is a criminal, a butcher . . ."

"No. He'll stay where he is. Can you imagine me letting him out now? With General Clark here? We've been trying to get some kind of hold on Thumb, some idea as to his location, to find some way of bargaining with him for the last three years. This is it. Clark smells a promotion. He'll be commander here officially by the time the negotiating begins, and there'll be plenty of glory in it. For him and for young Sampson. It's my considered opinion that both of them have fallen into this quite by chance, but that's neither here nor there. They have hitched their wagons to the star which is Juh, the son of Thumb."

"You said negotiations will be held. When?"

"We've sent people to some intermediaries who will contact Thumb as soon as possible."

"If they can find him."

"That's right."

"But it may take weeks, months."

"That's correct as well."

"While that little boy sits in the stockade like a criminal or caged animal!"

"I'm afraid so. I don't like it, but that's the way it must be, Miss Mary."

"But why?"

"Because we are at war. Things in war are not done so nicely."

"Colonel Shore," Mary said with emphasis, "things are meant to be done as nicely as possible at all times, in all places. That boy is no threat to you or anyone else. He's very small, quite young. Even if he tried to run, where could he go? Your soldiers would capture him in no time at all. Couldn't he at least live on the Apache reservation among his own people? The reservation is well-guarded at all times."

"Miss Mary, you are a good woman with the best of intentions. But no, it can't be done and you should realize that I can't change my decision. I am already being dismissed as incompetent. I should hate to have it also thought that I am a fool."

"May I see him?" she asked after a moment.

"For what purpose?"

"Curiosity, concern."

"I don't see what good it would do."

"But it can't do any harm either, can it?" she asked more eagerly, seeing that the colonel was weakening.

"No, Miss Mary," he said, reaching for his hat, "I don't suppose it could. If it will make you happy, we'll go and see the boy."

"And speak to him?"

"He doesn't speak English."

"But I speak a little of the Apache language."

"So does Bill LaPlante—more than you, I expect—but the kid wouldn't respond at all. Just sat there."

"But that doesn't mean we can't try," Mary said, rising, her eyes eagerly searching the colonel's haggard face.

"All right." The colonel put on his hat and tugged it down. "If it pleases you, Miss Mary. If it pleases you."

They went out together. The day was bright and hot. They crossed the parade ground, passing Captain Granger and Lieutenant Sampson. Both men saluted, murmured good day, and strode on. Mary didn't turn to glance after Scott Sampson, and the colonel noticed it.

104

"That surprises me. Is there something wrong between you two?"

"There was never anything at all between us, Colonel."

"No?" The colonel looked over his shoulder again at Sampson. "He sure thought there was, or was going to be."

"Perhaps he's found someone else to hang his fantasies on," Mary said in a tone not at all warm or generous.

"He . . . Oh, I see what you mean. Her."

"I was only hypothesizing."

"Yes," the colonel mused, "I saw a little of that the other night, but I didn't quite trust my eyes."

"It's really none of my concern one way or the other," Mary said, growing stiffer.

"No, nor of mine," Shore said. They walked on in silence, and after a time Mary noticed the slow smile growing on the colonel's lips. There was a twinkle in his eye as well as he indulged the hypothesis, perhaps finding consolation in the notion that the general's wife was flirting with the general's fair-haired heroic boy.

The stockade walls were twelve feet high. The palings cast narrow shadows at this time of the day—ominous, creeping things. Beside the gate stood two armed soldiers who came to attention as the colonel approached.

The colonel and Mary passed through a judas gate and into a hard-packed yard where the sun glared down. Three prisoners sat against one wall in a ribbon of shade, glowering at the colonel and the teacher. A guard lowered his weapon slightly, just in case. The prisoners didn't move.

Had they been drinking, fighting, deserting? Getting into predicaments with Bowie's maenads? They looked beaten already, perhaps knowing that a sentence of five years' hard labor in this country was the same as a death sentence.

Another pair of soldiers was posted beside the interior blockhouse. They were thick, humorless men, their eyes hard, expressions set. They had to be harder than the hardest prisoner, and they were.

"Open up, please, McCord. The lady and I want to see Juh."

"Sir . . ." The huge jailer hesitated. "I can't do that, Colonel Shore."

"What in hell do you mean!"

"The general, sir. He's in there. He told me no one was to enter."

"Damn General Clark," the colonel shouted. "I'm ordering you to open that door."

"Sir, I bet your pardon, he is the ranking officer."

"And I'm still commander of this post. I will be for four days. If you want to keep those stripes, McCord, open that door, and that is *not* a suggestion."

The sergeant hesitated. Finally he produced a huge iron key ring and sorted through it, finding the key he wanted. When he inserted it, the lock freed.

"It's not so important, really," Mary said. "Not if you're going to get in more trouble."

"Damn the trouble! There's a point to be defended here and it has nothing to do with you, Miss Mary. This is *my* post. This is *my* stockade. These are my men. I will have command over them until I have been officially relieved."

They walked swiftly down a stone-floored corridor, the colonel's boot heels ringing with each step. Mary saw a dark, bloated face peering from a cell-door window, saw hands wrapped around the bars set into it. Farther on they saw a lantern in the hall which cast a smoky light. They heard a voice—commanding, imperious, sharp, and angry.

The colonel entered the door, Mary in his wake. The general whirled toward them. His hand had been uplifted and now it hovered above his head indecisively. When he finally lowered it to his side, his face was flushed, his mouth drawn back by a rictus of fury.

On the floor before him was a small boy, huddled, crumpled. The side of his face was swollen.

"What is the meaning of this!" the general roared.

"What is going on here?" Colonel Shore demanded in turn.

"Colonel Shore, may I remind you—"

"Have you been beating that boy? Beating a ten-year-old child?"

"I have been doing nothing of the sort! And what business is it of yours, sir? You are forgetting rank, Colonel Shore, and you are breaching not only etiquette but also the military code."

"Have you been beating the boy?" the colonel asked again. His voice was a soft hiss now, very unpleasant to hear.

"Colonel . . ." The general puffed up a little and started to deliver a speech, but Shore cut him off.

"Get out of here. Out, or I'll have you thrown out!"

"You are forgetting yourself."

"I'm forgetting nothing. This is my post, sir. If you wish to beat up children on it, and think that I will tolerate it, you are sadly mistaken."

"The boy knows where Thumb has run to."

"Why don't we just torture him, then? Pull his fingernails out one by one, draw and quarter him?"

"I'm warning you, Colonel Shore . . ."

"Yes, I know that. I am going to retire very soon, sir. I would like to go out without a smear on my record. I wouldn't like to have it on my record that I had a superior officer placed under arrest for cruelty to a civlian prisoner. But I *will* if I have to. Do we understand each other?"

"Damn you, Shore!" The general tried to speak but couldn't for a time. Finally he calmed enough to spit out, "You'll be gone soon. Then the little bastard will talk. I promise you that."

He spun on his heel and strode out, leaving Shore and Mary in the silence of the cell. The lantern outside the door cast huge wavering shadows across the walls.

The colonel stood staring at the wall for a minute and then lowered his gaze to the boy. Juh was only ten, a Chiricahua Apache whose father was a killer, a warrior, a scourge. But Juh was only ten and he had been beaten by a high-ranking officer in the United States Army.

"I am sorry," the colonel said. Mary automatically translated. That much of the boy's language she knew. There was no response. The boy stared, simply stared. His Apache soul was cold within him, and the light in his eyes was cold. He was a warrior, of warrior stock. He would not cry and he would not speak.

"Can you handle him?" the colonel asked.

"What do you mean?"

"I mean can you watch him and take care of him? This is no place for the boy—you were right—it's just no place for a child."

"I can take him with me? To the school?" Mary asked in wonder.

"Take him with you. Don't let him go. This can't last—but for the time, you keep him. He'll obviously be safer with you than under my protection. Lock and key don't seem to be much help in keeping him safe."

"Colonel Shore . . ."

"Don't thank me, please. Don't congratulate yourself. I have the feeling we are both making a terrible mistake. I'll tell the guards outside to let you pass when you're ready." He looked again at Mary, at the child, shook his head and went out, leaving Mary and Juh alone.

"You are to come with me," Mary said in the boy's language.

The boy said nothing. Mary moved a step nearer and the dark eyes of the boy watched mistrustfully. She crouched down before him, hands clasped, pressing her skirt between her knees. She cocked her head and said, "You are not afraid of me, are you? No, you are Apache, you are afraid of nothing."

There was still no answer. Mary's hand stretched out and he shrank from it. The light in his eyes grew hotter. She could not read his thoughts, except to know there was anger within him, and fear.

"The army will let you live with me. I have a school where other boys come, Apache boys."

The child had nothing but contempt for that idea. He turned his head away. Mary's hand reached out, stroked his hair, and with a small growl Juh threw himself to one side to lie on his back, propped up on his elbows, his chest rising and falling too rapidly, staring at her.

"You have to go with me or stay here. Outside, the sun still shines. There is fresh air and the wind blows. You will die here. You need air and the sun. I will keep you with me for just a little while."

"Go away, woman. Are you white or not?"

"I am Indian."

"You dress white. You look white."

"I am Indian, though, Juh," Mary said, relieved that the boy had broken out of his silence, that deadly dark silence which cripples children.

"Why don't you go away?"

"I will when you go with me."

"I don't know where you are taking me. I want to go home. My father will kill them all. The soldier hit me. They burned our rancheria and killed many people. My cousin was playing with me. A soldier shot him."

"Come." Mary stood and stretched out a hand. "Come out of this darkness, Juh. It is bad here."

For a minute she thought he would not take her hand, that he would shrink away again into the dark silence. But finally he did rest his hand in hers, rise, and stand breathing heavily, as if he had been running. Then he dropped her hand. He challenged her with his eyes, but she would not respond to the challenge.

"I am going because I need the sun. I am going because then I can escape," he said. "I am going, but I am not going with you, woman, because I like you. I hate you. You are a soldier woman, a white woman. I tell you I hate you, and that is the truth."

"All right. Hate me if you want."

"Maybe I shall kill you."

"Maybe."

"You are not frightened?"

"Of course," Mary said, choosing her answer carefully. "You are Apache."

"Yes. I am Apache," Juh said. Then he looked around the cell and said, "Let us leave this place. Have you got ropes?"

"Ropes? For what?"

"To tie me up," the boy said with surprise. "If you do not tie me up, I will run away. So you need ropes."

"No. I won't tie you."

"Then I will run away."

"Won't you give me your promise? Won't you promise me that you will not run away if I don't tie you?"

"No. I can't make such a promise."

"Juh . . ." She crouched down and took his arms, looking into his eyes. "How can I take you out of here if you won't give me your word you will not run away?"

"I cannot."

"You can't stay here! This is a horrible place. The soldier who hit you will come back."

"I will not promise."

He looked small and very vulnerable for a moment and his lip seemed to tremble before he clamped his jaw firmly shut and his gaze became hard again.

Mary sighed and rose. "I'm sorry. I have to leave you, then."

Juh didn't answer. He stood there, arms limp, looking smaller yet, a child in a man's world, a stranger in a foreign land. Mary said, "I am sorry," and started out the door. She had her hand on the door and had begun swinging it shut before the small voice rang out.

"No, please. I promise. Don't leave me in here!"

Mary wasn't pleased with her own trick. It was

shabby. The child was afraid of the dark, afraid of the prison, afraid of the soldiers. She had made him more afraid in order to get him away from them.

He watched her with burning eyes, his fingers curling, forming into fists, his face pathetic and fierce at once as he revealed his anger; Juh was angry with himself for being what he could not help being—a small boy.

"You are ready to go now, Juh?"

He shook his head. "I have made my promise."

"Yes, and—"

"I have promised not to run away. That does not mean I do not hate you. I will go with you because I do not want to be here. But it does not mean," he said very slowly, "that I do not hate you, woman."

Mary pretended to ignore him. She took his hand and he allowed her to have it. She led him out and down the corridor, out the front door past the eyes of the jailers, out of the stockade and from the fort into the glare of sunshine. The hot wind blew over them and the boy seemed to blossom under the influence of sun and wind, to grow stronger by the minute, to warm—except for his eyes. His eyes grew only colder and darker.

At the schoolhouse Mary made a bed for the boy on the floor next to her own bed. He watched her expressionlessly, but when she was finished he dragged the bed out into the other room. Mary said nothing either; she simply dragged it back.

"Go out and play," she told Juh.

"Aren't you afraid I will run into the hills?"

"You gave me your word. I accept it. The son of Thumb would not lie. Would he?"

"I would not lie."

"Then go outside."

He went, looking more sad than sullen now. He went, and after a time, when Mary looked out she saw him standing on the porch looking wistfully southward, toward the flame-colored hills.

They ate in silence at the small unpainted table

Mary had placed in her room. When they were through the boy sat down on his blankets and watched the wall as she cleaned up. Later still Mary sat beside the table and read by the light of a candle. If Juh had any interest at all in her or her book, he revealed nothing.

When she had unpinned her hair, brushed it, and readied herself for bed, Juh crawled into his bed on the floor. For a moment Mary caught him looking at her in a different, softer way. Perhaps he was thinking of his mother—he must have missed her, though he only spoke of his father. At any rate, the softer light was there and then was gone, and Mary Hart knew that it was not for her that the boy yearned.

She blew out the candle and lay down on her bed, watching the ceiling. She couldn't even hear his breathing, and so she stuck out her hand to reassure herself. She felt his shoulder before he yanked away, leaving her hand dangling in the empty air.

It was a long while before she slept, and she awoke three or four times during the night to roll over and thrash. And each time Mary awoke, the eyes were on her—the child's dark, distant eyes staring up at her.

Morning was bright and dry. Kemo was on her porch an hour before school, his face eager, curious. She was so pleased to see a friendly face, she gave him a brief hug, from which Kemo predictably withdrew.

"Is it true?" he asked breathlessly.

"Is what true?"

"That you have Thumb's boy here. Juh?"

"Yes," Mary answered, "quite true. He'll be in class today and you'll see him."

"Thumb's son in class! Miss Mary, the Navajo boys will try to attack him. Thumb has killed some of their parents."

"They won't attack anyone in my school," she said with assurance. "We come here to learn, not to make war on each other."

"This is a crazy thing you have done, Miss Mary, the craziest yet," Kemo said.

"Perhaps. I don't think so, though."

"He might try to hurt you as well," Kemo said.

"He might. But he's just a little boy."

"A little Apache," Kemo said. "His father is bad, he is bad. He should not be here."

"But he is, so let us make the best of it."

Juh himself emerged from the schoolhouse and stood staring at Kemo with an unreadable expression. He wore his white cotton shirt, white cotton trousers, red sash, blue-and-yellow headband. All his clothing fit him loosely, all was stained and smudged, but still . . . well, Mary thought, that can be taken care of later, after he is more comfortable here.

The Navajo and Zuni children walked to the school, fewer seemingly than the day before, but not a great many fewer, Mary thought. At eight o'clock the soldiers arrived with their wagonload of charges.

The Apache swung down and stood awaiting a command. When they saw Juh, they approached him with a sort of wonder. They thought they knew him, but weren't sure.

"Are you Juh, the Chiricahua?"

"Yes."

"Your father! They haven't captured Thumb?"

"No. Be quiet now, the woman speaks our language." Juh's tone was almost that of command. He was small but perhaps he knew that he was destined to rule. To rule, if the kingdom of the Chiricahua could survive its simultaneous war with the Americans and the Mexicans.

"How, then—?" one of the boys began.

Juh cut him off. "Later we will talk," he said hurriedly. "Later."

Mary heard most of that and a few other fragments. They called her a name she didn't understand and she made a mental note to ask Bill LaPlante to translate.

Nochay was not there. Kemo had been right: the boy would not return after being bested by a woman.

"Corporal Killian, there's a boy missing today from the Apache reservation. The one called Nochay."

"Yes, Miss Mary." Killian touched his eyebrows with his sleeve. It was hot and already he was perspiring. "That one made a break for it last night."

"He jumped the reservation?"

"That's right, miss."

"But where would he go, alone?"

"Into the hills."

"He's only a boy."

"He'll make it. He'll survive. They're tough, these kids. He'll live off the land for a time, and eventually he'll find another band of renegades to hitch up with."

"Out there, in the summer heat, you believe he'll survive?" Mary asked in astonishment. She couldn't believe Killian would be so heartless as not to be concerned for the boy.

"Miss, he'll live. His people have lived here for centuries. He was raised wild. He knows the land, knows how to get water from plants, from sinkholes—tinajas—knows how to trap the dew and lick it if he has to, how to find food and shelter, how to defend himself and grow stronger and tougher with each day. It was the best thing, Miss Mary. You'd of brought him back here, he might have made trouble, a lot of trouble."

"Yes." Unconvinced, she looked to the desert flats and the rocky hills beyond. Nothing, she thought, lives there. It is a dry and savage land, a devil's landscape, hostile to human life. She only half-believed Killian. Even if the boy did survive, what kind of life could he have out there, scrambling over sun-baked rocks, chasing an occasional lizard to eat, dodging the preying things, fearing the snakes and the gila monsters and the desert coyotes, the scorpions and the centipedes, the forests of cactus, hiding from the eternal blinding sun.

114

Killian broke into her thoughts. "Miss Mary, as you know, the colonel's leaving tomorrow."

"Tomorrow? But . . ."

"A few days before schedule. He decided to report early to Fort Vasquez—who could blame him?"

Mary couldn't. That was for certain. Still, she was a little stunned.

"General Clark has already said there ain't going to be any more of this."

"Of what, Corporal?"

"Of having soldiers detached to guard schoolkids. This is the last day we'll be standing watch—or bringing the Apache kids over from the reservation, I guess."

"Why, he can't do that! How will the Apache children get here?"

"They won't, Miss Mary. They can't come by themselves, and we can't watch 'em."

"Well, I'll see about that! I'll talk to the general about it today."

"It'll be a waste of your time, Miss Mary."

"And the other children—will they stay if you're not here to guard them?" Mary asked. Would the Navajo, the Hopi, the Zuni all just run away? She hadn't had enough time, hadn't been given a chance to show them what an education could be like.

"I couldn't say, miss," Killian said. "I don't know. I guess we'll be comin' back for *him* one of these times soon." He lifted his chin toward the porch and Mary turned to see Juh standing expressionlessly, watching.

"What do you mean?"

"You can't think the general's goin' to let the kid stay out here with you. No, miss. He'll be back in that stockade in no time at all after the colonel's gone."

"Of course," she said distantly. "What was I thinking of. He'll take him back and the boy will die there, just die."

"It ain't that bad, miss," Killian argued.

"For him it would be. For a small boy who has always lived free."

"Yes"—Killian was looking at the boy now—"maybe so. I don't know. They ain't goin' to ask my opinion anyway."

"They're not going to ask mine either, but they're going to get it!" Mary promised.

"Well, that's all fine and noble, Miss Mary, but it won't do a thing to change the general's mind, and you know it as well as I do."

"Something has to. Something has to change his mind." There had to be someone to talk to, she thought, her mind working furiously. The colonel was going . . . Scott Sampson? Perhaps. He hadn't been around to see her, hadn't given any indication that he intended to pursue their relationship any further, but still he had seemed a kind man, generous-hearted. What he could do against the general's wishes she didn't know, but she could find out.

The children were all in the classroom now. All but Juh, who waited and watched woodenly. Mary nodded a good-bye to Killian, who went to look for a shady spot to spend the day. Then she went in, Juh following.

He sat alone, not with the other Apache; he sat alone and he was silent. No matter what he was asked, he would not respond. He was not a student, he was a prisoner.

The other Apache adopted the same attitude. Silent defiance became the rule. The children from the other tribes began to follow suit. Only a few answered questions or asked them, and the day was, for the most part, a failure.

"Too bad," Kemo said. "School is over." They watched the Apache going home, piling into the wagon to be driven away once more by the soldiers—perhaps for the last time.

"School is not over," Mary said resolutely.

"No one will come back now. No one wants to be a student."

"Kemo, it is not over, and will not be over until I am gone. And I am not leaving."

"No more Apache will come," Kemo said with certainty.

"I am going to the fort to see about that as well. I don't see why the army can't spare a few soldiers each day to help watch the Apache children. After all, they have to guard them on the reservation anyway. They may as well be in school."

Kemo didn't bother to respond. Mary was only half-convinced herself. But she would try. "Get my horse, will you, please, Kemo?"

"What about Juh?" Kemo asked. "You're not taking him with you?"

"No, I shall leave him here."

"Alone?"

"He has given me his word that he will stay."

"Miss Mary," Kemo said pleadingly, "you know I am your friend, but you do one mad thing after the next. Of course he will run away. Don't leave him here. There will be much trouble for you when he makes his escape."

"He won't make an escape. Believe me."

She turned to look at Juh, who was listening intently to their English conversation, understanding none of it—perhaps. Mary went to him, and crouching down, said, "I am going to the fort alone. You stay here."

"Yes."

"You won't . . ." she searched his eyes, those young, knowing eyes, and then stood again. "Goodbye, Juh," she said, knowing she was taking one of the biggest chances of her life, knowing that if he ran, General Clark would crush any chance she might have of continuing here.

She turned her back deliberately and walked away to where an unhappy Kemo stood holding the reins to her horse. "Miss Mary . . ." he began.

"I know."

"I will stay and watch him. I won't let him see me."

"I trust him, Kemo."

"Then you are making a mistake," Kemo said

gravely. "I am sorry, but you still do not know the Apache. Let me stay and watch him from the trees. I will see that he does not run away."

Mary answered hesitantly, "All right. Perhaps you're right. But I do trust him, Kemo. I do . . . it's just that there's so much to lose."

Then she was up and onto her horse, and with a single worried look at Juh she rode away through the trees toward Fort Bowie, which stood small and dark against the endless desert.

The ride was brief, invigorating. The wind was blowing hard out on the flats to the south. A milky shifting cloud of sand drifted toward Mexico from the hills. To the north and east it was clear, so clear that Mary could see the Peloncillo Mountains well enough to distinguish individual canyons and outcroppings of rock. The sky was incredibly blue near the horizon, but brilliant white overhead. Beyond Bowie nothing moved, nothing lived, nothing existed but the desert, white and red and violet in the shadowed foothills.

Bowie itself was dark and dismal. It seemed to be rotting away in sections, slowly losing ground to the desert. The wagon was still in front of the Shores' quarters and was nearly loaded. Two young soldiers were carrying out a leather-strapped trunk. Mary could see in through the doorway of the colonel's home, see that nothing remained there, not so much as a rug on the floor.

She got down from her horse, tried futilely to dust off her skirt, and went to the door. Rapping twice, she went into the room beyond, her footsteps echoed as they could only in an empty house.

"Edna?"

"In here, Mary."

She was in the kitchen with the maid, placing the last few pieces of silver into a wooden barrel. Edna looked grayer, more severe. Mary wondered how much of her professed desire to leave the desert was real.

"Come to say good-bye?" Edna asked.

"Yes. But I wish we didn't have to say it. Tomorrow, they tell me."

"It would be tonight, right now if it were possible." She threw down the forks she held, shrugged apologetically, and nodded toward the other room. "Into my parlor?"

Mary went with her into the empty room beyond. They went to the door and stood looking out at the blinding light. "Damnable place," Edna Shore said. "Heat and thorns and poisonous things."

"You'll miss it?"

Edna smiled. "Who knows? Maybe. Here I had enjoyable times. Here, once, I was younger. Here I saw a different future. I was closer to my husband. Everything changes. The future, the real future, won't be so bright as the dream the desert gave birth to. He's drinking a hell of a lot," she said abruptly.

"I'm sorry."

"Just a hell of a lot. Well, he thinks his career is over, that Clark will get him. He probably will," she said ruefully. "James Shore is a soldier, and if he's not a soldier, he's nothing. If they force him to retire, he'll die. He'll just wither up and die. Likely drink himself to death."

"But the assignment at Fort Vasquez . . ."

"That's just a spot to put him in until they ride him out—that's what James thinks. Maybe he's right. We've seen it done before. Now he's crossed General Clark himself. To his face. Well, maybe we're both pessimistic. Maybe it's old age coming on, or a fear of change. I don't know—what am I burdening you with all this for! You came to see us off, I'm grateful for that. How's everything on the reservation?"

"I don't know. I think the school can work. Sometimes I am sure it can. I need to talk to General Clark."

"Good luck. He won't talk to you, dear."

"But he must."

"He won't. As the colonel told you when you first

arrived, that school isn't army business. Has no relationship to the general's duties as defined by regulations."

"He has a moral obligation . . ."

"Clark doesn't know what that is."

Mary forged ahead. "Don't you see what I mean? The Apache, the other Indians who are brought here by the army—the army has an obligation to them."

"Honey, we feed them and give them blankets. They'll tell you that's more than an Apache would do for them. They're right. They don't see any obligation to educate them. No. If the BIA wants to do it, fine. That's their business, but it's none of the army's. Go through BIA channels, Mary."

"BIA channels! Through Ralph Justin? I haven't seen him for a week."

"Then write a letter to Washington. In a year or so maybe someone'll drop down to see what the trouble is." Edna Shore's tone changed, softened. "Look, I hate to be so cynical, dear, I truly do, but right now I'm fed up with the army, the government, the Indians, the lousy desert, and I don't have a lot of sympathy for the Apache, who killed some of the friends James and I made down here."

"I understand," Mary said quietly.

"Do you?"

"Yes. You apologized for laying a burden on me. I apologize for laying a part of my burden on you. It is not your problem, it is mine."

"But we're still friends?" Edna Shore asked, and there was something touching about the way she said it.

"Of course." Mary kissed her cheek and held both of the colonel's wife's hands. "It will be all right. Vasquez will welcome you and you'll be happy there."

"Maybe. Maybe you're right."

"If I don't see you again, good-bye."

"Stay and have some tea. We can dig the pot and two cups back out of the barrel."

"No. No, thank you, I can't. I have to be going."

"Going? Not back to the school. Going where, Mary?"

"Where? Why, to see General Clark, of course."

"The general? But I thought you understood . . ."

"It's a chance, Edna. I can't let it go untried. Good luck to you. Is the colonel here? I'd like to say good-bye."

"Riding. He's out on the desert riding. Alone with his horse and a whiskey bottle." Edna's smile was ancient and troubled. She turned to the desert beyond the fort and was still looking that way when Mary went out and walked deliberately toward the general's office.

Sergeant Hazleton was at his desk, looking as broad and gruff as ever. He brightened a little when Mary entered the orderly room, but his face clouded up again instantly.

" 'Morning, Miss Mary."

"Good morning, Sergeant."

"Colonel ain't here, Miss Mary."

"No, I know that."

"He won't be. The general's taken command, you see."

"Yes, I understand. Will you tell the general I wish to see him, Sergeant?"

"General Clark?"

"Yes, of course."

"But, Miss Mary . . ." He rose ponderously. "All right, miss. But don't expect much from this. You're not his favorite civilian." Hazleton looked toward the closed plank door behind him as he spoke. He added, "Not that I haven't always thought you were as fine as could be."

"Thank you. Now, will you please see if the general will see me?"

The sergeant tapped at the door as if hoping he wouldn't be heard. The general's voice summoned him and with a last glance at Mary, Hazleton went in. He was back in a moment. Somewhat astonished, he said, "The general says for you to go on in, Miss Mary."

"Thank you."

She bowed slightly, lifted her skirt, and went into the dark inner office. The general was there, and the sight of him contrasted sharply with her memory of Colonel Shore, who had always been slightly troubled, polite, interested. The general was openly hostile. Mary could read it on his narrow face before she had even seated herself.

"Good morning, General Clark. I would like to—"

"Where's the boy?"

"What boy?"

"You know which boy, woman. Juh, Thumb's boy."

"He's at the school."

"Alone?" the general thundered.

"No. Someone is watching him," Mary said carefully. "He thinks he is alone, however. You don't have to worry about anything, General Clark. He gave me his word that he wouldn't try to leave."

"He gave you his word," the general said with the thickest irony. "He gave you his word, and you accepted it. An Apache's word."

"Why, yes."

"A damned Indian's word of honor—they have none! But then, I forget that you're a squaw yourself, aren't you?"

"I don't think the word is conducive to—"

"A damned squaw who has come down here and stuck her nose into army business, taken away a valuable hostage by I don't know what trickery or coercion, and set herself up as guardian of the poor abused Apache Indians."

"General Clark," Mary said, heating up, "I have come here to establish a school. Any friction that may have developed between us is of your own doing. The boy, you will remember, was taken away by Colonel Shore and given to me because you were physically abusing him."

"That's a damned lie!"

"I was there!"

"It's a damned lie that I abused him. He tried to run from me, fell, and bruised his cheek."

"That's not what he says."

"Because he's a damned liar. The kid wanted your sympathy."

"Is that what your report will state?"

"There won't be a report. I wouldn't waste the paper and ink. I let you come into my office for one reason. I want you to understand how things are going to be now. Tomorrow, as soon as Colonel Shore is officially relieved at a brief ceremony, someone will come to fetch the boy. He will be placed in custody once more. Tomorrow there will be no more cavalry soldiers baby-sitting your Indian brats. Do you understand that!"

"You are making a mistake in both cases, sir. If you will allow me to—"

"Do you understand, woman? That is the way it will be."

"If I could explain—"

"That is all." The general gestured with the back of his hand and bent over a report on his desk.

"General Clark, please!"

"Go now. Remove yourself or I will have you removed," the general said, and his voice held a hard finality. Mary made a small gesture of futility spun on her heel and stalked out, banging the door behind her. Sergeant Hazleton didn't even look up. Mary walked blindly through the orderly room and into the bright sunlight.

Over. It was over. That was her first thought. Then her fighting spirit came back and she told herself: No, it's not over. I'll lose the Apache children for a while. Poor Juh will have to go back to the stockade, but I'll still have the Navajo and Hopi and Zuni children. Later perhaps the general will relent, or we'll have another change of commanders. Perhaps if I did write to the BIA . . .

"Miss Mary!"

The soldier was running toward her, pointing

eastward. Other soldiers were hurrying toward the gate to stand and look out. Then Mary saw it too, a colomn of dark smoke rising into the brilliant skies. She thought first of the Apache Thumb, but it wasn't that. With a dreadful sinking feeling she realized what it was, what it must be, before the soldier told her: "It's the reservation school, Miss Mary. It's on fire."

Before she got there, the school was burned nearly to the ground. Men and women stood around watching it. No one could have done anything without water, and that was sadly lacking. The roof caved in just as Mary rode up, ash and sparks rising skyward in a brief, violent fountain.

As Mary got from her horse, she found that her legs trembled. Her mind was blank with anger, frustration. She dropped the reins and moved through the trees and crowd of Indians, working her way to the clearing where the flames devoured her work, made ash of all her efforts.

Kemo was running to her, waving a hand. He arrived breathless and smudged. "He did it. He did it."

"Who?" Mary was staring straight ahead, feeling the heat on her cheeks, smelling the smoke, watching as an upright sagged and collapsed.

"Juh. Juh did it. I saw him go inside the school. I couldn't follow him in without him seeing me, so I waited. I waited a long while. I didn't know what he was doing. Then smoke began to curl out the windows. In seconds, there were flames, red and orange, and he ran out. He was laughing, Miss Mary. He was laughing and dancing around."

"All right," she said wearily.

"I know where he is. I'll take you to him," Kemo offered, "and you can beat him."

"It doesn't matter. I don't want to beat him."

"But he burned the school down!"

"It doesn't matter. It had already been destroyed. I was wrong to think I could keep it going. I was fooling myself. All along, I suppose. Everyone was right . . ."

124

"Miss Mary?" Kemo was worried. He had never seen her like this, never heard her talk that way. Perhaps she was in shock. Sometimes people acted like that when they were shocked. When Kemo's grandmother had found his grandfather scalped by a Chiricahua, she had taken off all her clothes and run into the hills. "Are you all right?"

She did not answer for a long while. She sighed deeply, poked at her hair with her fingertips, and finally said, "Yes. Yes, I'm all right. Where is he, then, Kemo? Where is Juh?"

"You are going to beat him?" Kemo asked with some enthusiasm.

"No. I just need to find him. He's my responsibility. Until tomorrow."

"He is this way." Kemo was looking at her oddly again. "Over here, come with me, Miss Mary."

They walked away from the fire, which still spun its fascination for the watching men and women, and moved through the oaks toward the arroyo beyond. There behind the willows they found Juh sitting against the earth, one arm around his knees, throwing stones into the arroyo bottom.

He looked up and with dark satisfaction said, "I did not run away."

"No." Mary stepped to him, and he cringed. "No, you didn't run away." Abrupty she scooped him up and carried him back to the Indian Agency office.

There was no one inside the building. The Indian secretary had gone home and Ralph Justin was out God knew where doing whatever he did instead of administrating the agency.

"What are you doing?" Kemo asked.

"We have to have a place to sleep."

"With him? You would sleep in the same house with him after what he did?"

"What am I to do with him, Kemo?" she asked a little wearily. "Tomorrow they are going to take him and put him in the stockade."

"Where he belongs."

"Maybe so. I don't think so, though. A young boy. You wouldn't like it, Kemo."

"They would not lock me up! I am a friend. I do not burn down buildings. I am not Apache." He delivered that speech in a somewhat impassioned manner. In Kemo's mind the gap between himself and someone like Juh was enormous. Juh was bad; Juh was dangerous; Juh was a criminal. In Kemo's mind there was nothing unseemly in locking up the Apache boy, in beating him.

"We will talk about it one day," Mary said. Now she was very tired, not physically, but emotionally. They had battered her and taken all of her strength away. A night's sleep, and perhaps it would return. A night's sleep, when the world seemed to vanish, its troubles hidden.

"I will wait outside," Kemo told her.

"No, Kemo. Go on home. Tomorrow we can speak. Tomorrow I will be myself."

"I do not like this idea—"

"I know that," she snapped. She was immediately sorry, seeing how hurt Kemo looked. "Leave me alone, please. I'm tired. Very tired."

Kemo didn't answer. He turned, went out, and slammed the door. Mary was left alone with Juh in the filthy Indian Agency building. She looked at him and saw him brace himself for the scolding, the beating that would surely come. She only turned away and busied herself tidying up. There was no sense in talking to the boy. He had his own code. There could be no changing it overnight, and this was his last night outside the stockade. Then what? A week or two, perhaps months before his father could be contacted. And would Thumb come as everyone thought, would he barter, or was he too much the proud warrior to yield?

Justin's room was a dungheap: piles of dirty laundry, empty cans, empty bottles, papers, and unidentifiable garbage swarming with insects. Mary got to work cleaning it. She would be there for only one night, but she wouldn't spend it in a place like that, or allow the boy to.

By the time she was finished, she was exhausted.

The work hadn't banished her unhappy thoughts entirely, but it had helped keep them at bay. Now, as she prepared for bed, they returned, darker and unhappier than ever. She was beaten; why couldn't she just admit it and go home? She had no school, no hope of getting the lumber to build another, and winter would be here before long. The Apache children would not be back. She had made an enemy of the military commander. Ralph Justin was worse than no help. She hadn't a single ally left with the departure of Edna Shore and the colonel.

And the boy. She sat on Justin's bed and looked at Juh as he slept or pretended to sleep in the corner, his knees drawn up, glossy dark hair screening his still-unformed face. His hands were small and dirty. His clothing was covered with soot.

So small, yet they were going to imprison him. Mary hadn't even been able to prevent that. In fact, she feared, she might have made things worse for him. Perhaps the general would feel obliged to prove to her that he could do as he liked with the young prisoner.

She couldn't go on thinking about these things, but she couldn't seem to chase them from her mind. They ran around and around past the windows of her mind even as she lay back in the darkness and tried to sleep. With the desert wind rattling the windows and the distant coyotes yipping and howling, the nagging worries prodded her as she watched the small prisoner sleeping on the floor in the corner of the room.

The night was warm and soft and her body was a turbulent thing filled with its flowing needs and wants, its savage ambitions. Laura Clark hungered for Scott Sampson and she rolled to him.

"Kiss me again, there," she said, and then she sighed, satisfied as his lips found her breast. She lay back, her hair in mad confusion, her arms looped around his neck.

It was madness and they both knew it. The grassy

bank beside the creek was far from isolated. Soldiers coming to and from town passed by. It didn't matter. They needed to lie there, to breathe in each other's breath and torment each other with their bodies.

"This will be the end of me," Scott said. "I know it."

"It's a beginning," she whispered.

"The general—"

"The general is old and soft and worn out." She touched his ears, his throat, his chest, his hard thighs. "You are young, the future is ours."

"We're bound to get caught. I can't help seeing you, I can't help wanting to touch you."

"Then do it," she whispered fiercely, "and let the old man be damned. You are my warrior, my man. You are on your way up, Scott, and I can help you. I'll see that General Clark helps you. He's old now, but once I thought he was exciting. I thought he was brave. I thought he was a man to walk beside, but now people laugh at him. Did you know that? His worn stories of valor, his promises, and his old man's dreams ... but you, Scott, you are young, and rank will come fast because you are a superior man."

Her mouth met his again, open, nearly feral. He kissed her and fell against her. The stars shone huge and bright through the oak overhead. The woman beneath him was eager and unashamed, demanding.

"You will kill them, won't you?" she asked very quietly.

"Kill them?"

"The Indians."

"If it happens that I must—"

"No. You *have* to kill them. All you can. They killed my parents, did you know that?"

"Yes, but—"

"They came and killed them and I saw them. It was night and very cold. There was snow and the

128

Sioux came from the reservation and killed my parents while they prayed."

Her eyes were distant, but her body was warm. She parted her legs and drew Sampson to her. "You will kill them all, won't you?" she said into his ear. "You *must* kill them all."

5

Mary awoke abruptly, her eyes wide and her heart palpitating. She looked around the room but it was silent. Juh still slept. The moon was peering over the sill of the single window in the bedroom.

She put a hand to her forehead, sighed, and lay back uncomfortably. What night-born menace, what half-dream had brought her awake like that? The entire unhappy panoply of problems came rushing back as she awakened. She sighed again, rolled over angrily, and lay staring at the wall. There would be no sleep on this night.

The wind whispered a jumbled night word and Mary's heart danced crazily beneath her breast. There was a shadow of movement, a soft and formless sound, and then a ghost of solid muscle and flesh, sinew and electric presence.

He moved across the room toward the boy in the corner, and Juh somehow knew he was there. At a touch on the shoulder Juh rose and started toward the door.

The thing, the man, the savage night creature moved to Mary Hart and bent low over her. She could see the moon in his eyes, see the interest dance across the moon's reflection, feel the warm nearness of controlled breath, see the rise and fall of a muscled bare chest.

She opened her mouth, and the hand, striking as quickly as a snake, was clamped over it. She tried to twist her head away but it was no use. His other arm was beneath her waist and she was lifted as if she weighed nothing. She kicked out and tried to poke her fingers into his eyes, to tear at his face, but with a muffled, amused grunt he turned and loped toward the door, moving lightly, as if he weren't carrying a living, thrashing human being.

Mary had been startled, afraid, but now blind panic seized her as she realized what was happening, *who* was taking her. It could only be Thumb, only Thumb who would come in the night and snatch Juh from the reservation. Only Thumb, who was a murdering savage, a violent, soulless monster of a man, who lived to spill blood upon the earth.

Mary struggled with all of her might, striking at his bare back with a desperately clenched fist, kicking, flailing, but it was all to no avail. She could hardly breathe; the hand clamped over her mouth and nose shut off the oxygen.

They were in the trees now, running softly. There was barely a sound as his moccasins skimmed over the earth, seemingly without crushing the fallen leaves. Mary could see nothing—only Juh, small and earnest as he ran, and the moon flickering through the intertwined wrought-iron branches of the oaks.

They were into the arroyo suddenly, where the air was cooler, damper. They half-slid down a bluff, wove through shoulder-high willow brush, and then Mary was on the ground, thrown roughly there to sit in her nightdress on the cold and rocky earth.

Juh said not a word. He was an Apache boy and he knew the necessity for silence, the value of speed, the obligation never to question the war leader.

Mary sat sputtering, gasping for a minute. They were hastily bringing two horses to where she sat. Good—they were going. They would be free, as they needed to be. Juh would not be in the stockade in the morning.

She did not fear Thumb—oddly. She did not consider that he might kill her. He had simply brought her here so that she couldn't spread the alarm too quickly.

"You don't have to worry about—" she began.

Thumb spun around, stepped to her, and forced her mouth open. He placed a rag in it, which Mary tried futilely to spit out. They didn't have to gag her!

He tied her hands behind her back with a rawhide strip. It was too tight. It was all so unnecessary, but then, Thumb didn't know that, she thought. Very well, she would wait a little while and then walk back to the reservation.

Thumb swung Juh up onto a spotted pony and handed him the reins.

Good. Go now, she thought. But Thumb didn't turn away and swing up on his own horse. Instead he lifted Mary in his arms, and she began to scream silently: *Not me!* What was he doing? Terror flooded her mind. She was horrified at the thought of being a prisoner, being forced to live a savage life in the wilderness, being made to live as the Apache did, to work as they did. She was needed here! The Indians of the territory needed her. There was too much to do. She was not an animal to be captured and taken away to be used as a beast of burden!

Thumb went to his horse with Mary in his arms, and stepping from a rock onto its back, he carried her with him, taking his reins with one hand as the other arm held her pressed to him, locked against his heated, solid body, which smelled of sage, crushed grass, and man sweat, of dust, paint, and leather.

He heeled his pony and it leapt forward into the brush, Juh following. They rode swiftly through the willows and up onto the desert flats beyond the reservation, where the sand was stippled with greasewood and cholla cactus. Mary's breath was bounced out of her with each running step the horse took. Thumb was a smothering force she couldn't escape. She saw Juh, grim and small aboard

132

the spotted horse, saw him look back and point and then cry out.

On the heels of that shout the rifle shots came. Mary just sagged against the horse, against Thumb's thighs. She was going to die; that was all there was to it. It was too bad she hadn't had the opportunity to do more with her life. She was going to die, shot down by soldiers in Arizona Territory, mistaken for a renegade Apache. Accidental death. There wouldn't be a report—it wouldn't be worth the paper and ink.

Thumb leaned low across her, gripping the mane of his pony as he muttered to it, urging the horse on to greater efforts. The bullets sang through the night, one of them notching the ear of the horse. The animal apparently didn't feel it; at least it didn't break stride.

Thumb veered suddenly left and then right, and the horse leapt a narrow arroyo, only to stumble, right itself, then plunge on. The moon danced crazily across the sky. Once she could see soldiers silhouetted against the moonlit desert background. Once she saw a flicking tongue of fire and then heard a bullet whip past her.

Thumb slowed his horse violently and Mary thought they were hit, but in the next moment the Apache yelled wildly, sending his horse back down a sandy bank. The pony went to its haunches, sliding down in a spray of sand as Mary was flung this way and that, Thumb's arm always holding her tightly. She prayed that he would just throw her to the ground to lighten the burden his horse was carrying, now that the soldiers were in pursuit, but she had no such luck.

Thumb's horse reached the bottom of the bank and he turned it, waiting for Juh, who was having a hard time of it. Finally the boy too reached the bottom of the wash and they hurried away to the east, through the long canyons that were white beneath the white moon, empty and haunting.

Mary saw the land flicker past, heard the drumming of the horses' hooves, smelled the sand and the sage, the dew on the chaparral, but none of it had any reality for her. She could not be here. She was Mary Hart, a schoolteacher from Dakota. In the morning she meant to see about getting started on a new schoolhouse.

She could not be in the arms of a Chiricahua warlord, riding onto the desert, hands bound, gagged. She would not allow it! She struggled again, but it was no use. She tried to kick free, to throw herself from the horse, but nothing worked. In the end she could only give in to the humiliation of it, closing her eyes to try to put a part of it out of her mind.

After the Apache slowed the horses, she wasn't quite as uncomfortable. But the slowing meant that they had eluded the soldiers, and there was no hope of immediate rescue.

Neither Apache spoke. Father and son simply rode on, following a perplexing maze of canyons and ridge trails, sandy washes and twisting game paths, making their torturous way through the broken hills.

When it dawned, they stopped atop a shelf of stone some three acres square in size. The plateau was overlooked by a massive rising stone face jutting skyward behind them.

Before them was only the desert, rose and violet in the dawn light. Endless mile upon endless mile. Thumb swung from the horse, lifted Mary down, and sat her on the ground, taking the gag from her mouth, and untying her hands. Then he went to talk to Juh.

Mary watched him go. She sat silently rubbing her aching wrists and her fingers, which had gone numb. Then she leapt for Thumb's horse, throwing a leg over, and kneeing it forward sharply.

Thumb was too quick, as quick as a cougar. He crossed the distance between them and gripped his pony's mane with one hand, Mary's arm with the other. She tumbled to the ground in his grasp as

134

the horse, frightened, and confused, danced away, tossing its head.

Thumb rose, hooked her under both arms, and dragged her nearer to Juh, where he simply released her, leaving her to lie there as he returned to talk to his son. Juh had gotten down from his horse and was crouched against the earth, holding the reins to his animal.

"Are you all right?" Thumb asked. Mary realized it was the first time either of them had spoken all night. The rising sun was red-and-gold flame beyond the two Chiricahua who rested in silhouette before it, father bent over his crouching son.

"I'm all right, yes," Juh answered.

"Tired?"

"No."

"But I think you *are* tired," Thumb said. Then he added something which Mary's knowledge of the language didn't allow her to pick up. There were moments like that throughout the conversation, but most of it she understood. She found Thumb's voice remarkably soft—not feminine, but nicely textured. The caressing tones seemed a repression of the terrible masculine energy in him, lurking behind the words. "Rest now," Thumb said, stroking the boy's head.

"You want to travel, let us travel."

"There is no hurry."

"The soldiers might come."

"Not up here, not without being seen. Are you afraid of the soldiers, Juh?"

"I am not afraid of anything, as you are not afraid of anything. Not of the soldiers or the snakes or Bad Lance."

"Did they hurt you?" Thumb asked, seeming to see through his son's words.

"No." Then there was something else Mary couldn't understand, something descriptive and violent. "Yes!" The boy finished. "They did hurt me. The man with the stars on his shoulders. He hurt me."

"And the woman?"

Juh blinked and looked toward Mary as if he had forgotten that she existed.

"How could she hurt me?" he asked. "A woman."

"Did she?"

"No."

"Did she try?"

"She wanted to make me read a white man's book, that is all. When they had me in prison, she came and took me to a place where the Indians must read white men's books."

But we had no books, Mary thought, managing to smile to herself. Thumb saw the expression and it puzzled him. He walked toward Mary, towering over her. She started to rise but he put a hand on her shoulder and seated her again.

He wore only a loincloth and a scarlet headband. His hair was to his waist. There was a long, jagged scar across his chest from his left shoulder nearly to his navel. His skin was copper-colored, and beneath it muscles rippled with each breath and small movement. He was quite tall for an Apache—not as tall as the giant Mangas Coloradas who was well over six feet, six inches tall, but as tall as many Americans, taller than all but a handful of the soldiers at Bowie. His black eyes stared out over high, sharp cheekbones. His nose was straight and unusually narrow. The forehead was high and smooth. He was a younger man than she had imagined.

"Who are you?" he asked. "Answer. I know you can understand us. I can see it in your eyes."

"I am Mary Hart and I demand that you release me."

"What are you?"

"A schoolteacher, as Juh has told you. I am—"

"What are you?" Thumb repeated. His hand remained on her shoulder. She still sat before him, and realizing that she was wearing only the chemise she had slept in, suddenly felt vulnerable and small. Yet he wasn't looking at her in an aggressive way at all. He was just looking. "You are not a white woman. What are you?"

"Cheyenne," she answered.

"I know the Cheyenne," Thumb said. "Once I killed some of them. Far north of here. They wanted to steal my horses and so I killed them all."

Presumably that was said to impress Mary. She did her best to look impressed, wondering at the same time what caused her to try to please the man. Was she afraid for her life? She thought not, though she knew she should be.

Thumb looked at her awhile longer, his eyes curious, as if he were seeing a creature new to him. She was an educated woman, a woman brought up in white culture; she must be unique in his experience. Juh had begun to move around restlessly, showing signs of fatigue.

"Why did you bring me here?" Mary wanted to know. "I am of no use to you. Why don't you let me go?"

"No. You are my hostage."

"Hostage!" She had to laugh at the idea. "What use am I as a hostage?"

"You are a woman, a teacher. Valuable to them."

"Am I?" She laughed again.

"Of course."

"No, Thumb. There's no one they value less at Bowie than me, and that is the truth."

"Of course you say that, but I know it is not true."

"But it is. The general is probably happy that I am gone."

"They trusted you with my son," Thumb said. "Do not tell me that they gave him to someone they did not respect."

"That was merely . . ." Her Apache wasn't good enough to allow her to explain that it was only due to circumstances. "It was just something that happened."

"Don't lie to me, woman!" Thumb spoke sharply, but he didn't appear actually to be angry. "They trust you with my son, with all the children. You are a person of much knowledge, a teacher. You are a woman, a young woman in your childbearing years. You are valuable."

Thumb's logic was impeccable. But it had led him to the wrong conclusion. Mary Hart couldn't imagine the general spending any time searching for her. He might look for Thumb, for Juh, yes. But any pursuit by the cavalry out of Fort Bowie wouldn't be for the purpose of rescuing the trusted, knowledgeable, childbearing woman.

Thumb was still watching her. Catching her eye, he turned away and went to his pony, taking a buckskin sack from a pouch in the soft saddle of the type the Apache preferred—buckskin stuffed with grass and buffalo hair.

"Juh, are you hungry?" Thumb asked loudly. Juh brightened, coming to his feet. "Look in the sack and see what you might find. There is water in the tinajas up on the bluff. Eat some venison and pinole. Fill yourself with good water. Then sleep, boy, sleep in the shadow of the rocks until the sun rises high."

Mary expected nothing and so she looked away across the rambling mountains to the forested uplands, the empty rivers and barren desert and playa, the turrets and towers, and vast eroded mesas and dunes.

"No help will come," Thumb said. Mary turned toward him. His shadow covered her briefly as he crouched and handed her a cake made of pinole—cornmeal and mesquite-bean flour—and molasses. "Eat and then drink. Juh will show you where."

"You treat your hostages well," Mary said sharply, but Thumb didn't answer. Indeed, when he rose and walked away it was as if she did not exist. He might have been feeding his horse, although when he did lead his horse to the small patch of grass growing on the ledge he did it with more concern and more tenderness than he had shown her.

Mary looked at the pinole cake, which was distinctly unappetizing in appearance, and began munching on it. Still she looked across the distances, not expecting help as Thumb believed, but simply looking, experiencing the unreality of being hostage in Arizona Territory when she ought to be teaching in a peaceful school somewhere in the north.

"Eat, rest," he said in a tone of command. "Soon we will travel on."

"Where?"

"Into Mexico. The mountains."

"Mexico?" Mary's heart sank. How would she ever get back from there?

"Eat, rest," Thumb said again. He sauntered off toward Juh, who was clambering up the bluff to search for the stony tanks which held water from the last rain.

Slowly she ate the bittersweet pinole cake and watched the blinding sun rise. She lay down and tried to rest, but sleep wouldn't come to obliterate the waking nightmare.

It seemed minutes later, centuries later that Thumb said, "Come, we must go."

Mary rubbed her eyes, sat up, and peered at the sun, which was much higher now. "When we get into Mexico will you let me go?" she asked.

"No."

"But why not? I won't be of any use to you as a hostage once we've reached the border."

"You will be of use. Listen, woman, the American and Mexican governments have a treaty which allows them to pursue Apache into each other's countries. If they can find Thumb's sign, they will follow Thumb. An entire army. All they want is to hang Thumb."

"But if they don't follow you? If you lose them in the desert?"

Thumb shrugged and looked away as if it were of no importance one way or the other. Mary noticed that her fists were tightly clenched, her fingernails digging into the palms of her hands; her heart was racing with anger and frustration.

"If you lose them in the desert and reach safety in the mountains, will you let me go?" she asked again. There was a long pause until he slowly turned his head toward her.

"A woman is valuable," he said, and then he turned his attention to Juh. "Come on, boy. Time to go. Bring the food sack."

Thumb mounted his horse and then lifted Mary up onto it, seating her in front of him. Juh looked very proud this morning. He glanced at Mary as if to say: I told you my father would come. I told you he was as tall as a mountain, as strong and swift as a stalking cougar.

They started off down the canyon where water had rushed off and on, carving the black stone walls of the arroyo, stacking huge boulders at the bends of the canyon, carrying bleached, broken trees from far in the uplands. There would be no hope at all of surviving a flash flood like that in this canyon, but it was not going to rain—the sky was white and hard. It hadn't rained since Mary had been in Arizona; she had been told years went by without there being rain. She had also been told of fearful flooding when it did rain on the land and a people unused to it, unprepared for it. Then the rivers, roaring and raging, would race across the land, battering it, sweeping away all in their path. Then the rain would stop and the rivers would die. Flowers would spring forth briefly from the moistened earth, from the cactus, and for a day, a week, the land would be dotted with color. But the sun would reclaim the desert quickly, the sun and the heat and the dry winds. It would again be a drab, savage place.

Mary let these thoughts trickle meaninglessly through her mind. Looking at the desert flats, she couldn't imagine them ever being damp, teeming with flowers.

The man behind her was silent. His grip on the

reins was sure, light. His arms imprisoned her, hard, sinewy arms decorated with silver bracelets. Now and then the wind would drift his long raven-black hair into Mary's face.

She was aware of the nearness of his body, the endless desert, and torpid sun, and nothing else as they rode into the dunes beyond the red-rock country.

By midafternoon Mary was praying for darkness, looking constantly to the sun and begging it to go down. Her head was ringing, her eyes sunburned, her lungs dry and papery. Still Thumb and Juh rode on. The boy seemed never to grow weary, though he must have been; he hadn't had much sleep and had eaten only a little.

"There's no one following us," Mary said once. "You don't need me for anything at all. Please let me go."

"When it pleases me," Thumb said quietly. Mary felt tears of fury well up in her eyes. She did not *want* this. She would not have it. She had chosen her own way, her own destiny, her own goals in life, and worked toward them. This savage had come from off the desert and taken her away from her civilized, orderly world.

"There," Thumb said, pointing. Juh sat up alertly in his saddle, looking southward toward a small dry lake, a *charco* where the mud had dried into a mosaic pattern. A patch of long-dead brown cattails stood on one side of the *charco*. What Thumb and Juh were happy about, Mary couldn't begin to guess.

The Apache got down from their horses and walked out onto the mud flats while Mary stood watching. They searched the ground carefully before beginning to dig, and in a moment found what they were looking for.

Juh stood up with a small living something in each hand. Mary saw legs, webbed feet, small unseeing eyes, and realized they were toads. From beneath the dried mud they had brought forth living creatures.

"You see," Juh called to her. "They live only when it rains. When the rain goes and their lake dries away, they burrow into the mud and sleep like the dead to await the next rain. That is how they pass their lives. From rain to rain."

"Yes, but . . . what are you going to do with them?" Mary couldn't help asking.

"Do with them?" Juh shook his head at the stupidity of the woman who would be a teacher. "We will eat them, of course."

They spent fifteen or twenty minutes digging up the hibernating toads. When they were finished Thumb built a small fire of mesquite wood and they began roasting them, skewering them on sticks. Mary turned away in disgust as they began to eat.

"You may eat, woman. Don't be afraid to ask," Thumb said between bites.

She couldn't have eaten if she wanted to. Her stomach was revolted by the idea and it had turned over twice, going sour and tight.

"Better eat, woman," Thumb said, and the sucking sounds he made as he devoured his meal turned her stomach once more.

"She does not wish to eat," Juh said.

"Why not? She must be hungry."

"It is not white food."

"Is that it? Oh, I see. It must be white food. Then the woman is going to be hungry for a very long time. . . . Woman, eat when there is food. You are Indian, you should know that. Eat when the hunt is good because there will be times when the spirits do not allow a good hunt. Don't the Cheyenne know this?"

"I was raised on a reservation. There was always food. We ate every day."

"This was a strange reservation, then. Those I know of do not feed the Indians at all unless they have to."

"That has nothing to do with me."

"Raised on a reservation, and you like the whites. You imitate them!" Thumb taunted.

142

"Please. You wouldn't understand, really."

"No. I am ignorant. I am not a white Indian. I would not understand."

"Please," Mary said. "I don't care to discuss it."

"Then I will be silent. What do I care if they have taken a Cheyenne girl and made her white? What do I care if they have sent you here to make the Apache white?"

Mary started to respond, but she managed to hold herself in check. She hadn't the command of the language to express herself properly anyway. Her arguments, phrased in a child's language, would only sound childish.

The sand was hot, and so she stood on the *charco*, trying not to listen to the noisy eating of the Chiricahua. She was sure they were eating like that on purpose, now that they knew the meal revolted her.

The sun was finally going down, sinking slowly toward the saw-toothed range to the west. The mountains stood out in stark relief, the shadows from the canyons creeping out onto the plains like spilled ink. A single star gleamed through the orange haze of sunset.

After they had eaten they withdrew from the mud flats. The fire, small as it was, might have drawn some tracker's searching eye. They rode toward the dunes as dusk settled and the sand was stained to deep purple. Finding a gap in the dunes, Thumb led them into a hidden valley beyond.

The sand rolled up to the mouth of the valley like an encroaching sea before being turned back by a force Mary didn't understand. Probably it was the wind, which seemed constant in the canyon due to some quirk of the land.

Within, the canyon was dark and still. They could hear but not feel the wind as it crept through the rocks above them, rattling the handful of scrawny and bent cedar trees.

They found water and grass. The water was silty, the grass dry, but it was remarkable to find any life at all on the desert. Thumb was proving himself to be the master of his own very small world.

Mary drank and then lay down as the Chiricahua took care of their horses, hobbling them with rawhide bands so that they could graze on the dry gramma grass but not wander far.

They spoke for a while, this father and son, the two savages, and it was a conversation which might have taken place a century ago, aeons ago.

Mary listened and pretended to sleep. Thumb had made a small fire and it glowed wispily, changing, shifting, casting moving shadows. It was a strange hour of night. Conflicting needs and emotions crept through the camp and made their bed with the Cheyenne schoolteacher. She wanted to escape, only to escape—and yet the nearness of the fire, of the soft-voiced man and his child, made the tiny camp nearly comfortable. Something inside her which was Akton and not Mary Hart seemed to be drawn out by the firelight, by the stars pendant in the sky above the canyon walls, and she had to beat it away.

She had to escape. There was too much left undone.

The fire burned low. Soon there was nothing left but the golden embers, memories of the heat of the dancing flames. When the last ember had winked out, Mary lay watching. The night breeze was cool. It searched her out and touched her with icy fingers. The stars were far too bright.

She rolled from her bed, hesitated, on hands and knees, and then crawled backward into the brush surrounding the camp. They slept. Her heart lifted exultantly as she studied the sprawled, sleeping figures of Thumb and Juh and determined that they were actually asleep, not feigning it. She backed away slowly until she was far from the camp, the rocks tearing at her knees, bare feet, and hands. She considered trying for the horses, but they were on the far side of the camp, which meant she would have to circle around through the dark brush-clotted canyon in the darkness. She decided not to risk it.

She rose slowly to her feet and went on, still backing away from the camp. She bruised her heel on a rock and then nudged a jumping cactus, the cholla, with her leg. The slight touch caused a section of cactus to break off and embed its hooked, needle-sharp spines in her flesh.

She just managed to fight back a cry of pain. She touched the cactus segment and succeeded in getting thorns in her fingers. She went on, removing the cactus from her fingers with her teeth. She could do nothing about the piece which clung to her leg, its itching, burning pain growing with each step as the thorns dug their way in deeper.

That wasn't important. None of it was important, not the pain, weariness, or the danger of falling, which she did often in the darkness. All that was important was getting free of Thumb, getting back to civilization, away from the desert.

She plunged recklessly downslope through the heavy sagebrush, which had been recently burned and smelled of charcoal. The rough sticks scraped at her flesh. Her face was lashed by an unseen branch.

Then she was at the bottom of the canyon, where she stood, hunched forward slightly, panting through an open mouth, looking back toward the camp, seeing no sign of pursuit, no indication that Thumb was awakened.

She started on. Beyond the canyon walls she entered the dunes and ran on, westward and to the north. Each step plunged her in sand up to midcalf and she was exhausted before she had crested the first dune. By starlight she couldn't see the trail Thumb had followed. But she had to go on, wading through the deep sand of the dunes, which appeared lik carved ivory, wave after wave of them beneath the silver stars.

The moon rose sometime later, an eternity later, as she climbed laboriously up the dunes and slid, scampered, and stumbled down the far side. She looked constantly behind, searching the sea of dunes for Thumb, but he was not there. He slept still, and when he awoke . . . why would he come after her, waste his time pursuing her back toward Fort Bowie, when safety lay in the opposite direction?

The dunes began to dwindle and flatten and then Mary was onto the red-sand desert. The night was cold. The moon glared down, huge and golden. She ran on, ran until her heart threatened to burst within the cage of her chest, until her throat was constricted, hot, and dry, until her legs were leaden, afire with pain. Finally she slowed to a staggering walk. Her feet were raw and bleeding. She was not going to look at them, did not want to know how bad they were. It didn't matter—they were going to have to do their service. They would have to support her, to carry her on despite pain and debilitation.

She stumbled over an unseen rock and went down painfully. She landed on elbow and thigh and the cactus still embedded in her leg was driven deeper. Her teeth had clipped the side of her tongue as she landed and her mouth was filled with the salt taste of blood. She rose and went on.

She remembered stories—what a time it was to have them return—stories her mother had told of hardship, of long treks after the buffalo or away from the soldiers, or from rival tribes. She remembered the stories of cold winters with the snow twelve feet deep outside the tipi, when there was nothing to eat for weeks, when the men went out to fight and the women had to find ways to silence the hungry babies and provide for the young and old alike. Long forced marches, long winters, long suffering. The wounded slowly dying, the dying crying out a last word. . . .

When her mother had told her the tales she had been too young to understand. She herself had not suffered and so she did not understand suffering.

The moon was high, seemingly hot, although the

night was cold, very cold. She went on, picking out for her landmark a peak with two notches that she had seen all day long. That way lay the fort, that way lay safety.

She let her mind drift as she wandered. She wondered about Kemo on this night. How had he taken the news? And Scott Sampson. Had he brought out a search party, insisted on being allowed to do it, or was he busy exchanging flirty glances with the general's too-young wife? Did General Clark just throw back his head and laugh when he heard that Mary was gone, or did he roar with anger because she had been the cause of his losing Juh? The Shores had been leaving, but perhaps they had stayed on, waiting to learn the news of her rescue or loss. Perhaps . . . perhaps she hadn't even been a ripple in their lives. Perhaps they had only been polite.

It seemed to be snowing. She broke stride, shook her head, and trotted on, her feet filled with pain. Of course it wasn't snowing, couldn't be. But the memory had come back from somewhere, a memory of long ago, a time she had thought her mother had only described to her until it had sunk into her mind. But it wasn't that way at all. *She* remembered. Why the memory had chosen now to come back, she couldn't guess, but she did remember—a hard and cold winter with the blood of the wounded on the snow and the wailing of the women in her ears and the sound of guns, the smell of powder-smoke in her nostrils. The dead. So many dead, and Hevatha vanished in the winter storm. She could remember her sister vividly, although she hadn't thought of her for years, had tried *not* to think of her twin lost during the plains wars. She had tried not to remember any of it, she realized. When her mother, Amaya, had tried to tell her of it all, she had closed her mind. Now the pain, the weariness, the dream snow seemed to bring it back. She whispered, "I am sorry, Mother. I am sorry, Hevatha. Twin."

There was no response from the cold and endless desert night, and Mary Hart ran on, her movements growing jerky, heavy, futile as the moon coasted over.

She was reduced again to a shambling walk. She looked behind her in terror as a coyote called to the moon. Thumb was back there—but no, there was nothing to be seen, nothing but the desert, which seemed to go on forever.

Mary wanted to halt, to sit down for five minutes, to catch her breath, to remove the thorns from her flesh, to bind her feet, but she didn't dare stop. She had to keep walking, keep moving away from the Chiricahua war chief.

My father was a war chief.

Another thought unbidden, this one rang in her skull briefly and then was blown away by the desert wind.

Saguaro cactus stood tall and stark, weird and powerful against the starry sky. The arroyo opened up before her, narrow and deep. She could not remember crossing it that day—was she heading in the wrong direction? No—there was her landmark mountain ahead of her still, black and crooked. It must be that the arroyo was deeper in certain places.

Mary walked along it hurriedly, still glancing across her shoulder toward the south and east where Thumb slept or had awakened and was racing his horse toward her. The arroyo was thirty to forty feet deep, the sides too steep to climb. She walked northward for fifteen minutes before she discovered a way across, or what she hoped was a way across. It was a frightening climb down, but there looked to be a way up on the far side.

She started down in a shower of stones and loose earth, falling, a stick tearing a gash across her shoulder. Mary bit back the cry of pain and went on, wiping her hair out of her eyes.

She reached the bottom of the arroyo and started up the far side. She climbed frantically. The sky was graying in the east. It couldn't be, but was.

Dawn was approaching, engulfing her in daylight, frightening daylight.

The darkness had offered some sense of security, some concealment from pursuing eyes. Daylight offered none. She could only hope she had run far enough, fast enough, so that Thumb wouldn't bother chasing her.

There should be soldiers ahead, a column of cavalry in pursuit of Thumb. They wouldn't have given up so easily. Not General Clark, not Scott Sampson; they wanted the Chiricahua leader too badly.

Up on the flats, once more Mary tried to hurry, to urge her wooden legs into a jog trot. She could feel the warmth of the sun on her back, see the desert flush to a delicate pink orange. Thumb would be awake . . . but if Thumb was awake, the soldiers would be up and moving as well, wouldn't they? Riding in her direction.

She fell, rolled onto her back, and lay holding her abdomen, panting. It was a long while before she could rise from the gravel of the desert basin and stagger on.

She was alone in the world. She walked across the face of the sun. It was hot and barren, white on white, deadly. Her throat was beginning to constrict with thirst, her mouth and lips to crack. It was well over a hundred degrees and the day had just begun.

Damnable desert, damnable sun.

A fine net of shade crossed her body and she looked in bewilderment toward the smokewood tree which tilted toward her. She started toward it, dazed, sun-bitten.

She sat beneath the tree, staring at her feet, which were all scab and blisters. One toe, the small one on her right foot, seemed to be broken. Red ants ran past her in rapid-fire motion, incited by the heat of the sun.

Mary found that her lips were gummed together and she had to pry them apart with her tongue. Her tongue itself felt like a wooden stick in her mouth.

Her mouth hung open now and she breathed noisily through it. Distantly a single black vulture rode the swirling heat waves across the endless desert.

Where am I going? She looked around at the vast emptiness. That way, yes, but how far? She shook her head violently, trying to clear it. She wasn't going to make it across that desert, not barefoot, she realized belatedly. If she couldn't walk out, she was going to die. She had no water. Water—there was no describing the joy that thoughts of water brought leaping to her mind. The velvet caress of water trickling down her throat, cool crystal beads of water touching her lips with their saving moisture.

She rose and went on, walking quickly before she could fall into the waking dream which was creeping over her, dreams of deep forest and soft rainfall and lush meadow grass. She walked on, her feet burning, her eyes rattling dryly in her too-heavy skull.

The soldiers would be coming. They would have to come soon.

Where are they, then? Mary peered at the wavering horizon, seeing strange curling images, images projected by the heat and her own thirst. Hundreds of soldiers appeared briefly and then were wafted away by the hot winds of the desert.

"Not you, too," she said. For beside her she thought she saw Thumb and Juh, riding silently. They kept on a parallel course with Mary, coming no nearer, saying nothing, not gesturing, and so she knew that they too were mirages.

But they would not go away. She closed her eyes and opened them, but still Thumb was there. She stared at the distant horizon, at the notched mountain, which seemed no nearer than it had at dawn. But when she looked back to her right, Thumb was still there. Now he was drinking something—water— from a skin, and he handed the sack to Juh, who did likewise.

"Go away," she muttered. The mirages taunted her, drinking, riding their horses easily, while ahead

150

of Mary lay only fifty miles of desert and mountain when she couldn't be sure of walking the next fifty yards.

"Go away!"

But they would not go away. The sun bored tiny holes in her skull and let the searing heat into her brain. Her body was dry; if she was perspiring, the wind was whipping it away before it could help to cool her.

There was no shade; there was only the sun; and the cavalry would not come. There were only the two Indians riding beside her, watching her.

She fell. She knew she could not get up, but she made herself do it and she lurched on. It was not yet noon.

It was impossible to walk through the heat of the day. Her feet seemed to have been set on fire. She found the shallow gully and lay down in the narrow, heated band of shade the wall of it offered.

She lay in the bottom of the gully staring at the tangle of roots growing out of the white earth like a snarl of thread, at the black beetle which tried to clamber up the bank and kept falling back. She stared at the receding shade, at the dirty cracked hand before her face which was her own hand, at the two Indians sitting on their horses above her, watching.

"Go away," she said through cracked lips, but her voice was only a dusty whisper and it had no effect at all on the watching Chiricahua.

She closed her eyes to escape the mirage, the blinding glare of the sun. Her head ached. Her body seemed to pitch and sway from side to side. Her blood hummed in her ears. But it was cool, somehow cool.

She opened an eye. Still they watched.

"Go away."

She slept then, somehow slept, or fainted away in exhaustion. At any rate she was no longer in that hateful, malignant world, that fierce white land fit for nothing whatever but dying.

She ran across the long meadows of spring. Flowers burgeoned everywhere. Bees hummed past her. On the distant peaks there were snowcaps. She lay in the grass and watched the stars fall from a crimson sky.

When Mary awoke, it was dark, very dark and cold. She tentatively moved an arm and found it stiff and awkward, swollen and sore. She sat up like a marionette at the hands of an untrained puppet master, her limbs uncoordinated and weak, her head bobbing heavily on her neck.

The stars were bright and cold. There was no moon.

She was dying.

Her body needed nourishment; more important, it needed water. No one survived out here without water. She was dying for want of water and she knew it. Oddly enough, she was no longer thirsty. Her body seemed to have closed up so that it wanted nothing. Her mind was alert, however; through the fog of a throbbing headache it insisted: *I need water.*

But there was no water, there was nothing but the night and the desert.

And the fire. She stared at the sky for a long while, trying to decide if her mind was playing tricks again, forming ever-more-intricate mirages in the dead of night. Thirst, she had heard, could do that.

The firelight remained, however. A small portion of the night was illuminated by its pale glow and Mary clambered cautiously out of the gully. Soldiers! They had come—it had to be the soldiers. She started mechanically toward the fire, slowing as she neared it, and realized that it wasn't the soldiers at all.

A lone Apache sat by the small red fire, feeding twigs to the hungry flames while a boy slept nearby. Beside Thumb was a water sack, and next to that his provision sack, which held pinole and dried venison. She halted, stared defiantly at the fire, at

152

the back of the Apache, and then she surrendered. She surrendered her pride to her body's needs and stumbled into the camp to collapse beside the fire, to have her head held while tiny amounts of life-giving sweet, pure water were poured between her parched lips by the man with the soft voice and bloody hands.

6

They rode southward into Mexico. Great mesas flanked their trail like enormous landships sailing the desert sea. They were red, eroded, capped with the green of sparse grass and an occasional bent, wind-formed tree. There was a narrow stream following the road southward. It had appeared from nowhere, springing out of the sands to take on life, to flow and glitter in the sun and provide water for horse and rider alike.

The land was red here, with less sand and more brush—mostly creosote and mesquite, but some sage and sumac in the gullies where the shadows haunted the land. Now and then there was a twisted, struggling cottonwood tree with its roots searching the shallow silver stream.

Thumb was silent, implacable. He held Mary to him or let her sit loosely before him on his horse, but she might as well have been a deer carcass or a sack of booty. They did not speak except at rare intervals, although father and son conversed.

The mesas merged into a vast plateau towering above them and they followed the stream through a gigantic red canyon. They moved slowly. Thumb and Juh's horses both had extra weight. Juh's spotted pony carried venison in a green deerhide. Thumb had killed it with a bow and arrow from horseback as the buck leapt from the stream where it had been quietly drinking and made for the brush.

Thumb's bow was of mulberry wood wrapped

with rawhide, his arrows of cane with steel heads, the bowstring of sinew. These weapons were a part of him, an extension of his mind and body. When he saw the deer, he prepared his bow, notched the arrow, aimed and fired quicker than Mary could have thought out the actions. The arrow flew true, catching the mule deer behind the shoulder, entering the heart, killing it in mid-leap, and so they had food.

The pinole was gone, so they gathered mesquite beans when they could and ground them into flour to make their cakes. They had much water now, but soon the river would vanish again and so Thumb sewed up the entrails of the deer and filled them with water, using this as a spare water sack. On the desert it was best to drink often while water could be found, to keep all that could be stored against drought and lack.

"Piñon," Juh said as they rode, and he pointed to the uplands, where piñon pine grew in profusion. The nuts of the piñon were one of Juh's favorite foods.

"We would have to climb, Juh. There would be no more travel today."

"Must we hurry so? Is there a big war waiting for us?" Juh asked.

"I hope not," Thumb said. "But Bad Lance awaits me."

"I do not like him. I like piñon nuts."

Thumb laughed. "Then you shall have piñon nuts. Who must climb, though? You or your weary old father?"

"I will climb—but look, there is a trail. And you knew it, too, didn't you, Father? There is a trail. It is cooler up there and it's nearly time for our night camp. May we go?"

"Yes, yes, let us go." To Mary he said, "Do you like piñon nuts, woman, or do the whites not eat such trivials?"

"I will eat them," she said with a shrug. She was subdued, and had been since the night she had surrendered herself to Thumb's fire, to his water-skin. Her feet had hardly healed, and still she was weak from her ill-fated trek.

"She will eat them, Juh," Thumb said. Juh wasn't listening. He had started his little pony up the winding trail. The way seemed too narrow for a rabbit, but the Apache ponies were skilled at climbing; perhaps they too wanted to reach the cooler uplands.

When they crested the plateau it was late. The breeze was dry but cooling as it swept over them, rattled through the pines, and raced away toward the desert of Sonora to the south.

Mary swung down from Thumb's horse as the Apache, leaping to the ground, led his son off into the trees in search of a stick to use to knock the pine cones from the low-hanging branches.

There was a horse, a chance to escape. Mary looked at it, wondering at herself. Was she that beaten? The woman who had always been admired or disparaged because of her stubbornness? But she knew it would not work. It was that simple. She could take Thumb's horse and Juh's as well, but she could not escape if the man didn't choose to let her go. Over a distance a man, a solid man, a strong man, could run a horse down.

Thumb was such a man.

She clasped her hands behind her back and walked through the pines, hearing father and son laughing, playing, teasing. She saw the squirrels leaping through the trees, winding around them, watching bright-eyed, seemingly unbothered by the humans' presence, except now and then one would chatter loudly as if decrying the theft of their piñon nuts.

It was warm and dry, but pleasant. The trees swayed in unison. She could hear Juh laughing. She walked for a long way—the plateau went on for mile after mile. When she returned, Juh was busy cracking the small brown nuts with stones. Thumb stood aside, watching. Then his eyes lifted to Mary.

"You may take the deer hide if you like," he said.

"What do you mean?" she asked. "What would I want it for?"

"For your feet, woman. To make moccasins—or don't you even know how to do that? For a skirt. You are walking around in nothing—whatever you call that garment you have on, it can do little to warm you; it does little to hide you."

Mary felt a flush creep over her skin and she turned away, folding her arms over her breasts, and her ragged chemise.

"She doesn't know how to make shoes, Father," Juh said.

"No? Perhaps not. What do you do, woman, wait for the man who has been out hunting to sit down and make your moccasins as well? No, you have stores, I have seen white stores. Once I emptied a white store of all its goods. There were many shoes, all different colors, red and yellow and green, but there were none a person could walk in."

"I will try to make moccasins when you are finished with the deerhide," Mary said. She was fighting back a small tide of anger. Knowing her anger wouldn't do any good, she stood meek and accepting before the Chiricahua. It seemed to please him, but to puzzle him as well.

"But you do not know how to make moccasins."

"I have seen it done. I need something on my feet. I will try to do it."

Thumb waved a hand. "Perhaps I can show you something of it, although I know only a little—it is not a job for a warrior."

"No," Mary agreed.

"Maybe there is enough for a shirt."

"Maybe there is."

Thumb looked at her for a silent moment and then turned away again, going to Juh to play with him, chasing him briefly, pretending that he wanted to steal his piñon nuts, which Juh shoved into his mouth as he ran.

Later father and son lazed the twilight hours away. Mary sat apart from them as always, listening but taking no active part in the conversation. She was, after all, a prisoner.

The night came on quickly; it was cool and brief. With the sunrise Thumb came to her. He was chewing on a strip of venison jerky. In his hand was the deerhide.

"Do you know how to clean this hide?"

"I have seen it done."

"You will need a scraper." He gave her his belt knife and she took it, holding it gingerly. "You must promise not to cut my throat with that," he said, and then the faintest hint of a smile lifted the edges of his mouth.

"I promise."

"Good. Now, let me show you what to do." He got to his knees and staked out the deerhide and began scraping it. Mary watched, remembering. Years ago she had tried to learn from her mother how to do this, but by the time she was old enough to become expert, that way of life was gone. They had gone to the reservation and there they did not have to scrape hides to make buckskin dresses. The government store had dresses of wool and of cotton that could be purchased with their allotment—those times that the allotment actually was distributed. . . . Mary felt the knife placed in her hand, felt Thumb's hand close around hers and guide it.

His chest was against her back as she knelt, his breath coming in small puffs as he showed her what to do. "One stroke and then another. You see?"

He paused then, paused for a single but very telling moment. He rose immediately afterward and said casually, "Like that. Do your best."

"Thumb . . . would you let me go now?"

"No."

"I am no danger to you, no help."

He didn't even answer except to shake his head and walk away. Mary looked at the deerskin staked out on the ground. Slowly she began to scrape at it, to peel away the clinging layer of fat, until her

158

temper boiled up and she stabbed the knife through the deerskin and sat back on her haunches glowering at the hide, Thumb, the day, all of it.

When she next saw the Chiricahua it was nearly full dark. She had given up the job of scraping the hide. Her fingers were sore, her hands blistered. She had cut out some of the leather and made a pair of crude moccasins—something to protect her poor feet, nothing more. The rest of the hide lay where it had been, slashed with Thumb's knife, ruined.

"You did not want a blouse, a skirt?" Thumb asked, picking up his knife from beside Mary.

"No. Not of raw deerhide."

"But this is just the material, woman. What you make of it is up to you."

"I will make nothing of it."

"But that is wasteful."

"I don't care." Mary shrugged.

"Nothing can be wasted." Thumb pulled up the stakes that held the deerskin and rolled up the ruined hide. "Something can be made from this still."

"Thumb?" She rose and stepped toward him in the darkness. There were no stars yet and the dying sun had left only a pale orange filament against the western sky. The wind spoke in the piñon trees. Thumb was in front of her, towering over her. "Will you let me go, Thumb?" she asked again, but the Chiricahua would not answer. He was gone again and Mary could only follow him back to the place where he and Juh had unrolled their blankets. There she too made her bed and lay down, feet and hands aching still, her body weary as always from the long days of travel.

In the morning they moved out silently. Thumb had seen his enemies during the early hours. He had seen their smoke and he had slipped down the long canyon to spy on their camp.

"Who are they?" Mary asked him.

"Mexicans. Scalp hunters."

"Scalp hunters!"

"Yes. It is me they want, but they would be happy with your scalp or Juh's."

"I'm not Apache!"

"Your hair cannot speak. It is worth fifty pesos to these men."

"A woman's scalp?"

"Yes. Mine would bring one hundred pesos—even if they did not know who I was. Juh's, I am afraid, would bring them only twenty-five pesos. That is, unless the bounty has been raised."

"That can't be. Civilized nations don't offer a prize for genocide. For murdering children."

Thumb looked at her with level dark eyes. "What world have you been living in, woman? I know you are 'civilized' yourself, but even in the civilized world you must have heard that Apache are filth, Apache are evil, Apache are less than human. There is a bounty for the bad cougars, for the coyotes when the American or Mexican ranchers want to put sheep on the land which belongs to the coyotes, to the cougars. There is bounty on the Apache when the Apache resist the loss of their land. The 'civilized' men want to push the Apache somewhere, out of Apacheria, but where can they go? The Americans have made their war on us, the Mexicans have made their war on us. There is nowhere left but the mountains, and one day they will drive us from there too. And so we fight. The army cannot beat us because they cannot catch us, and so they kill a little piece of the Apache nation at a time. Kill a woman, kill a child. Soon there will be no more Apache—that is the war the civilized people make against the Chiricahua. Now, be silent as we ride, or they will take your hair."

The wind crackled up the canyon. It was a cool morning and the chill of it seemed to creep into Mary's bones. The horses' hooves made a noise like thunder against the stone floor of the canyon, although they walked as softly as the day before.

Thumb was alert, tense, his head erect, neck

muscles taut. A vein across his throat danced with a steady, strong pulse. His breathing was shallow, controlled, his eyes bright and intent. Juh's spotted pony stumbled and Mary's heart skipped a beat. The boy looked worried briefly and then relief erased the expression. Thumb hissed between his teeth. A raven coasted past, black against the pale blue sky. They were deep in the shadows of the canyon.

When the first shot rang out, Thumb heeled his horse into a run, but the second bullet struck the horse in the hindquarters and it went down, rolling. Thumb practically threw Mary from the horse's back and leapt free himself. Bullets struck the earth around them as Mary crawled and ran toward the brush beside the trail. Thumb had caught Juh's pony by its hackamore and swung the boy down with one hand, pushing him toward the chaparral as the spotted pony reared up wildly and then ran, leaving them without any mounts.

A storm of bullets cut the brush around Mary's head as she caught Juh, pressing him to the ground despite his wriggling protests. Thumb stopped to snatch up his quiver, then ran toward them, weaving as he came, bullets peppering the earth behind and before him until he threw himself headlong into the brush to land beside Mary as the guns continued to sound from the canyon slope.

"Back. Move away from here," Thumb said. He yanked Juh to his feet, and moving in a crouch, wound his way through the brush, following a rabbit trail which twisted through the tangle of chia and manzanita, sumac and yucca.

They dipped into a small ravine and ran upstream, moving swiftly along the rocky bottom. They reached an area where stony ledges overhung the ravine—when it rained, there would be many small, sheeting waterfalls there—and climbed up to the ledge above.

Mary was first up, followed by Juh and then Thumb. She wasn't even frightened just then, nor did her body seem weary at all. She was ready to run all day if necessary, but Thumb wasn't going to run.

"Why are we stopping?" she asked.

"They'll follow us, woman. They'll track us down easily. Six men on horseback, and me with a woman."

"I'll keep up," Mary said with a stirring of pride.

"You would try, but you would not be able to. I have run every day of my life. You sit and read books to Indian children. Be silent now. Thumb fights his own wars."

"What, then . . ."

Thumb's face turned angry now; Mary didn't care for the expression at all. "I have told you to be silent," the Chiricahua leader snapped.

At a signal from Thumb they began to move forward—and upward—again. The day was still cool, the shadows deep. They startled a cottontail underfoot and it wound away through the brush, its tail bobbing.

Thumb moved in a crouch once again, looking behind him to make sure that Mary was following his example. Juh was still screened by brush at his height, but he bent over anyway, his young face earnest, too mature.

Thumb began to motion vigorously and Mary went to her stomach to creep forward onto a large black slab of stone which overhung the valley. They were now above the enemy. Mary saw them at once—three of them anyway. Mexicans in big sombreros, two of them wearing leather vests, searching the brush in the area where Thumb had entered it. Thumb's horse lay still on the ground, dead. They could hear voices, muffled and unintelligible, as the bounty hunters began to move with utmost caution into the brush.

Thumb wasn't looking that way—he had seen the three and marked their position; he was more interested in finding the others, the three he could not see. *They* could be anywhere, could strike at any time.

Black eyes searched the long canyon. The sun

had appeared over the eastern rim in a splash of golden-white light. Mary watched Thumb's searching eyes, his intent face. The eyes combed every inch of the canyon, moving methodically from side to side, up and down as the insects, warmed by the sun, began to fill the canyon with their hum and buzz. A rabbit hopped toward the rock, looked hesitantly at the strange beings who had taken his sun perch, and veered rapidly away.

Thumb tensed. His eyes sharpened. Mary saw the beginnings of a smile on his curved lips. She followed his eyes and saw the three Mexicans on the ledge below and to the east. They were lying in wait, providing cover for their *compadres* who searched the brush. Thumb looked to Juh and then to Mary, motioning that she should make sure the boy did not follow.

"There are—" She fell silent at Thumb's sharp gesture. There are six of them, she had wanted to say. Six armed men with rifles, but none of that seemed to bother Thumb. He looked at Juh and then slipped off down the brushy hill toward the three bounty hunters on the ledge. Juh scooted up beside Mary and lay watching intently, his hand clenched around a pointed stick he had picked up somewhere. Mary's arm went over his shoulders and he didn't seem to notice; he had eyes only for Thumb, only for the battle.

If there was a battle, and it seemed there would be, Mary could not understand how Thumb hoped to emerge victorious—perhaps he just wanted to make sure he drew blood. All of this was beyond her, outside of her ken. She had heard talk of wars as a child, talk of bloodshed and of death through arms, but such stories had always been discouraged by the chiefs, by the adult women. Nothing at all was gained through war but suffering, nothing through struggle but death—that was what she had been taught, that was what she believed.

Yet what could be done in a situation like the one she now faced? These men wanted her life. They wanted it so that they might cut a section of her scalp away and sell it for fifty pesos to the government of Mexico. They did not care what her ideals were, who she was, if she was or was not an enemy, an Apache, a warrior.

Juh stirred and she looked up, seeing Thumb almost recklessly cross a bare patch of hillside. Yet he was not reckless—from their perspective it seemed so, but Mary realized that the bounty hunters could not see him from their position.

A gun fired and Mary's body leapt as if it had been struck, but the bullet had gone in another direction entirely. The searchers in the brush had grown edgy, and one of them had fired his gun at a shadow, a ghost, an illusion.

A deep voice cursed proficiently in Spanish. There were several muttered words of explanation and the men went on. Mary could only occasionally see their sombreros above the brush, but she could always hear them; she always had a fairly good idea of where the hunters were.

That was not so with Thumb. Looking back in the other direction, she found she couldn't see the Chiricahua at all. She could not hear him. The three men on the ledge below lay patiently, not knowing that Thumb was hehind them.

Mary's hand tightened on Juh's shoulder. They had both seen Thumb suddenly. He darted forward and then snuggled to the earth between two upthrust gray boulders. They could see him notch an arrow, see him rise on one knee and sight down the arrow at the three men on the ledge.

Nevertheless Mary was shocked when the first arrow sang through the air and buried itself in the back of a bounty hunter. The man turned his head and tried to speak. Blood spilled from his lips. The two remaining bounty hunters sprang up in terror.

An arrow from Thumb's bow flew through the air and struck a second bounty hunter in the chest. He toppled over backward, but his rifle exploded with sound and flame as he fell.

164

The third Mexican threw down his gun and bolted for the rim of the ledge. Thumb's arrow took him in the neck and he reached the rim only to stagger and slump over, falling from the ledge to the arroyo bottom below.

From below, the rifles of the three remaining bounty hunters opened up, but they couldn't have seen Thumb, who was well back from the rim. Panic prodded them to fire anyway, at random, with a lot of noise and smoke but no success.

Thumb could be seen moving through the brush downslope. Mary discovered she was biting her lip, that her grip on Juh's shoulder had become a crushing one. She forced herself to relax. *Downslope*—he was going after them. Attacking three armed men alone.

Maybe he felt he had to, felt that if he did not kill the bounty hunters they would continue their pursuit until they killed the boy and Mary, Thumb himself. . . . He was into the stacked boulders on the flats below, and then, moving swiftly, shadow-like he was into the brush where the Mexicans, their guns silent, waited.

One of the scalp hunters suddenly broke from the brush, and Mary was sure Thumb had been seen; but he hadn't—the scalp hunter was running for his horse, bent on escape. He was too slow, too late. Mary saw him jerk, stand erect, twist, and fall. There was an arrow in his back.

The guns opened up again, this time in the right direction, although the two men still couldn't have seen Thumb. He was moving through the head-high brush above the Mexicans. From time to time Mary could see his headband, a patch of color against the grayness of the chaparral.

The Mexicans began to move. The two men split up and began working their way toward Thumb's position, figuring correctly that they would have to fight or die, be picked off singly as their friends had been. And there was a chance it might work. They were moving cautiously, easing toward Thumb.

Thumb couldn't fire his arrows through the thick brush. He would have to rise to do that, and if he did so the Mexicans' guns could cut him down.

They were good, these two, and they knew their work. They used hand signals to communicate. They seemed to sense that they had Thumb between them now.

The sun was growing warm. Gnats swarmed around Mary's face. In the canyon the shadows were receding. The scalp hunters were within yards of Thumb. Mary could no longer see the Apache warlord, but she was certain he hadn't moved from the last spot she had marked.

And the Mexicans were closer.

One of them lifted an arm and jabbed a finger at the clump of scrub oak where Thumb was—where he had to be—hidden. Mary felt her throat go dry, her stomach clench and unclench. Suddenly Juh leapt up. He leapt up and hollered, making a shrill, wavering war cry. The Mexicans spun in surprise or fear and leveled three shots at the Apache boy. Mary grabbed Juh by the seat of the pants and hauled him down.

Thumb used the distraction to good advantage. He moved, and quickly. Firing on the run, his bow held across his body, he sent an arrow into the ribs of one of the hunters. The other turned, dropped to one knee, and fired three times from his repeating rifle, but Thumb was at the Mexicans' horses already, taking shelter behind one of them, a strapping bay. The Apache cried out for the first time and Mary recoiled at the sound, thinking he was wounded. But it was only his own war cry, echoing that of Juh. Thumb was between two of the scalp hunters' horses, gripping their bridles. His bow was slung loosely over his arm. There was a single arrow in his teeth.

Mary saw the scalp hunter sight and fire. The big bay horse went down, tumbling into the brush in a cloud of powdery dust. Thumb was thrown free. He rolled to his feet, notching his last arrow

166

as he did. He fired at near quarters into the belly of the Mexican, who took the arrow in the abdomen just beneath the sternum. The arrow hit him with such force that the head of it protruded from his back beside his spine.

He lifted his rifle, tried to fire, and then toppled over into the dust to lie there unmoving.

Juh let out a cry of jubilation and rose to his feet to dance wildly, uninhibitedly. Thumb waved and shouted back—the words did not reach them, but the tone was elated, triumphant.

Mary stood shakily, staring at the canyon below. She had just seen six men die violently. If Juh and Thumb could be happy about it, she could not. She felt relief that the scalp hunters would no longer be pursuing them, but that relief was overshadowed by revulsion. Men had died. Men without names, without faces, but men. Dirty men, perhaps, criminals maybe—but men.

Juh stood looking up at Mary, beaming. She touched his sun-warmed dark hair lightly and started down the slope with him.

Thumb was waiting for them when they arrived. Dusty, streaked with perspiration, his muscular chest rising and falling with exertion and emotion. He crouched and stuck out his arms. Juh rushed to him and they embraced, Thumb rubbing the boy's head. Mary stood by, not looking—or trying not to look—at the Mexican who lay facedown nearby, his blood staining the dusty earth.

Juh had again begun an impromptu victory dance, jumping up and down with relief, with pride, chanting, "You killed them all, all of them."

"You are all right, woman?" Thumb asked Mary. She shrugged. She felt a chill pervade her body, and with it came a loosening of her joints, a strange sweet sickness. She had touched death, touched it again. *The men lying in the snow, the gray skies rolling eerily through the ranks of tall pines. A woman screaming somewhere, a man singing the death song . . . she knew them all, the dead, the wounded, the anguished, the bodies strewn about the ground. . . .*

Mary was looking up into the piercingly white sun. She blinked and shook her head. She touched her tongue to her lips and tried to sit up. She was resting on someone's lap, and now that someone stroked her forehead. She could not see his face, but he seemed gentle, very gentle.

"Are you all right?" Thumb asked. She recognized his voice with a start. His strong profile against the pale sky became clear and sharp. She tried to sit up again, pulling away from him as her head spun and the colored dots swarmed around inside her skull, buzzing like a hive of wasps. Thumb's hand was on her shoulder and she let it rest there, barely conscious of its intrusion.

"Are you all right?" the Apache repeated.

Mary, who was seated on the hot gravelly sand surrounded by sagebrush and horses, by nopal cactus—by the dead—nodded. "Yes. I'm all right. Thank you." She stirred again. "I'd like to get up."

"Sit there a moment. Juh, the water skin."

The boy was back with it in moments. "She is white," Juh said, trying very hard to put a sneer into his tone. "She is a Cheyenne. When she saw death, she fainted away. I am a warrior."

Mary paid no attention to his childish boasting. The water was soft and cool across her lips, and she swallowed greedily. Still Thumb held her, and when she tried to pull away, he tugged her back against his chest.

"Please. I am all right now, I told you."

"Yes?" Thumb said, peering into her eyes. "Except you tremble all over. What is wrong, Mary Hart?"

"She saw the blood," Juh said.

"No," his father answered. "I don't think so. I think she saw something else. Other death, other blood. Is that right, Mary?"

"I don't know." Mary stood, wobbling slightly as she came upright.

"You know."

"I've forgotten."

Thumb stood now, coming gracefully to his feet. He faced her, his head tilted to one side, his dark eyes still curious. "I don't think you've forgotten."

"I have, I told you," she snapped. "I've forgotten what I was thinking of. Juh is right. I just saw the dead men and I fainted."

"All right." Thumb shrugged. "As you will have it. Juh! Gather the scalp hunters' horses. See what they have that we can use."

There was much that they could use: rifles, ammunition, cooking utensils, knives, canteens, and in the pack of one of the men a bolt of blue cloth, perhaps intended for a loved one, perhaps stolen.

"This," Thumb asked, "do you think you can make clothing out of this, woman?" He let the bolt of cloth unfold and strike the ground. Mary only glanced at it, nodding. It was a light cotton cloth, aquamarine in color, very attractive. But she saw crimson, only crimson, splashed against the new snow, staining a dress front, masking a face.

Thumb watched her for a long minute, shrugged, and rolled up the cloth again. When they moved on they went in silence, riding south onto the desert once more, leading the captured horses as the day tramped heavily past.

They camped on a low mesa overlooking the desert, which had gone deep purple and gold, pale pink as the sunset flush spread across the empty, alien land.

Thumb and Juh ate in silence, and Juh, weary, and only now showing it, curled up to sleep. His father covered him with a light striped blanket.

"You did not eat, woman," Thumb said.

"No."

Twilight was a violet haze above the desert, the dark convoluted hills. "Is it this dream?" he asked, taking her arm above the elbow. "Is that what troubles you?"

"What dream?"

"The dream of blood."

"I don't know what you mean," Mary said. Again she was trembling, but she couldn't have said if it was because of the evening chill or because of the dream. Perhaps it was the touch of the man who stood before her, holding her arm, prodding her. The man who fed her, clothed her, kept her prisoner, dominated her, angered her, and in a way she did not yet understand, pleased her.

"Come, let us walk a way," Thumb said, turning her by her elbow.

"Walk where?"

"A little way. Don't be afraid. From higher we can see the sun still, see its colors and fire, feel the wind it sets loose across the desert to bring the night creatures to life."

They climbed in silence up a narrow crevice strewn with small dark rocks. When Thumb finally pulled her up to stand beside him on the pinnacle, Mary was facing the dying sun once more. In the canyons below, all was in deep shadow, but there, blazing against the western sky, was a magnificent display of red and orange, of gold which touched the few frail clouds, of violet seeming to fountain into the twilight sky from beyond the hills where the sun had returned to lie in its cradle to rest, to rise again in the morning, renewed, angry, heated, savage.

"Beautiful, is it not?" Thumb asked in a tone which revealed again his unexpected softness, his eye for the marvels of the desert, its raw and rugged beauty, the small and delicate fillips of nature, the challenging vastness of it all.

"Tell me of your dream," he said, and sat down on the ledge of sandstone, warm yet from the sun. He sat and plucked at the dry grass, watching the sun with narrowed eyes, waiting for Mary finally to seat herself.

"How do you know anything about it?" she asked.

"I know. I read it in your eyes. Don't you read eyes, read fear and love and anger and lies?"

"Yes, but . . ."

"I read that there was a dream, something you hid from me, from yourself perhaps."

She was silent a moment, thinking, remembering. "It was a long while ago," she began finally, and it was a relief to tell it, such a relief that as she spoke tears began to gather in her eyes and trickle warmly down her cheeks. If Thumb saw these, he said nothing. He didn't glance at her, but only watched the dying colors in the western sky. "It was a very long while ago.

"You laugh at me and call me white. I am not white; I am Cheyenne. We too fought our wars. We, the Sioux, the Shoshoni—all of the plains tribes. We fought and then we were defeated. We fought until the soldiers came in winter and attacked our camp and everyone was slaughtered, until my father was killed and my friends and my cousins and my uncles.

"We fought and then we died and I stood in a desolate place looking around me at the snow, at the crimson on the snow. My sister was gone. My mother was a wandering ghost. My father was dead and she had loved him . . . I was a child vagrant on the earth, small, undefined, and very afraid."

She looked at Thumb, but he hadn't moved. He did not turn his head and look into her eyes, her child's eyes which were now unfocused to look into the Cheyenne past.

"They took us then, and we went with them. There was no point in fighting. We went to live on the reservation with soldiers all around us. We had made a peace, but still we lived as prisoners. We could not have weapons to go out and hunt the buffalo. The government would care for us, always the government, but the government does not take care of people, it takes care of itself.

"I was young and I wanted to have a life. Around me the old way was dying, around me the old people were dying . . . my mother was a spirit woman walking through the shadows. She had been strong, so strong that an entire people could lean against her and be supported by her strength. She could lift my father to valor, and shame him to tears, love him so that he was as soft as she could be when the mood was upon her—I know all of this now. Then I saw nothing, for I was a child."

Thumb still had not moved. He might have been a statue carved out of the sunset-stained rock, an icon thrown up by his people to watch over the desert, to reflect the glory of the sun.

Mary rubbed wearily at her cheek. "I saw the old die, and I was young; I wanted to live. I wanted to have dreams. I wanted to do, to be, to have. And they were dying."

"You became white," Thumb said, finally speaking. He didn't say it with disparagement, but with curiosity, with wonder.

"Yes. I didn't do it on purpose. I didn't plan to be *American* and not Cheyenne. I didn't think as I changed my moccasins for button shoes that I was becoming another *thing*, another person. I was simply being what *was*. That which offered hope instead of the stagnation, the tragedy which was the old people, the old way. The Cheyenne way.

"I changed my buckskin dress for calico and my braids were pinned on top of my head. My mother watched me and said nothing. What was there to say? She was a wise woman and she knew about time, about generations which deny each other, one after the other. She knew about children endlessly repeating the very patterns they mock in the preceding generation, until we all seem very much the same, like beads in an endless necklace.

"My brother's name was Dark Moon until he changed it to become a man called Edward Court, a man who had his hair barbered and combed, who shaved although he had no beard, and wore bay rum and fancy suits with striped vests. A man who affected all of the externals of the white way but could not escape being Indian and so turned to drinking to fill up the hollow interior of his being."

172

Thumb guessed, "You weren't satisfied with the externals. You had to *become* something."

His perceptiveness surprised her and she glanced at him, wondering that she had underestimated his intelligence. Perhaps he had underestimated her, seen her as a prize or a novelty, a woman taken, to be toyed with, to be trained. Forgetting that she had lived a life of experience, had seen and worshiped and thought and dreamed and wanted and cried and touched . . . and needed to be touched.

"I was not satisfied with the clothing, with the hair styled after the white women's pattern. But I did not sit down and say, 'I am not satisfied so easily'—I only felt it. I saw that the Cheyenne were unhappy, that they were not free. I saw that the whites had won, that they were free. They lived in a time and a place that were suited to them. Railroads were running across the ancient lands, and whites had built them; telegraphs and steamships and buildings of concrete and tools of steel had been built by the whites, for them. The old ways of stone and hide could not last.

"I saw the castles of Europe, the art that was remarkable to one of my experience, and as I learned to read English, to understand it from the inside, I heard the subtleties, the desires, the power and longings of the white poetry which echoed—or formed, who knows?—my own longings. What else could I do but fall captive to the language, to knowledge, to education? Each thing I learned pleased my teachers, and when I surpassed them, or thought I had, my pride was unbounded. I had become a *person.* I did not sit on my haunches in the shade of the barren trees and dream of the buffalo days, of the timeless and primitive days when we would sled on our buffalo hides across the snowy hills, of the long hunts, of eagle pits and frost-glazed winters, of Manitou's eyes, of the long, long strand of beads which was the Cheyenne nation. I was doing, moving, teaching, becoming . . . walking with my head above those of the old and the dying and the ignorant and the dirty and the forlorn and loveless."

"But the shame of it all, Mary Hart," Thumb said. "What of that? Of knowing that the enemy had purchased you. Of knowing that your teachers were the killers of the People. What of that, Mary Hart?"

"It was not in my thoughts. I had forgotten. Each day drew another sheer veil across the memories, until there was no more memory, no past. . . ."

"Until today?"

"Until the other day when my feet walked a trackless desert, when I was a physical thing in touch with my physical world, my self, my soul . . . I can't explain it. There was no veneer of civilization protecting me on the desert, and without it I was as savage as you; without it I could remember, and I did."

"And then today you remembered blood."

"Today . . ." She pulled her hair back over her ears with her thumbs. "I remembered blood."

"And now what does the Cheyenne in you want, woman?" Thumb asked. "What does the memory of blood do to this white woman you have formed from your Indian clay?"

She shook her head. "I don't know. I don't know."

"What is your name?" Thumb demanded, nearly shouting at her.

"Mary Hart," she answered numbly. Was the world ever going to go dark, or would she have to sit forever in this coldly colored twilight, this world between light and darkness?

"What is your name?" His hand gripped her arm and squeezed it so that she nearly cried out.

"What is the matter with you?" she mumbled.

"Your name?"

"Mary—"

"Your name!" The hand tortured her arm. The sky seemed to go dark in one sudden gesture of surrender. "Your name, your name." He seemed to repeat it endlessly.

"Akton!" She screamed it out and then she screamed it again, feeling her shoulders tremble. "Akton."

Thumb took her by the shoulders and turned her to him. His mouth met hers, smothering the shout that was welling up again. He laid her back and she let herself be placed down against the sandstone where the warmth of day was still radiating. She lay there, her fingertips touching his bare shoulders, digging into his hard flesh.

She watched his head, motionless against the starry sky, saw his hair drifting in the light wind as he hovered, watching her in return, perhaps scenting her as she scented him, as she savored the man smell of him, the scent of horse and of sage. His head bent and he kissed her again, more gently so that his lips seemed to dance across hers, moving lightly, very nearly but not quite tickling her as she felt them brush against her own unskilled lips, very nearly but not exactly searching hungrily for the smallest response which would signal to him that, yes, she wanted him. The touch of his lips, the light pressure of his knee against her thigh, the nearness of him, was exciting, touching reservoirs of emotion deeper, more primitive yet than her Cheyenne heritage, the memory of man and woman meeting, coming together; the memory which sustains and is glorified and decried and hated and abused, but is needful, so needful to the heart of nature.

He slowly lowered himself and she felt his hair against her cheek, felt his hand loosen its grip on her arm and slide beneath her shoulder, felt his lips touch her throat where the pulsing had grown strong and regular as her head lolled back and her body slackened. She too needed; she too was a part of the memory of nature, of its want, of its way.

She lay still, hardly breathing for what seemed an eternity, not knowing how to respond, afraid to answer his kiss, to come alive beneath his hands, which now slowly, surely touched the warm flesh

175

of her thighs, crept across her breasts, and held her head as he kissed her with the controlled hunger of man. He wanted her, but all she had to do was speak out to stop him. Yet how could she stop him? When had she ever been touched, prodded, lifted to need, to want; when before had she needed a protector, a friend, a guide?

He stood and Mary saw him against the violet sky, stripping his loincloth. He was stark and bold against the night, a phantasm, an other-worldly creature, an opposite. A man.

Her heart began to pound violently and she turned half away from him, her hand to her lips as he lay beside her once more, kissing her ear, breathing softly into it. She started to turn away but her body, her being, the part of her which was female and needed to have its male half, responded with a shuddering need, with a trickling tear and a softening of her body.

His hands lifted her chemise, and though she felt herself go rigid, felt her heart striking out fearfully at her ribs, she could do no more to stop him than she could have done to stop the setting of the sun.

He was man against her, wanting her, clinging to her, and her head swam with need. She lifted her shoulders and he tugged the chemise over her head. Then Thumb, this savage and needful thing, was against her and she thought no more.

She thought of nothing; but her body, coming to its own sudden and demanding life, surrounded Thumb, stroked his head, his back and thighs, found his lips, met his kiss hungrily now, inviting him to take her and use her, to wander with her, to share her needs, to fulfill her, to do what he willed.

He was gentle and nearly timid even when her own actions had ceased to become halting, when her thighs met his, and her arms, wound around him, drew him more tightly to her. She clung to him as if only Thumb of all things was not of the night, as if only the savage man could save her from its deep and hopeless encroachment.

He was warm and close and his nearness was startling, overwhelming, intoxicating as he swayed against her in ways at once timeless and new. He kissed her abdomen, her breasts, her throat, her eyes, tasting her, seeming to marvel at her presence, at her welcome, at the comfort of her.

It was a long and gentle time, and when it was over it was not a thing ended but a thing begun. He slept against her and the stars blinked even more brightly and Mary watched them until her heart seemed to swell and open itself to him, until she had to cling to him as he slept, to hold him so tightly that he could not rise, could not escape.

"My name," she told the silence, the warmth, and the desert, "is Akton."

7

The mountains were dry and barren on the lower slopes, but as Thumb, Juh, and Akton rode higher into the tangled heights, that changed. There began to be trees here and there, and grass sprouting on the shady sides of the hills. They saw yellow limoncillos growing in patches where the soil was better, windmills or starflowers of rose and magenta hues dotting the hillsides where yuccas with their cream-colored clusters of blossoms reached for the pale sky above the Sierra Madres. This was the home rancheria, the last redoubt of the Apache in the Southwest—if it could be called that now that they were into Mexico. The land was strange to Akton's eyes. She had seen desert, but this was all brighter, more vivid, crowded with huge broken landforms and tiny delicate flowers, with miracles large and small. Or perhaps that was only the way it *seemed*. Akton saw things differently now. Her senses seemed to have returned to life, to have been altered, brought into sharp focus.

She rode beside Thumb now, on one of the captured scalp hunters' horses, and ahead of both of them rode Juh. He no longer accused Akton of being white, nor did he openly disparage the Cheyenne—but then, he was at that age when he was still a mirror of his father, reflecting his opinions, sharing them instead of battling against them as he would do when he was older.

Akton had managed to sew a crude dress of the

aquamarine material, a loose design with a full skirt and sleeves which went to the middle of her forearms. It was gathered at the waist with a belt made from the hide of the deer Thumb had killed.

Around her neck she wore a necklace of turquoise and silver. Thumb had taken it from around his own neck and given it to her. They did not discuss what it meant. Juh had said nothing, but he had certainly noticed. Yet Akton wore it proudly, a pagan symbol, a crude bit of heavy jewelry with polished but uncut stones, with a hand-cast silver chain. She wore it sometimes outside of her dress, sometimes beneath it so that it tapped incessantly, impatiently it seemed, against her breast, reminding her constantly of Thumb, of his touch, of his gifts of love.

There were pines along the trail now, and a quick silver stream gushed out of the rocks and wound its sinuous way down the gray slopes toward the desert below. Higher up yet, water seeped from the bluffs, sheeting down in thin waterfalls, like hundreds of small veils, and there red monkeyflowers grew in hanging bunches surrounded by fern and vines. Among these hanging gardens, larks piped, and they heard the calls of mountain quail.

Higher still, along the gray and forbidding ridge above the pines, Akton could see cedar trees combed and cut by the wild winds which scoured the canyons and rushed across the peaks. They were bent, gnarled trees clinging to an existence as sad as any the world has to offer. Yet they were tenacious and Akton frequently lifted her eyes to them. She had always appreciated tenacity, the will to endure and survive.

"Beyond the ridge is the rancheria," Thumb told her.

"I imagined your home was much closer to the border. When Juh was captured it certainly wasn't down here, was it?" Akton asked.

"No." Thumb looked to the ridge again before settling his eyes on Akton. It thrilled her to see the pleasure in his gaze as he studied her face, her eyes. "We were in Arizona, at the winter rancheria. For a time the army let us be, although they knew where we were. Then during a raid some people were killed, a child and a woman among them. The people came south again, back to the Sierra Madres. I, of course, remained to find Juh."

Akton nodded. Her horse had walked on another hundred feet before she asked, "Who killed them—the woman, the child?"

"This is a war," Thumb said a little defensively.

"Is it that kind of a war? A war where women and children are killed?"

"You have seen such a war—and the whites made it."

"Everyone made it."

"Still, you know that I speak the truth. The whites have made that kind of war."

"I know that." She leaned over and touched his hand lightly. "I also know that you would not make that kind of war."

"I am Apache. Chiricahua Apache. A wolf, a killing thing."

She repeated quietly, "You would not make that kind of war. It is not in your heart."

"You know me so well already, woman?"

"I know you so well, yes."

Thumb looked at her, at her quiet eyes and slight, knowing smile. Perhaps she did know him so well; perhaps their hearts had met secretly. Such things were possible, at least old Natash said that they were, and the old medicine woman was said to be a child of the gods.

"There is a man called Bad Lance—he is my cousin. He was born with the name Shashek, but when he was younger he and I were hunting the peccary, the wild boar. I had killed my boar, but Shashek had only wounded his with an arrow. As I was skinning out my peccary, his charged him from out of the thick brush. Shashek was armed with a lance and he plunged it into the peccary's back, but

180

the shaft of the lance was faulty and it snapped. The peccary ripped his leg and face with its tusks before I could recover my weapons and kill it. From then on, he has been called Bad Lance. From then on my cousin has blamed me for his wounds. If I had been less eager to skin my boar, perhaps he wouldn't have been mauled."

"That makes no sense," Akton objected. "It was his responsibility. He should have waited for you. Anyway, the lance broke. It would have broken anyway. How could you have done anything quickly enough to help him?"

"I didn't say it was sensible," Thumb said. "I only told you how Bad Lance felt about it, how he still feels about it."

"I see. It's a terrible thing when there's bad blood in the family."

"Yes, and with us it can only be bad for the tribe."

"Your cousin is also a war leader?"

"He's my chief lieutenant, yes. It is Bad Lance who is responsible for the tribe's well-being when I am gone, who leads them in their raids."

Who, Thumb was saying, was responsible for the killing of the woman and white children which had caused the army to mount an offensive, driving them out of Arizona. That would have been a command under Colonel Shore. It gave Akton a strange feeling of duality. She had liked Colonel Shore. Or Mary Hart had. Now she was here, the same person, only days later, on the other side of the border with a savage from another world, feeling perfectly comfortable. More than comfortable, in fact. She was content, happy.

But she had always sheltered a duality in her breast, always been half-white, half-Indian. The white Mary had had her way for quite some time; now the repressed Cheyenne girl, Akton, had risen to the surface. She had chosen this time—or had it chosen for her?—to dominate the creature, the woman, the two-souled being which was her self.

"Look!" Juh cried out jubilantly. He was pointing toward the highlands, where the twisted cedar grew. Now Akton could see them too, the Apache in white trousers and white shirts of manta, with red sashes and headbands. They held rifles over their heads in a gesture of recognition as Thumb rode the narrow trail toward the rancheria above.

"We are home," Thumb said. He looked at Akton and his expression was a welcoming one. His eyes told her, yes, this was *home* for himself and Juh, but he wanted Akton to find a home there as well.

Akton looked about, at the desolate, foreign land filled with an alien people whose ways she did not know, who lived crudely, savagely. She felt sudden, sharp discomfort—fear perhaps.

So long as there had been only the three of them, alone on an empty, nearly uninhabitable desert, she had found it simple enough to find a role, to be what Thumb wished without surrendering all of herself, without giving away her identity. But among strangers, perhaps hostile strangers, the role would become very different. They would require . . . what? Obeisance, servility? That she could not offer.

"What is wrong?" Thumb asked. Akton just shook her head. The Apache leader was buoyant, relaxed as she had not seen him before. Why not? He was coming home, a prince returned from an adventure in another land.

Akton felt her mouth go dry, her body tense. Here she would have to spend her entire life. She would labor beneath the Mexican sun, scratch out a living, wait for the endless war to come upon them again.

"I was not given a choice," she said, but Thumb didn't hear her. But she knew that was it. She looked at Thumb and felt her heart lift. She looked at his chest, his shoulders, his strong arms, his dark knowing eyes and long, raggedly cut hair, and she knew that she loved him, that he had come into her life with a gift, a great gift, with something that had been totally lacking. She had heard of, read of, dreamed in a girlish way of such things, but it had been nothing like the reality of his gift, hardly more than a shadow of Thumb's physical love.

Yet maybe the situation itself brought the wanting, the desperate urge to cling to another human being. Would she have felt this way toward him in another world, another time, with other men to choose from, with a choice? She didn't know. She was suddenly afraid, suddenly doubtful of everything once more.

The Apache came from out of the trees and rocks which pressed against the narrow trail. They were no longer mysterious shadows, but laughing, shouting people coming to greet their war leader and his son.

What they thought of Akton's presence, she could not tell.

They acted as if she weren't there. They jumped up to touch Thumb, calling to him. Juh slid from his horse's back to go among them, shouting to his friends, laughing with them.

Akton might as well have been invisible.

One old woman turned scornful eyes on her—or at least Akton thought it was scorn she saw in her look—and briefly evaluated her, then frowned and turned away. She was not a slave, not a captive, the woman seemed to acknowledge.

But she was not Apache.

They rode on over the crest and into a narrow, very long valley. Ten miles of bright, short grass stretched into the distance. Beyond, smoky peaks reached for the pale sky. A village—a rancheria, as they called it—of hundreds of wickiups was nestled in the heart of the valley, surrounded by pines. As many as five hundred horses wandered the grasslands. Smoke rose from the campfires along with the scents of pork and beef, or horsemeat. On a vast bonfire to the south, mescal was being roasted. The heart of the cactus was used as food and also to make a very strong drink.

They rode on into the valley and toward the

village. Now more women began to appear, and Akton was struck by how different, how *Apache*, they appeared. They were shorter than she was, their faces flatter, but they had a grace, a beauty that only life lived close to the marrow can impart. They watched her with the same expressionless eyes she had seen at the reservation school. Akton also saw children, the ache and fruit of the women's wombs, the joy and elation of their hearts and souls.

They all surrounded Thumb, Juh, and Akton as they walked their horses slowly through the village, the growing throng of welcomers forming a noisy tail behind them.

The wickiups, Akton noticed, were neater, more carefully made than those she had seen on the reservation. There everything had been viewed as temporary, an accommodation to the white man's whims. Here the branches were interwoven with care, the pine boughs layered to form a waterproof roof and walls. Skins were used on some of the wickiups, sewn together and fitted over the bent pole frames. These were made carefully, with great skill—what a shame it would be, after all, for the woman of the house if her man should wake up wet after a rain squall.

The houses were made with pride; the people carried themselves with pride. They knew what and who they were. A warrior nation living out its destiny.

Hundreds of years ago the Apache who spoke a tongue which was related to the Algonquian tongue drifted out of Canada—driven out, some said, by those who feared them. They came south, seeking who knew what—their destiny perhaps. They were hurried along their way by the plains tribes, who warred with them and chased them still farther south until they reached the great desert country. There too the Apache warred—through their own wish or through the simple need to survive—with the Pueblo Indians, with the Navajo and the Hopi, the Zuni and the Ute. They warred until they had established a kingdom of arms in the Southwest.

And then the Americans came, and the war expanded. The Apache had no fear of war; it was their life. But now it seemed there was no stopping it, now there was no winning, but only the gradual withering away of Apacheria.

"Thumb! My cousin, brother, chief!"

The dark, crooked man came forward wearing a lopsided smile revealing yellow teeth. His warmth appeared false to Akton, but Thumb did not seem to mind. He swung down, embraced the man, and turned to her to introduce him.

"And this is Bad Lance, Akton."

"Akton?"

Bad Lance frowned and his eyes passed over her. He noticed the crudely made dress, the breasts beneath it, the turquoise necklace suspended from her neck.

"What sort of name is this? Akton? What does this mean, cousin?"

"She is a Cheyenne woman, Bad Lance."

"Cheyenne? What of—?"

"What of whom?" Thumb asked, cutting Bad Lance off.

Bad Lance muttered something Akton didn't hear. Did Thumb still have a wife, then? Was Juh's mother alive? Akton knew that some Apache married for life, taking only one woman, while others were polygynous. Which did Thumb believe in? Why, oh why, hadn't she ever asked him? Why had she been content to sleep with him on the desert, to lie locked in his arms, to let him, her captor, become her lover, her savior?

"Thumb! Thumb!"

An old woman pushed her way through the crowd. Akton lifted her eyes and saw a hunched, gray woman wearing many bracelets. The years hadn't softened this one. Her eyes held fire, a slashing anger softened only by her apparent joy at seeing Thumb.

She went to Thumb and hugged him. Akton thought at first that this was the mother of the Chiricahua war leader, but she could see his face across her shoulder and he seemed to have little liking for her, although he smiled.

"Where is Juh?" the woman demanded. "Where is my grandson?"

"Juh!" Thumb waved a beckoning hand. "Come here, see your grandmother."

Then she was Thumb's mother ... or was she? Juh came slowly forward, his head hanging a little. The old woman picked him up and squeezed him.

"Mother Toonashi," Juh said as if he had just been introduced to her.

"Is that the way you greet the mother of your dear dead mother, Juh? Shame on you. And what if your dear mother were alive? She would beat you for being unkind to Mother Toonashi. Would she not, dear little warrior?"

"Yes, Mother Toonashi," Juh said, looking greatly relieved when the old woman put him down once again. Akton couldn't help but stare, thinking: "So this old woman is Juh's grandmother, the mother of Thumb's wife, his dead wife. Akton was pleased—ashamed, but pleased. His wife had died. Who she was, Akton did not know. She didn't want to know if she had been beautiful, intelligent, athletic, engaging, slim, fat, stupid, sexless. She was dead and that was all that mattered.

"What is this?" Mother Toonashi asked hoarsely. She was gesturing toward Akton and came to her horse. She looked up at Akton, gripping her knee with bony fingers, even at that distance smelling of wild garlic and yarrow soap, of age and charcoal and salt. "What is *this*?"

Not *who*, but what. What was this thing her son-in-law had brought from the north?

"Akton. Akton is her name. She is Cheyenne."

"The necklace!"

Toonashi was panting. Her eyes lighted oddly. her crooked fingers stretched out toward the breast of Akton. "She has the necklace my daughter made for you! The necklace Koti fashioned with her own hands, the gift necklace."

She reached for it suddenly and Akton slapped the hand away reflexively. When she did so, a small, nearly inaudible sound rose from the crowd of people gathered around them. Mother Toonashi sucked in her breath. Her arthritic hand remained poised in the air, talonlike, leathery.

Thumb spoke rapidly. "It is hers. I gave it to this woman. It was mine and so I gave it away."

"My daughter made it. Koti made it! Your dead wife. The mother of Juh." Mother Toonashi spoke as if she were having trouble breathing. She clutched her breast. "Have you no feelings for my Koti?"

"I must go on now," Thumb said stiffly. "Let us pass. We will speak another time. It has been a long journey."

"Have you no feelings for the memory of Koti? You give the necklace she made to a Cheyenne slut!"

Mother Toonashi moved swiftly over to Thumb and clutched his leg when he started his horse forward, moving through the throng with Juh and Akton behind him. Akton too felt the clawing hand of Thumb's dead wife's mother, saw the fury on her face—and the complacent satisfaction on the twisted face of Bad Lance. That one had a complacency that seemed to mingle darkly with deeper emotions. But when his eye met Akton's, his glance became lascivious and challenging.

She turned her head away and rode on across the grassy valley. No one followed, except for a few of Juh's friends, who raced the ponies for a way, calling out for him to return to hunt, to play, to tell of his adventures in the white land.

The wickiup they rode to was set apart from its neighbors. It had been built of willow branches and hides, and sat back among the blue spruce which lifted tufted heads to the pale sky. A cool breeze blew down the long, narrow valley behind the wickiup, where gray crags formed an infinite number of shapes suggestive of animals, clouds, spirits, and human beings. Akton could hear wrens in the trees, meadowlarks across the valley. Columbine, a subtle blue-violet, splashed color against the grass. The Apache had chosen well. This was a pleasing place.

"Come on," Thumb said. He stretched out his hands and swung her from the horse. His eyes were distracted; Akton found his touch wooden.

"Does it bother you so much?" she asked.

"What?" Thumb looked to where Juh had started running up the forested slope behind the wickiup.

"You know what—the meeting with Toonashi."

"It does not bother me." He took her wrists and held them, but his eyes were far away.

"The memory of your wife, then? The memory of Koti—that troubles you."

"No."

"Do you want the necklace back, Thumb? We were alone on the desert. Perhaps things were different then. Perhaps now it doesn't seem to be proper that I should have the necklace."

Thumb looked into her eyes with a direct and focused gaze. "I wanted you to have it. I *want* you to have it. I have not forgotten Koti, but she is dead. She was a good wife but she is gone. What I will remember of her needs no necklace to remain alive."

"You loved her."

"She was a good wife. She was Juh's mother."

Akton didn't try to dig any deeper. Koti was gone. What he felt for her, had felt for her, was only a memory. The weight of the necklace around her neck was suddenly oppressive. She carried not just metal and stone, but memories and conflict and sorrow.

"I will take it off if it means trouble," Akton offered. "If it means that you must quarrel with Toonashi."

"I gave it to you," he said sharply. "You must wear it, Akton."

"Then I shall."

He let go of her and stood, hands at his side, watching her eyes. The wind shifted his hair. His powerful chest rose and fell.

"If you would go, woman, then go," he said at last, turning half away. "I will not keep you prisoner any longer."

Akton moved to him and her hand rested on his shoulder. She kissed that shoulder, his arm, and said, "I will go when you cast me out, Thumb. Now I am your woman. The past fades quickly before the light in your eyes and I can't remember what I was before I was with you."

He turned and he held her, his head bowing, his grip strong, his body pressed against hers, thigh and chest and abdomen.

"I mean this," he said into her ear. "You may leave now. I will take you to the desert with two good horses and food and water. I will bid you good-bye and you never need to look back. You will never need to worry about war or want or the cold of night. You have people who will love you, who will care for you."

"No one can care for me as you can, Thumb." She kissed him with parted lips, feeling his body respond instantly, wanting her.

"Think twice, Akton."

"I have considered. I am sure."

"Then speak no more of the necklace. It is a gift from me to you. It symbolizes much. It was a loving gesture. If it was given to me with love, I hand it on to you with love also, with the wish that you will be my woman and remain here. But I will not hold you prisoner any longer."

"I will always be your prisoner, Thumb," she said quietly, and again he held her, clung to her, kissed her. It wasn't until they turned to enter the wickiup that Akton looked back and saw, across the meadow, among the trees, the hunched, crooked figure of an old woman watching.

The wickiup was twice as large as any of the

others she had seen. Twelve feet high, twenty-five feet across, it was dark inside, and dusty. But it had been well made, the willow uprights placed deeply in the ground, the curved framework formed precisely, lashed together with rawhide strips, the hides which covered it—deerskin mostly—carefully overlapped and sewn together.

"It is not like the white houses," Thumb said, "but it shelters us."

"It is not like the white houses," Akton answered with a private smile.

"It does not please you?" Thumb asked.

"It pleases me if you will fill it with gifts," she said.

"I will give you—" he started, moving toward her.

"If you will fill it with love, Thumb. Love for me." And then he turned her, taking her into his own bed, while outside the wind gusted furiously and the day passed into twilight.

And outside somewhere an old woman watched and waited.

Akton rose with the dawn. She slipped into her blue dress, feeling refreshed. The night of dreams, of love, had washed away the empty miles, the pain and the thirst, the doubts of the evening before.

She was now and would be for always his woman, and she knew it as she knew that it was the sun which painted the dawn horizon a vermilion hue, which flamed and streaked the dark morning sky.

She dressed and went out, pausing to look back at the males who slept wrapped in furs and blankets, at the young unformed face of Juh, who had been scored by fear, by loss, and who now revealed pride and courage and happiness even in his sleep. And she watched the other male, the man in his prime, his vigor and manliness evident even as he slept. He was a long and tawny creature, made for the desert, for a hard and violent life. He was a thing of muscle and copper skin and tendons flexing as he

190

moved, his veins full of crimson blood as he worked and fought and made slow, sweet love. His hair was black and long, his eyes firm and dark as he strode awake across the world. But in sleep they were nearly feminine, his long lashes soft and boyish.

They were alike, these two males, different sides of the endless balance of nature, of its renewal. The unformed gentle Juh and the warrior Thumb, hardened by time and war and need. Yet when they slept they were one, soft and hard; gentle and strong; prideful and giving.

Akton went out silently and watched the dawn exceed itself, become red and violet, gold and orange above the ranks of pine trees. A single strand of smoke rose sinuously from the camp across the valley—a lone woman, a dreamer, an early riser, one who longed for her man far away or dead or dying or lost or ill. . . .

Akton walked toward the dawn for a while and then turned away from it, climbing into the forested hills to listen to the gabble of the larks and the quail. She watched the dove wing low across the fiery sky and the ink of the night sky give way to the slowly climbing pale fingers of blue dawn. In the trees gray squirrels jabbered in their own tongue, scolding, mocking, teaching, sounding perhaps as man on earth must sound to Manitou in his starry sky.

She climbed and the fresh, clean morning brightened and became day. Above, rocky ledges thrust out from the bluffs. They hid small creatures who scuttled and goggled at Akton as she climbed higher, toward the sun which touched the rim of the bluff with copper and gold.

She was breathing heavily and her legs were knotting by the time she reached the pinnacle, but the sensations were pleasurable, the reward for having climbed worthwhile—the view from the bluff was spectacular. She could look across the vast and empty desert, which, now that she didn't have to cross it,

191

seemed enchanted, a magic place of pinks and pale purples at this dawn hour.

She sat down on a large rock, the dry, cool wind running across her body, caressing her as it murmured in the rocks, chanting piping songs that summoned the creatures of the rocks from their hiding places. They came, squirrels and lizards and wide-eyed pocket mice, and later a sleek, curious coatimundi.

"You are a woman I do not know," the voice from behind Akton said. She was only then aware of the shadow which fell across her, staining the rounded granite boulder where she had perched. The coatimundi looked at her for a moment longer before vanishing into the rocks. Akton turned to look at her visitor.

Small and thick, his face was peculiarly blank. Where had he come from? Was he, too, summoned from some secret lair in the rocks by the wind song?

"You are a woman I do not know," the short man repeated, coming nearer. He did not wear the usual white canvas shirt and trousers, but a black top and red pants that were very baggy. Around his head was a black headband with strange figures crudely embroidered on it.

"My name is Akton."

The man climbed up on the rock beside her, and folding his hands, sat for a long minute without speaking. His hip nearly touched hers in an unselfconscious way. He was noticeably without guile, without the focused intelligence of an ordinary man. Akton decided that he was a child in a man's body.

"You speak funny," he said.

"That is because I am not Apache. I am only just learning your language."

"There goes the coatimundi, Akton. Once I had one for a pet. It was better than a dog. It was silent and it slept with me. I fed it from my hand."

"I do not know your name," Akton said.

He forgot about the coatimundi and turned his

head to look at her with unusually round, protruding eyes. "Jak-jak."

"I am happy to meet you, Jak-jak."

"What are you doing up here? Only boys come up here."

"Like Juh?"

"Juh is my friend."

Akton said, "He is my friend too, and he told me that I would like it here, that I would enjoy seeing the morning born from here."

Jak-jak nodded silently. It was an explanation he could accept. He seemed to need some sort of an explanation. Those below—the grown-ups—did not climb the hill for the fun of it. Only the boys came, they and thick, slow Jak-jak, who was in his essence still a boy.

"I saw you with Juh and with Thumb."

"Did you?"

"When you rode in. I saw you and I thought: She is a beautiful woman, beautiful like the dawn or a quick fox."

"You were kind to think that."

"Not kind." The eyes again went to Akton's. "It was the truth—now I will admit it," he said, his head hanging as he peered up from beneath the fringe of his hair. "I came up here to see you. I wanted to know if you would speak to me."

"And now I have," Akton replied with a smile. His cheeks glowed with pleasure or pride or embarrassment. "And now we shall be friends. You shall be my very first friend among the Apache."

"You are going to stay?" Jak-jak asked, his head coming up, his mouth parting, preparing itself for any expression from dismay to joy.

"I am going to stay," Akton said, and his expression blossomed forth as pleasure. He reached out a hand to touch her, but withdrew it before he did, as if realizing that such familiarity wasn't allowed, as if he believed it would somehow be sacrilegious to actually touch this creature from the north who had completely captivated him at first sight.

Akton found the gesture touching and disconcerting at once. She had done nothing to call this man's admiration to her. The last thing she had expected on this morning, when she had desired only a moment's solitude, was to beguile a strange child-man and draw from him pledges of devotion.

"I will watch over you," Jak-jak said. His voice was very serious, his eyes nearly morose.

"Thank you, Jak-jak. But Thumb will watch over me, I am sure," she replied.

"Thumb. You are his woman?"

"I think so. I think he wants me to be."

"His wife?"

"Not yet. I don't know. It will come if it does."

"I will watch over you," he repeated slowly.

"I appreciate your intent, Jak-jak, but I have a man who will protect me."

"Thumb is a warrior. He does not know what secret plots live in the camp when the war parties are gone."

"I am sure . . ."

"When Thumb is not here, secret things are done. Only Jak-jak sees and only Jak-jak can protect you, Akton, beautiful Akton."

She was beginning to grow uncomfortable. Was he as harmless as he seemed, or was there a place where his madness could become a violent thing? Her first impression might have meant nothing. She was looking for a way to slip away from him when Juh appeared, clambering over the rocks, as agile and quick as a coatimundi himself.

"Hello, Jak-jak," he said. "Hello, Akton." His greeting, she was pleased to notice, had lost its mockery. It was a pleasant change, but she was happy to see him for other reasons.

Jak-jak immediately rose and waved to Juh. "I will race you to the yellow rock," he called out. Juh turned and started climbing toward a high outcropping on the far side of the ledge. With a startled yip, Jak-jak leapt into pursuit, running after Juh with all the enthusiasm of a young boy, with all the

ability of one. He was quick, this round man, and apparently very strong beneath his smooth layers of flesh.

Akton watched him pull himself up over a rock and run on before she herself rose. She dusted herself off, then looked for a moment longer at the desert, which was now paling beneath the hot sun, becoming a world of white sand and dark mountains. Then she turned toward the long valley to the south, where the Apache made their home, where children were suckled and raised as the elders planned war or "secret things."

What had Jak-jak meant by that exactly? Akton couldn't guess and she didn't want to waste her time pondering it just then. It was a dark notion and the morning was bright. Below her Thumb waited, strong and handsome. She felt a sudden longing for him, as if he were miles from her, as if she had never known him and never could. She started down the rocky slopes, hearing Jak-jak and Juh calling to each other higher up, and the wind whining through the empty, bright day.

Thumb was waiting outside the wickiup, dressed only in a loincloth, his hands on his hips, his eyes combing her appreciatively as he waited. He lifted his arms and she went to him to be embraced, to smell the clean, herbal scent. She savored the feel of her breasts swelling against his chest, responding to his power and grace, his need for her.

"We will be married," he said as if it had only just occurred to him. Akton knew it hadn't, knew that he had given the matter long thought.

"It might mean trouble for you."

"Why? Old Toonashi, you mean? She is half-mad, I think, with age and remembered grief."

"Walk with me a way," she said, and he looked at her oddly before lifting one shoulder in a shrug, putting his arm around her waist and leading her through the pines surrounding the wickiup. Across the valley they could hear children shouting. Cook-fires rose in silent concert all across the rancheria, and warriors on horseback raced down the long valley, calling mock insults to one another.

When they were into the trees across the narrow arroyo, Akton stopped. She pulled away from Thumb and leaned against one of the great trees, her hands behind her back, plucking at the pocked bark as she spoke.

"I am not Apache. What do your people think of this? What do they think of their war leader bringing home a Cheyenne woman, one who was 'white'?"

"I do not care what is said, Akton—"

"Maybe not. Perhaps *I* do. What do they say privately now, Thumb, that they will say openly later? What *could* it mean to a man of rank to marry an outsider, a foreigner? I want to understand."

"Nothing will be said," Thumb answered grimly.

"Publicly."

"Nothing will be said," he repeated.

"But they will think . . . what? What will they think of you for having brought me here? Toonashi I can understand. She grieves still for her lost daughter, for your wife. But the other leaders, the other men of rank—I have to know these things, Thumb!" she said, coming away from the tree. "I am not the sort of woman who can be content with a life of sheltered ignorance. I want to know what I am doing to your life, what sort of bargain we are entering into. Will it hurt you, will it harm Juh? If it will, I will go away. You have told me that I can; if it will make your life difficult for me to stay here, to be with you, to live as your wife, then I will go."

"What are you talking about, woman?" Thumb asked, and he took her wrists, pulling her to him harshly. "You can only make my life difficult by going. By going you can only hurt me. What has happened to you, Akton? Where have these dark thoughts come from?"

She looked away, shaking her head. The violence of his reaction told her that she had guessed right.

Her presence, Thumb's determination to marry an outsider, could very well endanger his position.

"No one will challenge me. No one dares," he said.

"Not Bad Lance?"

"Bad Lance sees himself as more powerful than he is. He sees himself as war leader. He doesn't realize that the council would never give him such power."

Akton thought she detected some doubt in Thumb's pronouncement, but she said nothing. Instead she asked, "Who is Jak-jak?"

"Jak-jak!" Thumb laughed. "A child. When he was young there was a raid by the Papago and the whites—Arizona Rangers—and Jak-jak was struck on the skull. Since then he has not aged. He is still a child."

"The Papago say that the Apache are their blood enemies. They say that the Chiracahua want to kill them all."

"The Papago speak the truth," Thumb said coldly. He looked away briefly to the jay which hopped along the low bough of the pine tree overhead. "This raid I spoke of—Jak-jak was struck on the head, as I told you. What I did not say was that others were struck on the head. The rangers, the soldiers, overran the Apache rancheria. Then, while the Americans held their weapons on the Apache, the Papago took the prisoners and crushed their skulls with great rocks. Men, women . . . children. They were crushed flat."

There were no tears, but the emotion in Thumb's voice was far worse than any simple weeping.

"I am sorry," Akton said in a near-whisper.

"She was killed there—six years ago."

"She? Your wife, Koti?"

"Yes. Killed."

"Thumb—"

"Do not speak of it. You understand how it is difficult for us to think of peace now. This thing happened. Other things. A trader who sold us pinole for furs. In the pinole was poison. Strychnine, it was called. Many people died, many young people. It makes it difficult to think of peace. Another man gathered young warriors to trade them whiskey for gold, gold from our Sun Place. When the warriors were drunk on whiskey, a cannon loaded with nails and glass and rusty iron was unveiled and touched off. All of the young warriors died. It makes it difficult, Akton, to discuss peace...."

And then he was silent and she held him, whispering, "I just don't want to make things more difficult. Your life is a battle, against the elements, the enemy armies, time, and the way of the coming world. I don't care to make it harder."

"But you can only make it easier, Akton!" Thumb said with surprise. "You can only be a comfort, a person who will share my burden, a woman, a lover, a wife, a confidante."

"And not a problem?" she asked, and Thumb's mouth lifted into a faint smile.

"Perhaps a small problem. They will not like it."

"Then—"

"Then they will have to sulk and gossip and grouse, for this marriage will be, Akton. I will have you."

"And I," she responded, "*will* have you, Thumb, my warrior." She leaned her head against his warm, strong shoulder, listening for a long while to the pulsing of his heart, to the wind sighing in the pines.

"I want to see the shaman," Thumb said.

She looked up and blinked into the bright sunlight. "The shaman, did you say? The medicine man? What for, Thumb?"

"I want him to read the omens. I want him to tell me that it is propitious for me to marry you."

"And what if he does not tell us that?" Akton teased.

"Then I shall denounce him for a charlatan in front of all the tribe."

He was only joking, and Akton knew it. "It's important for the shaman to bless us?"

"It may be. It will quiet some of the criticism."

"You do expect it, then?"

"A certain amount." Thumb kissed the top of her head and held her for a moment, thinking his own thoughts. "Besides, Cochinay is a good man for you to know. Let us see what he thinks of you as well as what his spirits think of you."

"And then you may decide what to do."

"I have decided already, woman. You know that I want you, and so I will have you."

"You are so certain of that?" she teased, pulling away from him.

"As certain as I was the night I saw you lying in your bed on the reservation," he replied.

"You couldn't have known then . . . not like that."

"I did know, Akton. Something in my heart clutched at me and said: Take this woman. And so I did."

"But you couldn't have . . . the way you treated me then . . ." Akton shook her head in wonder.

"I knew," he answered, "but it wouldn't have done to let you know that. What would you have thought of my madness?"

"You loved me then? On the first night?"

"Then, and now, and tomorrow, woman. I knew, Akton; my heart is a knowing thing and it said that we should love forever. And so we shall."

She believed it as she kissed him and felt his love in the way he held her, tender and needful at once, strong and sheltering. She looked into his eyes, his black, black eyes, and she believed it.

They found the shaman before his wickiup, high up a desolate canyon where only a few wind-flagged cedars grew, blistered and scored by the never-ceasing winds. He was outside of his wickiup, this man Cochinay, and he watched them come.

He was as thin and withered, as wind-twisted as the ancient trees around him. He wore a loincloth wrapped loosely around his narrow hips; his hair was white, and he wore it down to the middle of his back. When he looked up it was with toothless anticipation, as if senility had dogged him down by the ankles. But there was quick cunning in the eyes that Akton finally met with her own gaze. Perhaps the knowledge went beyond the plane on which they dwelt. He seemed distracted, as if things somewhere *beyond* caught his attention and held it, leaving him little time for the things of this earth.

What he said by way of greeting was: "Ah, the Cheyenne woman has come."

"You knew, Cochinay?" Thumb asked, not astonished, but merely curious.

"I know. I know. A star fell. So I read the sign in the entrails of a bat from the high cave. It was indicated. I opened the bat and read there: A Cheyenne woman is coming. It was indicated. And so she came."

"Her name is Akton," Thumb said, "and I have brought her here to marry."

"Stolen away?" Cochinay said with a dry little chuckle.

"Yes. Stolen away."

"A lioness tamed now."

"I think scarcely tamed," Thumb said.

The old man laughed again. Rising from his crouch, he touched Akton's necklace, her hair, her cheek.

Akton looked into his eyes, holding herself erect, although there was something alive in those gnarled hands which was frightening in its vague implications.

"Yes, scarcely tamed," the shaman said, laughing to himself.

"I wish to marry her," Thumb repeated.

"Of course, of course—beautiful."

"Her soul, too, is beautiful, Cochinay."

"Yes," he snapped, "I know this!"

"So we have come to you for your blessing."

"The spirits bless. Manitou blesses. I read the signs, the paint."

"Then will you read the signs to us."

200

Cochinay asked, "Does it matter? A man does what he will for a woman when he loves, when he dreams he loves. What do the words of an old man mean?"

"I am a man of rank, Cochinay. It will bode ill for the tribe's unity if the gods do not approve of this woman."

"But still you would marry."

"Yes," Thumb agreed. "Still I would marry. I would take her and bind her to me. I would make her my prisoner to keep her, to share one moment of silent belonging, one kiss, one touch, to have one hour with this woman who *is* me, who is my other half, as I am hers."

Akton had never heard Thumb speak in that way. She looked at him in wonder. Perhaps he *had* always loved her. From first sight or beyond. Perhaps all of time and all of the spirits had agreed that these two should be together. She had come to Arizona from a northern land to find him, to unite with him. Was all of that an accident? Were there accidents of that kind?

She could only stare; Cochinay chuckled again at Thumb's passionate speech.

"And so, you see, you do not need a blessing."

"Thumb wishes to make it easier for us, for me, and he wants to act as is becoming to one of his rank," Akton offered.

"Yes." Cochinay looked at her for a long time. When she thought he would answer, he only laughed. "Let me show you now what I have been doing."

Akton looked at Thumb, who only shrugged, his mouth drawing down. The shaman took Akton's hand and turned her, taking her a little way up the slope toward a sheltered stony nook. Thumb followed after them.

A crow sailed overhead, cawing raucously. Cochinay glanced at it as if it had spoken to him in a tongue he knew but did not care for. When the crow's shadow was gone, they went on.

Underneath the small nook, which was shadowed

and gray, water seeped out. The nook itself held six alcoves, and in each alcove was a straw man.

Each straw man was life-size, made of poles and shirt and trousers, stuffed with straw. Each wore a bizarre mask and headdress.

The masks were of leather, painted weirdly in designs Akton couldn't understand but which reminded her of creatures of the mountains, of the bear and the badger, the snake and the eagle. The wooden headdresses surmounting the masks were in the shape of stylized antlers. But they were like no antlers ever seen on a wild creature. Rather they were like the antlers of an antelope racing across the night sky in silver-blue haste.

"The hunt dance," Thumb said.

"Yes. The hunting has not been good since we came again to Mexico. We have offended nature, and it returns our contempt as it always must."

"Who will dance?" Akton asked.

"The youngest, the strongest, the boldest. And they will do this thing as it must be done. It is not a ritual but a coming together of man and all that surrounds him, of spirit and nature and wild things, do you understand? No? It must be done so that each man becomes a part of all things, so that the tribe can come into concert with the right ways again. Do you understand that? No? Well, perhaps you were white too long."

How did he know that? Akton wondered.

"It will be done properly so that man and nature, the Apache and his spirits, the spirits that are in him and in the mountain things, concur. We have done a wrong thing. We have walked with too much pride, knowing that we are strong upon the earth; but forgetting that nature and man are the same, we have scorned the spirits again, scorned the wild things and the other people of the earth alike, believed that a simple prayer could control the rain and the wind as a deer can be killed simply with an arrow. Things are not so simple. It is necessary to restore unity."

He went on for quite a while, speaking of things vague and ephemeral as the sun rose high, and Akton, fascinated by the manner of speaking Cochinay used, listened spellbound as the rhythmic words tumbled past.

When the medicine man was through and Thumb had started to lead her away from the grotto, Akton stopped and turned back and spoke. "But what of the blessing?" she asked. "What of the answers to our questions?"

"Cheyenne woman," Cochinay said, "do you think I would spend time talking to someone whom I did not favor, to a woman who had wrongly captured our great war leader, to a person who was not one with nature, to one whom the spirits did not trust and love? I had asked a blessing before you came. I only wanted to see you, to see if you were what the spirits had promised. Go now, and when it is time let me hold each of your hands and pass your souls from one to the other, completing the unity which is already yours. Go. You have love and completion— what do you care for the others, who cannot understand any of it?"

Akton watched as the shaman turned sharply away and walked off through the rocks, chanting and lifting his arms to the bright skies, lost in mysteries or fantasies they could not understand.

"Well!" Akton laughed. "And so everyone knows me. And everyone believes that my soul is beautiful!" She shook her head. "Did you make him promise to say that, Thumb?"

Thumb was grave. "No one can make Cochinay do what he will not, say what he will not. He sees your soul, Akton, that is all—as I saw it. Yes, it is beautiful and we know it. Do not mock yourself."

"All right," she said soberly. "I won't, although I know myself. I know that I am only a woman, one subject to pique and fits of temper, to sulking and pettiness—hardly a beautiful thing. But if you think it, I am pleased. If Cochinay thinks it, I am flattered. But I care for none of the flattery; I only care for you. If he has blessed our union, then I am content, pleased that someone considers my soul more perfect than it is."

"I am pleased that we will marry."

"Are you, Thumb?" she asked, turning to him, the wind in her hair.

Thumb put his hands on her waist and drew her gently to him. His lips touched hers as he spoke. "I am, woman. I am, and you know it."

"Is there much to be done?" she asked.

"Not so much, no."

"And when . . . when then can we begin?"

Thumb laughed, and together they walked down the slope toward the valley.

They had reached the flats when the riders came toward them. There were six warriors and they sat on their ponies in a way that told Akton that it was Thumb they wanted, that war had come again.

Thumb went to them and Akton could only stand watching his eyes narrow, seeing the sharp, decisive movements of his hands.

When he returned he told her, "I must leave."

"Not now, so soon," Akton protested, but she knew her protest was futile and so she forced herself to be silent, to accept the way of a soldier's woman.

"The Mexican army has been seen ten miles south. Perhaps they look for the camp of Thumb, perhaps not." Thumb looked briefly beyond Akton's shoulder, to the desert highlands. "But they will find Thumb. They will not come here, not *here*."

Then he held Akton so tightly that she could not breathe, and kissed her head, but he was gone again before there could be any real comfort in his touch. He was marching to the wickiup, marching to snatch up his war tools, to go out onto the desert, to kill or die.

Akton stood watching and then she did what a soldier's woman must do. She followed after him to prepare a little food for her man to take with him, a little food and a warm blanket.

He was gone in an hour. Gone, and the camp was empty, strange and nearly hostile. People moved around her, an old woman with a bundle of sticks on her back, a young man with a bow slung over his shoulder, his carriage graceful and erect. Two young women laughing together, blankets over their heads, holding hands. Akton knew none of them. If they knew who she was, they did not like what she was. She realized suddenly that she was no one here without Thumb, and the idea made her sad and angry all at once. This must not be allowed to continue—but what could be done? Nothing, it seemed—nothing but wait, watch, and dream.

No, she told herself abruptly, strongly. It would not be that way. Akton was strong, she was more than Thumb's war prize, and she would somehow make them realize that, make them realize that she had come to stay, to be an Apache.

8

The rancheria was a different world without Thumb. Akton was an alien walking among people with dark and searching eyes, among the wives and widows of warriors, among the Apache children, the old and crippled men. She spoke to them but their answers were terse. What had they to talk about? What did the Cheyenne woman know about their war, their pain, their fears and way of life?

She considered leaving during those first few days, and it would have been easy. Take a horse and ride away to the north. No one would have tried to stop her. Why would they bother?

Yet how could she go? Her life had changed dramatically in a few weeks. Thumb had become her lover; he was to become her husband. Could there be a life without him? She had to know that he would come back safely, had to assure herself that he would.

Besides, there could be no return for her—the woman who had left Bowie days ago was no longer alive. Mary Hart had been left out on the desert somewhere, trying to return north, struggling toward her white dreams, her white way of life. Akton was no longer that woman. How it had happened, how she had changed so completely, she did not know. She only knew she was no longer Mary Hart, and Akton, the Cheyenne woman in love with a Chiricahua warrior, would find no place in the white world.

She wandered the desert mountains, sometimes with Juh, who delighted in showing her things like a saguaro cactus twenty feet tall where a family of pocket mice lived. They had tunneled from the base of the great cactus to its very tip, where three small, nearly round holes provided lookout spaces for three members of the family at once. Their bright-eyed heads emerged, whiskers twitching furiously, and then withdrew as they grew afraid of Akton and Juh, who wasn't above winging rocks at them.

He showed her the plants and the herbs, the sego lily with its edible bulbs, the forests of cholla, and jumping cactus which Akton remembered all too well. He showed her where the cactus wren, agile and swift among the thorns, made its home safe from any predator. He showed her the tracks of the coyote and the prowling cougar, huge padded tracks, the sign of the desert badger and the armadillo.

He showed her how the Apache used the nopal cactus. It was dried and used for fuel, or the spines were burned off and fed to the horses. Candy could be made from its red fruit. If a pad of nopal cactus was sliced open and used to stir silty water, it caused the sediment to coagulate into tiny lumps, thereby clearing the water faster. Pads of the cactus were sometimes bound to wounds to heal them. There was so much to learn. She knew that the coatimundi, looking like a raccoon but with a long snout, was friendly and mischievous and lived in the paloverde trees which had leaves nearly without substance. They looked like mere skeletons of trees. And the sight of the smoke tree—so called because from a distance its wispy branches resembled smoke rising from the desert—meant that water was beneath the surface of the land.

She learned the desert mountains and the ways of the creatures that lived there. She learned the way of the Apache and the legends of the old warriors from Juh. But he was a boy and became tired of her company and went off to play with the other children. Akton wandered alone in the desert mountains day after day, waiting for the war party, which did not return.

And at night she lay awake in her wickiup, her hands on her abdomen, certain now that within her a small seed was growing, certain that Thumb would one day have another son.

A son without a father? She turned her face and a single tear raced to the blanket beneath her head. The blanket which was the door to the wickiup was folded back, and through the gap Akton could see the cold, knowing stars above the mountains.

"What is it?" Juh asked from across the wickiup. "Are you awake?"

"Yes. I heard you. You cried in your sleep."

"No," Akton said.

"You did. Is it for Father that you cry?"

She hesitated. "Yes. I love him, Juh."

It was a long while before the darkness answered. "I love him too."

Then Akton heard the small movement, saw the shadow before the stars, and felt the small body slip in beside her. He lay there silently, wanting only the comfort of another human being. Akton stroked Juh's hair until he fell asleep and his soft, childish snoring fluttered in her ears, bringing a smile to her lips and a small comfort to her heart.

The next morning the first summer storm came roaring across the flats and struck the mountains with the fury of a vengeful god.

When the rain came, Akton was in the hills watching the clouds come scudding toward her, as if hypnotized by them. She had never seen it rain on the desert and in her heart perhaps she believed it never could. It was mesmerizing to watch the great blue-black towers of clouds tumble and froth, to see the gray rain falling on the desert flats as the wind swept the storm toward the mountains.

When the rain came, it came in hard and fast. The first few large drops seemed unrelated to the clouds, like cool, harmless darts thrown against her body as she sat on the rocky ledge above the rancheria. Then suddenly the world was dark and the storm was a roaring menace smothering the earth with a tumultuous cape. The rain lashed against her with vicious force. She could hardly keep her eyes open against the deluge, which was like gravel flung into her face. In moments her dress was soaked through and the sultry heat of minutes before had become the damp chill of a driving storm.

The gorges filled with running water. Where it seemed water had never run, frothing white-water freshets hissed their way toward the valley below, where already silver ponds had made their appearance.

The wind was fierce, the rain bitter. Lightning burst explosively across the skies and the rumble of thunder rocked her eardrums and brought her to her feet. She stood, her hair hanging limp, dress saturated with cold water, feeling suddenly threatened by the massed forces of a dark and seething nature.

"And this is the way for the mother of an Apache prince to prepare herself?" the voice from beyond and above Akton said.

She spun around, astounded. Above her on the rocks, lashed by the rain and wind, white hair twisted and tangled, wearing only a loincloth, stood the shaman, Cochinay.

"Cochinay!"

"Do you not consider the child in your womb? Perhaps this one is the one to lead our people to victory, to freedom," the medicine man said.

He was quite serious, but there was a hint of dry humor in his voice. But how did he know? Akton wondered. How could he, when Akton only suspected that there was within her womb another life, a young Apache?

"What are you doing here?" she asked.

"What is the wind doing here, the rain?" Cochinay asked, waving toward the heart of the storm. "I am the same. The same force, the same existence. As are you."

"Yes?" She laughed. "And so you know what the rest of existence knows?"

"A part of it," Cochinay said, coming over the boulders to stand beside her. He put his hands to her abdomen and looked into her eyes as the rain fell, a gray veil between them. "I know that there is a warrior alive within you."

"Perhaps," Akton said with less irritation than she would have thought she might feel. Who was this man and what business was it of his? "If you know much," she said, "then tell me where Thumb is, tell me when he will return."

"Doesn't your heart tell you?"

"No."

"I don't know either," Cochinay said, and Akton felt strangely, inexplicably desolate as he said that. "I do not know except that there is war upon the desert and a warrior has gone forth."

"The rocks on the mountain know that," Akton said with some anger. "Where is your magic, your knowledge?"

"Are you so lonely," the shaman said, "that you must lash out against an old man who suffers from imperfect vision, an old man who does not know what the spirits have in store for the warrior Thumb?"

"I'm sorry," Akton said. "Truly sorry."

"Come, now, come out of the rain. This is no place for a mother to be."

He was there beckoning, and then he was gone. It was as if the rain had washed him away, as if the banks of cold, seeping clouds had taken him. Akton stood for a moment longer, and then, feeling cold, feeling the cut and thrust of the wind, she started down the slope.

The rancheria was still. One old woman, her head covered, scuttled across the space between two wickiups. Nothing else stirred. Akton went into Thumb's wickiup to find it deserted and cold.

Juh was no doubt with a friend. He spent much time away from Akton, not out of antipathy, but simply because no matter what she was, she was not his mother and his father was not there. The wickiup would always be empty to Juh without Thumb . . . as it was empty, barren without Thumb for Akton.

She sat inside the wickiup listening to the storm, watching the rain fall, and wondering what she had become. What sort of life had she chosen? What would become of the living creature, the man within her? She sat cross-legged and watched and waited, dreaming her waking dreams of Thumb's love, of his arms enfolding her, his lips meeting hers, his body warm and strong in the night.

And the rain hammered down gray and dismal and endless.

The time without Thumb stretched on toward infinity. When dawn came, silver and orange, the air was clean and warming. The storm had broken but Thumb was not there yet. The war lived somewhere on the desert; he would perform his duty.

He would fight and the Apache would lose only a little ground and then a little more and the years would tighten around them. They would be isolated on this small mountain and then the enemy would come, perhaps it would be the Mexicans or the Americans, but they would come. . . .

Akton shook her head, not wanting to drown in such dark seas. Still the memories returned—oddly enough, stronger and clearer than ever in her life. The memories of blood, the fear of the guns, the soldiers, the wailing of the women. The time when the Cheyenne had died.

She climbed the rocky bluff in the early hours as dawn still colored the sky, and the desert, vast and clear, now stretched out before her. She stood atop the highest point she could reach, and as the wind raced over her, she thrilled in its force and vigor, her hands against her abdomen, touching the shelter of the life in her womb, as she looked out toward the east, toward the war.

Then she turned and watched the beauty of morning, the beauty of the long valley where the people rose and washed and started about their work.

Everyone had somewhere to go, something to do, Akton realized. Everyone but her. Was that what kept her apart from the Apache? It wasn't all of it, but how could she know them, be with them, share their troubles, standing apart as she had been?

"I will not stand apart," she said, and with a nod of resolution started down the rocky slope. She would work with the others, she would weep with them and laugh with them. The memory of Koti must not shadow her or Thumb. She would be a good Apache, a respected woman.

The women were among the oaks, crouched down, waiting to begin their work. They had tall woven baskets with them for gathering acorns to be ground with stones and made into pinole or acorn soup. As Akton came among them, eyes lifted and then fell away again.

"I want to work. Where is a basket for me?" Akton asked.

There was no answer. The women returned to their gossip. Akton repeated her question. "I want to work, Apache women, where is a basket for me?"

The woman who answered was narrow. Her hair was oily, cut off haphazardly. She rose from her crouch to snap, "Go back to the Cheyenne lands and find a basket."

There was a lot of laughter following that remark. "Back to the Cheyenne land," one crone repeated. "You have told her something, Shima-awa."

"I won't leave until someone gives me work," Akton said. No one responded to that. She might not have existed.

"Come," a new voice said finally. "Share my basket, Woman of Thumb."

"My name," she answered, "is Akton."

"You may work with me, Woman of Thumb," the

Apache woman said. She was young, reedy, and small. "It will lighten my burden, will it not?" She looked around her, but no one answered, although one woman muttered the name "Toonashi."

As if some signal had been given, the women rose in unison then and started out of the trees toward the hills beyond the camp. Akton stood watching them, feeling their dislike, their suspicion.

"Come, Woman of Thumb," the small Apache said. She had her split-cane basket on her shoulder. She smiled at Akton. The smile showed crooked teeth, a generous mouth. Her eyes were very large and as inquisitive as a small animal's.

"I would like you to call me Akton, that is my name."

"A very hard name to say. I call you Woman of Thumb—that is a good Apache name."

"Akton."

The Apache girl smiled again. "So it is, Akton. I will practice the name. Come, we will go to work."

"What is your name?" Akton wanted to know.

"Oh, me? Just call me Tiny. That is my name."

"Tiny?"

"Yes," she laughed again. "I am very small, you see. Tiny thing. It means I have a big soul, says the shaman."

They started toward the hills, Akton following Tiny, who had a lively step despite what appeared to be a deformity of the hip—that was not unusual among the Apache or any other tribe. The midwives frequently disjointed a baby's hip to make delivery easier.

The sky still held color in the east as they started up a long rocky slope past great oaks that overhung the trail.

Tiny spoke as they went. "Now, this tree belongs to the family of Hava-hanku. Now, this tree was given to her father when he was very brave in one war with the Comanche. Now, this tree belongs to Shima's family, the one you made angry back there."

"How did I make her angry?" Akton asked. "I just wanted to work with them."

"Now," Tiny said, speaking as if to herself still, "they were angry because you are not clean and you came to them and asked to share their work, which is clean."

"Not clean . . ."

Tiny went on, "How can a haunted person be clean? Now, that is something that cannot be."

"Haunted?"

"Here is the tree of my family," Tiny said. She turned, putting a hand to her narrow breast, panting a little from the climb. A great oak tilted out from a huge jumble of moss-stained boulders. Acorns, small and pointed, littered the ground.

"How am I haunted, Tiny?" Akton asked.

"What? Well, now, Koti is with you, behind you, beside you, saying, 'Who is this foreigner who has come to take my husband?' and so you are haunted. Koti is with you."

"But why should she disapprove! I love Thumb. I want to be good to him, to comfort him in the night, to feed him. What makes me dirty?"

"Oh, well, that is because you are a foreigner. All people who are not Apache are soiled. Dirty people."

Tiny shed her gray blanket and knotted her hair, tying it with a length of rawhide lace. She began working, picking up acorns, sorting out those which had been bored into by insects, those which had lain since last season. Akton followed her example, keeping silent for a time, although questions nudged her mind, troublesome questions. She was dirty and so no one liked her. She would always be dirty because she was a foreigner. Was there no way to break the circle?

Now and then Akton could see other women working on the hill and on the ones adjacent. They sang as they worked or told stories. Some prayed.

"Now, then," Tiny said, hunched over still, working quickly, effortlessly, "I will tell you the story of Slip Over. Now, he was a man who took a young wife. Now, Slip Over was very stupid and his wife had to tell him everything, for he wasn't smart at all.

"Once Slip Over went to the pond, to the reeds, and he saw that everyone was making himself a basket. Now, that was good, thought Slip Over, and he sat to make himself a basket from the reeds. Only Slip Over didn't cut the reeds like everyone else, and when he was through weaving his basket, it was still rooted to the ground. He was a very stupid man. His wife found him tugging at the basket when everyone had long gone home, and she said, 'Oh, you stupid thing! You don't know anything, you ought to die.'

"Then the wife of Slip Over said, 'Now, make us a proper basket to gather acorns in, and break off the reeds, don't be stupid,' and she went away to their wickiup, leaving Slip Over. Then Slip Over wove a basket and he filled it with acorns and he went home, but he didn't walk the trail like a normal person. Instead he burrowed into the ground like a squirrel and dug his way home. When he came out into the wickiup his wife nearly had her heart stop. She hit him with a stick and scolded him.

" 'Oh, you stupid thing. You don't know anything. A person doesn't bring acorns through the ground like a squirrel. You must use the trail. You don't know anything, you ought to die.' "

Akton laughed. She stood up and pressed her hands to her back. Tiny kept working, talking.

"Then what happened was this. Slip Over's wife said, 'You must use the trail,' and so Slip Over went down into the ground again and back to the head of the trail. Then he put the basket of acorns on his back and went home and his wife found him there, just standing outside the wickiup. She said, 'Oh, you foolish thing, when people come up the trail with acorns they should put the basket down and go inside and sit and rest.' So he went inside to sit, and he just sat. He sat and would not move.

"His wife said, 'Oh, you foolish thing, sometimes when people come up the trail with acorns, they move around and eat.' She made his food and he ate. He ate and he ate and he ate!"

Tiny looked up and shook her head seriously. "He was very stupid. His wife told him, 'Oh, you foolish thing, you ought to die. Sometimes people quit eating when they have enough. Then sometimes men and women play together.' So Slip Over tickled her and hugged her and rolled around with her until the wife was very tired. She said, 'Sometimes people have to stop playing, don't you know anything? You are so stupid, you ought to die. Sometimes people just like to sit down and talk.'

"And so they sat down to talk and he talked until his wife said, 'Oh, sometimes people just sit quietly,' and Slip Over just sat, he might have been dead. He sat and he stared until his wife said, 'Oh, you stupid thing, sometimes people lie down.'

"He lay there and he lay there through days and his wife said, 'Oh, stupid thing. You don't know anything, you ought to die. Sometimes people fetch wood and make a fire.'

"And Slip Over went to the trees and brought wood and wood until it was stacked to the sky before the wickiup and his wife had to make him stop. Then they went to sleep and it began to rain and water leaked in their wickiup and Slip Over's wife woke him and said, 'Now it is raining and water is leaking in our wickiup. Go out and fix the leak, you stupid thing.' And Slip Over went out and after a while the leak stopped but he did not return. He did not and did not return and after a while his wife went out to find him. Instead of fixing the leaky roof with brush, he had laid his body against the hole and fallen asleep there. He almost died of the cold as he lay there wet and shivering.

"His wife took him back into the wickiup and warmed him and said, 'I'd like to know what makes you so stupid. You ought to go off and die. You don't know anything, you crazy man.'

"And that is a true story from a long time ago, so my grandmother told me," Tiny said. "I heard the story here while I worked with her."

Akton straightened up again, feeling the sun on her face, the wind against her body. There was history in these hills and Tiny had brought a moment of it alive. Only a moment, so that Akton could hear the whispering of generations of women, see their faces in the shadows. Then she saw something else.

The wickiup had been on a ledge above the tree and so Akton had not noticed it before. There was no wickiup now; only a pile of burned sticks, ashes, and rocks.

"There was a house there," Akton said.

"Yes. A wickiup."

"But it burned."

"Yes. Thumb burned it. Burned it down."

"But why!"

"Why? Koti's house. It was Koti's house and his, and so he burned it when the sickness took her."

"Here? But I thought you said this was the tree of your family, that you had lived here."

"Yes," Tiny said, and she smiled again, "did I not say that? I am Toonashi's other daughter. I am Koti's sister."

The day passed easily with Tiny's storytelling and singing, but by sunset Akton was exhausted. She had never done anything approaching such work, and although the Apache women looked as fresh as when they had gone out, Akton was ready to return to her wickiup and sleep before the sun had gone down.

They had heard nothing from Thumb's war party and without men the camp seemed subdued, cheerless. The wickiup was empty.

Thumb was making his war. Juh was gone somewhere. He still barely tolerated Akton; now she knew the reason. It is because I am *unclean*, Akton thought, and the idea at once amused and frustrated her. She ate a little pinole, a little venison, and lay down on her bed.

I am *haunted*.

That much, perhaps, was true. She was haunted by Koti's spirit and would be as long as she was among the Apache who had known and loved Thumb's first wife. Perhaps it didn't matter to Thumb that his new woman was Cheyenne, but the people cared. The people who were to become her world. The people. The Apache.

There had to be some way to appease the spirit of Koti, there had to be some way to become clean, to become accepted so that she could have friends, family, a life which would not leave her an outsider.

What of Thumb's life and position? Perhaps he had broken no law by bringing Akton here, but his reputation must have been shadowed by it in certain ways. His judgment was questionable; perhaps he seemed a man ruled more by passion than logic—to bring a Cheyenne woman home to lie with when there were Apache women of good rank to be had.

These thoughts rang in Akton's head, robbing her of needed rest. She was alone and Thumb was making his war. Her body ached and she did not want to be alone. She was haunted and could find no way to appease the spirit.

"There must be a way," she told the darkness, "there must be."

"He broods, he is angry," Sagotal said, and Thumb lifted his eyes to the small dark man near the low red campfire. Yes, Bad Lance was angry.

"Let him brood."

"It is no good, Thumb. We cannot fight when we argue among ourselves, when we must wage battle like this—Apache against Apache."

"I can do nothing about it, Sagotal. I am leader. If Bad Lance will not listen, then he must be punished."

"It will not do any good to hold to pride," Sagotal said with emotion. The big Chiricahua crouched down beside his war leader. "Speak to him. I will tell him to come to you."

"I will speak to him. When he comes and admits his mistake."

That was all Thumb said; he would say no more, and Sagotal went away. Thumb had too much pride at times, but then, what could be done? The warriors must obey the war leader. To do otherwise would be to lose control.

Sagotal walked past the fire of Bad Lance without looking into his scornful eyes.

"It does no good to speak to the man," Bad Lance said.

Sagotal did not answer. The warrior Nantje, seated beside Bad Lance, thrust another handful of twigs into the fire. The night was cold on the peak. Out on the desert they could see the fires of the Mexican army, although the Mexicans could not see theirs, small and sheltered as they were. The enemy was there, but Thumb did not attack.

"There may be no blood," Nantje said as if to the fire, but Bad Lance heard him.

"Not if Thumb has his way. And why not! There are enough Chiricahua arrows to kill them all."

The reason was simple and had been explained to Bad Lance patiently. The Mexicans seemed to be veering away from the redoubt in the mountains. They did not know for certain where Thumb's camp was. To make war on them now would be to tell everyone exactly where the camp was, and then the camp would have to be abandoned.

"It is the woman. He wishes to return healthy and sleep with her," Nantje offered.

"The woman." Bad Lance scowled. "Maybe she can be used for our purposes. *I* am rightful leader now, not Thumb. Where was he when we fought at Los Alamos? Where was he at Three Creeks? With his woman in the north. I have proved I can lead."

Nantje said nothing. He followed Bad Lance. Bad

Lance had promised him much, and so the two planned together. The council would be turned against Thumb somehow; somehow leverage would be applied to cause them to doubt Thumb.

"The woman," Bad Lance repeated. "She is our tool." And then the scowl was gone from his face and he looked up with fire-bright eyes, nearly smiling at Nantje.

Thumb had kicked dirt over his fire and curled up in his blanket. Bad Lance made him tired. Bad Lance and his ways. He wanted to be leader again. He talked behind Thumb's back—that was a shameful thing to do. But Bad Lance had always been that way, always jealous. The people paid no attention to him. They had no cause to.

Thumb was restless. He rolled onto his back and looked at the stars, the stars as bright as her eyes. He longed for Akton's body, for the touch of her hair against his cheek, for her hand on his chest, her thigh against his, her soft, curiously accented voice whispering.

Akton could not be there and so he would wait. He would wait for as long as was necessary, but not for a night longer. She was his woman, she was his love.

Morning was bright and dry and warm, the desert flats painted varying hues of deep violet, of pale orange, the mountains streaked with sinuous shadow.

Thumb told them: "Rise. Today we fight."

"But you said we would not," Nantje said.

"I told you we would not attack the column of soldiers—we will not. We will attack their nest."

"Fort San Miguel!"

"Yes."

"But, Thumb, it is mad."

"No. It will be done. Must I explain everything? How many soldiers can be left to guard the fort? You saw the column of Mexicans here. We will destroy their nest, their supplies, the walls they hide behind, and we will destroy them by doing it."

Thumb's voice had risen with passion and now

he drew a spontaneous cheer. They had come to fight, these men; they needed to fight. Very well, he would give them their battle, he would give them their blood.

What Bad Lance still did not understand, would never understand, was that the Apache could only fight as guerrillas. There were too many Americans, too many Mexicans with too many guns, and so the war must be fought on Apache terms. But Bad Lance wanted glory and he did not understand. And so he would always be a bad leader. "Let us go. Hurry and eat. See to your horses. Now!" Thumb whipped their spirits higher with the lash of his voice. The young warriors like Sky Fight and Hapata were nearly leaping with enthusiasm. Hapata had lost his father to Mexican guns. Very well, today he would avenge that death.

Bad Lance stood nearly immobile until he was the last warrior; then, glowering still at Thumb, he turned away and strode toward his horse.

"You see!" Sky Fight said enthusiastically. "Now Thumb is back, now we make the great war."

"Never, never with Thumb. He is cautious. He would not fight the column of soldiers because there were too many."

"You cannot be saying that he is afraid." Sky Fight, who had been painting his face, turned with astonishment.

Bad Lance, his hand on his spotted war pony's mane, shook his head. "I said nothing like that." But there was something in his tone of voice that sent another message. Sky Fight could only watch, frowning, as Bad Lance swung onto his pony's back and heeled it savagely. He raced away to catch up with some of those who had left early. Sky Fight thoughtfully finished painting the yellow snakes on his cheeks, and then, putting away his medicine bag, he too mounted his horse, wondering at the breach between the two Apache leaders.

They rode southward and then west through the Yaqui Pass. The day was long and hot, the sands white and gleaming. At noon they found the fort and the little town which rested beside it near the glinting creek. The fort was of adobe, as was the town. The creek provided just enough grass for the army horses, enough moisture to keep a grove of dry, twisted sycamores alive on the northern edge of town. It was from those trees that Thumb meant to attack.

"How is it done?" Sagotal asked. He was staring at the fort, his warrior's eyes taking in the lay of the land, the natural and manmade obstacles and aids without conscious thought. Already each Apache knew how the river twisted through the trees, that the low bluff west of the fort offered a sniper good position, that the great, red yawning canyon to the south was a blind canyon.

"Feint from the south," Thumb told his lieutenant. "Set fire to the town and then withdraw."

"Into the canyon?" Sagotal asked.

"Yes. The canyon."

Bad Lance didn't like that idea and said so. Patiently Thumb explained to the crooked man who now wore white and black paint, "They can leave their horses and climb. The army knows it is a box canyon; they will be running over each other trying to get out of the fort and kill the Chiricahua. But Sagotal will only draw them away from the fort for us. We will come from the trees and I will see that the fort is burned, that all the army supplies are destroyed."

"That there is *blood*," Bad Lance said.

"Yes," Thumb answered grimly, "that too."

Sagotal and his chosen few slipped off toward the south, and Thumb settled on his haunches to wait, to watch. When the signal, made with a mirror in the sunlight, was flashed from the canyon, Thumb rose. He nodded, and leaving his war pony, picked up his weapons and led his warriors down toward the sleeping Mexican town.

They were ghosts moving across the white land, the only color splashes of red starflowers, the crimson of the Apache headbands. They worked across the narrow silver creek and into the huge sycamores, where the sun fell against the earth in mottled patches. The grove was a small one and they were through it in moments, going to the earth to lie and watch and wait, hearing the creek behind them, the dry wind rustling in the trees, the distant calling of quail.

It was half an hour before the first smoke began to rise from the town, a feathery wisp which darkened and thickened into a column of black menace. The first shouts went up from the pueblo a moment later and then the first gunshot, which accelerated Thumb's pulse narrowed his eyes, and tightened his grip on his bow.

They saw the gates to the adobe fort open, saw the soldiers, some of them half-dressed, rush out toward the town. Bad Lance started to rise, but Thumb held him back.

"Not yet, brother," Thumb whispered. The black eyes of Bad Lance glared back, but the Apache said nothing. He looked at Thumb's hand on his arm, the hand which controlled, restricted, led.

The hand lifted suddenly and a ululating cry rose from the throat of Hapata. It was followed by a dozen more, and another dozen as the Apache ran toward the fort, firing at the few astonished, unprepared soldiers.

A man with a mustache, his brown uniform stained and faded, went down as Thumb's arrow found its mark. Thumb was in the forefront, as a leader must be, and already he could see that it was good, that it would mean victory.

He was inside the wall now, leading his men past a few dazed rearguard soldiers. The Apache warriors struck them down as they fought back or tried to flee.

In their own storeroom the Mexicans had the means to finish the destruction.

"There," Thumb shouted after the door had been battered down. "Kerosene, gunpowder. Destroy this place, burn it to the ground. Hurry, though, the soldiers will soon see they have made a mistake chasing Sagotal. Hurry, now!"

Outside, the fort was already burning. Mexican soldiers lay scattered across the parade ground. Smoke rose from the town beyond the walls.

"Now!" Sky Fight called eagerly, a fresh scalp tied to his rifle barrel. He stumbled as he came up beside Thumb, who stood watching the confusion of their victory. "The fuse is lighted."

Thumb looked to the storeroom, nodded, and took to his heels, jogging toward the gate with Sky Fight beside him. Some of his warriors carried booty, others wore captured jackets or hats. Bad Lance had no trophies. He stood watching Thumb's approach, and then he started away.

"Now," Sky Fight said joyously, "we have won. Now Bad Lance has seen!"

"Seen what?" Thumb demanded.

"Nothing, seen nothing," but the young warrior had gone too far, he had revealed too much. Thumb stopped, grabbing Sky Fight by the arm as the fire raged behind them.

"What are you saying? Does he still speak about me?"

"He speaks ... Thumb, the powder kegs. We have started a fuse."

"Still says I am afraid to make war."

"Please, Thumb! Yes." Sky Fight nodded. "So he says."

"Then he will no longer accept his part in this war, he will no longer be my lieutenant and right arm. Very well," Thumb said slowly. "Then it shall be Sagotal."

Thumb turned and looked at the burning fort, the town. Beyond the town he could see dust as the Mexican army rushed back toward San Miguel. It was a victory, and it should be proof that Thumb was still a good leader, but perhaps victory was what Bad Lance despised most. Perhaps it was defeat he wanted for Thumb, no matter what it meant to the Apache. Perhaps, Thumb thought, he is just a little mad.

"Thumb!"

The war leader looked to the storeroom and then, with Sky Fight again by his side, sprinted from the fort as the powder caught and the explosion flashed heat and flame and rolling thunder across the desert.

They trotted through the trees and across the creek and back to where their horses stood. By the time the Mexicans reached the knoll, the Chiricahua on fresh ponies were gone with the smoke that drifted away from the burning town on the desert wind.

The work went on and Akton worked as hard as anyone, for she was determined to become part of the tribe. She worked but she made no friends. There was only Tiny, and what would she have done without Koti's sister?

"Now, all the women used to go and harvest rice in the ponds while the water stayed, before the sun dried the ponds to mud," Tiny said as they worked. On this day they weren't picking rice but harvesting the sunflowers. The seeds were used in cakes but also for medicinal purposes. Pressed into oil and mixed with tobacco leaves, the seed of the flower was a healing poultice, useful, Tiny said, for healing sunstroke.

"Be careful there," Tiny said as Akton reached out to brush away a spiderweb. "Never do that. A spiderweb is for healing wounds. A gift from the small spider; don't destroy it for nothing."

"I'm sorry," Akton said. She lifted her head and wiped her eyes with the back of her hand. Her apron was filled with sunflower seeds. The day was hotter than ever. Briefly, habitually she looked to the distances, hoping for some sign of Thumb, but there was nothing to be seen but a distant dust devil racing across the flats. Never depleting her supply of lore, Tiny called the dust a furious, wandering soul.

"Now, they were harvesting rice," the Apache girl finally went on, "and the women had put their babies' cradleboards in the cottonwood trees to hang in the air. They worked and they sang and told love secrets. One woman whose name was Yoimot had no baby and so she sang alone, not listening to the love secrets. She was angry perhaps. She stood up from her work and saw a beautiful butterfly and she thought: I will catch that butterfly and it will please me. She stood and ran after it but she could not catch it. She wore a deerskin robe and she thought: Perhaps I cannot catch it because I have my robe on. So she threw it away. Still she chased the butterfly across the hills far from the rice pond and the village of her people, the Chiricahua. Still she could not catch it and at last she took off her apron and ran naked after it. She chased it until night came and then she lay down beneath a river and slept.

"When she awoke in the morning, she found a man beside her. He said, 'You have followed me a long way,' for he was the butterfly. 'Maybe you would like to come with me to be among my people and stay with me,' Butterfly-man said, and she agreed. She had forgotten her work and her own people.

"She climbed onto his back," Tiny said, "and flew with him to his land, clinging very tightly to him. They went through a long hidden tunnel in the mountain and then suddenly they were in bright sky far above a beautiful flowery valley. And all around Yoimot came other butterfly-men, so pretty! She looked at this one and then at that, reaching for them until finally she lost her grip and fell to the ground. She was dead. She never returned to her tribe. This is a true story told to me by my grandmother long ago when I worked with her in these hills."

Akton stopped working. The wind shifted the great heads of the golden sunflowers. Tiny came to her and said, "Eat some seeds, we will rest. And look, yucca. The blossoms are good. The plant is for soap and mats. Did you know that?"

"I'm afraid I don't know much of anything," Akton said, "but I'm trying to learn."

"To be Indian."

"To be . . . Apache," Akton answered.

"Oh." Tiny shook her head as if that were a tall ambition. "For one who is not Apache, it is hard."

"But there must be a way, Tiny."

"You are haunted."

"Yes," Akton said impatiently, "but I don't want to be haunted, I don't want to be unclean. There must be a way."

It was a time before Tiny answered. She stood munching on raw sunflower seeds, watching a crow sail past. Then Tiny smiled. "There is a way. I will tell you someday."

"Now! Tell me now, Tiny, please."

"First you must cleanse yourself. In the sweat lodge, rid your body of poisons. Then you must eat nothing while you pray. Then you are clean. Then you must come to the house of Koti."

"The burned house?"

"Just so. That one. You must place flowers there. I will show you which ones. Then you must tell her that you love Thumb and Juh and will take care of them. Then . . ." She hesitated, shaking her head. She bit at a seed, found it rotten, and spat it out.

"And then what, Tiny? Please tell me."

"It is no use."

"Let me decide that, please!"

"The mother must give her approval."

"Toonashi?"

Tiny answered with a shrug, "Just her."

"Won't she? Isn't there a chance? I'm going to marry Thumb, Tiny. Cochinay has given his blessing. If I go through the purification, if I ask Koti for her approval, won't she give her blessing?"

"I do not know," Tiny said. "Maybe." She lifted her eyes and gave a quick hopeful smile.

"You don't believe it, do you? And if she doesn't,

227

then the tribe will always turn their backs on me because I was not welcomed into the family by Toonashi."

"But maybe she will, maybe she will . . . once you are clean."

Maybe. Akton was determined to find out. She would do this for Thumb, for their unborn child, for herself. She would do all she could to become one of them, one of the People.

Tiny helped Akton prepare, and Cochinay gave her the prayers. While a strange rainless desert storm darkened the mountains, for three days Akton purified herself, sitting naked in the sweat lodge, an airless, lightless place made of mud and thatch.

The sweat rolled off her body; her head swam. She had been shown how to keep the stones hot, how to dip water and pour it onto the stones to cause more steam to rise, and she did that. And she prayed.

She did not know the prayers, she felt foolish at times, but she tried. She fasted and sweated and placed nothing but spring water in her mouth, and she chanted. The long prayers, the healing prayers, the Apache prayers:

My poor heart is lost
My poor heart longs for the joy of the sky
My poor heart aches for my lover gone away
My poor heart wishes to see those who have died.
My poor heart wishes for goodness before my
    time is lost
Let it rain, let the grass grow, let it all be good
Let my poor heart not be lost and so alone.

The prayer meant nothing to her at first. She spoke it endlessly, sitting steeped in rising steam. She sat and she prayed. *My poor heart is lost.* Then abruptly it was as if the steam had been wafted away by a cool morning breeze and Akton stood alone on a mountain peak wearing white doeskin robes. She stood alone and she could see for miles, to the ends of the earth, and toward her came the man with her heart and they met. That was all. They met and then she was not alone and she had found the joy she needed.

When Tiny found her she was lying sprawled on her side in the sweat lodge, and the small Apache woman had to drag her into the open, into the fresh air.

When Akton finally could sit up, she sat gasping, her head hanging, her limp hair across her face. She looked up slowly and took Tiny's hand, smiling.

"And," Tiny said, "something was learned."

"Something was learned."

Akton wore her best dress when she went alone to the house of Koti. The storm remained. The sky was deep, deep orange and the wind raced down the slopes, twisting the fringes of Akton's dress, shifting her hair. She carried a small wreath in her hand: limoncillo and windmill flowers woven together. It was a delicate thing, made with great care. Akton had failed many times and torn it apart in frustration, but Tiny had laughed and urged her to try again until at last she had made a small crown, one which might be used by a fairy princess.

It was for Koti.

Beneath the tree the wind was slightly stilled. Above, the ashes were lifted by the breezes. Clouds formed a constantly changing dark background, and thunder rumbled.

"I've brought you this," Akton said. She looked around, temporarily embarrassed. There was no one there, however, no eyes, no ears—none but those of Koti.

"I've brought you this. I wanted to say: I do love Thumb. And Juh. And I mean to take care of them. I know," she went on, "I don't have the skills you had. I can't weave or make a decent basket or fix pinole, but I'll learn—I will learn and I'll make them happy.

"I'll love them."

Then Akton put down the wreath and walked

quickly away, not listening to the small sounds formed by the wind, to the distant words.

It was done, then! She was clean, she had spoken to the ghost of Thumb's wife. She had done all according to the law. There was only one thing left to do.

Toonashi was at her wickiup. Akton knew she would be there; she seldom went anywhere, not even to work. Only sometimes she crept close to Akton's own house, spying, wishing evil perhaps. Who knew?

Akton touched her temple nervously. The wind was still strong. A cottonwood dropped a small branch. Beyond the tree Shima watched—Shima, who showed no signs of becoming friendly: Tiny said that the young woman had wanted Thumb. Probably that was so.

Akton stepped to the lodge entrance and spoke "Toonashi, it is Akton, the stranger. I wish to speak to you."

"Go away, dirty thing."

"Toonashi, it is Akton. I have purified myself. I have spoken to your daughter's spirit. I have—"

The blanket covering the entranceway was thrown back and the Apache woman, her gray-streaked hair tangled wildly, appeared. Her hand was empty but she held it as if she clutched a skinning knife.

"You speak my daughter's name, you Cheyenne whore!"

"I have been purified—"

"Purify a Cheyenne, a white thing! Go away. Leave my sight!"

"Toonashi. I have come for your blessing to marry Thumb."

"Then you have come," she answered very slowly, the words taut and aggressive, "to the wrong wickiup."

And Toonashi was gone, the interview ended. The day grew darker yet.

Akton was not a woman to cry, but that night she cried; that night she cried and prayed again: *Let my poor heart not be lost and so alone*. And in the morning the sky was bright, the village alive with sound, and the man was there at her door, the man with her heart, and they met and she was not alone.

Thumb was home and the land was no longer dark and the world no longer empty.

He held her and stroked her hair and murmured words of love and she clung to him. "How did it go?" she asked him later, when their hearts had been replenished. "How was the battle?"

"It was a victory. We will be safe for a time, a little time." There was an unhappy expression in his eyes, and Akton asked about it.

"Bad Lance. He still opposes me. He is still bitter."

"Can he harm you?"

"No. Not now." But there was doubt in his voice. She knew it but didn't press him. If he wanted to tell her more, he would another time.

'I have had my own small battles," Akton told him.

"Oh?"

"With Toonashi." And she told him about the purification and Toonashi's rejection of her.

"She had no right!" Thumb said angrily. "You have done what you should have done—more than you should have. She had no right to send you away." His eyes softened. He reached out for her hesitantly. "You went to Koti?"

"Yes."

"And what did she say?" Thumb asked.

Say? Had Koti spoken, or had it only been the wind? Akton kissed his chin and answered, "She said to love you and Juh, to be the best Apache I can, to bring to Thumb another son."

They went into the wickiup then and drew the blanket down and they slept together.

The days passed peacefully. Thumb hunted in the hills and Akton went with him. They spoke and lay together in the grass and made sweet love, and the days fell away, drifted by the wind.

"When will we marry?" she asked him, and Thumb put his lips to her naked belly, to the belly which grew with each day.

"For him?"

"For me. For us," she answered as his lips kissed her rounded abdomen.

"It should be now. Today," Thumb said. He sat up, his fingers still on her stomach. "But I cannot."

"Why?" She touched his dark hair, sweeping it back from his strong face.

"This is the time when I married Koti, Akton. This was our moon, and I do not want you to share it."

She understood that. She understood it, and it didn't matter. She lay back again in the long grass on the empty hillslope and drew Thumb down to her. It did not matter. Let this month be Koti's. She would have him for a long time after, for every other month, for every other year.

It did not matter if she was not Apache yet. She would soon be. They would learn that she had come to stay—Shima, who wished to marry Thumb, Toonashi, Bad Lance. They would learn that their world was now Akton's as well. She had come to live with them. This was where her man dwelt.

That was the time of well-being, but it could not last. One day the runners came again and Thumb was summoned to the council hut. When he returned he told her, "There is an army on the desert," and she began to pack his war bag.

"Where will you ride?" she asked, not looking up from her work. It did Thumb no good to see the sadness on her face. Their time had been so short. Would there never be a time for them?

"Las Conijas," Thumb told her. "A man named Rodriguez has Delshay trapped near there. Delshay is Mongollon Apache, our ally. He is a cousin of my father. He too has come to Mexico. I have heard stories that some of his young warriors had taken to raiding Mexican pueblos, taking slaves sometimes.

This was against Delshay's orders—he hoped to find peace in Mexico," Thumb said with irony.

"And so you take up Delshay's war," Akton said. She rose and handed him his war bag.

He lifted her chin and looked into her eyes. "There is duty, Akton, beloved. I am the man my people have chosen to protect them. We have sworn to help Delshay when help is needed. I do not forget an oath; that would be shameful indeed."

"Yes," she said, and her eyes were suddenly misted and she turned her head away, but Thumb brought it back and kissed her deeply. He kissed her and held her and then he was gone again. The blanket at the entrance to the wickiup was opened and light poured in, nearly blinding Akton. Then it fell shut and it was dark and she stood watching nothing for a long while, feeling the emptiness that no song, no prayer could alleviate.

9

The Apache warrior ran in a crouch across the flat red rock that overlooked the long valley below. He went to his belly and wriggled up beside his war leader, Thumb.

"There are sixteen men," Bad Lance reported.

"So few?" Thumb looked darkly doubtful.

"I counted them," Bad Lance hissed.

"Then the others are in the canyon." Thumb rolled onto his back and looked toward the broken hills. They had crumbled and fallen, those hills, been thrust up and folded and had the sparse soil on them washed away by rain, blown away by wind. Were the Mexicans there? Rodriguez was very good. He was not an imperious regular-army officer who followed the book, riding to battle with trumpets blaring and colors flying. He was a militiaman, a great landowner whose home at Sonoita had been raided by White Mountain Apache under Bonito. His wife had been killed, his children taken and sold into slavery, his hacienda burned. Rodriguez was far worse than a professional soldier; his was a holy war. More than once Thumb had had occasion to curse Bonito's excesses.

"We would have seen them." Bad Lance was tense, anxious. Below them lay the remains of Delshay's ruined camp, to their right the long canyon where Rodriguez' men were sheltered. Bad Lance thought it was now time to attack, yet Thumb was worried. Rodriguez wasn't the sort of man to separate his force unnecessarily, and sixteen or fewer men was too tempting a target.

"He wants to draw us in," Thumb guessed.

"What would you have us do, cousin? Wait, run?"

"Quiet. Your voice is a swarm of warnings to the enemy."

"What," Bad Lance repeated, his voice soft and angry, "would you have us do, war leader? Wait?"

"Yes. Wait. Wait a little while, Bad Lance."

"We know where they are now! Perhaps more soldiers will arrive while we wait. Delshay cannot move from his camp. And we *wait*?"

"We wait," Thumb said.

He settled down against the sun-heated rock, hearing Bad Lance's exclamation of disgust. He squinted into the sun, watching the canyon and Delshay's camp, which had been made among the rocks. The Mongollon leader was still alive—they had seen him earlier, briefly. Delshay always wore a blue headband because of a sky dream. When he had shown himself, he shouted and cursed the enemy as he stood bare-chested before his wickiup.

Rodriguez had known what an inexperienced fighter would not have known, that Delshay was risking his life so that his warriors might locate the positions of the enemy guns. Rodriguez had not allowed a shot to be fired at the Mongollon chief.

Sagotal was a huge man with a badly scarred face—half of his face, in fact, had been burned by fire during a daring escape from a white prison. Now the warrior slipped up beside Thumb and looked at him with glowering eyes. The eyes meant nothing. Sagotal was loyal, would always be loyal. "It will be dark in one hour," he said.

Thumb glanced at the sky and nodded. The day was still bright, and after the rain, the rocks, silvered with water, glittered brightly. But Sagotal was right. The day would end soon.

"Rodriguez might slip away."

"Is that what Bad Lance fears?"

Sagotal shrugged. "What do I care what he says?" He grinned. "Yes, he says this."

"Rodriguez won't run. Not so long as he thinks there are Apache to be killed."

"We could take him this afternoon, Thumb. He does not know we are here, could not know."

"He knows."

"How?"

"He knows. Why doesn't he attack Delshay now, finish him? Why did we count fifty pony tracks and now we find sixteen men? Why does Rodriguez hold his main force in a canyon with no retreat possible? He knows."

"It is our chance, Thumb, our chance to finish this menace. Last month on the Desierto de Altar it was Rodriguez who slaughtered Kataka's people."

"I know who it was," Thumb answered, grim.

"We wait?" Sagotal said.

"We wait."

Bad Lance could not wait. He sat in the shade of a huge boulder glaring at his cousin. A warrior sat beside him, scratching at his arm.

"Why do we not attack?" the warrior asked. "We rode fifty miles to sit in this canyon and watch the sun."

"My cousin has become a different man. Where his warrior's blood has gone, I do not know. The woman has changed him."

"What woman? Oh, the Cheyenne woman. Where did she come from, Bad Lance?"

"From the north, from the white lands. And Thumb wants to marry her! A white Indian. She has robbed him of his senses and his courage—he is afraid to fight, I tell you, afraid that he won't live to lie with her in his wickiup."

"I have seen that happen. My own brother would not fight. He wanted to be with his new wife to make babies."

Bad Lance was watching the sun, noting as Sagotal had that there was little time left. "One hour and it will be dark. And then this Rodriguez will be able to slip away."

"No." The warrior shook his head with anger. "Not again. Not this wild one. He has done too much harm already. Next it may be our camp and not Delshay's."

Bad Lance didn't answer, but when he looked away there was a thin smile on his lips. His expression would have revealed much, if anyone had seen it. In Bad Lance there was contempt, ambition, bloodlust, but most of all, jealousy. He was born to be war leader, not Thumb. Their grandfather had seen the two infant boys and it was said that he had given his blessing to Bad Lance—but time and the chicanery of Thumb, the coward Thumb, Thumb who would not even come to his aid when the terrible peccary gored him, making of him a cripple, had robbed Bad Lance of his birthright.

Now he heard the warriors in consultation, heard muttered complaints—why had they ridden so far, why waited in the rocks for day upon day, why slipped into this position to merely watch? What kind of war was this? Was it true, as some were saying, that his new woman, the Cheyenne woman, was a witch who had robbed Thumb of his war pride?

Then Nantje, good, savage, loyal Nantje, said what Bad Lance had hoped to hear. "Who led us while Thumb was gone to find his son? Who led us while Thumb was in the desert with this Cheyenne woman? Who led us when we found the caravan from Nogales and grew rich on its spoils, drunk on its liquor, happy with its women? It was Bad Lance."

"It is true," Bad Lance heard them say, but he didn't go to them right away. He waited, letting the heat and the weariness work on them, letting each one's complaint rub against the other until they had honed their discontent to a steely sharpness. He waited until they came to him to beg him.

"Bad Lance. We have come to fight. What way is this for a Chiricahua to fight? The great one,

Cochise, would scorn us if he could see our band. The Mimbres, Geronimo would turn his back on us. Why haven't we a leader like those among us? Why do we not fight, and break them, and tear our enemies apart?"

"What would you have me do?" Bad Lance asked casually. He picked up a pebble, rolled it between his fingers, and tossed it away. "My cousin is war leader. Thumb's word is the law."

"Law?" Again it was Nantje who acted as an unknowing spokesman for Bad Lance. "The law is that we war to protect our people, that we fight when the enemy is near, that we do what we must to stay free. Not cower in a dry gully waiting for darkness to come and cover our shame."

"What would you have me do?" Bad Lance asked again.

"Lead us."

"It is Thumb's war."

"Thumb's peace."

Bad Lance played the reluctant leader for a long while, but he let himself seem to be slowly convinced. The warriors wanted to fight, they wanted triumph, blood. They needed only a word to shatter their patience, and Bad Lance gave it to them.

"Yes." He nodded. "I will lead you." He lifted his eyes. "Who will tell Thumb? Who will tell my cousin?"

Nantje leapt forward. "I will," the Apache said. Bad Lance again smiled inwardly. Nantje was a man who needed a leader, any leader. Once he had chosen one, he was fiercely loyal, even blindly so. Bad Lance, who had known him from childhood, as he had known all of them, had carefully nurtured Nantje's loyalty and devotion. The tall warrior was brave and his deeds well known. The younger men followed where Nantje led, and now he led them to Bad Lance.

With Thumb's return, things had changed. Bad Lance had enjoyed being war leader, enjoyed his position of power. And he had won great victories.

Then Thumb had returned, and things had been as they always had been—Thumb had assumed leadership. The people had come out to welcome him in a way they had never greeted Bad Lance, even when he had brought booty and prisoners to the home camp. Thumb had shamed himself with a foreign woman, and even that was accepted—in public.

They had turned their backs on Bad Lance, but now the current of the stream had turned, and swiftly. It was Thumb's own doing ... perhaps he *was* the coward Bad Lance had named him.

"Go on, then," he said to Nantje. "Do it. Tell him that we are proud and we must fight and not cower."

A subdued murmuring, a stifled cheer, a mutter of agreement rumbled among the warriors. They were Apache; they must fight.

Nantje strode away, carrying his feathered lance in his hand. Thumb watched him approach, and he looked beyond Nantje to where Bad Lance stood with the warriors surrounding him.

"Look at this," Thumb said to Sagotal.

"Yes." The big scarred man frowned. "This was inevitable."

"What do you mean, Sagotal?"

"Your cousin. Bad Lance has been speaking against you since you left to find Juh."

"Speaking against me?"

"Thumb, my leader, my friend, for a man who is brave in war and knowledgeable on the desert, for one who knows the wind and the wiles of the snake, you know little of the wiles of man. Your cousin has always hated you and he always will."

"But I am war leader."

"Yes. Now. While you were gone, however, Bad Lance was our leader. He tasted power and liked it. Now I hear mutterings from those nearer to Bad Lance than I am."

"What sort of mutterings?"

"That Bad Lance should be war leader. They say

that you have tainted yourself by touching a white Indian."

"Tainted!" Thumb came angrily to his feet. "They don't even know Akton. Who here has even talked to her?"

"That doesn't matter, Thumb. The woman is only an excuse to turn the warriors against you. Any excuse would have done equally well, but when you appeared with the Cheyenne woman, the word went swiftly around the camp that you had left us to fight alone while you lived in the north with a white Indian."

"That is foolish. Absurd! I went to look for my son—who would deny me that? The woman ... well, she was a gift of the gods, a happy thing that happened to me. If you knew her, Sagotal ..."

"I do not need to know her, Thumb. I am your lieutenant. I see into your heart; I see into Bad Lance's," the scarred man said. "I know where I must stand."

Nantje had arrived, and he stood before Thumb, his chest rising and falling with emotion. He felt righteous indignation, but still had respect for the war leader, for the chief who had fed Nantje's family from his own stores when Nantje was unable to hunt because of a wound he had taken in battle with the American army.

"What is it, Nantje?"

"The day grows short. The enemy is before us. We wish to fight him, Thumb."

"We will fight him—when I say it is time."

Nantje looked behind him as if to assure himself that Bad Lance and the others were still there, supporting him. He shrugged. "If you do not wish to fight ..."

"When it is time, we shall fight."

"Perhaps Thumb is frightened now—" Nantje burst out, but he got no further as the huge hand of Sagotal shot out and closed around Nantje's shirt and the warrior was hurled to the ground in the grasp of the scarred giant.

Nantje reached for the lance which had fallen from his hand as he fell, but Sagotal was stepping on it already, staring down at the tall painted brave.

"I will kill you, Sagotal," Nantje said, his voice strangled and hollow.

"Perhaps." Sagotal stepped back, leaving Nantje's lance to him, and the warrior rose with it in his hand. But he hadn't the heart to attack the scarred giant, and he backed away slowly.

"We are going to attack. Bad Lance will lead us. We are with him and we will follow him—all of us."

"No," Sagotal said, "not all. I know the law. I recall the oath I have taken. I will do as Thumb says."

"Then stay with him and share his shame," Nantje shouted. He turned away quickly, as if afraid the huge man would leap at his throat. But Sagotal said nothing, did nothing.

"And now what?" Thumb asked, turning to his loyal companion. "Have I lost them for good?"

"Perhaps," Sagotal mused. "Perhaps they wish to follow Bad Lance. That is as it must be. But they are fools. I know this."

"Thank you."

"You don't have to thank me for the truth, for loyalty you have deserved a hundred times over."

"What should I do, Sagotal? Change my mind? Lead them?"

"And give in."

"Once."

"It would not be once, but a hundred times. Tell me this, Thumb, who is correct? Where does Rodriguez have the bulk of his soldiers?"

"I don't know, but they are not where my cousin thinks they are. He risks death for all that follow him."

"Then why speak of compromise?"

"Because they fight. They go to fight and I am not with them, Sagotal."

"You can go only as a subject of Bad Lance. To go is to hand him the bow of leadership."

Thumb nodded. Sagotal was right. It hurt, but he was right: no matter the outcome of this battle, Thumb could now have no part in it. Looking up, he was gratified to see the Brothers coming. The Brothers, as everyone called them, although they did not share blood.

Star Voyager and Pale Eyes had been together since they could walk. One had never played without the other. They had refused, when still very small, to sleep apart, so each boy's parents had to be satisfied with seeing their son on alternate nights in their wickiup. Star Voyager and Pale Eyes had continued to be together always. When they married, they married sisters. Their sons were together always.

Now they came to Thumb, these tall young men. "What shall we do?" Star Voyager asked.

"What you will."

"Bad Lance wants to war. You do not?"

"No."

"Out of fear, Thumb? Because the woman has cast a spell over you, because the omens are not right?" Pale Eyes met Thumb's gaze boldly.

"Because Bad Lance errs. Rodriguez has more soldiers. Where, I do not know. Fight if you wish—they will call you cowards."

"You are our leader. We took an oath."

"Go," Thumb said. "I release you."

"No. What is right must be done. Let them go. You are our leader," Star Voyager answered.

Thumb looked toward Bad Lance's party. No one else came. No one else had the courage to be judged a coward. He lifted his eyes to the sky, where the sun had begun to redden behind the towering thunderclouds that for days had obscured the mountains—at the rancheria they must have had much rain. It was darkening. Bad Lance had to go now; Thumb seated himself on a large shattered boulder and folded his arms, letting them go, watching them.

From far below, a cry rose from the burned Mongollon camp and Thumb felt the thrill of battle rise in his veins, an emotion that he had to fight down. "You are wrong, my cousin, wrong," he whispered to himself.

Behind him thunder rumbled as the desert storm neared. Bad Lance and his followers were into the rocks now, and like ghosts in the dusky light, had vanished into the shadows. Beyond the rocks, Rodriguez waited. Minutes passed, slowly, heavily, like the ill-fated steps of a giant. Nothing sounded from below, from the Mongollon camp or from the canyon where Rodriguez was concealed.

And then the thunder came again, but it wasn't from the skies. The guns rumbled in the canyon, many guns, and Thumb simply turned his head, looking away. The Brothers stood beside each other, gripping their weapons tightly, leaning slightly forward, the guns summoning them like war drums. But they stayed; they would honor their oath. Sagotal turned his back. No one knew what was in the giant's mind just then.

The guns spoke and the thunder from the desert storm grew louder and soon the two had collided as the clouds roofed the canyons and the rain began, dark twisting rain which fell in sheets as night settled, and the guns, if there were any still firing, could no longer be heard.

"Now?" Sagotal asked at last. He stood before Thumb, rifle in hands, watching his leader, whose face was set, soaked with rain, whose eyes blazed like dark coals from out of a shadowed face.

"Now it is time to go," Thumb said.

"Is the battle over?" Sagotal asked.

"For us."

They walked to the small gorge where they had left their ponies. Some of the Chiricahua who had participated in the attack had returned for their horses. They were jubilant, loud, scarcely able to control themselves. In the darkness Thumb could barely see them, but he could feel their exuberance like a wave of energy, a storm of feeling and war fever.

"What has happened?" he forced himself to ask. He was, after all, a Chiricahua. He needed to know how the battle had gone.

"Victory," a voice they recognized as that of Nantje called out, boisterous, boastful. "We killed them all."

"Rodriguez?"

"He was not there."

"Not there? But this was his siege."

"He must have run away. No matter. Next time we meet, Bad Lance shall kill him, too."

"There were no more Mexicans, no reserves?" Thumb demanded.

"None. Sixteen men. Easy prey. We are riding into Delshay's village. Do you want to come with us, Thumb?" Nantje asked in a way that nearly caused Sagotal to lay hands on the warrior again, "or are you now content to go home."

"Now," Thumb responded, "I am content to go home."

Thumb, Sagotal, and the Brothers mounted their ponies and rode out as the rain tortured the dark earth with thousands of slender silver arrows. They rode up the winding canyon until the Chiricahua leader halted his pony atop a rocky hill and sat looking back down at the valleys below, at the battlefield, which appeared and disappeared through the dark veils of rain and cloud, occasionally displayed brightly as lightning flashed.

The wind pushed against them; Thumb did not ride on. "What is it?" Sagotal wanted to know.

"There were more Mexicans. I know it."

"They did not fight. There were none."

"There were!" Thumb insisted. "What happened, I don't know, but it was a trap, a trap Rodriguez failed to close properly."

"Why would he do that?" Sagotal asked. "Why

would he sacrifice his own men? Why leave them unprotected, trapped in that canyon?"

"I don't know. I only know," Thumb insisted, "that there were more men, that Rodriguez laid a trap for us, one which he did not choose to close." Thumb drove his fisted hand angrily against his own thigh. To himself he added, "And now, because Rodriguez has done this thing, I have lost leadership of the tribe, surely lost it."

For at home again, the council would see only from a distance, and from a distance Thumb's act would seem indecision or even cowardice, while Bad Lance had won a victory over Rodriguez and rescued Delshay.

"I'm riding back," Thumb announced.

"Back? Back where, Thumb?"

"To the canyon there. The canyon where Rodriguez had to have his second force sheltered."

"You can't think he is still there, watching his people be killed?"

The rain was a heavy screen between the Chiricahua leader and his lieutenant. Thumb shook his head. "I don't know. I only know I must see."

"Then I will go with you," Sagotal said.

"No. Ride home. Take the Brothers and go. Why should you endure my shame any longer?"

"Shame? What shame is there in leading wisely?"

"You know what they will say."

"And who listens to old Limp? Your cousin is as crooked in mind as in body. Everyone knows this. He envies you. Everyone knows this."

"Yes. He envies me. He hates me. And now he has the material to make his hatred work for him. Now he has the tools in his hands that he needs to cut down his cousin Thumb."

In the end the Brothers headed home through the storm, having been convinced by Thumb that they could do no more good for him. Sagotal and Thumb started the long ride around the rocky hills toward the mouth of the canyon far away. The rain was relentless, the wind a clawing, shrieking thing, whispering curses and words of impotence in their ears. Once lightning struck so near at hand that Sagotal's horse threw him and ran off, and the air was filled with the scent of sulfur like the springs at Las Colinas. It took fifteen minutes to find the pony and another fifteen to calm it so that Sagotal could mount again.

They rode on, the hills forming dark clusters, menacing and mysterious against the sky. The saguaro cacti towered over them nearly thirty feet high, lifting supplicating arms, praying to the skies. They were monuments to the dead, giant warriors waiting for darkness to come to life and walk the desert before morning froze them into their grotesque shapes once more.

The mouth of the canyon yawned darkly and Thumb halted his pale horse to sit waiting for Sagotal a few lengths behind on his balky pony.

"Is this the one?"

"Yes," Thumb answered. "Ride carefully."

"Thumb, there could be no one there! Rodriguez could not have allowed his people to be killed."

"Ride carefully," Thumb repeated sharply.

Inside the canyon the force of the wind was blunted, but it moaned and whined as never before. The floor of the canyon was now a narrow creek. The rain drifted past overhead, swirling down.

Thumb rode slowly into the canyon, and as lightning struck again, Sagotal saw him nod, saw his mouth set grimly, saw him swing down.

"What is it?"

"Come here, Sagotal."

Sagotal too slipped from his pony's back, and he walked to where Thumb crouched, feeling uneasy despite his certainty that the canyon was devoid of human inhabitants on this cold and angry night.

"What is it, Thumb?"

"Here."

Sagotal crouched beside Thumb, and the Chiricahua leader took his friend's hand and touched it to the soft earth. Sagotal let his finger lightly search the impression there. A horse had passed this way. A shod horse, one wearing iron shoes; it had to have been a white man's horse. In another few minutes the rain would destroy the track or the rising creek smother it, but it was there now. Someone had been in the canyon.

"One track," Sagotal said dubiously.

"When you find one tooth, you have found the cougar." Thumb rose. "Come on."

They walked their ponies. It was too dark to see anything unless the brilliant illumination of savage lightning exploded above and around them, and that was too white and temporarily blinding to be much help. But Sagotal noticed that Thumb was no longer looking at the ground. He had found all the proof he needed to settle his own doubts.

They climbed upward through the rain until Sagotal was cold and each blast of the wind seemed a torture. Thumb did not stop. They climbed, and feeling their way along a dangerously narrow trail, they came at last to the outcropping which offered an overview of the valley below, where Delshay's camp had been. Squinting into the violent storm, they could see the faint red and yellow glow of bonfires as Delshay and Bad Lance celebrated their victory over Rodriguez.

"Anyone here could have seen everything," Sagotal said. "They could have seen—"

"They could have seen our position. Yes, Rodriguez saw us. He saw his own people trapped. He did not come to their aid. It wasn't a courageous act, was it? He ran away. He ran away, Sagotal, and he took my leadership with him."

"He could have been here, Thumb. Probably was. I don't deny it, but . . ."

Thumb had crouched down again and now he held a small dark object up to Sagotal. It was short, tubular. It was a while before Sagotal knew what it was. He had to have it pressed into his hand and lift it to his nostrils before he knew by smell and touch that what Thumb had found was a cigar end—tobacco rolled in a tube, as the Mexicans used it. Since the elements hadn't yet caused the thing to disintegrate into a handful of flaky leaves and be blown away by the wind, washed away by the rain, it was very new, very new indeed.

"Rodriguez. Thumb, forgive me, even I had my doubts."

"I knew he was here, felt it," Thumb said to the skies.

"I shouldn't have doubted."

"I knew he was up here waiting to attack us, but he wasn't going to attack. He was afraid, and he ran."

"I had my doubts."

"That means nothing, Sagotal." Thumb put a hand on his friend's shoulder. "I had only my feelings. How could I have shared those with you?"

"But you knew."

"I knew. I did not guess, I *knew* . . . for all of the good that will do me now. If you had doubts, the others had more. If you are convinced by a hoofprint, a sodden piece of tobacco, they will not be. The evidence will no longer exist in a little while, and there will be only my word—and yours, which will not be accepted, since you are my friend—against the word of Bad Lance, the victory of Bad Lance, who made a bad choice and was rewarded for it."

"They should have all been killed! You were right."

"Yes." Thumb threw the cigar end down and was silent for a long minute as the rain roared in across them from the west. "I was right, but Bad Lance was victorious. Rodriguez was cowardly, but I am named coward."

"We will tell them all."

"Tell whom? Those who matter were here, they saw. Only you and the Brothers stood with me. The ones who counted, the warriors, fell in with Bad Lance, and the victory has proved their judgment right. I have lost my position." He shrugged and said more lightly, "Maybe that doesn't matter to anyone but me, Sagotal. The men need a leader they trust at a time like this, a perilous time. They fight for a man they believe in, that they love. And if it is Bad Lance they choose, well, maybe it is for the best. Maybe they will fight harder, be bolder."

"And maybe," Sagotal said dismally, "today we have seen the beginning of our end."

"Don't think that way, Sagotal. There is no end to our people. The Apache will always prevail. Let our enemies bring their guns and their soldiers onto the desert. We shall prevail—we always have. We are the People, we are the brave ones, we are the chosen of the gods!"

Lightning flared up and Sagotal saw the pale, bold face of Thumb lifted to the rain, saw the clenched fists. And then the lightning blinked out and Sagotal wondered if perhaps the gods did not sometimes have to close their eyes.

10

The storm had gone. In the morning, the sun had risen and there wasn't a thread of cloud to mar the pale sky. It was dry and hot and empty in the valley, as if it had never rained—could never rain—and the people were hot and dry and irritable. And, most of all, they were anxious for the warriors who had gone away and not returned.

Akton walked the slopes of the rancheria's hills, smelling the unique scent of the warm pines, exuding eternity and fragrant promise, a knowledge that they and their kind would be there yet, clinging to the mountains a hundred years from now, a hundred hundred years from now, when Akton, when man himself, was gone. Man—who loved and warred with equal impatience and sought adventure and security, who wanted all. But there could be no reproduction of all of the aspects of humanity possible, all the savage, kind, stony-eyed softness of him, his will both to create and to destroy in seemingly endless conflict—perhaps, in its eternal ebb and flow, in endless harmony.

Akton thought of these things until her head ached and she could think no more. She sat on the narrow gray boulder with the twisted black and leafless oak and looked down across the deep and narrow valley toward the blue-white desert beyond.

"And so, the child grows," the voice of the shaman said.

"Slowly." Why Akton was not surprised to find

him there she didn't know, but she had expected him. Cochinay was a part of existence, of the wind, the rain, the stones, and the swaying trees which rattled their branches in the capricious breeze.

"Now it is slow. Soon, with a rush toward existence, it will swell and develop and demand its own being, wanting to come forth. And then," the old man said, sitting beside Akton, "the world will drag down this new thing, this person, this godly creature, bright-eyed, alert, dedicated, lost. Then it will become as we are and wish to feed its belly and find someone, anyone, to lie down with."

"Pessimism?"

"Life has repeated itself too many times," Cochinay said cryptically.

Akton didn't reply. She had thought these thoughts before, and her head spun with them. Now she only wanted to feel life, warmth, movement in her womb, to know she was creating in the only way that lasts; to feel the growing tenderness, the milk building in her breasts, the swelling ache of her belly. To feed her belly and lie down with her man, her Thumb. As Cochinay had said, as Cochinay knew. But she did not know which was wrong and which was right, to think these thoughts that snarled upon themselves like a thousand spools of thread, multicolored, endless, or to feed her belly . . . and lie down with her man.

Perhaps Mary Hart would have known. Akton did not.

"Soon you will marry."

"When he returns."

Cochinay nodded. The old shaman asked, "Why are you here? Why are you among us?"

"Because of Thumb."

"Only that?"

Akton couldn't answer. She didn't know. Perhaps she was there because a memory had stirred in her blood, a racial memory that prompted and demanded . . . what? What could such a memory demand?

"Because of Thumb," she could only repeat.

"Then be careful."

"Be careful?" She turned toward him. "I don't understand you, Cochinay."

"It doesn't matter. Be careful. Time exists only to baffle us. We seek to slow it, to stop it, but it rushes on and we are confused by it all."

"Are you confused by it, Cochinay?"

"I do not live in time, woman," he said, and there was a hint of reproach in his voice. Akton understood none of it, and when he was gone there was nothing of the conversation left in her mind but the warning. Be careful.

The dance of the hunt was held later in the day. Cochinay was in charge, but he was hidden by his paint and his bison headdress and so Akton never saw his face. She saw instead the dancers with the wooden antlers performing precisely as Cochinay had told them. To do otherwise, would be to go mad. With them danced a clown, a small mocking creature—perhaps to remind them that they were after all only small and impotent humans and their dances, their pleas, were only that. To remind them that they had no real power in this vast and god-centered universe.

Akton stood apart and watched. The sun was setting, forming a brilliant golden star above the peaks. The sky to the east was purple. The dancers moved and sang, seeming to swim through the ritual, to throb with each drumbeat, to react to each whistle of the high thin flutes. Dreamlike they moved, no longer seeming supplicants of the gods, but their puppets. Night came nearer and the shadows reached out from their feet—twisted, misshapen things, pools of night in which the lost dancers traveled.

Jak-jak was behind her, Akton knew. He had become her own shadow, seldom speaking, seldom drawing near. At first she had feared his presence, wondering at the man, as simple as he seemed. But he was content to be a shadow on the earth, and he had needed another form to give him life—he had chosen Akton for his soul, his substance.

"Here they come; they come now!" someone yelled, and heads lifted and turned, eyes widened, hearts stirred.

"Who is it? The warriors?" someone asked, tension strong in the voice.

"They come now. There was a signal fire."

"How many? Are they well? Did we find victory?"

There were suddenly so many voices questioning that none of the questions could be answered. It would have been impolite to leave the dance, and so no one did, but they stood seeming to tilt toward the long canyon waiting, seeing the dance only with one eye, hearing the drums hardly at all above the roaring of the blood in their ears.

Someone was approaching; was it Thumb? There were only a few horses—had it been a defeat, a terrible and crushing defeat with the hearts of brave loved men stilled?

Still no one broke from the ranks of watchers, those who stood and listened to the drums and watched the feet of the dancers. There was a comfort in being among the many. Knowledge could be put off for another minute, another single second—the knowledge that someone had died, as someone always did. The knowledge that now there would be no hunter in the wickiup when winter came, that the bed would be a cold and sterile place.

"Who is it?" a child called out, breaking the spell, and they all started that way, though the hunt dance continued. "Who is it?"

"Two men only."

"Which two?" someone asked hoarsely.

"The Brothers. It is the Brothers," a voice answered.

"Just them? The Brothers?"

Akton felt her head grow lighter. The drums were in her skull and around it, in her blood and in her heart, lifting it to greater excesses. But she would not show the excitement, the anxiety. It was not fitting.

"Just those two?" she couldn't help asking in turn, but no one answered. She was the stranger, the foreign woman, the Cheyenne from the north, the white Indian.

An old man hobbled toward the Brothers, waiting for them to swing down and tell the news of the raid. His name was Cha-lipun and he had been council chief for forty years. He was erect and proud, but his legs had been crippled when the cavalry shot a mule from under him and the animal, rolling, had crushed his knees.

Now he was the council head and it was his duty to discover what had happened, if the general apprehension had any basis in fact.

People were shouting at the Brothers. "Where is Sa-shonay? Where is my son, Nanni-Chaddi?"

The Brothers didn't answer. They gave their horses to boys who would rub them down and put them out to graze, and they went away with Cha-lipun and the other council members.

"What has happened?" Jak-jak asked. He was at Akton's shoulder, his head hanging forward, his heavy body poised as if to dash off in any direction.

"Nobody knows. Only Star Voyager and Pale Eyes have returned. They've gone to the council lodge."

"Why? What has happened?"

"I don't know, Jak-jak! No one will say. I don't know what has happened, if Thumb is even alive . . ."

"A tear. Don't cry. I'll find out. Do you want Jak-jak to find out what has happened?"

"Yes, but how can you?"

"I can. Jak-jak can. I can get behind the council hut and listen. If you want—"

She pushed his broad shoulder. "Yes," she urged him, "go on, Jak-jak. See what is being said."

He nodded, grinned, and bounded off, determined and devoted.

"What has happened?" Juh asked, just now reaching Akton's side.

"I don't know. Jak-jak is going to try to overhear what they say."

"Don't worry," Juh said solemnly, and he stood facing her, surprisingly taking her arms. He was so small in stature, but very solemn and brave. "Father is all right. I know this. I would know if he were hurt. So too would you, Akton."

"Perhaps . . ." Still she felt hollow, dry, withered as she watched the hunt dance go on—and on.

"Grandmother sees," Juh said quietly.

"What do you mean?" Akton turned and glanced toward the trees. She saw her only briefly, Toonashi vanishing into the deep shadows. Toonashi, who had not been to speak to Thumb since he had brought home the Cheyenne woman and given her her daughter's necklace. Toonashi, who lurked in the shadows, watching the wickiup, watching Thumb and Akton.

"What does she see, Juh? What is it she waits for?"

"I don't know. I only know Grandmother sees." And then he was gone, running off to be with his friends. He was still at that age when his mood could change from the ponderous to the buoyant within seconds. The hunt dance was over and now there would be a feast, offering more food than anyone could eat, to prove to the spirits of the hunt that the Chiricahua had faith in their willingness to bring more game to the mountains. Thumb was not back, yet Juh was cheerful, leaping across the camp with a rowdy band of children. Well, if he had no fear for Thumb, why should she? Perhaps she *would* know if Thumb were dead. Perhaps the pain in her womb would be so great that she too would die from it; perhaps her heart would open and break apart. She told herself that Juh was right, that she would know, but still the anxiety would not go away and she waited eagerly for Jak-jak's return.

He was back within fifteen minutes, his broad face excited, eyes eager. "All is over. Thumb behaved with cowardice."

"Liar!" Akton spat out. She barely restrained the hand which had risen to strike Jak-jak's face. "You are a liar," she hissed. Jak-jak's face fell. Akton was instantly sorry, but still the anger throbbed within her.

"I am not lying, Akton," Jak-jak said. He was a child, reproached for something he did not understand. "I heard them speaking."

"The Brothers?"

"Yes. They told Cha-lipun, but he argued."

"Told him *what?*" It was exasperating to talk to Jak-jak. She touched his shoulder. "Walk into the forest with me and tell me all that you heard."

Jak-jak's unhappiness was washed away by her touch. He started into the trees, Akton falling in behind him. As she walked she watched the bald, misshapen plane on the right side of his head and wondered both at the cruelty of the act and at the resilience of the human animal.

Then, too, she looked for Toonashi. Where was Juh's grandmother? Where did she lurk and what did she want? Jak-jak halted in a small alcove where towering pines grew up out of huge gray granite boulders, the roots of the trees having split the rocks hundreds of years ago.

Jak-jak sat on a fallen, barkless log. "They say that Thumb is . . ."

"You may say it."

"A coward."

"Who says it, the Brothers?" Akton demanded.

"No, no, not the Brothers. They told what happened, as they were bound to, and the council said that Thumb had failed his people."

"How? What did the Brothers say? Tell me!"

Jak-jak told her. At second hand, told through the lips of Jak-jak, it all sounded surreal and improbable.

Akton shook her head. "No. Something has not

been told—or perhaps there is something I do not understand. That Thumb sat in fear while an inferior force attacked the Delshay camp, that Bad Lance had to turn against him in order to protect the Mongollon allies, is not something I can accept."

"It is not Thumb," Jak-jak said, wagging his head heavily.

"No. Precisely, it is not Thumb."

"And that is why they say it, Akton." Jak-jak looked instantly diffident. He broke off a piece of gray wood from the log and sat staring at it unnaturally.

"That is why they say *what?*"

"I do not know, Akton."

She was on her feet and strode to where he sat, her feet braced, her eyes flashing. "Say *what*, Jak-jak?"

"That it is you, Akton," Jak-jak, scarcely audible, mumbled.

"What is me? Do I understand you, Jak-jak? What are you saying?"

He burst out with, "They say that you have taken Thumb's soul, that you are Cheyenne, that you are worse—a white Indian, a reservation Indian."

"Who says all this? The council or the Brothers?"

"The council."

"They do not even know me! Old Cha-lipun? I have never even spoken to him."

"Then someone has spoken, then someone has been saying these things before today, Akton."

"Someone . . ."

"Bad Lance, I think it is he."

"Yes." She sighed and turned away, folding her arms angrily. "It would be Bad Lance. If only I had known more about these jealousies, these old antagonisms when I arrived . . ."

"You could have done nothing."

"I could have gone."

"Without Thumb? You could have gone from your man?" Jak-jak asked incredulously.

Akton stretched out a hand and touched his large, misshapen head. She smiled. "No. I could not have gone. You are right," and the happiness returned to Jak-jak's face. "But what can I do now?"

"You can do nothing. Wait until Thumb returns. He will tell them the truth," Jak-jak said positively.

"He is all right—Thumb?" she asked hesitantly.

"They say so. And Bad Lance. It will all come out. Thumb will tear their lies to shreds. He will stand among them and speak the truth and no man will dare to call him a liar, a coward."

"No. No one would dare," Akton said. Again, briefly, she touched his head and then her hand fell away. She stood looking off into the forest, wondering if she had been responsible for this, or if some senseless fate had driven Thumb northward, had caused him to fall in love with a Cheyenne woman and destroy his own life.

It had not been destroyed, however; no—she would not allow it to be destroyed. Thumb would not allow it. It was as Jak-jak said. Whatever had started this lie, Thumb would return to destroy it like a malevolent serpent. He was a warrior, he was a man—hadn't she seen him kill six scalp hunters alone? A coward! Anyone who knew the man would realize that such an accusation was a lie, that cowardice was against his nature, that it was as foolish to call him a coward as it was to name the rattlesnake a rabbit or call the moon the stars or say of the night that it was too bright.

Thumb would come and the lie would be crushed....Why, then, was she worried? Why, then, did she feel guilt as she returned to the village and walked among the feasting Apache? Why, then, did she wonder: Have I come onto the desert only to ruin what was Thumb's way?

When Thumb did come, he was nearly alone. He rode into the camp and with him was Sagotal, the scarred giant. Akton was there watching, and Juh, expectant and proud. But Akton noticed the difference immediately.

When she had come home with Thumb there had been rejoicing, pleasure, adulation. Now there was nothing. No crowd had gathered to welcome the chieftain. The word had spread quickly among the people of the rancheria.

"Thumb."

He swung down and kissed her wearily, holding her to him as he hugged Juh with his other arm. She looked into his eyes and knew he was troubled. She didn't ask him anything, not then, not with Juh beside them. Juh, who would not understand. He would not believe any rumor of cowardice, but he would be stung by the accusations.

She waited until Juh had taken his horse and Sagotal had gone away, until they were alone. Then Thumb said, "Come," taking her up onto the wooded slope where he sat in the late shade and watched the spring burble forth and wind its serpentine way down through the rocks.

Finally he said, "They have come and brought their stories."

"Yes." She shrugged, dismissing all of that. "Something was said. The council demanded an explanation from the Brothers. They told them what they knew. Apparently it was little enough."

"They told them that Bad Lance named me coward."

"So it seems." She rested a hand on his knee, his scratched, hard-muscled knee.

"I do not apologize to you. You do not believe it."

"No," Akton said, "I only wonder that anyone does."

"Bad Lance must have spoken against me much."

"While you were gone. Yes."

"And then I brought you home—have you heard the stories, Akton?"

"That I am a witch woman? That I have seduced your courage? Yes, I have heard." She leaned her head against his shoulder. It was cool beneath the trees. Sundown was beginning to form itself, the sun to color, the shadows to gather.

She waited, not wanting to ask what had happened. She was curious to know how the lie could have begun, but she didn't need his explanation as reassurance. She, who had known him only briefly, had an absolute trust in Thumb. She was witnessing a power struggle she didn't fully understand, one that apparently went back to the days of Thumb's youth, to the terrible day of the bad lance.

"We found Delshay's camp . . ." Thumb began suddenly, and he told her all about it, about the trap he feared, about the hastiness of Bad Lance, his implacability, his need to lead, to challenge Thumb whether right or wrong, about the evidence in the canyon. "A hoofprint, a cigar end—if these can be called evidence. But I know that I was right."

"And Sagotal knows!" Akton said brightly. "His word must be honored."

"Sagotal is too close to me. They will never believe what he says. They will say that he speaks only for me."

"Yet they would believe Bad Lance."

Thumb sighed. "I don't know. I only know that I did what I thought must be done to keep us from being massacred by a waiting enemy. Let the council decide what my act meant. Let Cha-lipun tell us what must be."

"What could happen?"

"Bad Lance would be war leader. I would be shamed."

"No—it isn't just!"

"It doesn't matter. Perhaps they want a new leader. I have considered that. Perhaps the warriors wish to follow Bad Lance and not me. It was he who led them when I was gone. I only regret what this might do to you."

"To me?"

"Yes. They are blaming it on you. You will have to carry the blame, not me."

"It's senseless."

"Yes, but they find my cowardice senseless."

"As it is! That ought to tell them that it is a lie."

"They would rather find a reason for it all. *You.*"

"This is absurd."

"It is a time, Akton, when we have much to suffer at the hands of foreigners, from those not of the tribe, of the People. We are fighting, but we are also dying, losing a little each day. Everyone knows this. The whites are killing us. The Americans, the Mexicans—you are perceived as white. You lived with them, you speak their tongue, you taught their reservation school, making other Indian children white . . ."

"Thumb, Thumb! You know that I love you, that I want to be whatever you would have me be. I do not think anyone could consider me white! I was never a war-maker anyway, never a soldier, only a teacher. I am here because I love you, not because I want to ruin you."

"I know that. What they think is a different matter. I am sorry for all of that."

"I don't care, Thumb! I really don't care at all if no one ever speaks to me again—I have you and I have Juh. I have a few friends. Jak-jak likes me and he will not change his mind; I think Cochinay knows that all of this is nonsense. What do we care for the rest of them?"

"What do we care?" Thumb repeated. But it was clear that he did care. It was a time of war, a dark time. He could not simply desert them, his people. Or could he? What else was there to do if they did not want him? He was gloomy, dark-eyed, leaning on his fisted hand, staring out at the mountains.

"What will we do, Thumb?" she asked quietly, touching his cheek with the back of her hand.

He took the hand and kissed it, smiling. His answer was calm and deep and soft. "Marry. We shall marry, Akton. Now."

"Is the time right?" she asked, looking up, still needing reassurance. Was this all right? For her, for Thumb, for the people of the rancheria?

"The time is right. When can it be better? When our troubles are fewer, smaller? Perhaps that time will never come. I want to have you and so I must, so long as you will still have me."

She didn't speak to answer. She kissed his lips softly and then clung to him, curled against him on the rock as darkness settled and Thumb looked off into the east, reading his future among the desert shadows.

She had no one to tell her what should be done. She had no female friends, no relatives. She knew only to wash and comb her hair and dress herself in the blue dress, to put a wreath of white flowers on her head. When Thumb came, singing with his friends, she was ready.

Outside in the sunlight he stood in white linen, crimson sash around his waist, his long hair brushed back, a silver necklace embracing his bronze throat, bracelets on his arms, rings on his fingers, new white buckskin moccasins on his feet.

With him were the Brothers and Sagotal.

"What is it you wish?" Akton asked, coming forward.

"A wife to be with me and love me and lie down with me and have my children, one who will sleep beneath the stars or in the finest wickiup with me, who will share my feasts and the poverty of an empty cup, one who will walk the long trails and tell me when I am wrong and comfort me when I am lonely in the night."

Akton felt a tear stream down her face. She didn't bother to wipe it away. She went to Thumb and took his hand. Juh stood by looking solemn in his best linen trousers and shirt.

Not knowing the formula, Akton said simply, "Take me, then, for your wife, Thumb. I will lie with you and comfort you and be with you and no one shall part us until the day we both die—and even then our hearts, our souls will walk the long

Hanging Road together, the deep and mysterious valleys among the stars. There our love will still endure."

He took her then into the mountains, his friends following, singing a marriage song, Sagotal thumping a small drum and laughing—it looked as if he and the Brothers had been drinking mescal. The sun was bright, swirling through the pine trees. Thumb's hand gripped hers tightly, too tightly, as if to keep her from floating away. At times she wasn't sure that she might not do that. The day was ethereal, colored with lights which did not belong. Bells and whistles, distant ringing horns sang in her ears. Her body was impossibly heavy, her breasts weighing her down, her feet barely moving up the long slope as her head, like some soap bubble atop her shoulders, weightless and thoughtless, kept threatening to drift away.

The wedding house was in the tiny valley high above the rancheria. Cochinay was there in buckskins, his white hair braided and tied. In his hand was a stick with the secret face of happiness carved upon it. This he shook at the wickiup Thumb had built as he danced around it.

The wickiup itself was half-hidden in the bower, the pines towering all around it. It was festooned with bright flowers—lupine and starflowers, columbine and black-eyed Susans, their scents mingling in the still-warm air. Inside there were provisions for a week's stay. Somewhere beyond, above the chanting of Cochinay, Akton heard the sounds of falling water.

Their friends were invited in and Akton gave them food. Sagotal had become garrulous and overly gay. When he left he had to be supported by the Brothers. Then they were alone—Akton and Thumb, her husband. Juh had looked on in wonderment. He knew what was done when a man took a wife, but for his father to take one was just a little confusing.

Finally Cochinay had offered to show the boy the

mysteries of the skybird, the heart of the stone, the place where the clouds wished—although that meant a journey of three days from the rancheria—and Juh had gone away with the shaman, content, adventurous, proud.

"And so we are left alone—finally," Akton said. And at last she was someone who lived for another person. There were needs other than her own to consider, other stomachs to feed, others who needed love. Needed her love—and what a remarkable thing that was. To be needed for the gifts she carried within her, gifts that ached to be released and given away, inexhaustible gifts.

Thumb was tall and strong and sleek, a mountain cat. There was tenderness in his eyes, yet also a distant look. Perhaps that would always be there.

"Is it the council you think of?" she asked.

"The council?" He laughed. "What does it matter to me? Let Bad Lance tell them all he wishes. This is my wedding day. You would concern yourself with this on this day, Akton?"

"You are my husband. What concerns you concerns me. We have thousands of days to share. There will be only one council to decide your fate."

"My fate," he said, moving to her, "is to be with you, and if there are a thousand days with you, then each is precious. Each is of more value than the council."

He held her and she sagged against him; her body, which had felt heavy and weary, seemed to melt into his. He held her up, supported her weight, kissed her ear, her scalp, clung to her, showing her that for this moment she was needed, would always be needed.

"Come with me," Thumb said, and he took off his shirt, tossing it onto the bed he had made for her. Akton followed him out of the wickiup and up along the mountain trail. Mist seemed to hang in the air, rubies and sapphires floating down through the deep blue trees, and the headiness, the strange disembodied sensation returned so that Thumb had to take her hand and lead her.

She could feel the heat of his body, see the movement of his taut muscles beneath his mahogany skin, smell the yarrow soap and wild-lilac scent about him. His grace was a physical thing, as were his needs and wishes and thoughts—his eyes transmuted thought to physical reality. His grip was sure and strong, and it too transmitted need and want, hunger and tenderness.

When they emerged from the trees, Akton saw the tiny pool, the pencil-thin waterfall dropping from the heights, casting rainbows in the air as it sang its magical, untutored, endless song.

Around the pool the trees stood tall and straight. Around the waterfall rose gray stone bluffs crowded with hanging gardens, with red fern and agave, with aster and scarlet trumpet. Was there a world with war beyond the forest, out on the desert somewhere?

You have always dreamed too much and wanted too much and wished too much and lived too little in the dream, she told herself. She turned to the man and let his fervid embrace take her.

Through the red fern was the pool where the waterfall sprayed down from the heights. There Akton undressed with Thumb watching her, merging mentally with her. She placed the blue dress aside and stepped into the pool, which was of stone. It was five feet deep in the center, but sloped gently so that Akton was able to wade into the water, the surface taking her reflection, distorting it into a nymphlike memory of her.

Thumb was naked on the shore and he watched her until she lifted her hands, which streamed beads of crystal, and he stepped into the pool to join her, wrapping his wet, warm arms around her. He found her mouth with his own and turned her slowly as their damp hair intertwined and her breasts were flattened against his chest. She pushed away from him, laughing and a part of it was coquetry, but another part of it was a genuine shyness—oddly she now felt as if she had never been naked before him, never had his hands upon her body. Now she was another person, a wife. And as a wife she did not know what to be, how to act. The beginning of this new life, the passing of the old, had left her without a role she could accommodate. She was now the wife of Thumb—where the girl Akton was, or the woman Mary Hart, she did not know.

She laughed and hid her face, as embarrassed as a young girl, when Thumb dived into the water, bare thighs and buttocks gleaming with moisture. He rose before her to offer himself to her, to cling to her as he forced her head back with his kiss.

The waterfall fell over them, a misty veil, a sheltering magical thing, warm and soft and exciting. He drew her nearer and met her body with his own, lifting her higher, finding her need with his own. They stood together in the waist-deep water, breathing raggedly, wondering at the presence of the other, at the difference, the sameness.

At sunset they sat on the ledge, and Akton, facedown, watched the pool swirl and overflow its stony cup. Sundown gilded the pond and crimson flecks stained the water, seeming to reflect the red fern, which now seemed full and lush in shadow.

Thumb's hands were strong and loving. He rubbed the backs of her thighs, her back, her shoulders, at times straddling her, bending low to kiss her neck, her spine, the sleek and golden flesh of her.

"And so I have lived," Thumb said. "I have lived, now that I've been joined to you. Now that we are a man and his wife, our souls have found a union. Now I may die and walk the Hanging Trail, and those I meet may look upon my face and say, 'He has lived in joy.'"

Akton rolled onto her back and he bent low, his eyes delighting in her smile, in the softness and form of her breasts, in the slender curve of her graceful neck, in the darkness of her eyes, eyes which watched him in return, taking in the strength of him, the sinew and woven muscle, the manliness of him. She tugged him down and his weight was against her, reassuring and alive.

"What could please you more, Thumb?"

"Nothing." He propped himself up on his elbow and stared at her, his finger tracing the curve of her mouth, her nose, her eyebrow, still damp with the pool's water. A jewel of water stood there, catching the slanting rays of the late sun. "What do you mean?"

"Is there nothing?"

"Only a child. A child by you, a living son from your womb, a warm creature I have planted there with my eagerness for you," he answered.

"A son . . . or a daughter? For I feel that it is a daughter, Thumb."

"You feel . . ." He sat upright, his eyes going to her abdomen, which was still very flat. "Is it so?" he asked.

"It is so, Thumb. And now are you happy? Now are you very content?"

He lay beside her, his eyes closed, not speaking or looking at her. She knew that his joy was complete. He held her and the day bled away into crimson and orange. When it was dark she picked up her dress and they walked, wound together, back to the wedding house, and Akton's white flower wreath floated silently on the dark water of the pool.

When their week was over and they were full with lovemaking and feasting on each other, they came down to the rancheria and found Juh. Then all three went back to the wickiup to live. It was then that the trouble started.

Sagotal brought the news. The scarred giant seemed hunched, his massive shoulders lifted apologetically. Thumb rose from the ground outside the wickiup where he and Akton had been sitting, and he welcomed his friend.

"I greet you, Thumb," Sagotal said. "I am sorry to bring you bad news."

"Bad Lance?"

"Yes—I could not bring myself to trouble you while you were in the hills."

"Don't apologize. Bad news can always wait."

"Yes—and it *is* bad."

"The council has decided?" Akton came to stand beside Thumb, who slipped his arm around her.

"They have decided for Bad Lance."

"And named Thumb a coward?" Akton asked.

"They have decided that Bad Lance should be war leader," Sagotal said. "They stopped short of charging Thumb with cowardice."

"Didn't they listen to you, to the Brothers?" Thumb asked.

"They listened. What could be proved? Who saw the hoofprint but me?"

"It wasn't much," Thumb said. He looked skyward and sighed. "It does not matter what they say. I know."

"Thumb, it is bad for the tribe."

"I know this."

"Very bad."

"They say . . . they say it is Akton's fault, you know." Sagotal shrugged as if such a thought had never entered his mind. "They still say that she has bewitched you."

"Who says?" Thumb demanded.

"The women. Everyone. I hear the tales. Then, when you decided to get married immediately and didn't come down to defend yourself at the council meeting . . . well . . ."

"There was no defense to be made," Thumb said. He was obviously angry. "What could I have said? Should I beg with them?"

"No, Thumb."

"If they could think I was a coward after all I have done for them, all of the battles I have led us into and out of again . . ."

"They admit that you were brave, Thumb. But it's . . ."

"It's Akton still."

"Yes."

"Then I don't care to defend myself. I don't care to argue with them. Should I defend the woman I love, this harmless and good-hearted creature, this woman who is wise and dignified above any of them? I would not waste my breath."

"And so Bad Lance is war leader."

"And so he is. What do I care? I am content with my woman and my son."

But he wasn't, not entirely. Thumb chafed under the new restraints, those which kept him from leading the war parties as they rode out onto the desert and returned with tales of battle, with a few less men each time.

Akton found him in the trees, watching the stars through a gap in the pines, and she went to him, holding his hand, saying nothing. Finally he turned to her and said, "This is not good, Akton, not good at all. Bad Lance is a fool and a pirate and a butcher."

"Something has happened?"

"Something has happened. Disaster, I'm afraid."

"War?"

"If it can be called that," Thumb said grimly. He told Akton directly. "Bad Lance found a wagon train heading for Tucson from Nogales. Ten slow-moving wagons, a very easy target, a very simple one. There were no guards. He took his men in."

"They attacked a white wagon train?"

"Yes, Mexicans headed for Tucson and safety. Sonora is no longer safe for anyone."

"There was much killing . . ."

"Much killing. Akton, the wagon train was filled with children. They were orphans from a Catholic mission school in Nogales. Accompanied only by nuns and an old priest."

"Surely—"

"But he did!" Thumb banged his fist into the tree behind him. "He killed them, every one. And there was torture. There was rape." He shook his head. "Don't you see, Akton? It is over now. This will inflame the whites like nothing else could have done. We are defeated and the enemy has not yet risen on the horizon. We are defeated, and it is the beginning of the end."

11

Bill LaPlante stood squinting into the brilliant light of day. Behind him the sutler filled his order for tobacco, cartridges, a canteen. The scout was watching the main gate, where the column of irregular soldiers led by a man in a fancy uniform entered the fort.

"That's trouble, I'll wager," LaPlante said.

"What's that, Bill?"

"Nothing. Rodriguez, that's all. There'll be something come out of this, wait and see. Just wait and see."

"He's here."

Sergeant Lou Hazleton leaned into his commanding officer's dark, musty office. It was difficult to make out the man behind the desk. He might have been asleep or dead—but this would wake him up. He was a man who lived to fight, to kill the enemy and with his blood buy rank.

"Send him in," Sampson said.

Hazleton backed out and Major Scott Sampson rose to open the window blinds. The light he admitted was brilliant, white, piercing. It drove into his skull, where the angry residue of last night's whiskey slept in dark pools.

Rodriguez flounced in wearing his blue uniform, red sash, and showy saber. He would have made a fine portrait in oils for someone to hang above the family mantelpiece. He made a hell of a soldier. His specialty was unarmed camps—women, children, and old men. Everyone knew it, even if Rodriguez thought no one did. His own mind held the picture of himself as a valiant warrior, a conquistador. He was handsome, though turning slightly to fat. He wasn't exceptionally clever, but he had one remarkable asset—an army of five hundred men he had raised himself, which he paid out of his own pocket.

"General ... Pardon me, sir." Rodriguez halted and blinked into the bright sunlight. "I was expecting the general. General Warren Clark."

"The general has been transferred. Promoted to a larger command."

Scott Sampson walked around the desk, saluted, and briefly took Rodriguez' damp hand. Then he perched on the corner of the desk in a position calculated to allow the sunlight to gleam on the gold oak leaves he now wore. He had reached that rank more quickly than anyone since the Civil War, General Clark having twice promoted him personally. He had earned his rank through bravery—and there was no denying that Scott Sampson was a brave officer. Since that first engagement when he had driven his reluctant, lackadaisical army to meet and defeat Thumb, he had piled success upon success. He shone in this desert Hesperia. Colonel Shore had been much loved, but he was indecisive, and thus ineffective. General Clark had been resting on his laurels, and it wasn't possible to defeat the Apache by reputation alone. Major Scott Sampson, still extremely young, already much blooded, was destined for great things.

What did it matter if he awoke in a sweat at night to stand naked before the window and stare out at the purple hills, his heart pounding as he thought of Thumb, of the things he had seen, of the wild, mad things he had dared and would dare again as battle fever washed over him.

"Darling ..." Behind Rodriguez the door opened

and he turned, his smile deepening as the beautiful blond woman entered. Even the Mexican immediately noticed the dancing light in this woman's eyes, and understood by the way her glance lingered on a saber or a holstered pistol that she was a woman who needed dangerous men and attached herself to them. She was the reason General Clark had departed so quickly, and the reason Scott Sampson lingered so long in the desert.

"I am sorry," Laura Sampson said. "I didn't realize you were busy, Scott."

"I am sorry, Mrs. Clark," Rodriguez said with a deep bow. He had met the general's wife before; but as soon as he had bowed he knew he had made an error.

"This is my wife, Laura," Sampson said abruptly, pridefully. "Perhaps you have met Señor Rodriguez."

"Yes," Laura said, and she gave him her small hand. Her smile was cool as she thought back to the story she had heard, about Rodriguez running from Thumb, abandoning his own men to the slaughter of the Apaches. "Please, Scott, go on—I only wanted to know if we would still go riding."

Scott answered briefly that they would, and then Laura was gone. Left were the two men who had somehow come to know each other intimately in those few moments.

"Have you heard, Major Scott—of the attack by Thumb on the orphan train?"

"Yes. Sit down, please. Cigar? No? Don't mind if I light one, do you?" Sampson lit the cigar, waved out the match, and hid himself behind a screen of blue smoke rising in the strong flat rays of sunlight.

"It occurred on American soil," Rodriguez went on, "or of course I would not have troubled you. This is the sort of incident we prefer to revenge ourselves. The children were all Mexican, save one, who was French. The nuns were Mexican, the priest Spanish."

"How bad was it?" Scott Sampson asked, turning

his back to stare out the window at a squad of soldiers going through their drill. He always wanted to know how it had been, to assure himself perhaps that they needed killing, that the bastards deserved it. He paid no attention to Rodriguez' excuses for coming to the U.S. Army for help—the man was a coward. No one could have blamed the Mexican. He had fought long and as well as his mental and physical resources allowed. But he was afraid of Thumb, as were all on the desert—all but Sampson. All but Scott Sampson, who ached and hungered for the man, who had wanted Thumb since the day he had arrived at Bowie.

"It was bad. All orphans, all dead. Mutilations. Babies scalped."

"We'll let the newspapers know immediately," Sampson said.

"Of course, but . . ."

"It'll draw a hundred volunteers from this area alone. Three hundred easily if we can wait a month. The people of Arizona won't stand for this."

Scott Sampson remained standing at the window, staring out at his men, his tools of war. Something was bothering him, however; Rodriguez asked what it was.

"Thumb. This doesn't sound like Thumb."

"They were Thumb's people."

"I thought they were in the Sierra Madres. That's a long way to ride for a single raid."

"Thumb rode this far once for a single boy. His son."

"Yes." And for the schoolteacher—what was her name? Mary Hart. "If it was Thumb's band, there should be other raids in the area. They will gather whatever wealth they can—horses will be their chief interest. Horses are mobile wealth, food and transportation all in one." Sampson seemed to be talking to himself.

Rodriguez interjected, "If we were to leave now, there is a chance we could ride Thumb down."

"I'm waiting for civilian volunteers!" Sampson snapped. "I want the community, the state, the civilian mind behind us. Besides, if it was Thumb, he'll still be here, in the hills—he won't ride south just yet."

"And if he does?" Rodriguez asked.

"What sort of charter do you have?" Major Sampson asked.

"Pardon me?"

"What does the government allow you, Señor Rodriguez?"

"Full freedom. Carte blanche. I ride when the army has no post nearby, when they cannot follow, when they are without resources. My *charter* Señor Major, allows for all contingencies."

"Good." Sampson nodded. His own standing orders, according to the treaty in existence with the sovereign nation of Mexico, allowed for the continued pursuit of the hated Apache by an army from either side of the international border. They would have him. This time they would have Thumb.

"We may ride now?" Rodriguez asked.

"I want the volunteers. I want an army massed under me which none on this desert can stand against. And I don't care if my soldiers are scum or convicts, Indians or Mexicans or men without a country. I am going to have Thumb. I am going to ride my horse across his broken body and from then . . ."

And from then he would ride the tide of his victory to high places, to plateaus of success Laura had never dreamed of, to the rarefied and honored bright pinnacles. Thumb was the way to all of this. To have Thumb's head was to have the key to the halls of success. And Sampson would have Thumb's head!

"Rest your people, Rodriguez," Sampson said. "Rest them and feed and water your horses. The volunteers will come. We will have our man. Hazleton!" Sampson roared. "Get Lieutenant Sharpe in here—I want him to write a dispatch for the news services."

Bill LaPlante didn't like it, but it wasn't his place to say much. In the first place, Bill thought as he sat in on the meeting with Major Sampson, Lieutenant Sharpe, Captain Holt, and Captain Granger, it couldn't be Thumb's work. That was obvious to a man who had been hunting and running from Thumb as long as LaPlante had—and it should have been obvious to Sampson. But Sampson had an obsession about Thumb; he always had. He also had a grudge, unspoken, against LaPlante. The scout knew how things had really been on Sampson's first mission. He had seen the dry-mouthed, wide-eyed green officer stumble on one of Thumb's rancherias. LaPlante had seen the fear in Sampson, and knew that now that fear had to be subdued by constant doses of valor.

No one asked LaPlante for his opinion at the meeting. And, as he had always said, as long as he was taking army money, he figured he was army personnel—let the officers figure out what they wanted to do, he would help them the best way he could. Although this didn't seem to be a project he could do much to aid. Granger, who had been there the longest of any of them, ended up voicing LaPlante's own misgivings.

"It's not Thumb," the captain said.

"Of course it's Thumb," Sampson answered offhandedly.

"Against a wagon trail full of orphans?"

"He wouldn't know that until he hit them," Sampson said.

"He would know," Granger said. "Thumb would know."

"Maybe you think it's Geronimo, then, Pat?" Captain Holt, the owner of the regimental racer said, needling his friend.

"No, I think Crook has pretty well got Geronimo

located," Granger answered seriously. "But I think we're guessing wrong here."

"And if it isn't Thumb?" Holt asked.

"Well, we'd have to get them anyway, but I like to know who it is," Granger conceded.

"It is Thumb," Scott Sampson said, and no one contradicted the major. They all knew how much he wanted to find the Chiricahua who had become a phantom, at least in Major Sampson's mind. Thumb was the ghost who had come and snatched his son away and taken the schoolteacher to keep him company or tutor his son.

Granger wasn't comfortable with things yet. He tugged at his mustache ends and said, "These civilian armies aren't so easy to deal with, Scott."

"If you mean my people," Rodriguez said hotly, "we have been for three years in the field . . ."

"No, Señor Rodriguez, I didn't mean you. I was thinking of the Arizona volunteers. With Colonel Shore we ran a pack of them—LaPlante will recall—and they turned out to be worse than the Apache."

"That's not even humorous, Granger," Sampson snapped.

"It wasn't meant to be, sir."

"White men worse than the Apache!" The major's outrage was real.

"They weren't much better, then. They were taking scalps, and they weren't all warrior scalps, either."

"I don't blame 'em," Sampson was hot. "Did you read the dispatch on the Phillips family? No? Look it up. Phillips, his wife, and two children attacked by a band of Geronimo's men. The entire family killed except for the older girl, who was hanged on a meat hook, the hook entering her skull. They found her alive and took her into Silver City, but she died hours later. As for the Apache women— when Jim Cooney and Chick were killed by Mongollon Apache, hidden observers saw squaws stick pieces of wood into their bowels while they were alive, then crush their heads to jelly with rocks. I saw a report here from Crook concerning a party of twelve settlers literally hacked to pieces with knives. Any man who wouldn't kill a squaw as quickly as a buck or a rattlesnake knows nothing of the Apache women, Granger."

There wasn't much Granger could say. He had been raised a strict Baptist, however, and his moral conviction was that you did not prove yourself better than a savage by becoming a savage yourself. He was a good soldier and a strong man, but he had seen children killed on both sides and he knew that he would never stoop to that. He looked at Bill LaPlante and caught a sympathetic glance. LaPlante understood him. They knew.

"These people in Arizona are tough and fearless," Major Sampson was going on. "They'll fight and they'll take orders—you can ask our friend Señor Rodriguez here if a civilian army can't be effective. After all, what's the final difference between a civilian and a soldier? Only a uniform, perhaps."

Sampson nodded appreciatively at his own statement. "Only a uniform," he repeated. Then he gave them their orders, keeping all forces close to the post, having Sharpe issue a news bulletin calling for volunteers, ordering the reservation guard increased in case some of the wild young bucks there chose to try to break away and hook up with Thumb.

Outside, Captain Granger stood with Bill LaPlante awhile. The sun was warm, the shadows long. The Mexican volunteers Rodriguez had brought with him clustered together near the sutler's store.

"Is someone going crazy in the territory, Bill?" Granger asked at last. "Maybe me?"

"Maybe you, maybe me," LaPlante said, turning his head to spit. "Maybe the whole damned territory."

"Everyone wants war . . ."

"It's always been that way, Captain. It's easier to tear down than to build. Look what skill it takes to build a town, how few brains to set the torch to it."

Granger shook his head. "Damn all, it's not Thumb, Bill!"

"No. No, it ain't."

Granger's eyes slowly shifted to the scout. "I thought I was the only one who believed it."

"Hell, we all believe it. Except maybe Rodriguez, who don't seem to have the brains or just don't care."

"Scott . . ."

"Major Sampson knows. Believe me, he knows."

"Then why . . . ?"

"You'd have to ask him—but then, he wouldn't tell you, would he? I guess he wants everyone to think he's going against Thumb, the best and the bravest the Chiricahua have."

Granger fell silent, turning away. It wasn't his way to speak against a superior officer. "I hate to have the civilians in on this, Bill, damn me I do."

"I know it."

"They volunteer for a few reasons: they expect to profit or they want to be known as brave men or they are just plain cruel. Some of them want vengeance for families and friends hurt by the Apache. None of those are very good reasons for joining up."

"They don't necessarily make you a good soldier," LaPlante agreed.

"Well, I don't like it, but that's the way it's going to be, I guess. I've been a long time on the desert, Bill, maybe too long. I've turned into a complainer."

"Or a thinker," LaPlante amended.

"Maybe. At any rate, I've got things to do. A discipline problem in Baker Company . . . I'll be seeing you, Bill."

"Yes, you will."

Granger started away, then halted and said, "Bill, it doesn't smell very good, does it?"

"No, Captain. No, it doesn't smell very good."

LaPlante watched him go, narrow and weary but erect. Maybe Granger had been out here too long, but then, how long had he himself been here? And it was worrying him as well. There was a fever building, like the fever that strikes before an illness, the plague or cholera. And there didn't seem to be anything a man could do to stop it.

The following week, the first company of volunteers came into camp. They were drilled by a veteran sergeant, although they seemed to want to make a joke of it all. Bye Courtney brought the majority of them in; the big merchant was spending out of his profits to stop the Apache. They had hit his supply trains, and plenty often, and now Bye Courtney saw his chance.

The Mexicans, the U.S. Army, and the concerned citizens in Arizona were joining together to finish off the Apache once and for all.

Bill LaPlante watched the army grow, and with each new man, thought it was growing in quantity but not in quality. The bad ones had begun to drift in, seeking whatever there was to be had. Jack Wethersfield had come, bringing his moronic brother. Theotis Lee, the unreconstructed rebel with the reputation of a man hunter, had come with old Bib Stoddard, who had been adopted by the Basin Ute and then run off when he had killed his new father-in-law after a night of heavy rum drinking.

Major Scott Sampson was euphoric, watching his army grow. He might have been Napoleon gathering forces from far and wide; they were rabble and worse, but Sampson was bothered by none of it. He surveyed the scene and thought with pride: Damn Crook and his war with Geronimo! Scott Sampson's was going to be something to print in the papers, to summon banner headlines even in the East, where careers were made and broken.

Outside the post proper there was a tent town where the waiting fortune hunters and Indian-haters drank cheap whiskey and gambled. From time to time they rode in armed bunches over to the reservation, where they amused themselves by shooting over the heads or at the feet of the unarmed Apache there.

The army regulars had to drive them off, but as

Bill LaPlante noted, it all seemed to be done in the spirit of good fun. The soldiers saw nothing wrong with "hoorahing" the tame Apache, who, after all, had done plenty of that themselves when they were free—and worse.

LaPlante's mood didn't get any brighter as the days went on. There was a rape on the reservation, a shooting in which a ten-year-old boy was hurt. Apparently the Apache boy had grabbed at a soldier's weapon and been hurt when it accidentally discharged, but the facts couldn't be ascertained. There were bad feelings everywhere. By now the word of the wagon-train massacre had reached all quarters and there were mutterings among all the civilians concerning retribution—and it was easier by far to contemplate retaliation against the unarmed reservation Indians than against Thumb, who was known to be armed and on the warpath.

Major Scott Sampson was doing nothing to cool the situation down. In fact, he seemed to enjoy fanning the flames, perhaps building up his own future role as savior of the territory. He had given two interviews in the Tucson newspapers condemning Thumb, swearing to hang him before month's end. There were a lot of flattering adjectives applied to Sampson in those interviews, and he had clippings of them in his desk.

Bill LaPlante moved around in worried distraction. Captain Granger was morose. The Indian scouts led by Yellow Sky repeated that this was bad magic, a bad war, but they wanted their pay.

LaPlante wore his buckskins again now. The days were growing cooler. He carried his rifle with him wherever he went, out of lifelong habit; he was holding it when he heard the exchange between Bye Courtney and Jack Wethersfield in the tent town.

". . . Any damn squaw," Courtney bellowed. He had a jug in his hand and he was plenty drunk, although it was only nine in the morning.

"I never had one," Wethersfield said. He took a

deep drink from the jug. His idiot brother, Luge, watched with pride and excitement as Wethersfield performed the glorious feat of opening his mouth and swallowing.

"The tame ones are a little safer," Bye Courtney confided, leaning forward to tap Wethersfield on the chest, a gesture Wethersfield didn't much care for, by his expression. "There was a schoolteacher here on the reservation. Now, she was a sweet little chunk."

"Had her, did you?"

"Partner, she couldn't resist. She was tame, but her Indian blood rose when she saw the plenty wampum in my purse!"

That was enough for LaPlante. "Talking about the lady you tried to rape during a post dance, are you?" he asked in a quiet drawl.

Bye Courtney swung around. The eyes of all the men who had been sitting or standing in a circle, passing the jug, settled on LaPlante.

"Who asked for your two cents, LaPlante?"

"Nobody. I'm chippin' it in free. I happened to like the lady you're referring to, that's all."

"That Cheyenne . . ."

The rifle in LaPlante's hands seemed to train itself on Bye Courtney of its own volition. Courtney was suddenly staring directly down the menacing black bore of the weapon.

"She was a lady, and I imagine she's dead now. She was trying to do a job here, and she paid for it. She was too much woman for ten men like you, Bye Courtney. You got drunk and tried to have her, and if I hadn't been there, maybe you would have, I don't know. But I won't hear you telling lies about Mary Hart."

Bye Courtney's swollen tongue moved around inside his mouth, but no sound came forth until he whispered, "By God, I'll kill you for this."

"Not so long as I'm looking at you, you won't," LaPlante said. Then with disdain he turned his back on the men and walked away, hearing a stifled chuckle from one of them—Jack Wethersfield, he thought.

"Damn them all," LaPlante said to Captain Granger later that day. "This tries a man, it really does."

"Yes." Granger looked into the distance, then back to the headquarters building, where Scott Sampson was planning his war. "It tries a man, Bill. Why don't you pull out?" the officer asked abruptly.

"I don't know. Thumb, I guess. I can't stomach some of what he's done—this orphan train. Courtney's a pig, but he's no butcher. There's a war. We've got to decide which side we're on. Besides," LaPlante said, spitting, "I'm a warrior. What else can an old warrior do but fight, Captain?"

"Dry goods?" Granger, who had an uncle in the business, suggested facetiously. Both of them laughed. There was little humor in the laughter, but what other weapons did they have?

The next morning the great army of retribution moved out. Sampson gave them all a stirring speech first, about the pride of the nation or some such nonsense, and they rode out.

There were cheers and a brass band—three pieces from Bowie—along with several dozen civilians holding children and waving flags. The regular-army unit rode out first with Sampson at its head. Behind them came the Indian scouts, fifteen strong, and then Rodriguez' army followed, all pomp and splendor, fancy epaulets and crimson sashes, tall hats and brass. Last came the civilian army, ragtag, lively, jocund, and half-drunk.

They were going to war. Bill LaPlante watched and shook his head. The tuba racketed on deeply in four-four time as they were going to war. The jug passed from hand to hand. Major Sampson turned in his saddle and waved a hand, urging them forward. The wind lifted the horses' manes and teased the feathers knotted into the Indian scouts' hair. They were going to war. They laughed and sang and hurried on, perhaps fearing death might not wait for them.

Sagotal brought the word to Thumb of the approaching army of whites, both Americans and Mexicans, and their trained Indian scouts.

"Bad Lance wants to engage them—four hundred soldiers. Four hundred, Thumb!"

"He would have to."

"We can't stand against them."

"We can't run. Are our scouts sure they know where the rancheria is, certain that they are marching this way?"

"Certain. An Arapaho scout was captured. He told us that the Americans knew where the rancheria was."

"Where is the scout, the Arapaho?"

"Dead, Thumb."

Akton had appeared from the wickiup. Her hair was parted and braided and shone glossy blue-black in the clear sunlight. Her cheeks were glowing, scrubbed. Her dark eyebrows, arched questioningly, drew together slightly as she listened, leaning nearer to Thumb and holding his arm.

"There is to be a council meeting, Thumb. They want you there . . . but not as war leader," Sagotal told him.

"Very well, I will come."

"Thumb, perhaps the women and children should begin packing provisions."

"Yes. They should."

Sagotal wanted to say something else, but instead he spun on his heel and trotted off toward the village. Akton still held Thumb's arm, still silently watched him.

"Did you hear?" he asked.

"Yes, I heard him. What will happen, Thumb?"

"Ask the spirits," he said with some irritation. "I do not know. My cousin has brought death upon the tribe."

"Tell them that," Akton said. "Tell the council."

"It will do no good. The past can't be undone."

"They can't attack us here, can they, Thumb?" Akton asked. "In these mountains? With our narrow passes—why, I've heard you say it would take a vast army to rout us from these hills."

"And now," Thumb responded, "they have come with a vast army. Mexicans and Americans together—perhaps they will join with other forces, the Mexican army, who knows? Yes, Akton, they can attack us here, although it will cost blood, much blood, for them to do so."

"Sagotal said . . ."

"Yes. I want you to begin packing. You and Juh. I will make sure you have the best horses."

"Yes." Akton noticed that Thumb was looking down, and now she did too. She had been holding her abdomen without realizing it—her abdomen, which had begun to swell with his child.

"You can travel?"

"Of course," she laughed. "I am Apache."

"Not quite," he answered, kissing her, "but very nearly, very nearly."

Then he sighed, let his hands fall away from her, and started into the wickiup for a shirt. He wanted to be present at the council meeting, to see what was decided, although no one would ask him for his opinion. The mood of the people was warlike, and they had judged Thumb a coward.

Akton watched him tug on his linen shirt and start toward the council lodge. She stood alone, watching him for a very long time, feeling small and futile.

She wanted to pack the provisions as Thumb had asked, but it seemed impossible to start just then, to decide what to take. Perhaps he would return to tell her that it was unnecessary, that it had all been a mistake. Where were they to go anyway? If the mountains weren't safe, what was safe?

She started up the slope, moving through the trees. There was no war in the trees, only the singing of the bluebirds, the hum of the bees, huge and droning. Without realizing where she had been walking, she found herself near the waterfall, where the marriage house stood in disrepair, but still solid and well-constructed, as was their marriage.

She walked on, smiling, looking for traces of those days so few, so recent, and yet so long ago. At the waterfall she walked out onto the gray outcropping, where the sun warmed her as blue-gold dragonflies hummed past and the silken fall raced past into the stony pool.

There it was silent and still and perfect, if anything without Thumb could be called perfect. After a little while, feeling lazy, she stripped off her blouse and lay back on the stone to doze in the sun, which stunned and muted her senses, her thoughts and anxieties.

She lay there and was conscious of the life around her, of the dragonflies and the softer buzz of the bees, of the bluebirds and larks in the forest, of the cicadas singing in the grass, of the softer sounds emitted by the sun, by yawning flowers, grass springing into existence. There was the indistinct, silent sound of the pines growing, of the sap in them swelling, flooding the tree with life as the blood in Akton's body flooded her own body in ways dynamic and minute, passing to the infant within her womb. As she breathed in the sun and the wind and the pines, she knew the world around her was transmitted to the child, Thumb's child, becoming racial memory, a need to be free, to walk the long-shadowed hills.

She heard and felt these things, and heard, too, the voices from out of the past, the many who had suffered, laughed, battled, loved, cried, and clung together in the long winter—all of them. She saw them, and heard as well the voices of those to come, the many in the long chain of proud unborn, the handsome, wistful, praying, angry many who would stand and see the desert, and perhaps when the wind was right, when the hour was right, remem-

ber her, whom they had never known but only
dreamed of.

The old woman shrieked and threw herself at
Akton. Her knife flashed through the air, the sunlight glinting on the cold blade as Toonashi screamed
and struggled to kill the Cheyenne woman.

"Slut! You carry the bastard child. You have
brought him down, brought shame on my family
and my grandson!"

The first shout was all that had saved Akton. She
had rolled to one side, and as Toonashi slashed at
her belly with the knife, Akton managed to evade
her. The knife struck stone, and the steel, brittle
and razor-sharp, shattered against it.

Akton struck out at Toonashi with her elbow,
and the older woman took the blow in her eye.
Howling with pain, Toonashi tried to stab Akton
with the broken blade of the knife. Her own hand
was cut in the effort, and blood stained the rock in
huge drops.

"You have ruined it all! My people, my daughter's husband, my grandson. Whore, witch! Cheyenne! White thing!"

She tried again to attack Akton, but the advantage of surprise was gone, and the rush of energy
which had flooded the old Apache woman's body,
suffusing it with murderous strength, was now wan-
ing. She was only an old and sorry creature, small
and hunched and bitter.

"I want to kill you," Toonashi said, but her voice
was a whisper and Akton knew what she meant—
she was an old woman who wanted to kill the force
of time, to destroy the insanity of the moving stars
and of the sun, which brings life and then carries it
away at random into the void. Love can follow, but
it cannot be answered as silence surrounds the place
where there had been joy, as the heart in the night
is alone, listening to its own beating. Then hate
needs to find an object, the frustration of life, of
death, of need and want, and being must find an

outlet, subtle or violent, near or distant, imagined or real.

It was futile, all of it, because war and time and the stars continued while the dear ones with their sweet flesh and laughing eyes altered or passed away or ceased to smile upon those who needed, hoped for, yearned for the silent expressions of love and life. The signs that we too lived and were loved and would fade away and wish—for only a moment in time—to be remembered.

"Toonashi," Akton said. "I don't wish to hurt you. It wasn't I who made your daughter go away. It wasn't I who hurt you, who made your heart ache. Thumb loves her still in his way. I know he does. So does Juh—I have not taken from you, but tried to give to them. . . ."

But the old woman was not listening. She was in love with the dead and wanted no more to do with the living.

"You killed her . . ." Toonashi said, and slowly backed away into the trees while Akton watched and wondered where the blame lay.

She picked up her blouse and pulled it on. The broken knife blade clattered against the stone. Akton looked around her at the waterfall, the deep, dark trees, the blue sky above it all, and she shook her head. War, death, hatred had come to this place, too, and destroyed it forever. It was finished just as the desert, pure and pristine, was to be destroyed so that it would never exist as it had for future generations.

She stood and looked at the knife blade. Then she turned and walked away. There was a war growing like a secret canker on the desert.

Juh was at the wickiup, looking graver, than ever. He had begun packing buckskin sacks with food, with venison, pinole, maize, and honey cakes.

"Where have you been?" he asked with a hint of the authority which should be, might be, his one day if the people could survive this onslaught—but how could they survive? The world was in turmoil, changing. Technology was colliding with the primitive beauty of their way, and there could be only one victor.

Akton had once believed that only she understood that, but now she knew that Thumb was aware of it all, aware of the certain defeat. Yet he fought on.

There was no other way.

She had seen the reservation from one side, but now saw how it was to the free people. The reservation was death, slow, shameful, and prideless. Could Thumb endure such a life?

Never.

"Here he comes," Juh said, and sprang to his feet.

Akton turned and saw her warrior. He entered the wickiup and stood before her, lost in some smothering concern.

"Thumb. . . ?" Akton asked, hesitant.

He was abrupt. "Pack the provisions. Did I not tell you to have everything ready?"

"What has happened?"

"Nothing has happened . . ." He caught himself, hearing the tone of his voice. He went to Akton and held her silently for a long, long while. "It is time. The white army is coming. Bad Lance will engage it. You must retreat to someplace safe."

"Safe? Where, Thumb?" Akton laughed without humor. He stepped away from her.

"I don't know," he said, disgusted.

"You . . . you are going to war?"

"I am a warrior," Thumb said.

"Will it be a victory?" Akton wanted to know. He wouldn't answer her. "Will it?"

"It will be a battle. That is all a warrior ever knows. Pack your provisions."

"How long do we have?" Akton asked.

"A day or two."

"We can spend it together."

"No! Go now. Quickly."

"Not without you!"

"Akton . . ." He took her by the nape of the neck, his strong fingers wrapped in her heavy dark hair. He opened his mouth, his lips parted to speak, but then he simply turned away. He walked from her as she held out a hand, then dropped it limply to her side.

"Woman," Juh said sternly, "we must make ready. Didn't you hear what my father said?"

"Yes." Akton watched Thumb for a moment longer as he strode away across the meadow. Her voice was firm as she said, "You must show me what to do then, Juh. I don't know so much as you do about this. Tell me what must be taken and what left behind."

They began to pack. Across the rancheria the camp was breaking up. The horses were herded together now. If need be, they would be left behind. The Apache could fight on foot, and in rough country it was preferable—a man can go where no horse can hope to follow. The wickiups were left standing. They needed only food, water, the babies.

Akton had little to pack, less than the others. The necklace she wore in a buckskin pouch inside her dress so that it wouldn't bounce and flash. She had little else, she had lived such a little time among the Apache. She had little but the child in her womb.

Juh had a small bow and arrows with him. She had seen whites laugh at the small ones with their tiny bows, but she had seen Juh kill a rabbit, a squirrel with that bow. An Apache warrior's bow could kill at a hundred and fifty yards. Juh's had considerably less range, but it too could no doubt kill if necessary. It was no toy, the eye behind it no untrained child's eye. He had hunted with it since he could walk, and it was no joke for him to be carrying it with him.

He was armed. He was a warrior. He had seen others of his age fight and die.

Thumb returned before they had joined the others who were set to march away from the trouble. He held both of them. His face was placid but there was a tenseness in his grip.

"Which way do we march?" Juh asked.

"North."

"North, toward the army, Father?"

"They won't suspect it. Besides, we have word now that a Maxican army is approaching from the south."

"Oh, Thumb!"

"Several days off yet, but approaching. Besides, to the south the land is flat, and that won't do, will it, Juh?"

"No, Father."

"The land is our ally, the desert our friend. We can live upon her and find water where our enemies cannot. They are blind to her wealth. The desert kills as surely as an arrow, yet it succors, it succors."

Akton clung to him. She kissed his chest, nipping at it with her teeth, and when she stepped back she smiled. It wasn't a very brave attempt perhaps. Thumb placed his hand on her abdomen and said, "Be careful, then. The women are taking the horses. Cha-lipun will be in charge. He is too old to fight. Juh, you are responsible for our family."

Juh nodded seriously. His father's hand rested briefly on his narrow shoulder. "Akton . . ." Thumb said, but he could say no more. He turned away, snatched up his war bag and his weapons, and walked from her, his stride measured, his body erect. He was, after all, Apache.

"Now, woman," Juh said, "we must go." But it seemed to Akton that there were tears standing in the small boy's eyes. She might have been wrong, for he turned away quickly and shouldered his sack of provisions.

They walked to where the women and children, the aged and the infirm, waited with blankets around their shoulders, with their lined faces empty of expression. They did not fear the war, but now they were weary of it. And for the first time, doubt had begun to gnaw at them.

"Women, men!" Cha-lipun called. They turned to look to the council chief, frail and small. "Please, we go now. Let us go quietly. The enemy is near. Let not our sounds give away our warriors' intent."

The horses, Akton noticed, had had their hooves muffled with leather shoes. Everything that rattled or squeaked had been lashed securely or padded. The children would not cry. They were Apache and had been trained from birth to be silent: a cry might give the tribe away, and the tribe was all that mattered.

Jak-jak was an eager, bouncy presence among them. He had wanted to go to war, but as always, he had been left behind, something he didn't understand but didn't resent. After all, weren't Juh and the other boys here as well?

"I'll guide you," he told Akton. "If you are tired, you can ride on my back. I'm strong. Strong as a horse, I heard someone say, so you may ride me."

"Thank you," Akton said, forcing a smile that Jak-jak accepted as genuine.

"We go," Juh said, and he lifted his pack again. The horses were being led out. Some of the women were riding. Akton could have had a horse, indeed Thumb's blue horse was there among them, but she preferred to walk.

She watched the procession stream past, oddly colorless, faceless. A few she knew, nodded to. Cochinay was there, appearing exhausted. He had danced all night for victory.

Toonashi was there, blanket over her head, shadowing her face. But if she saw Akton, she did not look toward her. The woman moved as if she were suddenly very old. Tiny had to guide her mother by the arm—Tiny, who was so small and frail herself.

"Come now," Juh commanded. "Don't lag or they will talk against you."

And so they started on. It was hot, airless, and the rancheria fell away into the gray and yellow mountains. Heat lightning crackled and thunder rumbled in the distance.

They walked on and Akton let her senses go flat

so that she hardly smelled the dust or saw as the pine trees gradually passed from the scenery.

She saw only the shadowy, blanketed figures around her, felt only the life within her, and she walked on, placing one foot before the other—so that they would not talk against her.

Behind her, yet another world fell away.

12

They heard no guns all that day, but it did nothing to calm their fears. War surrounded them. Tired and thirsty, they made their camp in a narrow, rocky valley. Boys were sent up into the rocks to act as lookouts, and a cold meal was shared.

Akton sat in the darkness, feeling the heat from the stones around her and the chill of the night breeze. She stared at the stars. There was confusion in her soul on this night. What had happened to her, and where was she going? What were any of them bothering to fight for?

Surrender. Then they would not have to walk, to go thirsty, to sit in the dark and cold of night without a good glowing red fire.

But perhaps it was Mary Hart who considered these things. Mary still loved her comfort above freedom. Mary's pride was personal and not of the race, for the tribe.

She watched the stars and recalled her long dreams. Dreams of ages past and of women faceless yet familiar, warm and knowing, their eyes upon her. She saw cold nights and hot days, laughing people, and sunlight on a sparkling stream. Whose memories these were, she did not know. She remembered them now. She knew it was worth the good fight.

She did not sleep that night, but stayed awake, watching and remembering, waiting and dreaming.

Dawn was slow in coming into the canyon, but by

the time the sun had risen the next morning they had been on their way for an hour. They moved softly across the sand on the canyon bottom. They were a slow procession moving northward, a lost people wandering on the earth.

The gunshot was distant, but paralyzing in its effect. They stopped, heads lifted, and froze in their motion.

"Hurry on," Cha-lipun scolded them. "Do you think your warriors fight so that you may stand and listen, be captured and tortured?" He struck some of them with a length of cane as he passed. They hurried on, trying not to listen to the gunshots, which had increased and multiplied and gathered menace.

Scott Sampson sat his horse looking up the gorge where the bulk of the fighting continued. The cavalry unit had been ambushed by Thumb's men, and in the first terrible minute Sampson had seen half of his force go down.

The white-stockinged bay horse he rode sidestepped nervously and Sampson struck its head with his fisted hand in frustration.

"What do you want to do, sir?" LaPlante asked, reining in beside the officer. Dust streaked LaPlante's face.

"Where are they?"

"Everywhere. Find a rock, there's an Apache behind it."

"Damn all!"

"Are you planning on retreating?"

"It's not much your business, is it, LaPlante?"

"No, sir, I don't reckon—except some of those boys up there are friends of mine."

"I won't retreat." Sampson was grim. His dreams of a great triumph were being shot to pieces under the hot morning sun. Sweat trickled down his throat. "It's an act of cowardice to retreat." Sampson was talking to himself, so LaPlante didn't answer.

Captain Granger rode in with his arm hanging,

his forehead smudged. Crimson blood ran from his sleeve onto his hand. He didn't bother to salute. "Retreat, sir?" he asked.

"No, damn you, do you all think I'm yellow! Where's Rodriguez?"

"He's holding back. The civilians, those who didn't turn tail at the first shot, are with him."

"Turn tail! We had people turn tail?" Sampson was beside himself.

"Some of the civilians, sir. Maybe half. The rest are with Rodriguez."

"We should be counterattacking! Where's Rodriguez? What the hell kind of soldier is he? We should be counterattacking!" Sampson spun his horse, spurred it savagely, and rode toward the Mexican, who had his people barricaded up a feeder canyon.

LaPlante watched him go, then asked Granger, "Want that arm bound up, sir?"

"What?" Granger looked at his wounded arm as if he hadn't noticed it before. It seemed to be pretty badly shattered. "Oh, yes. If you think you can do anything."

"He won't back off, will he?" LaPlante asked as he swung down and helped Granger from the saddle. He propped the wounded man up against a boulder. The fighting in the gorge had settled to a sniping exchange. "He just won't quit."

"Not Scott. He's got a lot riding on this," Granger said through the pain, which had now come to stay. He panted and let his head loll back. "It's Scott Sampson's jihad, and God help the soldier who doesn't express the wish to die on his shield."

Sampson had found some who didn't seem eager to do that. Rodriguez was waxen but stood straight and tall. Sampson wasn't satisfied with the appearance of a soldier the mustached Mexican offered him.

"Damn you, reinforce me, Rodriguez!" The captain stayed mounted. His bay, growing more excited with each shot, danced into the Mexican and shouldered him roughly.

"It is suicide, Señor Major! I can't order my people to charge up that gorge!"

"The hell you can't. Where did you get your reputation, Rodriguez, squaw-hunting?" The Mexican stiffened with anger, but Sampson forged ahead. "I want some help up there or I'll see that your name is known for what you are—a stinking greaser coward!"

Rodriguez put his hand on the hilt of his saber and for a moment Sampson thought, hoped, the man would try to use it. He would have happily put a round through Rodriguez' head.

"Get your people on the move!" Sampson ordered, spurring his horse again, drawing blood.

He rode away in a flurry of dust, and the officer next to Rodriguez said, "Pay him no mind. He is mad. Mad with war and ambition. I think he is afraid, my general, very afraid."

Rodriguez, who was still trembling with rage, could not even speak. This man had *ordered* him to do something! This American officer, this child!

"What do we do, General Rodriguez?" the officer asked, carefully using the title which Rodriguez had conferred upon himself. The officer was hardly prepared for the response.

"Attack. We attack!"

Sampson found the Americans standing around up the feeder canyon, smoking cigars and drinking. Bye Courtney came forward with a bottle in his hand. Sampson uttered a strangled cry and kicked the whiskey to the ground. Courtney got back up, his face flushed with alcohol and anger.

"What in the hell are you doing, Sampson!"

"Trying to fight a battle. What are you doing? You say you want Thumb dead, his band crushed— what are you doing hiding here?"

Jack Wethersfield and his hulking brother, Luge, had come up to stand beside Courtney. All of them held guns. Beyond the canyon wall the fighting continued.

"The Mex stopped, we stopped," Courtney said.

He had puffed up a little with the backing of his friends. The idiot, Luge Wethersfield, was wide-eyed with incomprehensible delight. At least the moron wasn't responsible for his actions. Bye Courtney was—he had been strutting around Bowie, bragging for weeks that he was going to show the army how to take Thumb.

"Where are Stoddard and Theotis?" Sampson demanded.

"Went home, I guess," Bye Courtney said with derision.

Those were two men Sampson had been counting on for leadership. Damn all, what had caused them to turn yellow? "I want you men to get around to Snake Canyon—"

"Now wait a minute!" Courtney objected.

"Snake Canyon! We're going to push and push and push until Thumb has to take to his heels. They're afoot, and when they make their run, they'll be slower than cavalry. You are the cavalry I'll use to cut them off. They won't see you if you continue up Bull Creek and wind back through the cotton-woods."

"Listen, Sampson . . ." Courtney began again.

Scott Sampson reminded the merchant of something. "You signed certain papers when you volunteered for this expedition, Courtney. An oath of loyalty. You run out on me or refuse my command, and it's virtually treason. I don't know what the technical charge will be, we'll let a court decide, but damn you—I *will* bring charges! I swear it. I've got good men dying, half my force gone."

"And you'd throw away the other half just so you don't fail, you bastard," Jack Wethersfield muttered, but Sampson didn't hear him. He turned his horse and with a last warning glance at Courtney rode off in the direction of the battle.

"The man's mad," Wethersfield commented. "I can think of ways a hell of a lot easier to impress a woman anyway." He asked Courtney, "What do we do now, Bye?"

298

"How the hell do I know?" Courtney growled. "Have another drink and ride up the canyon. The bastard's just crazy enough to try having us hung."

Thumb didn't like the trend of the battle. From atop the flat rock where he stood watching, he could see the apparent confusion in the enemy ranks. There was milling, retreat, many casualties. One man, apparently their commander, kept riding furiously back and forth, trying to whip his people into a fighting frenzy.

Still Thumb did not like it.

"He has won," he told Sagotal. "Bad Lance has won the day. He has met them and defeated them. Now we must slip away. It will shatter the confidence of the Americans."

He left his rifle with Sagotal as he slipped from the rock and, moving in a crouch, worked his way to where Bad Lance was sheltered in the cleft of a huge split boulder which was bright with green moss on the inside surfaces.

The crooked man turned savage eyes on his cousin. "What is it?"

"We should withdraw, Bad Lance."

"Withdraw! We have the enemy beaten. Thoroughly beaten."

"Yes, I agree."

"*I* have beaten him," Bad Lance said challengingly.

"Yes. Let us consolidate our victory."

"By withdrawing!" Bad Lance laughed. He looked at Nantje, who was, as always, beside his leader. Nantje smiled as well.

Thumb was persistent. "We have him beaten physically and mentally. The enemy will run now. It will be a long while before he can raise another large army. To remain in the canyon is to risk more casualties to no end. We have won. It has always been our way to lose as few warriors as possible, to inflict as many casualties as possible on the enemy and then slip away—why would we now go against the wisdom of the centuries? Why now stay and fight on, Bad Lance?"

"To crush him! To crush the enemy." Bad Lance's fist clenched. He twisted his hand and held it in front of Thumb's face. "To kill him and drive him away forever. To show them all that Bad Lance is the greatest of all, that Geronimo means nothing beside him, that Cochise and Victorio and Mangas Coloradas are only shadows of Bad Lance, the Chiricahua!"

Thumb could only stare at his cousin. What was Bad Lance thinking of? "I am not important, Bad Lance. Not now."

"I know that!" his cousin answered sharply.

Nantje was still smiling and it was insufferable. Thumb ground his teeth together. "What I mean is, you do not have to prove that you are a better war leader than I am. Not now."

"No. That much is taken for granted," Bad Lance said. A spate of firing from the canyon below turned his head. A small contingent of cavalry was making a desperate attempt to break out of the canyon.

"Stay. Here you die," Bad Lance said softly, and he raised his rifle.

"Bad Lance," Thumb said, "it is time to go." He touched Bad Lance's shoulder as he was sighting down the barrel at a blue-uniformed figure far below.

Angrily Bad Lance slapped Thumb's hand away. "Leave me alone! Coward. Now you will see—see what I always knew! I am war leader, I am the genius of battle. I am the only one who can lead the Chiricahua to victory. Only me! Only I can save the Apache."

"Bad Lance . . ." Thumb's voice was quiet, but there was deep menace in it.

"Just because you wish to run, to run to sleep again with your Cheyenne slut."

The rage boiled up in Thumb and he leapt at his cousin's throat. The rifle in Nantje's hand exploded with smoke and flame and a deafening roar and Thumb felt the searing pain across his skull as he fell, his face scraping against the granite beneath him, the last sound in memory the laughing of Nantje, maniacal, deep, following him down into an empty place which smelled of death.

Bad Lance nodded. It was good. Thumb had become a coward. "Is he dead?"

"Not yet." Nantje, who was concerned for his own sake, looked up from the body. "I shot his head."

"Don't worry, my Nantje. A white bullet did that. I saw the man shoot Thumb—then I shot him."

Nantje smiled with relief. Bad Lance had returned his attention to the battle below. There were dead and dying white soldiers everywhere. A runner came in with a report. Moving through the rocks, he came to where Bad Lance crouched. The runner glanced at Thumb's body, his eyebrows going up, but he said nothing of the fallen former war leader. "Bad Lance, the Americans are leaving. The civilian soldiers. They have run."

"You are sure?"

"I saw them with my own eyes. Riding toward the Snake Canyon."

Nantje interrupted excitedly. "That is where the women and children are, Bad Lance! We must hurry there."

"Yes," Bad Lance said, waving a disinterested hand. His attention was only on the scene below him. There were no reinforcements for the white soldiers now. Only Rodriguez, and he would not fight. He had proved it that day at Delshay's camp. That had been a glorious day. Bad Lance had used that situation to his own ends. This day would be more glorious yet. He had it in his hands to crush the strength of the U.S. cavalry in southern Arizona. He could accomplish what Geronimo and Cochise had never been able to do, what Thumb with his hit-and-run tactics had not had the courage to do.

"Bad Lance . . . the women." Nantje's wife was

new to him. Nantje wanted to save her. Bad Lance stared at his friend coldly and thought: "He is a fool. His woman is making a coward of him as Thumb's Cheyenne woman had made a coward of him.

"Pass the word to attack."

"Attack! Bad Lance—"

"Tell them this: Let not a white man live to see the sun go down in this canyon. They must be dead, every one. Dead and their bodies scorned."

"Bad Lance, we will lose many people. The soldiers are in the rocks."

"Then we will lose people!" Bad Lance snapped. "We will win glory and freedom on this day. It will be the last time an American army will dare pursue the Chiricahua into Mexico—because they will remember Bad Lance! Bad Lance, who broke the Americans' back."

"Bad Lance . . ." Nantje wanted to argue but saw there was no point in it. His gaze fell to the body of Thumb. If the war leader doubted Nantje's loyalty, he could make much trouble. Nantje did not want to die at the hands of his own people. "I will take the word."

"You, runner, work northward. Tell the warriors there to prepare themselves. At my signal we go into the canyon. At my signal we destroy the enemy, destroy him!"

Scott Sampson, his face sweat-streaked and dusty, rode to where LaPlante crouched beside a badly wounded Captain Granger.

"What's happened, LaPlante? They've stopped firing."

"Pulled out, I'd say," LaPlante offered. "That's an Apache's way, always been Thumb's way. Inflict maximum enemy casualties, take minimum losses yourself, and pull out."

Sampson's voice was anguished. "He *can't* pull out. He can't retreat."

"Likely he is, sir."

"I'll pursue, dammit."

"Not through those boulders with cavalry."

"It can't happen—I won't let him! I've got him, I tell you. He can't retreat through the Snake Canyon, not once Wethersfield and Bye Courtney get there. But they haven't had time . . . If he doesn't break off the engagement . . . Damn the Apache!"

Granger was lost in pain but his eyes exchanged a look with LaPlante. Scott Sampson was ranting now. He was nearly over the edge.

The canyon was suddenly filled with war cries. LaPlante's head came up as he grabbed for his rifle. Sampson's horse leapt forward as the major rode wildly, joyously toward the suddenly erupting battle.

LaPlante stood and said to himself, "Crazy, crazy." Granger, lying on the ground, couldn't be sure whom LaPlante meant—Sampson, Thumb, or himself.

They wore their death masks, but when they removed them they had no faces at all. They stood around and chanted the song of death and bid you to join them. Yet the woman called from a high hill. She stood in sunlight wearing a blue dress and she was smiling down at Thumb, who crawled back out of the black and fearsome tunnel of death to the light calling her name.

"Akton . . ." But she wasn't there.

There was no one there. What was happening? He lifted himself and his head seemed to split open with pain. At the same moment the roar of the many guns came to his ears and his heart lifted wildly.

He tried to come upright but he could only stagger and fall, dragging himself finally to the edge of the outcropping. Blood fell from the wound on his skull, dribbling from his right ear. He watched the horrible thing below—the thing which was war untempered by reason or object or sanity.

The Apache ran afoot toward the position the white soldiers still held behind the rocks. The soldiers' guns fired again and again, and the Apache fell one after the other until the earth was stained with their blood. As Thumb watched, Sagotal was shot, and the faithful giant fell, sprawled against the ground, to rise no more.

Still the Chiricahua were winning. They had numbers, they had the will to fight, and the American soldiers were already decimated.

The sound of cavalry turned Thumb's head. He half-rose in astonishment, in dread, in frustration. Rodriguez was leading a charge of his Mexican irregulars. The sunlight glinted on his saber, his red sash splashed him with color. He was finally a warrior, motivated by who knew what. Thumb could see the outcome now. There was no victory possible for the Apache. But there was escape, still escape.

"Run! Flee to the rocks," he cried aloud. He was erect, blood running into his eyes, streaking his chest. "Withdraw!" he shouted to the hard and empty sky, but Bad Lance would not order a retreat. His warriors charged on, running into the Mexican cavalry, which trampled over them, which added its firepower to the American unit's guns. Star Voyager went down. Rodriguez seemed to be hit; he sagged in the saddle. The Apache were among the cavalry, but they had no chance against the horses. They were now encircled, and it was only a matter of time.

Looking around, Thumb found his own rifle on the ground and started downward. If he must die on this day, he wanted to die among his people, fighting beside them. But his knees buckled and he fell against the hard and rocky earth, to lie still, peering through nearly closed eyelids at the exploding white ball of the sun.

Scott Sampson was beside himself with exhilaration. He had won! He had defeated Thumb, had crushed his band of Chiricahua, had secured himself a reputation none could gainsay.

He walked the field now, his saber in hand. Mexican cavalry, American soldiers, Apache warriors, and horses lay strewn madly across the earth. Smoke still hung in the air. Rodriguez was dead. They would build a monument to him in Nogales, seated on a muscular bronze or marble horse, his saber raised, his visage noble and courageous in death as it had never been in life.

Captain Holt, looking dazed, found Sampson and walked silently beside him as they reviewed the casualties, the cries of the wounded following them. The two men were together when they found the Apache with the twisted face, the crooked leg.

He lay looking up at them with flat, dusty eyes. "Tell them . . ." he managed to say in English, "tell them it was Bad Lance."

Scott Sampson put his saber tip to the Apache's throat and plunged it in. Then the two officers walked on, Holt scarcely glancing at his commander.

Bill LaPlante found them and reported, "Sir, Captain Granger died."

"You said they'd retreat, LaPlante. You said Thumb would pull off. You see . . ." The saber described an arc of exhibition. "He did not!"

"Did you hear me, sir? Captain Granger is dead."

"I knew he wouldn't retreat. He couldn't. And when he attacked, I knew we would have him. I only had to whip that cowardly Rodriguez into motion. Had to insult him. Well," Sampson went on, standing with his saber behind his back and rocking on the balls of his feet, "it worked. Good tactics. Rough, but necessary. You'll do well to remember that, Captain Holt!"

But Captain Holt didn't answer. Nor did LaPlante, who simply turned and walked away, finding his horse where he had left it. He mounted to ride northward alone, to ride out onto the desert, where the world was cleaner, leaving behind the smoke and stench and the memories. They had paid him and so he had done his duty. Now, Bill LaPlante decided, it was all over. They didn't have enough money to pay him anymore.

It was still, very still. They hid behind the rocks and the gray, broken cottonwoods, watching and listening. Juh was beside Akton, and with them was Jak-jak. The Americans were half a mile farther down the canyon, coming nearer. Why they were coming, they did not know, but Akton knew there were many of them, a part of the army Bad Lance had gone to meet. She repeated Thumb's name as if it were a talisman. She could not bear to think long about him, to wonder—but she could speak his name, keeping him well by doing so.

They had heard no shots for a long while. Only the wind through the shattered trees broke the stillness. That and the whispering sounds of hooves, the creak of saddle leather.

Akton hugged Juh to her, or tried to—the boy was alert as a wild thing, his eyes and ears alive only to the movements of the hunters.

A baby cried and was instantly stifled, placed to the nipple. Heads turned that way. A collective breath was held. The soldiers came then.

They were civilians, not soldiers really, but warriors. These men had come out to protect their families or homes—some of them. Others sought glory as the Apache always had in war. Akton felt herself sink lower. A leaf blew past her face, dry and brown, and the movement caused her heart to jog.

They were faceless creatures, these hunters, their features hidden by the shadows cast by their hat brims. They were heavily armed but seemed to Akton undisciplined for an army. Their voices drifted to her.

". . . Gonna come over that hill and try to get out this way."

"You heard the *commander!*"

"Little . . . give me the whiskey."

"Why don't you all shut up, if . . . hear you for miles."

"What do you care? I say we sit here for an hour or so and then ride back. Hell with this. If Sampson wants . . ."

And then it happened. A dry branch broke from

the cottonwood overhead and fell, drawing the eyes of the whites. One of them cursed savagely, seeing a bit of color. His hand reached for his sidearm, but before it had been drawn from its holster Cha-lipun rose up, drawing his bow.

"No!" Akton screamed, but the arrow flew true and took the rider from his saddle. His horse reared up and then galloped away, dragging its rider, whose boot had stuck in the stirrup. Akton heard someone scream, and scream again, and it was a time before she realized it was herself. The guns roared and the old dream came back, the Cheyenne dream, the dream of war and death and Mother running with them through the snow as the soldiers came, of the crimson blood, of Hevatha, her laughing sister, being lost, of the horses slowly freezing.

The smoke from the soldiers' wildly firing weapons concealed the white army and their rearing mounts. Cha-lipun was dead. Cochinay, shirtless, was dancing on a log, his hands held high, his white hair streaming in the wind, cursing, laughing, chanting, praying until the bullets washed away his song.

"No, Juh!" Akton screamed. The boy had risen up, bow in hand, ready to fight, to die as a warrior should.

"Leave me be, woman," he shouted, and slapped her hands away, tearing free to race toward the white army.

Akton sprang to her feet and raced after him, dragging him down. They fell into the dust, Juh kicking, fighting her wildly. From the corner of her eye she saw Tiny hit by a bullet, saw her go down and lie still.

Akton was screaming in English, "Stop it, stop it! We are women and children here. Just women and children!"

But they kept firing. Surprised, frightened themselves by events, half-drunk, they shot at anything that moved. When they discovered that they weren't being shot at in return, they did not halt but continued at a fevered pace. Guns were placed against the breasts of the old women and touched off. Toonashi was ridden down by a man on a white horse. Jak-jak stood in the middle of the wild, brutal confusion, watching with wide, dark, horrified eyes until the man in the green jacket tried to ride down Akton. Then Jak-jak roared with anger and leapt at the man, pulling him down as the horse veered away. It was a short fight; as Akton watched, another white soldier shoved his rifle barrel against Jak-jak's thick back and pulled the trigger. Jak-jak, harmless and fat and childlike, jerked and fell dead, his spine splintered.

Juh lay still but his eyes smoldered. His anger was with Akton, not with the whites. He wanted to fight, but she would not let him rise. Now he tried again, yanking his bow out of her grasp, but Akton got hold of the sinew string and pulled back until it cut her hands and finally the bow broke.

Juh fell onto his back, still as death, as Akton covered him with her body. She saw a soldier fire point-blank into a girl younger than Juh. The bullet caused the body to leap, the blood to spray from it. Akton was no longer frightened—she was mad with rage. Furious, wanting a gun in her own hands, wanting to fight back, praying that Thumb would arrive and hack them all to pieces before her eyes.

"Filthy bastards!" she shouted at them until she was nearly hoarse, her body trembling with each explosive shout. "Pigs, criminals, fiends!"

In front of her a hulking man with the face of an idiot was undoing his trousers as he stood over the young wife of Nantje. And around him blood was still being shed. It was insane, a depraved and broken world, a world of white devils.

"Well . . ."

He stood over her, huge, drunken, and red-faced, smudged with black powder smoke. Bye Courtney.

"Remember me, *Miss Hart*? Surely you do. Everyone figured you were dead . . ."

Juh tried to break free, and Bye Courtney kicked

308

him savagely in the head. The boy collapsed. Akton shouted out something that was not human, but the sound of an enraged wild thing, and she sprang to her feet. Courtney slapped her down again, and she fell into the dust, her mouth filled with blood.

"I wasn't good enough for you, remember, Miss Hart? And then some Apache buck took you—how did you like that, Miss Hart, how did you like lying with a filthy Indian buck?"

He reached down, grabbed her hair, and pulled her up. His face was twisted with savagery of a sort Akton didn't understand—passion and hatred mingled. The one seemed to stimulate the other. Behind him Akton could see the moron atop Nantje's wife. She was still, unmoving. Dead or alive, Akton didn't know. A dead child lay on the other side, ignored by everyone.

Mad. The world had gone mad, with beasts masquerading as human beings. Everything that moved on two feet was not a man, but a hunting, stalking, dirty carrion beast.

Bye Courtney ripped her blouse open. Simultaneously she saw the cloud of approaching dust, saw the blue of the cavalry, and she recognized the man at the head of the column. Scott Sampson.

Akton simply stood there as Bye Courtney stepped away from her to face the soldiers who were riding in at a gallop. Sampson looked older, his face narrow and lined, sun-browned, hard. The boyishness was all gone. War had done that; the love of war had made him one of these. Only his regulations, his training, kept him from being a killer as they were.

"There's nothing but squaws and kids here, sir," the captain beside Sampson said before they had even reined up. "Old men."

Sampson's face was pale. With righteous anger or the fear that this would taint his victory, Captain Holt didn't know. He saw Sampson go stiff. He swung down and walked to Luge Wethersfield, who was sitting on the ground with his pants undone.

Sampson kicked the man in the face so savagely that Luge's mouth and nose spewed blood before he was spun around and lay still in the dust. Then Sampson's eyes found Akton and he frowned darkly for a moment before recognition dawned.

"Mary Hart!"

Her eyes were haunted yet hard. He gave her the blanket from his roll to cover herself, yet she seemed not to care one way or the other.

"How is the boy?" was all she asked.

"Thumb's boy," Sampson said as he hunched down. "Look, Holt, it's Thumb's boy! By God, this'll turn General Clark green—I've got the kid back."

"It doesn't matter anymore, does it?" Holt said.

"No." Sampson managed to laugh. The carnage hadn't entirely ruined his sense of humor. "There won't be any negotiations with Thumb, will there? Ever again."

"What do you mean!" Mary Hart flew at him, clinging to his shirt, her blanket falling free, her mouth open, eyes wide. "What do you mean that it doesn't matter?"

"He's beaten. Thumb's beaten, Mary—you don't have to be afraid. We just about wiped out his army today."

"And Thumb. Dead? Tell me!"

"Not yet," Sampson said. Akton felt her stomach release its knotted tension. Sampson smiled, although it was a faraway expression, one for himself alone or perhaps for the blond woman back at Bowie. "But he's badly wounded. We've got him, and his best hope now is that he will die, because if he lives, he'll only live to hang."

Akton stepped back, her face stony, her eyes dark and expressionless. Sampson said, "Holt, see that Miss Hart is taken care of. She's had a rough time of it, no doubt, a prisoner of the Apache."

Then Akton did the unexpected. She threw back her head and she laughed, shook with laughter, hysterical, wild laughter which broke off into momentary tears before she recovered herself and stepped back, shoulders straight. Sampson and Holt looked at each other, Scott Sampson shaking his head significantly.

"Move the prisoners out," Sampson ordered finally. "Check them for weapons—women and children too."

"The dead, sir?" Corporal Killian asked. "What do we do with the dead women and children?"

"What dead, Corporal?" Sampson said stiffly.

"There, sir. The women . . ."

"*What* dead, Corporal?" Sampson repeated. Killian turned and walked away without saluting.

As Akton watched, the women, the old, the children were searched. The civilian men stood to one side continuing to drink. Nothing more had been said to Wethersfield or to Bye Courtney, who stood smugly watching.

Juh stood shakily beside Akton, but when she tried to put her arm around him, he pulled away. She knew why—he had wanted to fight, honor had demanded that he fight, and Akton had not let him. She had broken his bow. Things would not be the same between them again.

Jak-jak lay dead; Cochinay lay dead. Where was Thumb? They said he was alive. If that was the truth, where was he?

She asked Killian, who remembered her from the school, but he could only shake his head. He was lost in his own hell at the moment, a hell where women and children were not only killed but also not even given the dignity of a burial. Lies would be told about this day.

The Indians were lined up and once more they began to walk northward. They were silent, an empty, dying people moving in slow procession out onto the endless desert. An hour later they came across the other column of soldiers. They had with them the captured and wounded Apache warriors. There were only a few, a very few—they had intended to fight to the death, and most of them had.

Akton scanned their ranks anxiously, seeing no sign of Thumb.

Then her breath caught, her body tensed. She gripped Juh's shoulder as the boy started forward. It was Thumb—it had to be Thumb they carried on a makeshift litter between two horses. They couldn't see his face, only the army blanket thrown over a wounded man, the Apache moccasins protruding from underneath, but Akton knew it was Thumb.

Akton clutched at the necklace around her throat. She left the column and started forward.

"Back in line, woman," someone shouted.

"Damm it, she's a white woman," Killian said.

"No one's supposed to go across to the other column."

"Miss Mary . . ." Killian shook his head. "Don't go, please."

"I want to see Major Sampson."

"He won't talk to you."

"I have to see the wounded man there, the prisoner. Isn't that Thumb?"

"I don't know," Killian said. "Maybe so. Orders are that no one goes to the other column."

He held her shoulders, and although she strained against his grip for a while, she gave it up soon. They wouldn't let her go to him, and so she stood with the others, watching as the beaten, wounded warriors passed by in ranks, some with hands tied.

Cries of anguish, words of grief, questions and bleak answers were exchanged among the people in the two columns despite the halfhearted efforts of the cavalrymen, exhausted and blood-weary themselves, to keep silence in the ranks.

And as they passed the news of death to each other, one column to the other, the death song began. The young cavalry soldiers turned to watch, knowing the anguish—their friends too had died that day—until the order came down again from Scott Sampson that there must be no communication between the warriors and the women and children. The columns were separated more widely still, diverging as they marched northward, always northward. One woman tried to break free, to run to her husband, but she was clubbed down by soldiers on horseback and there was no more of it.

The day was white and endlessly prolonged. Akton was aware of nothing but the sun, the red sand, the litter that hung between two horses. Whoever it was that lay there, he did not move, so far as she could tell from across the distance that separated the two columns.

Juh was beside her but silent now, even scornful. The rest of the people seemed to have lost their faces, in the Snake Canyon perhaps. They had blankets over their heads, and the shadows smothered them. They were not people but a memory of people, or so it seemed to Akton as she trudged on across the endless flats, scarcely alive herself.

"Miss Mary," Killian said as he slowed his salt-flecked horse and walked it beside her. "Captain Holt says you don't belong in with these people. Major Sampson wants you to ride with the soldiers. We've a horse for you."

She shook her head, not looking up, seeing nothing but the legs of his bay horse, the sinews and veins and bones and hooves and muscle of it.

"Miss Mary. . . ?"

But she didn't answer, and after a while he rode away. They trudged on.

At night they camped on the open desert, miles from any shelter. The horses were restless as the wind blew and the stars shrank in a cold black sky.

Akton sat and watched as the wind drifted fine sand over them. The soldiers spoke in low voices around the fire, and the scent of coffee drifted toward them. The people sat huddled in the night, and from across the camp came the sounds of pain and despair.

With the dawn, they marched. One woman had escaped during the night. Where could she have gone?

They walked on as the rising sun bled crimson tears for the lost people.

They walked on and the desert warmed and glared and tossed angrily as the wind scoured it. The cavalrymen tied their yellow scarves across their mouths and noses. Then the wind abated and still they walked. They walked into eternity; northward. One hour, one day, someone said they were no longer in Mexico, and then on another day they saw Fort Bowie and the reservation, and the wails of mourning and defeat and despair went up again.

They walked past the fort and onto the reservation, and then it was over.

13

The winter was not cold. Only twice did it freeze, and once snow lightly dusted the peaks above Apache Pass beyond Fort Bowie.

Akton waited and pleaded and stood alone on the reservation. Beneath the trees where once there had been a school, she waited and watched. Below, there were a fort and a stockade. A prisoner waited there—ill or well, she did not know. They wouldn't tell her.

She wrote letters, many letters, to everyone she could think of. They mailed the letters for her but no response ever came. She had to see him, had to know.

Nothing happened. Days passed. The Apache did not speak to her. Juh spent his time with other boys, his face growing tight and foreign as he saw Akton.

She knew Thumb was down there somewhere, and something was happening, for soldiers of high rank arrived by stagecoach and stayed. But it was maddening not to know *what* was happening, what could be done.

It was the middle of February when a friend arrived, perhaps the only friend Akton had in the world. Rising, dressing, washing her face, Akton emerged into the bright cold sunlight brushing her long glossy hair. And there, waiting for her, was Edna Shore.

"Hello, Mary," the colonel's wife said. Akton

dropped her brush, going to the older woman to hold her, to feel the comfort of her body.

"Mrs. Shore," Akton said. "You actually got my letter. You came!"

"What's all this, and what in God's name are you doing on the reservation in those rags? Mary"—she examined her at arm's length—"what are you doing to yourself, and why?"

And Akton told her.

"But this is all foolish," Edna said, "staying up here when you belong down on the post—or in town at a boardinghouse. And you mean to tell me you still care for this man, this Thumb?"

"He is my husband."

"Yes, dear, but that means nothing. Not now. Not when you're back in civilization."

Akton started to respond, but there didn't seem to be much point in it. She simply shrugged. Even Edna had her prejudices.

"You're thinking about the baby," Edna said, "but what good is it going to do to have it known that the father of your child was some bloodthirsty savage?"

"He was not," Akton said very softly.

"All right." Edna hadn't become less blunt—nor had she become less compassionate. Now she kissed Akton on the cheek, holding her briefly. "But that is what people will say."

"Yes, and no matter what I do, people will say it. I can turn my back on Thumb and let them pity the poor unfortunate woman I have become, let them pity the child. Or I can keep my head high and tell them what this baby is—the son of a prince."

"You can tell them what you want. They'll hear only what they want to believe, Mary."

"Yes. And so we must endure, the baby and I. For now I must see Thumb. I must! I want to see him, and then I want to speak the truth about what happened. I must make them listen to me."

"It's a little late, Mary."

"What do you mean?"

"The trial was held two days ago. The sentence

was passed. Thumb is an enemy of all civilized people."

"What do you mean, what are you saying!"

"They sentenced him to death. He'll be hanged."

"Hanged?" Again, inappropriately, Akton laughed. Edna studied her curiously. "How can they hang him? Who was on trial? Thumb, only Thumb? And what of Scott Sampson and Bye Courtney and the Wethersfield brothers? Cowards, thieves, murderers, rapists . . . what of them?"

"The major has received a letter of commendation and some private promises of a promotion to come. I think Bye Courtney was given a citation for valor and the thanks of the War Department for raising a civilian militia in time of need."

"This is preposterous! I demand to be heard."

"I don't think that is possible, Mary. You are Thumb's wife, and prejudiced in the extreme . . . or you are mad due to your capture and mistreatment at the hands of the Apache. I have heard both opinions expressed. I've tried to do as you asked, you see, tried to have someone interview you—no one cares to. They're busy congratulating each other, toasting victory."

"Perhaps Colonel Shore . . ."

"Colonel Shore passed away last month, Mary. Yes"—she smiled gently—"It was the whiskey . . . that and a broken heart."

"I want to see someone. I must be heard!"

Edna could only shake her head. "Who is there to talk to, Mary?"

"Then . . . I must see Thumb. I have to see him. They can't keep me from him."

"They can."

"Do they think I'm going to smuggle him a weapon?"

"Would you? If you could?" Edna asked, and Akton had no answer for her. Yes, she would have done that, would have killed for him, laid down her own life, done anything at all. But there was nothing whatever to do, and that was worst of all.

"Still you must try, you must ask for me," Akton said. "Talk to Scott Sampson. He can't hate me so much. Talk to anyone you may know among the officers who have come. Please!"

"All right. I will, Mary." Edna removed a tear from the corner of Akton's eye with her thumb. "But don't hope too much, dear. Please."

"I have to hope, don't I? What else is there for me?"

"All right." Edna, gray and frail as she was, stood straight and took in a deep breath. Resolve colored her cheeks. "I'll try again, Mary. I'll ask, beg, threaten—there're a few skeletons hidden in a few closets, and I know where some of them might be. I'll try."

"Thank you."

"Well, don't hope for a lot, dear," Edna said, holding Akton for a last moment. "Everything has been twisted and blown out of proportion, it seems. The papers back east have made a real hero out of Scott Sampson. I've seen full accounts of the battle in a Philadelphia paper—and a differing one in a Kansas City paper. But everywhere Sampson's a hero. He's a hero here and in the East. Arizona will name streets after him, and perhaps a town. I'd be surprised if anything can halt the momentum this thing's built up. The good have been rewarded, and symmetry requires that the guilty be punished."

"Guilty . . ." Her voice was very small. "Of what?"

"Guilt in war," the colonel's wife said, "consists of being on the losing side."

"Maybe. You will try?"

"I promised. I will."

"At least ask if I can't see him."

"Yes. Mary . . . you can't stay out here."

"Why not?"

"You're not Apache. It's not necessary, not right."

"It is," Akton said, "both right and necessary, believe me."

And there was nothing more to be said after that. Edna Shore held her cloak tightly against the blasting wind and walked to where her buggy and driver waited. Then she was gone, the wagon bouncing away toward the fort, toward the stockade where Juh had once been held, where his father now waited.

The world was a prison. The Apache were its inmates. The day grew colder yet.

The next day the soldiers came and Akton's heart leapt with confused emotions. They were going to take her away, they were going to let her see Thumb, they were going to give her an interview with Scott Sampson or his superiors. . . .

She didn't know the men who came. Their sergeant said, "Miss Mary Hart, you are living illegally on an Apache Indian reservation. You are requested therefore to gather your belongings together and prepare to move."

"Prepare to move, when?"

"Now, miss, it's an order."

"Where are you taking me?"

"Temporarily to the guest cottage on the post, miss."

"But I don't want to go there."

"Orders, miss. One thing we can't ignore, you know." He smiled. He was at least trying to be polite.

"I can't believe they can make me stay on the post," she said in frustration.

"I don't think anyone's trying to bully you, miss, or make you do anything at all you don't want to—except leave the reservation. You're just not authorized to be here, and the new Indian agent and post commander have decided you have to be moved. Now, as far as going to the cottage, I guess you don't have to at all, but if you wanted to be near the post . . ." The big sergeant flushed surprisingly. "I'd heard you wanted to be near the post for a time yet."

Akton looked at the man, looked past him, seeing war and the decent men like this soldier who had chosen it or had it chosen for them. What she saw was nameless, dark and bloody. Only Thumb mattered, she decided. Thumb, Juh, and the baby. There was no point in being recalcitrant. The cottage, as the sergeant had pointed out, would keep her on the post, able to hope for an interview with Scott Sampson, perhaps able to see Thumb. Thumb! And how long had it been since she had seen that strong and vital man, that thoughtful, resourceful, brave creature? He was always present yet never near enough in her thoughts.

What was the matter with her? She had been sitting hoping, wishing. Why, the old Akton, Miss Mary, would have marched right up to Scott Sampson's door and on in, telling him that he had no right to keep her separated from her husband, and that if he didn't allow her to see him, she would tell the world, the *world*, what had happened at Snake Canyon, not a whisper of which had yet reached the newspapers and probably never would.

"I'll be with you in ten minutes," Akton said. "And I'll be going to the visitor's cottage to stay. Please wait outside."

"Yes, miss." The sergeant touched his hat bill and went out to fill a pipe and light it.

The private first-class with him said, "I don't get it, Sarge. That 'Pache woman speaks better English than I do."

"Yes, she does. Better than me. Except she ain't Apache."

"No? Then what is she, Sarge? What exactly?"

"A woman, son. Just a woman," the old sergeant said.

Akton was as good as her word. In ten minutes she reappeared with her sack in hand. There wasn't much in it: a few articles of clothing—moccasins, a buckskin shirt, the turquoise dress; some pinole, which she hated to waste, having acquired the Apache's thrift with food and water; and the necklace. She had touched it tenderly, feeling the silver and turquoise trickle through her fingers as she placed it in her sack. It was a terrible, marvelous sensation, like life itself seeping away.

"I'm ready. But may I stop and see someone?"

"Yes, miss. I expect so."

The wickiup they stopped at was small and shoddy, as if it had been thrown up in the expectation that with morning it would be torn down again, or moved away from. Juh was there, before the wickiup. He was plaiting a rawhide quirt. As Akton stepped down from the soldier's wagon, he looked up and his eyes were as dark and empty as they had been when he had been in the stockade.

Now he was back. The world was a prison.

"Juh?" She walked toward him, smiling.

He got up and walked away, leaving the quirt behind him on the ground. She didn't follow him; there was no point in it. In his mind perhaps she had reverted to being of the white world. Perhaps it was simply that he would never trust another human being again, no one who was not Apache at any rate.

The sergeant, who had gotten down as well, stood holding the reins to his team. He watched Akton for a long moment. "Well, miss?" he asked at last.

"We can go," she answered. She looked again at the wickiup and then away, to the distance, to the shadowed mountains and the empty land.

The wagon rolled through the main gate of the fort. Everything was the same. Akton saw men in blue, traders and idlers, a few "blanket Indians" loafing near the sutler's store. A group of soldiers was performing a mounted drill. Farther across the parade ground a wagon with six or seven men in it was starting out for some duty or other, probably to collect firewood. The flag still flew, the stockade still stood, guarded, bleak, having a mysterious and dark life of its own.

"Please stop at the commander's office, Sergeant."

"I was told to take you to the cottage, miss."

"I want to see Scott Sampson."

"Major Sampson is probably pretty busy, miss."

"I'm not a child," Akton said. "Don't speak to me as if I were."

"All right, miss," the sergeant said with some anger. "I won't. I'll tell you this. Major Sampson won't see you. He doesn't want to have anything to do with any Indian unless he's dead."

"I see." Akton bit her lip in irritation. "Nevertheless, I will see him. Unless I've been dismissed for letting myself be kidnapped, I'm still an employee of the Bureau of Indian Affairs. I think I am entitled to an interview."

"You might think so, Major Sampson might not."

"Halt the wagon!" Akton said so loudly that heads turned.

"Miss . . ."

"Am I a prisoner? If not, stop this wagon or I'll jump. Take my belongings to the guest cottage. I know you have your orders, but I'll not be treated like this."

The sergeant looked at the woman. Dressed in a buckskin skirt and white blouse, hair braided, she was fiery, denying any notion of the servility of a reservation Indian, the usual stature of a woman. It would almost be a pleasure to see her tangle with Major Sampson, who was pompous, demanding, and just a little cruel. What could they do to him, after all? Take a stripe? No, the major wouldn't like it, but he couldn't do a lot. A little facetiously he said, "Yes, Miss Mary. As you say."

The sergeant pulled back hard on the reins and stepped on the brake handle. The enlisted man in back slid across the bed of the wagon with Akton's luggage. Akton lurched forward, caught herself, and climbed down, her black eyes scolding but amused.

She smoothed her skirt unnecessarily and strode purposefully toward the commander's office. Eyes followed her from everywhere, some of the soldiers calling out taunts or encouragement or obscenities she didn't hear or care to hear.

She marched on into the orderly room and halted before the desk of First Sergeant Lou Hazleton,

322

who looked up with astonished eyes, and then stood respectfully.

"Miss Mary. I heard. I'm sorry for it all, but happy to see you're well, just happy for that."

He took her hand in his huge red weathered ones and then let it go almost sorrowfully. "Was there something . . . ?"

"I want to see Scott Sampson. He's in, isn't he?"

"Yes, but—"

"Sergeant Hazleton. You and I have been through this with Colonel Shore and with General Clark, haven't we? I'm not going to give this up, not going to go away. I want to see Major Sampson. He knows who I am and what I want . . . maybe. If he doesn't, he's going to find out right now. There's no time for diversions or for long waits, for anything at all. I'm going to go in there, I'm going to see him. With or without you. Do you want to be seen throwing me out of the orderly room by main force?"

"Miss Mary . . ." Hazleton was stung by the last remark. "It's not a thing I'd do, and you know it; but I'm a soldier, you must understand that by now, what it means."

"I think I do," she said coolly.

"There's no way I'm going to talk you out of this, is there, Miss Mary?" Hazleton asked dismally.

"No . . . no, there isn't."

"No . . ." He studied her again. "I don't suppose so." He took a slow breath and with a glance skyward went to Sampson's office door and knocked. Akton heard the muffled summons, and with a last look back Hazleton went in.

Akton was right behind him. She wasn't going to wait for a refusal, and if she gave Sampson the chance, that was what was going to happen.

Scott Sampson sat behind his desk, looking gray and weary. The young freckled man who had come to Arizona was gone, long gone, left to die on some distant battlefield perhaps.

His wife was also in the room.

Laura Sampson lifted her green eyes to Hazleton

and let them shift contemptuously to Akton. Her features were pinched and hard, from boredom with her life, her husband, and herself. Perhaps there still hadn't been enough blood.

"Sergeant—" Sampson began.

"Don't blame him." Akton pushed past an unhappy Lou Hazleton. "I assume you remember who I am," she said, standing before Scott Sampson's desk, her hands on her hips, her head cocked to one side.

"Thumb's squaw, aren't you?" Laura Sampson asked icily.

"I remember you, Miss Mary, of course," Sampson said, half-rising. He smelled of whiskey and defeat. "But I can't do anything for you."

"I haven't asked for anything yet."

"Edna Shore has been here. Twice. She's with General Currier right now, unless I'm mistaken. I know what you want, yes. To see Thumb."

"That's right."

"That's impossible. I'm sorry."

"I demand to speak to an investigator—one of these general officers who've come down here to applaud each other, to cheer you."

Laura Sampson leaned her head back and looked at the ceiling in bored disbelief.

Sampson shook his head. "There's no point in that."

"You won't allow it?"

"I said," he replied, his eyes bloodshot, suddenly cool, "there was no point in it."

She pressed ahead. "Because of Snake Canyon you won't let me talk to anyone."

"I don't know what you're talking about."

"I'm talking about slaughtered men and women!" She leaned far forward, her fisted hands on Sampson's desktop. "I'm speaking of children murdered, women raped—"

"I don't know what you mean!" Sampson exploded. "I never fought a battle in Snake Canyon."

324

"You attacked what you thought was a remnant of Thumb's force."

"I found you and the Apache women and children there and escorted them without incident to Fort Bowie."

"Leaving the dead behind."

"There was no battle there!"

"Bye Courtney was the militia leader. He was drunk and incompetent, but he didn't mind shooting down unarmed Indians."

"That's enough of this!" Sampson said, turning away, running a hand across his forehead.

"Did you bury the dead?"

"Sergeant Hazleton—get her out of here."

"If you didn't bury them, maybe someone will find them."

"Please, Miss Mary . . ." Hazleton took her arm, but she shook him off. Sampson was staring out the window. Laura Sampson sat to one side, too weary, too bored.

"Someone might find the bodies and issue a true report. The newspapers might get the whole story—"

"Out of here, Sergeant Hazleton!" Sampson roared, spinning back from the window, his face pallid, his eyes bulging, his finger thrust toward the door.

"Miss Mary . . . please."

"Hazleton, damn you!" Sampson screamed.

Hazleton took both of Mary's arms and dragged her from the room. She didn't struggle, but she continued to shout at the cavalry officer.

"You let that happen! You knew what kind of men they were! You saw it, but you didn't report it. You didn't want to blemish your grand reputation! The dead will be back to haunt you one day. You can bury them now, but it's too late. They'll be back to haunt you all!"

Hazleton had pulled her into the orderly room and he managed to close the door with one hand. He no longer needed his strength to hold Akton. She had given it up. Hazleton could feel the anger drain out of her, feel her go limp, surrender to reality, inevitability, exhaustion.

Then she was all right again. She was Miss Mary—no, Hazleton thought, she wasn't. She was someone else, someone he didn't know, yet still admired. She had very nearly caused him serious trouble, and she knew it. She apologized very properly but emotionlessly.

"I am sorry. I won't bother you again, Sergeant Hazleton. You don't have to worry about me coming around again." And then she was gone.

Hazleton went to the door of the orderly room to watch her stride off across the parade ground in the direction of the visitor's cottage. He watched her and when he could no longer see her, he shook his head and returned to his desk. The rest of the day was going to be anticlimactic.

Akton walked to the cottage. It was a joyless stroll. The soldiers turned their heads to look, but she was only peripherally aware of their attention.

"Fool," she told herself over and over. "Stupid fool."

She had told the truth and vented her wrath. But that wasn't the point of going to see Scott Sampson. She wanted to see Thumb, she needed to talk to someone who could stop this miscarriage of justice. Instead she had made an enemy of Sampson, threatened him, shut the very doors she had needed open.

It was the weariness perhaps. The warm days and cool nights of watching, waiting, wearing herself out with worry. Knowing that nothing could be done—deep inside, knowing that, still needing to hope. She had ruined everything in Sampson's office, but would he ever have helped anyway? She thought not. And so she had erupted. It was the weariness.

When had life become this vast turmoil, this endless and bitter confusion? Where was the peace some people found, the peace she had not dreamed of since she had had her life wound up with the fate of the Chiricahua?

326

Where was the peace of the Apache?

Edna Shore was in the guest cottage in a wooden rocker by a cold fire, watching the flames that did not exist, the fire that had gone out. Her hands were pale, heavily veined, inert on the arms of the rocker. She spoke without turning her head. "They told me they were putting you in here."

"You were with a general. General Currier," Akton said.

"That's right."

"There was. . . ?"

"There was no luck. Currier is here as an observer. He doesn't care to interview Indian survivors."

"Did you tell him. . . ?"

"I told him everything you told me!" Edna Shore said with a burst of impatience. She too was weary. She stood slowly, carefully, as if she had suddenly become brittle with age. "I'm sorry, Mary."

"No. I'm sorry. What could I expect?"

Akton's head was hanging. The older woman moved to her and held her tightly for a moment. She murmured, "We should have known better than to fall in love with warriors."

"Tea?" Akton withdrew and offered the other woman a false smile. The expression was returned.

"If we've got everything we need, yes! There was a silver service once, but a visiting congressman's wife took it with her when she left."

There were a teapot and spoons, but they weren't silver. There were also cups and a pot to boil the water in, and the two of them, these warriors' wives, sat in silence while the new fire blazed.

"What will you do, Mary?"

"I will see Thumb."

"They won't let you. You know that."

"He's my husband! I have his child in my womb."

"That carries little weight, I'm afraid."

She was determined. "I will see him. I'll demand it, and in the meantime I'll write letters. To Congress, the President, the commander of the western army. General Crook is supposed to be a fair man."

"Mary, Crook is in the field. A letter might take a month to reach him. And what could he do by then? The execution . . . it's been set for sunrise the day after tomorrow."

"The day after tomorrow!" Akton felt her body go numb. It seemed to have been drained of blood. Her head hummed furiously.

"I'm sorry, Mary."

"Yes . . . yes. So soon? How could it be so soon?"

"We have busy men here to witness the execution, Mary," Edna said. "They can't spend much time waiting to watch a man die."

Mary didn't respond. She was watching the flames beneath the teakettle, watching as they too withered and died. The gold and orange ropy strands faded and shrank and fought to survive, fought but were strangled by the lack of fuel, of oxygen. By time. She sat there with her folded hands on her swollen abdomen and watched, never even noticing when Edna got up, kissed her on the forehead, and went out into the afternoon, which had grown cold and blustery, darkened by the forming clouds.

There was no night, only the following morning, which burst angrily against the window as Akton sat in her rocker, a dead creature which breathed in and out. She had strength, but not the will to use it, to rise, to fight, to challenge existence and its fatal decrees.

I am his wife. I am capable of doing *something*! she shouted inwardly. But what? She rose and nervously paced the floor of the cottage as the sun tormented her tired eyes. Outside, soldiers marched in cadence. Someone shouted a command.

Akton went out and walked to the visiting officers' quarters. There were two soldiers with rifles outside the building as she went up to it, her fists involuntarily clenched with determination.

"What is it, woman?" one of the soldiers, a Southerner with blue eyes and a hooked nose, asked.

"My name is Mary Hart. I want to see General Currier."

"The general left orders not to be disturbed," the soldier responded. There was humor in his voice: she was only an amusing nuisance.

"I want to see him."

"Sorry, woman."

"Now!"

She stepped onto the porch and was pushed back. She stumbled and sat down hard in the dust, letting out a cry of rage. She rose then, shouting at them in the Apache tongue.

"Get out of my way! Shall I cut your throats for you?"

The soldiers laughed again, and then the door opened and a man wearing a blue shirt and suspenders emerged, a cigar in his teeth. The soldiers snapped to attention.

"What the hell's this, Private?"

"Squaw woman making trouble, sir. Wants to see you."

Currier, for that was who it was, looked at the woman sitting in the dirt, at the dusty, dark-eyed, but beautiful woman. He turned sharply away, snapping at the guards, "Keep her the hell away."

"Yes, sir."

"General Currier!" Akton cried.

The door slammed and he was gone. Someone would die, but that didn't mean the general should have to be disturbed. "You heard him, woman," the Southerner said.

His friend was a little more gentle. "Please, miss. You'll only get yourself in more trouble. You heard the general—we can't let you hang around here."

He started down off the porch as if to help Akton to her feet, but she rose and dusted herself off before that could happen. She stood for a minute looking at the closed door, at all the closed doors.

"Please, miss?"

Akton turned and walked away. The soldiers should not be allowed to see the mist in her eyes.

Her stomach ached and she paused for a minute in the center of the dusty parade ground with soldiers, mounted and afoot, singly and in groups, passing by. One young man smiled. He reminded her of Scott Sampson when he first arrived in Arizona. She breathed in deeply, holding her abdomen. A soldier started to approach her, his face concerned, but she turned sharply away.

Head down, she walked on, her stride angry, heavy, her heart racing, the pain in her womb growing more insistent.

It was darker suddenly, very dark. The clouds must have drifted in.

She lifted her head and saw the log wall, saw the guards, the iron-barred gate. She was standing in the shadow of the stockade. Standing where the light never shone. It was as if she could not move, as if some force had drawn her there to taunt her. She threw back her head and she thought she screamed. She believed she had, that she had called his name, called for Thumb, called to God, to Manitou, to empty, passive, and blameless Eternity to stop this.

All she remembered for certain was waking up in the guest cottage, feeling the cool damp cloth on her forehead, seeing Edna Shore's kind, grave face by firelight.

"It's dark," Akton said.

"Yes."

"It's night again. This is the last night, isn't it?"

"Yes."

"I've got to get up." She struggled to sit, but Edna pushed her back as if she were a small child.

"You have to rest."

"I'm all right, am I not? I am all right?" Akton felt sudden panic. "The baby . . ."

"You're all right. Yes. Just exhausted. You've worn your nerves out. Broken your strength."

"The baby must be all right," Akton said, lying back to watch the ceiling. "You understand that. The baby must be. The baby is Apache, Edna." She

330

took the old woman's hand and crushed it in her own. "You do understand that?"

"I understand. Sleep, dear. I understand."

"You'll wake me?" Akton asked.

"You won't want to be awake."

"Yes. Yes, I do wish to be awake. At dawn. I want to know when it happens. It's necessary, Edna," she said, her eyes dark and feverish as they pleaded with Edna Shore's eyes.

"All right. Sleep. I'll wake you at dawn."

"If you promise." Slowly the grip she kept on Edna's hand relaxed.

"Yes. Sleep now. Sleep, dear thing, sleep. I'll wake you with the dawn."

Dawn, when it came, was suffused, soft and red and deep violet through the heavy clouds which had gathered to mourn the day. Akton sat up in bed, her eyes on the wall, her heart seeming not to beat. Once they heard soldiers march past, and once a trumpet, and then, many plodding heavy minutes later, a faint, distant cheer.

The child in her womb leapt; a brilliant red ray of sunlight smeared itself against the window, seeming to strike the fireplace, where a log cracked and fell into the golden embers, sending up sparks.

Then the child was still. It was a wise and mysterious child; it knew. Thumb was dead.

14

"**W**hat does this prove? What is the good of it, Mary?"

Edna Shore was beside herself. The Indian woman, burdened with the weight of the child in her distended abdomen, continued to move around the cottage, sorting out the few articles she would take with her.

"It's a long way, Mary. A long, long way to Florida."

"Yes. A long way. But that is where the government has decided to send the Apache so that he may never have a home to fight for again."

"Mary, you are not Apache."

She continued to pack, tossing small unwanted items into the fireplace. She stopped now, finding something of interest. As Edna watched, she went before the window to stand silhouetted there. In her hands was a necklace of silver.

Without lifting her head, Akton answered. "My baby," she said, "is Apache. He will go where his people go."

"But you could stay here with him! Go back to Dakota. Anywhere. It will only mean grief for the baby."

"My baby will be raised to know what he is, what she is. The baby will be raised with its people."

"I don't like it. I don't understand it," Edna said in exasperation, "but you're a grown woman. I'm not even related to you."

"No"—Akton came to her—"but you are a mother to me all the same. You wish to help me, I know that."

"Why, yes, dear. Come back to Colorado with me! We'll have the baby there. The colonel, bless him, left me a small restaurant. There are quarters above it."

"No. I am going to Florida. A place I know only from books. Why we are going, I don't know; but the Apache are going. I am going."

"Mary ... they don't even care for you, those people."

"Thumb cared."

"But Thumb is staying here," Edna said carefully. "Here, on the desert."

"Here he lies buried, but he is not here. He travels with his people; he is alive in their memory. And so his child must go—to know who its father was."

"You won't reconsider?"

"No, not now. It's too late."

"No, it *isn't*. Listen, Mary—

There was a tap at the door and a soldier entered, peering around the corner first. "Mary Hart?" he asked. "I was sent to drive you to the Tucson train station. The wagon's out here."

"Mary?" Edna tried again, holding her shoulders, looking into her eyes. "It's a long way on a train in your condition."

"Miss?" The soldier nodded at the single bag she had packed. "Shall I take this?"

Akton looked at Edna again, kissed her cheek, and said, "Yes, take that bag. That's all there is."

Outside it was clear and cool. In the wagon sat Captain Holt, going home. He glanced at Akton and then looked away as the driver helped her up. They didn't speak the entire trip to Tucson, and when they had reached that city Holt swung down, snatched his bag from the wagon bed, and strode off without looking back. The driver helped Mary Hart down. The train was half a mile outside of town, and so she walked. They had left the long gray train beyond the city limits because of threats to the Apache's lives. When Mary arrived, half-dragging her bag, dusty and dry-mouthed, she found the train ringed with soldiers.

"Where the hell did you come from?" a soldier asked.

"My name is Akton. I'm supposed to be on the train."

"What band?" the man asked. "What tribe."

"Chiricahua. Thumb's band." Her voice caught a little, but she managed to say it with pride. The soldier shrugged and led her through.

There was a doctor there, a small man with a wispy white beard who looked exhausted and slightly ashamed. He caught the soldier's arm as they passed.

"Find room for that one in a Pullman," the doctor said.

"Where are the others?" Akton asked.

"In the freight cars, but they're locked in now. Besides," he said, looking at her belly, "you may need me before we get to Florida."

The soldier was indifferent. He found Akton a seat in a Pullman car where Apache sat on the floors, crowded two into every single seat. She was placed next to a window, an older woman evicted despite Akton's objections.

And then she waited, waited to be away. There was a reservation for the Apache in Florida. There she would live, there likely give birth to her baby. A reservation—she could not escape them. Perhaps the baby would. Perhaps the baby would one day leave the reservation and come back to Arizona. What would it find here? A different world, certainly, but perhaps some memory of Thumb would linger here. Perhaps the ghosts of the Apache would always live on the desert, the great, empty, too-beautiful desert. The train lurched forward, steam hissing from a valve somewhere, machinery clanking, and Akton leaned her head back, closing her eyes. She did not want to see the desert slip away from her, for he was out there. Thumb was there, waiting, and she would never return.

There was nothing here but memories. Nothing but the lost thoughts and the empty wishes, the things of the mind which lived upon the desert, mysterious and fugitive, shadowy, without substance. A time had come, and it had gone again, the time of the Apache. It had come and then drifted on, leaving only these things—these memories, these shadows, invisible but real. The way of the Apache, like the way of the wind that was eternal on the desert, lived on in her heart if nowhere else; and in her heart and the thousand hearts of those who had survived, it would continue to live until the last memory had gone, blown away by the last bitter wind.